PASSIONS IGNITE

PHOENIX RIDGE FIRE DEPARTMENT
BOOK 5

EMILY HAYES

1

LUX

The soft morning light filtering through the blinds stirred Lux Valentine from her sleep. Her eyelids flickered open, slowly taking in the familiar sight in front of her: a powder-blue wall with abstract white designs streaking on it—her bedroom.

Lux stretched and blinked furiously again. The sheets felt warm against her bare skin, and she could feel them tease against her nipples.

A soft sigh caused her to turn. It was Phoebe, twisting and turning but still sound asleep. Lux turned her head slightly, taking in the peaceful sight of Phoebe—the gentle rise and fall of her breasts, the soft curve of her lips.

Phoebe always craved fiery, sensual lovemaking, and Lux wasn't a stranger to fire. She was chief pilot at the Phoenix Ridge Fire Department.

With a sigh, Lux slipped out of bed, the cool hardwood floor satisfying under her bare feet. The room was a jumble of discarded clothes and half-empty wine glasses.

Her eyes caught sight of the digital clock on the wall: *10:23 am*. Being a helicopter pilot meant she had less free time on her hands. Phoenix Ridge was a forest fire hazard in summer, so firefighting from above was essential. Something none of her previous girlfriends ever understood.

Lux shrugged as she walked over to the wardrobe. What she shared with Phoebe was a fling, but it didn't mean they couldn't have a great time during it.

Her mind drifted aimlessly as she thought about her relationships in the last year. They've all been similar. No matter how much she tried to make it into a serious relationship, it never worked. They never saw how important working as a firefighter was to her. Lux felt like they never really saw her—the real her; they just liked the idea of her.

She had long decided to ignore relationships

completely. What mattered to her was her job at the fire station, nothing more.

Lux slipped into her uniform.

As she pulled on her boots, the loneliness she kept tucked away floated to the surface. In the quiet moments, she wondered when—*if*—she'd ever find love. She managed to shrug off the thought and focus on getting dressed.

A sleepy voice called out from the bed, "Lux?"

Phoebe blinked, her eyes still heavy with sleep.

"Hey," Lux replied, a small smile tugging at the corner of her lips. "Someone looks like they had a great time."

"It's always a great time with you," Phoebe said. "I never want it to end."

Lux paused, then continued getting dressed. She walked over to the mirror in the corner and fixed her tie. She could still feel Phoebe's eyes following her intently.

"Leaving already?"

"Got to be at the station, Phoebe," Lux said. "You know how it is."

"Yeah, yeah. You show up, we make love, then you disappear."

"Make love?" Lux snorted. "We fuck, Phoebe. I don't make love." She turned around. Phoebe propped herself on one elbow, pushing her hair out of her face.

"Forgive me, Lux." Phoebe rolled her eyes. "I forget every time."

"We've talked about this a million times before." Lux turned back to the mirror. "I can't deal with a relationship right now."

"And why's that?"

Lux sighed. She had gone over this so many times with Phoebe. She just didn't have feelings like that for her. Yet, every single time, Phoebe always got clingy afterward.

"Phoebe, darling," Lux said, "I can't commit to anything serious right now. Maybe sometime in the future, but right now, I can't."

"Can't make it official, you mean?" Phoebe asked.

Lux paused, her hand freezing mid-air. "Official?" she echoed, her smile fading. "Did you hear anything I just said?"

Phoebe nodded, her gaze unwavering. "You know, like...a real couple."

Lux let out a laugh. "Come on, Phoebe. You know how I am. I'm not the relationship type. The only fires I don't fight are the ones that come with relationships."

"Maybe it's because there are no fires to fight."

Lux chuckled. "That's a nice one. See, you get it."

"I don't. I mean, why not?" Phoebe pressed. "What's so wrong with wanting something more?"

Lux sighed, running a hand through her hair. "It's not you, Phoebe. It's me. I-I can't do relationships. I've tried, but they never work out. They either distract me from my job or suffer because of it. Either way, it never works."

"Why not?" Phoebe said, her voice now tinged with anger. "Is it because you're afraid of getting hurt? Or is it because you don't care about anyone but yourself?"

Lux winced, the accusation hitting a nerve. "That's not fair, Phoebe. You know I care about you."

"Do you?" Phoebe retorted. "Or do you just care about what I can give you?"

The room fell silent. Lux turned back to the mirror and tugged her tie one last time. Talking about this with Phoebe wasn't worth it. She felt a pang in her chest.

"I've always felt sorry for you, Lux," Phoebe said. "You hide behind your humor and carefree attitude, but deep down, you're scared. Scared of letting anyone in, scared of getting hurt."

Lux's jaw tightened, her fists clenching at her sides. "You don't know anything about me."

"I know enough," Phoebe said. "I know you'll end up alone if you keep pushing everyone away. I know you'll never find happiness if you don't learn to open up and let someone in."

"You're only saying that to hurt me." Lux chuckled, but it didn't reach her eyes. "That's not fair, Phoebe."

"No, *you're* not being fair."

"You knew how things were with me before now. Why make it an issue now?"

"Because I'm not built for all this, Lux." Phoebe walked out from the bed, her breasts bare. "I know I agreed not to get attached and all that. It's just supposed to be sex and nothing more. But you're you, Lux. How could I not fall in—"

"Just don't," Lux interrupted. "Trust me, you can't love me."

"And if I do already?"

"You won't be the first to say it," Lux said. "But trust me, you'll get over it."

"Is it that evil to let yourself love someone? Are

you so certain you want to live the rest of your life alone?"

"I've got Mira, honey," Lux said, watching Phoebe's face squirm.

"Mira? Are you—?"

"Mira is my favorite helicopter at the station," Lux clarified. "You don't even know that, and yet you think you love me?"

"You love your job more than you love me."

"Finally, you're starting to see it."

"You're not getting any younger, Lux. You need to find someone to spend your forever with."

"Thanks, Mom. I never knew being thirty-four meant my life should end."

"I didn't say that."

"Of course, you didn't," Lux retorted. "Shut the door when you go. You know where to leave the key."

She turned and walked out of the room, not slowing down until she reached her white truck in the driveway. Her smile wore off the second the door thudded shut behind her.

Was Phoebe right? Would I die alone?

Phoebe's words echoed in her head as she started the truck's engine. Phoebe didn't understand it. No one ever did.

As much as she wanted to find love, she knew she'd never see it. Not while she's still tucked this deep in her job. She'd talk to her father about it, but then again, he wouldn't know. He had devoted most of his life to his job after Mom had died all those years ago.

Perhaps there's nothing wrong with me after all. It's just the deal with the job. You either give it your all or it takes yours.

Sam would understand, but he was working in the city. Besides, she wouldn't want to call him over anything as petty as a spat with someone she was not even in love with.

Love. Lux chuckled again.

"Oh, well." She eased her truck out of the driveway and headed for the station.

The sight from outside the window soon drowned the thoughts from Lux's mind. She drove just fast enough to get past the sights of houses lining either side of the road.

She smiled at the ragged forests sprawling in the distance. The rugged hills were always a beautiful sight, except, of course, when the fires began.

They scorched much of the greenery, but the town always won the fight against the fires every season. Even these very green expanses she drove past had thick smoke drifting from them about this time last year. Now, it's lush again.

Lux wondered if that was why the town was called Phoenix Ridge. It always rose from the ashes. A thin smile crossed her face. Hopefully, her love life would one day rise from the ashes too.

Soon, even the distant forests faded from her mind as she drove into the fire station parking lot, a sprawling complex of red brick and steel that hummed with activity.

Lux took a deep breath. The smell of burnt coffee and engine oil hung in the air.

Inside, the atmosphere was charged with a nervous energy. Everyone knew what season it was, and as much as they anticipated it, no one could say they loved it.

She parked her truck and looked around. The crew, a mix of seasoned veterans and eager rookies, was preparing for the day's drills.

"Another day, Lux," she said as she descended from the truck.

"Morning, Chief," a voice called out.

Lux turned to see Jay, one of her most experienced pilots, grinning at her from across the room. Her tangy-orange hair sat messy on her head.

"Jay," she replied, returning her smile. "How's the morning treating you?"

"Can't complain." She took a swig from her coffee mug.

"I can't say the same for your hair," Lux replied. "Get a hat or something."

"It's that bad?"

"Like a hornet's nest."

"Just another day in paradise." Jay patted her hair and fell in step with her.

Lux chuckled. "If you consider dodging wildfires paradise, you're right."

"It'll be fire season soon," Jay said. "Chief Thompson is already giving everyone hell down here."

"You think Becky Thompson is hell? Wait until the fires start."

"Trust me, I'm not eager for that," Jay said.

As Lux made her way toward her office. She caught her breath before going to the simulation room. She couldn't afford to have unprepared pilots with fire season so close.

"Alex thinks there might not be any fires this year," Jay said.

Alex, Jay's wife, was a beautiful woman with

brown eyes, and Lux remembered meeting her on a few occasions at some town events.

"She thinks? She must be psychic." Lux raised her eyebrows.

"She hopes," she said. "She'd rather have me home with her, you know."

"How sad," Lux said. "She has to put up with your bland jokes for the rest of her life."

They both laughed.

"You sure have been having a great time yourself," Jay said. "I can see that look in your eyes."

Lux chuckled. "You kidding? Love's not on my agenda, Jay."

"And fires are?"

"You know it," Lux said. "Fire is where my real passion lies. Big, wild, aggressive, beautiful fire. That is my true love."

A flash of movement caught her eye.

A tall and athletic woman who Lux hadn't seen before stepped off a black truck, her dark hair pulled back in a tight ponytail. She wore the standard-issue navy blue fire department uniform, but an air of authority set her apart from the rest of the crew.

She looked around with the eyes of someone

new to the environment, but her head was still held high with confidence.

Lux found herself staring, her breath catching in her throat. The woman's features were striking: high cheekbones, piercing brown eyes, and mouthful lips that hinted at a hidden sensuality. She moved with a grace that belied the strength in her muscles, her every step radiating confidence.

Lux's heart hammered in her chest, an unfamiliar flutter of attraction taking hold.

"She's new," Jay said, appearing at Lux's side. "A lieutenant, I think."

Lux snapped out of her daze. "Not bad. We could do with the addition."

"You think she's hot, don't you?"

"Don't be ridiculous," she retorted, regaining her composure. "The only thing hot around here is the fires we're going to fight."

Jay chuckled. "Oh, come on, Chief. It was written all over your face."

Lux rolled her eyes. "I was just...observing."

"Observing, huh?" Jay teased.

Lux shot her a warning glare. "Drop it, Jay."

Jay held up her hands in surrender. "Alright, alright. I'll leave you to your...observations." She sauntered off, leaving Lux to grapple with the unexpected surge of attraction.

Lux glanced in the newcomer's direction again. But as she turned, the woman suddenly stopped and looked directly at her. Their eyes met, and Lux felt a jolt of electricity shoot through her. The woman's gaze was intense and unwavering, and Lux could not look away.

Time seemed to slow down as they held each other's gazes. Lux's cheeks flushed, and warmth spread through her body.

The woman's lips curved into a polite smile. Then, just as quickly as it had begun, the moment was over. She nodded and continued, leaving Lux standing there, her heart pounding.

2

ZOEY

Zoey Knight glanced at her phone. A text message notification flashed on the screen. Dad.

Settled in already?

Zoe sighed. Her father was "settled" somewhere on a Montana ranch, vacationing with her mom. She was in a new town, unsure if she would ever settle in.

Her thumbs hovered over the keypad, thinking of how best to reply.

She heaved and looked around.

The room was sparsely furnished. A desk was pushed against the far wall, a chair tucked neatly under it. A stack of unopened boxes leaned against the wall beside a file cabinet.

The fluorescent lights above hummed quietly, casting a stark white light over the space. The walls were painted a dull beige, and a single window offered a view of the parking lot.

Her thoughts were riveted to the woman she had seen when she arrived at the station. Their eyes danced together in unison for what felt like an eternity. How long did she stand there, staring?

Not now, Zoey, she warned herself.

It was way too early to be attracted to anyone. She wasn't even sure she was attracted just yet. It didn't work that way, right? She hadn't come down to Phoenix Ridge only to find solace in the arms of the next woman who smiled at her.

Lisa, her older sister, would tease her for always having fickle emotions and craving a life forever with anyone who smiled at her. She liked to argue that she wasn't a hopeless romantic, but then she knew, as did Lisa, that she was.

At least, she used to be. Romance was not necessary anymore.

She ran her fingers over the smooth desk surface then glanced at the empty shelves on the wall. The office felt sterile, impersonal. A place that didn't yet feel like home.

Her phone buzzed to life. The caller ID was one she didn't expect. Jamie. She smiled. Jamie was her younger brother and favorite sibling.

"Hello, Jamie." She pressed the phone against her ear.

"Hey, Z. How's my little big sister doing?"

"Holding up, I guess," she said. "Dad just texted."

"You must be the only middle child in the country who gets this much attention."

Zoey laughed, even though she'd argue that they only cared this much because they feared she'd fall apart if left alone. At thirty-one, one would think their family would cut her some slack.

"I guess so," she said. "How's the army treating you?"

"Not bad," Jamie replied. "Snuck off just to check up on you."

"That's sweet."

"I'll be heading back out now. You're fine, right?"

Zoey rolled her eyes. She hated being asked that. It's been three months, and she still gets asked this. "I'm fine."

"You know it wasn't your fault, right?"

Zoey paused. "If you believe that, you don't have to say it."

Jamie chuckled. "Typical Zoey. You always have to be a—"

"Say 'wise ass,' and I'll whip yours from over here."

"I was gonna say 'loving older sister,' but you took the words right out of my mouth." Jamie chuckled. "Take care, Z."

"You, too, Jamie."

The line clicked. She smiled, but it only survived the next few seconds.

There was a knock on the door. Zoey turned as the door creaked open and Fire Chief Becky Thompson stepped inside, holding a thick folder.

"How's the office treating you?" Chief Thompson asked, her voice no-nonsense but not unkind. She was an average-height woman with a head of sandy-colored hair streaked with gray and lines around her eyes, and she was renowned for running a tight ship.

"It's fine," Zoey said, glancing around. "Still getting used to it."

"You'll settle in soon enough," Thompson said, setting the folder on her desk. "These are the files you asked for. Reports from the last few years. Thought you might want to go over them."

Zoey nodded, eyeing the folder. "Thanks."

"Take your time," Chief Thompson said, straightening up. "No need to rush. Just ensure you're ready for the drills tomorrow and the command ops meeting later, Don't forget to take a peek at the simulation."

"Command ops?" She raised a brow.

"It's our fancy word here for the tactics room. That's where we decide on strategies and the like. You'd like it there."

"So, it's straight to work then."

Becky smiled. "I know what you're capable of, Lieutenant. Can't wait to see you in action around here."

Zoey nodded. "Can't wait either."

Becky lingered for a moment, then gave a curt nod and left the room, closing the door behind her. Zoey stared at the door momentarily, then turned back to her desk.

She opened the folder, flipping through the details of Phoenix Ridge and its history of wildfires. The paper felt thin under her fingers, the text dense with numbers and details. She tried to focus, but her mind wandered back to Forest Vale, her previous station.

Chief Thompson said she knew what Zoey was capable of. She wondered if she knew that she made a poor call once and lost a child in the process. Did she also know how much it had hurt her? So much that she opted for a transfer away from Forest Vale to help her deal with it?

Even now, she wasn't even certain she had dealt with it. How does one deal with the fact that the error they made led to the death of a child?

Zoey's body shuddered. She walked over to her seat and sank into it.

"Get yourself together," Zoey said to herself. She sighed again.

The door opened again, this time without a knock. A young woman walked in. She was very beautiful with thick dark hair in a long, messy plait and a kind smile.

"Lieutenant," she said, then took a step back. "I'm sorry, I should've—"

"Knocked? Yes, you should have." Zoey said. "Pilot?"

"Firefighter. The name's Leilani Silva. Chief Thompson says I'm part of your team."

"You'd have to remember to knock next time if you're going to remain a part of my crew."

"I will, Lieutenant." Silva nodded.

"What's the rest of the team like?" Zoey asked.

"Most of the team like you already."

Zoey shrugged. "I didn't come here to be liked." She came here to make sure no one else died under her watch, but she didn't say that. "There's a lot to catch up with around here." Zoey pointed to the files on her table.

Leilani walked over, standing beside the desk as she glanced at the open folder. "I can go over them with you if you'd like. I can tell you about many of them firsthand."

"That would be helpful," Zoey said. "You've been here a while?"

"Seven years," Leilani said. "Started as a rookie, worked my way up."

"Impressive," Zoey said, watching her closely. "You must know this place inside out."

"I do," Leilani said, pointing toward the door. "I should get back to the rest of the team."

"I'll meet up with you guys soon," Zoey said.

Leilani left, closing the door softly behind her.

Zoey exhaled and looked around the room again.

She turned back to the folder, this time focusing on the reports, determined to make this place home—or at least safe. At the moment, it felt way too dull inside.

Needing fresh scenery, she headed outside into the hallway, her boots echoing on the concrete floor. The walls were lined with framed photographs of past crews, smiling faces, and scenes of controlled chaos.

A few people walked past her, everyone seeming to be in a hurry. They were trained to be this way. To be ready for any and every eventuality. She wondered how they dealt with it when something came along that they weren't prepared for.

Zoey spotted Chief Thompson a few steps ahead, deep in conversation with someone dressed in a pilot's uniform with short, messy hair. Becky Thompson's own strawberry-blonde hair was neatly cut in a bob and her uniform was immaculate. Thompson turned just in time for her eyes to meet Zoey's.

"Lieutenant Knight," she called to her. "Join us."

Zoey walked over to meet them.

The pilot with messy hair nodded toward her as she approached. "Welcome, Lieutenant."

Zoey matched her smile. Something about her looked familiar.

"Thanks, and you are?"

"Jay Summers," she said as they shook hands.

"Pilot?" Zoey asked, glancing at her hair.

Jay seemed to catch her eye. She patted her hair as she replied, "Yeah."

"Lux Valentine keeps these pilots in line." Chief Thompson chuckled.

"Lux Valentine?" Zoey asked.

"She's the chief pilot around here," Jay said. "We both saw you step off your truck this morning."

The memory raced through Zoey's mind. She recalled those blue eyes that held hers, the curl of her lips that moved slightly as they held her gaze, and the beauty—and defiance—that lurked behind it.

Zoey frowned. She hated the thoughts that swarmed her head. She hated the fact that she wasn't even settled in and some very attractive woman who looked like trouble—the chief pilot, to make it worse—was filling her head with thoughts of passion. Passion, Zoey certainly wasn't sure she desired.

"I don't think we've been introduced," Zoey said.

"It won't be long now. Which reminds me, I should go meet her in simulations." She nodded toward Chief Thompson. "Chief?"

"Alright, Jay."

Jay walked off, and Chief Thompson turned to Zoey. "Come, it's about time you meet your team."

Inside, firefighters milled about, some checking equipment, others conversing.

"Lieutenant Zoey Knight, I want you to meet some of the team," Chief Thompson said, waving her toward the open room.

A tall woman with a no-nonsense expression was the first to approach. Her uniform was crisp, and her hair was pulled back into a tight bun. "This is Captain Ramirez," the chief said. "She handles most of the ground operations. She'll work with you."

"Nice to meet you," Zoey said, extending her hand.

Ramirez shook it firmly, her gaze sharp as she looked Zoey over. "Welcome to Phoenix Ridge."

Zoey nodded, not quite meeting her eyes. The

room felt too warm, the air heavy. She forced a smile, her mind drifting back to Forest Vale, to the faces of her old team, the way they had looked at her after the fire where they had lost the girl. She swallowed hard, pushing the memory down.

"And this is Captain Hallie Hunter," the chief continued, introducing her to a serious-looking woman with a tired smile.

"Good to have you here," Hallie said, her handshake quick but firm.

"Thanks," Zoey said, quieter now. She could feel the weight of the room pressing down on her, the unspoken expectations. It was the same as Forest Vale, only her previous comrades didn't hold any silent judgment.

A familiar face walked over to meet them. It was the nice firefighter, Leilani Silva. "Hello, Lieutenant Knight."

"Leilani, we meet again."

They shook hands.

"I see you've met Silva here," Chief Thompson said.

"Yeah, I already did."

Leilani nodded and walked toward the hoses. The chief led Zoey through more introductions, each blending into the next until they reached the large bay where the trucks were kept. Zoey's eyes scanned the area, taking in the equipment, the orderly rows of hoses, and the gleaming trucks. It was all so familiar yet foreign at the same time.

As they reached the end of the bay, Zoey spotted a group of pilots near the far wall. One of them, the woman from earlier with dark hair and intense blue eyes, caught her attention. She stood apart, her arms crossed over her chest, whispering with another pilot.

"That's Lux Valentine, chief pilot," the chief said, following Zoey's gaze.

Zoey almost said she recognized her from earlier, but she didn't. The other pilot next to Lux listened attentively, nodding intermittently. It looked more like a rallying of directives than a conversation. Lux's body was striking, and the curl of her lips switched from sensual to a snarl constantly. Her blue eyes were hard, and her dark hair was in a neat bun. Her body was beautiful, lithe, and athletic with beautiful curves.

Zoey nodded, tearing her eyes away from Lux. "Looks like she knows her stuff."

"She does," the chief said. "But she's not the easiest to get along with. Stubborn, to put it mildly."

Zoey shrugged. She could see that Lux Valentine was difficult. It was written all over her face, defiant stance, and tense shoulders. Lux looked like she seriously needed to loosen up. "I'll keep that in mind."

Zoey glanced over her shoulder at Lux one last time. She quickly dismissed the thought. Relationships hadn't worked out for her before. There was no reason to think this time would be any different. And as beautiful as she was, Lux Valentine looked exactly like trouble. Trouble with a capital T.

The chief studied her for a moment. "Get settled in. We'll need you at command ops tomorrow."

Zoey closed the door behind her, leaned against it, and closed her eyes. The room was quiet, but her thoughts were loud. She took a deep breath and pushed away from the door, looking to clear her head.

She'd need a clear head to contribute tomorrow, which meant she'd need to stop thinking of Lux Valentine in any way other than professional.

3

LUX

Lux woke up the next day more tired than when she went to bed. She rolled over and patted the empty space next to her.

She recalled Phoebe's words but quickly discarded them. It was of no use. She'd rather have just a cup of coffee in bed with her. She certainly didn't need a partner.

She picked up her phone. Two missed calls from Dad. It's been a day since she last heard from him. Perhaps she could stop by at his place before heading back to the station for the meeting at command ops.

She returned the call, and he picked up after a few rings. "Hello, princess."

"Princess?" She chuckled. "I'm Chief Pilot Valentine now, Dad."

Her father's laugh floated into her ears from the other end of the line. "My bad then. How're you, little princess?" He stressed the word "*little.*"

"I'm fine, Dad. Sorry I missed your calls. Are you okay?"

"Younger than I've ever been. I'm sure I'd be better if you came to see me."

"I could stop by before going to the station."

"That'll be nice. Your brother is far off in the city. You don't want me to grow old so soon, do you?"

"You're still too young to think of aging, Dad," Lux said. "I'll see you soon."

"I'll hold you to that."

Half an hour later, she entered the coffee shop off Main Street. The place was small but cozy with mismatched wooden chairs and tables scattered throughout.

She once frequented this place when she had dated Sarah. They'd come here every weekend before she went to the station. It was beautiful, at least for the months it lasted. Soon, their time here grew shorter and shorter. At first, by an hour, then to mere minutes.

She wasn't surprised when Sarah asked for a breakup. It all didn't matter anymore. That was nearly half a decade ago. Now, all she craved was coffee.

She approached the counter, nodding at the barista. "The usual, Flora," she said. "Black."

"Sure you don't want our special for today?"

"Only if you can convince me that the day is special."

"Every day is special in Phoenix Ridge." Flora chuckled. "Something special coming up."

Lux leaned against the counter, waiting for her coffee. Her eyes wandered over the few patrons scattered around the shop. Most were familiar faces, townspeople who started their day with the same routine as her.

As she scanned, her gaze landed on someone familiar sitting at a corner table—the new lieutenant at the fire station. Dark ponytail. Big, expressive brown eyes. Full lips. A body made for sin. Very attractive. Zoey something, wasn't it?

Maybe Flora was right; today might be special after all.

Lux watched a little longer. Zoey sat alone, her hands wrapped around a mug of coffee, her eyes fixed on something outside the window. She looked out of place in the relaxed setting, her posture stiff, her eyes distant.

"A cappuccino for Phoenix Ridge's best pilot," Flora said, smiling at Lux.

She placed it on the counter with a quiet clink, but Lux didn't move to grab it immediately. Instead, she watched Zoey, curious as she was interested in what lay behind those pretty eyes.

Lux finally picked up her cup and walked across the room slowly.

"Morning," Lux said with her most seductive look, stopping at Zoey's table.

Zoey looked up, her eyes widening, then quickly becoming neutral. "Morning." Her voice was calm but had a hint of something guarded in her tone. It was as though she had been lost in her head and hated the interruption. Lux didn't mind. She nodded toward the empty chair across from Zoey.

"Mind if I sit?"

Zoey hesitated for a moment then gestured to the chair. "Go ahead."

Lux sat down, setting her coffee on the table. The chair creaked slightly under her weight. She studied Zoey, trying to get a read on her.

"How are you settling in?" Lux asked, even

though she already knew the answer. It was an easy way to start the conversation.

"If I had a penny every time I've been asked that, I'd be a billionaire by now."

"I doubt there are that many people in these parts," Lux said with a little laugh. Zoey didn't join in. Lux curled her lips in a warm smile nonetheless. "You seem to be finding your way around quite well."

"I guess so."

Lux motioned toward the coffee in Zoey's hand. "Great coffee, right?"

Zoey nodded. "Best I've had since I've been here."

"You've had coffee elsewhere?"

"No."

Lux chuckled. "You're funny."

"Yeah," Zoey said, taking a sip of her coffee. "Why do I doubt that?"

Lux nodded, leaning back in her chair. "What do you think of Phoenix Ridge so far?"

Zoey glanced around the coffee shop then back at Lux. "It's quiet. Different from Forest Vale."

"Forest Vale, huh?" Lux said, pretending to be surprised. "I've heard it's a bit rougher up there."

"It has its moments."

"Phoenix Ridge isn't so bad once you get used to it. There's a lot to like about this place. And it isn't so quiet, I promise you that. Not once fire season starts. We will be very busy."

Zoey looked at her, saying nothing. Her beautiful brown eyes were framed with long, thick lashes, and they were hard to read. There was stuff going on there; Lux could see that for sure. Lux could also see the curve of her full breasts under her shirt, and she liked it. She ran her eyes over them appreciatively, knowing Zoey would notice.

Zoey didn't react. Women always reacted to Lux's moves.

Hmmm. A tough one here. Maybe she isn't gay?

Even the straight ones usually reacted to Lux. She had that effect on women.

Lux smiled slightly, taken aback by Zoey. "I'm guessing you haven't had much time to explore yet."

"Not really," Zoey said, her expression unchanging.

Lux felt herself getting more annoyed at Zoey's lack of reaction.

"So, how are you finding the station?" Lux asked, her tone casual.

"It's fine," Zoey said. "Still getting to know everyone."

Lux took a sip of her cappuccino, studying Zoey over the rim of her cup. Zoey was very attractive, no doubt about it. Her features were sharp, and there was a quiet intensity about her that Lux found intriguing. Oh, and her resistance to Lux's charms. That had to be a challenge.

She put her cup down. "I know it can be tough being the new person. Especially in a place like this where everyone knows each other."

Zoey's eyes met Lux's, and for a moment, Lux thought she saw a crack in the armor. But it was gone as quickly as it came.

"I'll be fine," Zoey said, her tone polite but firm.

Lux nodded, leaning back in her chair again. She wasn't going to push. "If you need anything, you can always ask. People here are friendly, even if they don't seem like it initially."

Zoey offered a small smile, but it didn't reach her eyes. "I appreciate that."

There was a brief silence between them. Lux could feel the awkwardness settling in, but she wasn't ready to walk away.

"What brought you to Phoenix Ridge?" Lux asked.

Zoey hesitated again, her fingers tightening slightly around her coffee mug. "Just needed a change of scenery, I guess."

Lux nodded, sensing that was all she was going to get. "Well, I'm glad you ended up here. We can always use good people."

Lux caught Zoey's wince at the mention of *good people*. Did Zoey feel like she wasn't good? A modest firefighter. That was unusual.

"Thanks," Zoey said.

Lux went to finish her coffee, but the cup was empty already. She stood up, adjusting her jacket. "I should get going. Got a lot to do today."

Zoey nodded, looking up at her. "Sure."

"I'll see you around."

As Lux left the coffee shop, she glanced back at Zoey one last time. She had finally remembered her surname: Knight. Lieutenant Zoey Knight. She was still sitting there, her big brown eyes again focused on something outside the window. Lux felt a bit puzzled by her and her complete lack of reaction to Lux.

Zoey was attractive. Damn, she was hot. Merely staring at her brought up wild fantasies in Lux's mind. But there was something about her that felt distant, almost unreachable. Lux found herself both frustrated and intrigued by it.

As she walked back toward her truck, she couldn't shake the feeling that there was more to Zoey's story than she was letting on. Maybe it was just the newness of the town, the strangeness of being in a place where everyone already knew each other.

Or maybe it was something else, something that Zoey wasn't ready to talk about.

Whatever it was, Lux decided to let it go, at least for now. She had her own life to focus on, her own responsibilities. But as she reached the station and stepped inside, she couldn't help but glance back down the street, wondering if she'd see Zoey Knight again before the day was done.

She held that thought as she started the truck heading straight for her father's house.

The drive was short as she wound through quiet streets lined with trees and modest houses. She had grown up in this neighborhood, every turn familiar, every yard and front porch a part of her childhood.

Her father's house was a small, single-story home with white siding and a neatly kept lawn.

The flower beds out front were filled with blooming roses, their vibrant colors standing out against the green.

She parked in the driveway and got out of the truck, taking a deep breath as she approached the front door. The screen door creaked as she pushed it open, the sound familiar and somewhat nostalgic.

It reminded her of the many nights she had stood on the other side of this door, crying for her mom to come back to her. Losing her mom when she was so young had been devastating, and Lux had carried the trauma of it her whole life.

She often thought of what might have been, what her mom might have been like. How they might have had a great relationship now that Lux was an adult. She wished so deeply that things had been different.

They—Lux and her father—soon became inseparable, so much that she wanted nothing more than to be a firefighter, just like him. She walked inside.

The house smelled like freshly baked bread and coffee, a combination that always made her feel at home. The living room was cozy, filled with well-worn furniture and awards sitting atop the shelves. Her father had been a pretty outstanding firefighter in his time.

"Dad," Lux called out as she walked inside. "You in?"

"Kitchen!"

Lux made her way to the kitchen where her father was standing at the counter slicing a loaf of homemade bread. He was a tall man with graying hair and a friendly face; his eyes crinkled at the corners when he smiled.

Lux smiled and took a deep breath as she watched him. He wore an apron over his plaid shirt and jeans, his hands moving with practiced ease.

"Hey, kiddo," he said, looking up from his work.

"Hey, Dad." Lux leaned against the counter. She watched him for a moment, then walked over and hugged him from behind.

"Want a slice?" He held up a piece of bread. "There's nothing like warm, homemade bread."

"Sure." She took a slice and bit into it. The bread was warm and soft, the crust just the right amount of crunchy. "This is good."

"Glad you like it," he said, grinning. "I'm trying out a new recipe."

"It's a winner!"

He poured them both a cup of coffee, and they sat down at the small kitchen table. The table was old, the wood worn smooth from years of use. Lux's father took a sip of his coffee, his eyes on her, full of the same warmth and affection that had always been there.

"So, how's work?" he asked, his tone casual but interested.

"It's good." She set her cup down. "Busy as always."

"Anything interesting happen?"

Lux thought about Zoey, about their brief conversation at the coffee shop. She wasn't sure how much to share, not wanting to make too big a deal out of it.

"Not really," Lux said, keeping her tone light. "Just the usual stuff."

Her father nodded, taking another sip. He didn't press for more, just smiled at her, content with whatever she was willing to share. That was one of the things Lux loved most about her dad—he never pushed, never demanded more than she was ready to give.

"How about you?" Lux asked. "How's everything here?"

"Oh, you know" He waved a hand absentmindedly. "Same old, same old. I went fishing yesterday and caught a couple nice ones."

"Yeah? Did you cook them up?"

"Of course," he said, grinning. "Saved you some for later."

"Thanks, Dad." She smiled back at him.

Lux's phone rang, cutting into their conversation. She recognized Chief Thompson's number.

"Work calling?" her father asked, his tone light.

"Yeah, Chief Thompson," Lux said. She knew her father knew Becky well and respected her.

"Already?"

Lux shrugged. "You know how it is, Dad."

"Well, don't let me keep you if you need to get going."

"Yeah," Lux said. "But I'll be back soon. Maybe this weekend?"

"I'd like that." He stood up.

They walked to the front door together, and Lux hugged her father before stepping outside.

"Drive safe."

"I will," Lux said, giving him one last smile before heading to her truck.

4

ZOEY

Zoey walked into command ops, her mind still on the conversation she'd had with Lux Valentine earlier in the cafe.

She sat two seats to Lux's right, and Zoey saw Lux's beautiful blue eyes darting around. Every once in a while, their eyes would meet. Zoey did her best to keep her face expressionless.

What expression is there to hide anyway? *Attraction? Lust?*

What was the use in being attracted to someone like Lux Valentine, anyway? Women like Lux—everyone wanted them. She hadn't missed how Lux had put the charm on her or how her gaze had travelled over her body and lingered.

A gaze meant to seduce. And it had.

But Zoey would never let on that it had. It was pointless being attracted to Lux. Zoey had seen her type a million times. Lux was exactly the type of woman you would do well to avoid.

Their eyes met again. Zoey looked away, her eyes darting in front of her.

Becky Thompson stood at the front of the room, her expression serious as she reviewed some notes while waiting for everyone to settle in.

Zoey nodded at a few of the firefighters she recognized from her first day. She momentarily missed her old team, their faces flashing through her mind unbidden. She shook off the memories, focusing on the present. This was her team now.

Becky cleared her throat, drawing everyone's attention. The conversations died down, and all eyes turned toward her.

"Alright, let's get started," the chief said, her voice calm but firm. She looked around the room, making sure everyone was focused. "Zoey, meet Marcia Foxwell, our chief engineer. Marcia, Lieutenant Zoey Knight."

Zoey stretched her hand toward Marcia but she simply nodded curtly at her, ignoring her hand.

. . .

"She didn't mean any insult," Lux whispered to her. "That's just Marcia."

"Oh," Zoey said.

"We've got a lot to cover today. First, I want to talk about the state of our station and where we stand in terms of resources."

Becky clicked a button on the projector remote, bringing up a slide that showed a list of their current assets: trucks, equipment, helicopters, and personnel.

Zoey leaned forward slightly, taking it all in. The numbers weren't great, but they were about what she had expected. The station was under-resourced, like most of the others she'd worked at.

"We've got a total of three helicopters," Chief Thompson continued. "Two are fitted with the necessary gear for fighting fires. Water tanks, thermal imaging, the works. The third is still waiting on some repairs and upgrades, so it's not fully operational yet."

She turned to Marcia. "How soon can we get the third chopper operational?"

Marcia shrugged. "A week? Maybe two?"

"That's not ideal," Chief Thompson said.

"My team is working on getting that third chopper up to standard as soon as possible," Marcia added.

"Get it done. In the meantime, we'll have to make do with what we've got."

She paused, giving everyone a moment to digest the information before moving on.

"In terms of personnel, we're stretched thin, as usual. We've got a solid ground team, but we're short on pilots. Lux, as chief pilot, is doing the best she can with what we have, but it's going to be tough."

She clicked to bring up the next slide, which showed a map of the region with several areas highlighted in red.

"These are the possible hotspots we're most concerned about," she said, pointing to the map. "There's a big one to the north, near the edge of town, and another out to the west, near the forest. If the winds shift, we could be looking at a pretty serious situation."

Zoey felt a knot of anxiety tighten in her stomach. She'd seen too many situations like this before—understaffed, under-resourced, and on the brink of disaster.

"We'll need to prioritize our response," Chief

Thompson said. "We can't be everywhere at once, so we need to be smart about where we deploy our resources."

Lux leaned forward, her eyes on the map. "Chief, if I may," she began, "I think we need to focus our efforts on tackling the fires at the hotspots. We've got two choppers that are fully equipped, and I can take one of them to the northern area while the other handles the west. If we concentrate our ground teams there as well, we can hit the fires hard and hopefully contain them before they spread."

Zoey's eyes narrowed slightly as she listened to Lux's suggestion. It was a solid plan, tactically speaking, but there was something about it that didn't sit right with her.

"We can't ignore the evacuation and rescue operations," Zoey said. "There are still people in those areas, and if we focus all our efforts on the fires, we're leaving them at risk."

Lux turned to Zoey, a snarl forming. "We're firefighters, Lieutenant Knight. Our primary job is to put out the fires. If we don't, there won't be anyone left to rescue."

"I beg to differ, Chief Valentine. Our primary objective is to ensure the security of lives and property by putting out fires."

"And when the fires intensify?" Lux's face was defiant and her shoulders tense as hell. She looked ready to fight. Zoey kept calm.

"I understand," she said. "But I've seen what happens when a team is too focused on fighting the fires and not enough on getting people out. We can't afford to make that mistake."

"And how do you suggest we do that?" Lux asked. "Expend all our resources on rescue operations?"

"We don't need to expend. We prioritize evacuation and rescue operations," Zoey said. "We can assign a few teams to tackle the fires, but the majority of our efforts should be on getting people out of harm's way. Land attacks in these areas could be dangerous, especially if the winds shift."

Lux's expression didn't change, but Zoey could see the stubbornness in her eyes. "And what happens if the fires spread faster because we're too focused on evacuation? We could end up with an even bigger disaster on our hands."

Zoey felt her frustration growing, but she kept it in check. "I'm not saying we ignore the fires, Lux," she said. "But we have to be smart about this. If we lose people because we didn't get them out in time, that's on us."

Chief Thompson cleared her throat, interrupting their argument. "Alright, let's take a step back here, you two," she said, her tone calm but firm. "Both of you make valid points, but we need to find a balance. We can't afford to ignore either the fires or the people in those areas."

She looked at Zoey then at Lux. "I want both of you to work together on this. Come up with a plan that addresses both concerns. We need to be coordinated in our response if we're going to handle this."

Zoey nodded. She wasn't sure how well she and Lux would work together, but she knew they didn't have much of a choice. Disagreeing with the fire chief immediately after disagreeing with the chief pilot would only make her seem unreasonable.

The tension between her and Lux was electric. Zoey did everything she could to dampen her thoughts, but her eyes kept flicking to Lux's hands and strong, capable fingers. Fingers that might...

Lux glanced at Zoey. "Alright," she said, her tone clipped. "Let's figure this out."

Becky continued with the rest of the meeting, outlining other details and updates, but Zoey's mind was only half aware of her words.

When the meeting finally ended, the team slowly filed out of the room, but Zoey stayed behind. She watched as Lux gathered her things, her movements quick and her face giving nothing away.

As Lux headed toward the door, Zoey stopped her. "Lux, wait a second."

Lux's gaze didn't waver, but Zoey could see the slight tension in her posture. "Can we do this later? I've got a crew waiting in simulations."

Zoey nodded. "Okay."

Lux turned and left the room, and Zoey didn't get the chance to go over the interaction.

The fire chief walked over to her, her expression thoughtful. "You handled that well."

"I'm sorry, Chief. I didn't mean to create a scene."

"A scene?" Chief Thompson waved her hand dismissively. "Nonsense. I love it when reasonable points are going around my strategy room. I also love it when someone is brave enough to challenge Lux Valentine."

"Reasonable points?"

"You and Lux would make a pretty great team."

Zoey snorted. "We would've had each other's

throats if you weren't in the room."

"I did mention that she was stubborn."

Becky Thompson laughed heartily. She took a few steps toward the door, and Zoey fell in step with her.

"I'm glad I have you two on my team, you know?" Chief Thompson said. "You're two smart, capable women who know how to get things done."

"Thanks," Zoey said. "I just want to make sure we're doing the right thing."

"I know you do," Chief responded. "And that's why I have confidence in you. But remember, this isn't just about what you think is right. It's about what's best for the team and the people we're trying to protect. You and Lux are both strong leaders, and I need you to work together, not against each other."

Zoey nodded, understanding the weight of her words. She was still getting to know this team, and she knew she had to earn their trust. Pushing her agenda too hard too soon could backfire, and she didn't want to start on the wrong foot.

"I'll work with her," Zoey said, trying to sound more confident than she felt. "We'll come up with a plan that makes sense for everyone."

"Good." She gave a reassuring nod. "I know it's not easy, but I'm counting on you both."

Zoey watched as the chief left the room, feeling the pressure of responsibility on her shoulders. She took a deep breath, trying to shake off the lingering tension from the meeting. She couldn't afford to let this get to her—not now when there was so much at stake.

She headed out of the meeting room and down the hallway toward her office. Her mind raced, trying to piece together a plan that would address both the evacuation and firefighting efforts. She knew Lux's suggestion had merit, but she couldn't shake the feeling that they needed to prioritize getting people out first.

As she reached her office, she found herself pausing at the door, her hand hovering over the doorknob. The memories of her old team, of the child they'd lost, came flooding back. She pushed them down, focusing on the present. This wasn't Forest Vale, and she couldn't let the past dictate her decisions here.

At least, she hoped so.

Zoey stepped into her office, the familiar surroundings helping to ground her. She moved to the desk, sat down, and pulled a notepad toward her. She jotted down ideas, trying to find a balance between the different priorities they faced.

She spent the next hour working through different scenarios, trying to find a happy medium between fighting the fires and ensuring the safety of the people in the affected areas. Every time she thought she had a solution, a new problem would arise, and she'd have to start over.

"Come on, Zoey. Think," she said aloud.

She leaned back in her chair, rubbing her temples in frustration. She couldn't do this alone; she needed to talk to Lux and get her input to find a way to make this work. As much as she wanted to prove herself, she knew that this wasn't something she could tackle on her own.

Zoey let out a deep breath. They had to get on the same page, for the sake of the team and the people they had to protect.

But first, she needed to get Lux Valentine out of her head, as ironic as it all sounded.

5

LUX

Lux stood in front of the simulation room, the hum of machinery filling the space as her pilots gathered around.

The room was dimly lit, the large screens on the walls displaying various terrains and fire scenarios they would be navigating today. She ran a hand through her hair, her mind going back to Zoey and their spat in command ops.

She hated that it was still gnawing at the back of her mind, even as she tried to focus on the details in front of her.

Oh, and obviously how attractive she found Zoey. That wasn't distracting *at all*.

"Listen up," Lux said. "Today, we're running through a series of scenarios that could realistically happen, given the current fire season. I want everyone to treat this as the real thing—no cutting corners, no messing around."

She walked over to the control panel, her fingers hovering over the buttons as she set up the first scenario. The screen flickered to life, showing a dense forest with thick smoke rising from the treetops. The simulated fire spread rapidly, with several hotspots scattered across the terrain.

"Let's start with a basic containment strategy," Lux said. "We've got a fire line here"—she pointed to a section of the screen—"and I want you to establish a perimeter around it. Remember to coordinate with the ground team and keep an eye out for any spot fires."

The pilots moved to their stations, their fingers flying over the controls as they began the simulation. Lux watched them closely, noting their movements and decisions as they navigated the scenario. She could see the tension in their shoulders, the way they leaned forward, fully immersed in the task.

As they worked, Lux's mind drifted back to Zoey. She couldn't shake the image of her standing tall and defiant in the meeting, her eyes flashing with determination. Lux found herself annoyed by the way Zoey had challenged her.

She wasn't used to being argued with when it came to tactics, and, to an extent, it excited her. She tried to push the thought away, focusing on the simulation.

"Jay, you're coming in too hot," Lux called out, her eyes on one of the screens. "Pull back and give yourself more room to maneuver."

Jay nodded, adjusting her controls as she pulled the helicopter back. Lux nodded in approval, her attention shifting to another pilot. "Jeanine, you're drifting off course. Stay focused on the target area."

Jeanine corrected her flight path, her movements precise as she guided the helicopter back into position. Lux continued to monitor the simulation, her eyes scanning the screens for any signs of trouble.

But even as she worked, she found herself replaying their argument over and over in her mind, analyzing every word, every look. Lux was used to conflict—she thrived on it, in a way—but this felt different. Zoey Knight was different.

It wasn't just the argument that bothered her; it was the way Zoey had looked at her, the way her lips had curved into a slight smile when Lux had finally agreed to work with her. Lux found herself drawn to Zoey in a way that she hadn't expected, and it was unsettling.

She shook her head, trying to clear her mind. "Focus," she muttered under her breath, her eyes narrowed.

The first scenario ended. "Nice work, everyone. Let's move on to the next one."

She set up the next simulation, this one featuring a residential area on the edge of a forest. The fire was closing in on the homes, and the pilots needed to work quickly to protect the structures and evacuate any residents.

As the simulation began, Lux's eyes flicked to the clock on the wall. Time was ticking by, and she knew they needed to get through several more scenarios before the day was done.

The pilots worked efficiently, coordinating their efforts as they tackled the fire. Lux could see their progress, the way they communicated and adapted to the changing situation.

Her mind wandered back to Zoey. As much as she didn't want to admit it, there was something about Zoey that intrigued her, something that made her want to know more. She found herself wondering what Zoey was doing right now, whether she was thinking about their argument too. Whether she was thinking about her.

"Chief V!" one of the pilots called out to Lux, pulling her out of her thoughts. "We've got a flare-up in sector three. Should we divert resources to handle it?"

Lux blinked, forcing herself to focus. "Yes, divert two units to sector three and make sure they coordinate with the ground team. We need to contain that fire before it spreads."

The pilot nodded, relaying the instructions to the rest of the team. Lux watched as they executed the plan, their movements precise and efficient. She felt a sense of pride in the way they handled themselves under pressure.

As the simulation came to an end, Lux let out a breath she didn't realize she'd been holding. The room was silent for a moment, the pilots catching their breath as they took in the results of their efforts.

"Good job, everyone," Lux said. "You handled that well. We'll pick this up again tomorrow and run through one more scenario."

The pilots nodded, standing up from their

stations and stretching. Lux watched them for a moment before turning back to the control panel.

The door to the simulation room flew open. Jolted, Lux turned to meet Zoey, her gaze fixed in Lux's direction. Her heart thumped unreasonably fast, no matter how much she willed it to slow down.

There was something in Zoey's eyes that Lux couldn't quite place—something intense, something that made it hard for her to breathe.

"Lieutenant," Lux said, "you just missed the simulation."

"Good," Zoey said, walking toward her. "I came here to see you, not the simulation."

Lux raised her eyebrows and then signaled her pilots to leave. They all exited the room. Lux walked out from behind the control panels, taking a few steps in Zoey's direction.

"Was there a simulation room like this in Forest Vale?" Lux asked.

"A simulation room? Yes. Was it like this? No."

Lux chuckled. "So, no then?"

"No."

"Actually, I guess I did come to see the simulation," Zoey said, pointing to the control panel.

"What about it?"

"I figured I'd better understand your views if I saw your simulations firsthand."

Lux nodded. It wasn't an apology. It wasn't an admission of guilt either. It was one strong woman speaking to another.

One strong, beautiful woman.

"My team just finished their rounds. It's just us now."

Lux could feel the tension between them, but she pushed it aside, focusing on the task at hand.

"Let's start with a basic scenario." Lux moved to the control panel. "We'll go through a forest fire situation, similar to what we've been working on. I'll walk you through the process."

Zoey stood beside her, close enough that Lux could smell the subtle scent of lavender on her. It was distracting, but Lux didn't let it show. She set up the simulation.

"First, we establish the perimeter," Lux said, pointing to the screen. "The helicopters will focus on containment while the ground team handles evacuation."

Zoey frowned, her eyes narrowing slightly. "I think we should prioritize evacuation first. If we can get people out safely, then we can worry about containment."

Lux's jaw tightened. "If we don't contain the fire, it's going to spread faster than we can evacuate. We need to prevent it from getting out of control."

Zoey shook her head. "Containment isn't going to matter if we lose lives in the process. We should focus on getting people to safety."

Lux's frustration flared, but there was something else too. Something about the way Zoey's lips moved when she spoke, the way her brown eyes, like warm hot chocolate, stayed locked on Lux's, unwavering. Lux felt a strange pull, a distraction that made her want to look away, but she didn't.

"The wildfire isn't predictable," Lux said. "We have to contain it first or we're risking everyone."

"And if we waste time on containment while people are trapped?" Zoey's voice was calm, but Lux could see the intensity in her eyes. "That's not a risk I'm willing to take."

Lux's eyes darted to Zoey's lips then back to her eyes. Her mind raced, and she kept getting caught in the way Zoey was standing, the way her body seemed so close, almost brushing against hers.

"We're talking about lives here," Zoey continued. "I understand the need for containment, but I think our priority should be the people."

Lux wanted to argue, to push back, but she found herself hesitating. She couldn't get past the way Zoey's voice sounded, strong but soft, commanding but somehow gentle at the same time. It was throwing her off balance.

"Fine," Lux said after a moment. "We can run the simulation your way and see how it goes."

Zoey nodded, stepping closer to the control panel. Their arms brushed, just barely, and Lux felt a jolt she didn't expect. She turned away quickly, staring at the screen.

Zoey's fingers moved over the controls, setting up the simulation to prioritize evacuation. The scenario started, and they both watched as the screens displayed the spreading fire and the rescue operations in action. Lux could feel Zoey's presence beside her, the heat from her body almost making Lux's skin tingle.

"We're losing too much time on these evacuations. The fire's spreading faster than we can handle."

Zoey didn't look up, her attention trained on the screen. "We're saving lives. That's what matters. Be patient."

Lux clenched her fists, her frustration mixing with something else she couldn't quite name. "But we're not containing the fire. It's going to get out of control if we don't act fast."

"We'll get it under control," Zoey said. "Once we know people are safe."

Lux was about to argue more, but she caught sight of Zoey's profile, the curve of her jaw, and the way her hair fell just slightly into her eyes. She looked so composed, so sure of herself, and Lux found herself caught in the moment, forgetting what she was going to say.

Zoey glanced at her, and Lux quickly looked away, pretending to focus on the simulation. But her mind was still on Zoey, on the way she looked, the way she sounded, the way she made Lux feel something she didn't want to acknowledge.

The simulation ended, and Zoey turned to Lux, a small smile on her lips. "See? We managed to handle both. People are safe, and the fire's contained."

Lux nodded, trying to hide the turmoil inside her. In some ways, Zoey had a point, but she wasn't going to admit that. "I still think containment should be the priority."

Zoey's smile widened a fraction. "We'll find a way to balance both. We're on the same team, after all."

There was something in her eyes, something intense, something that made it hard for Lux to breathe.

"Maybe you're right," Lux conceded. "About finding a balance. It's just...this job is dangerous."

"That's why we have to be smart about it."

Lux nodded, her eyes flicking down to Zoey's lips and back up. She didn't mean to; it just happened, like some magnetic pull she couldn't resist. Zoey took another step forward, and suddenly, they were standing too close, their breaths mingling in the space between them.

"Zoey," Lux began, but she didn't know what she was going to say. The words died in her throat as Zoey's eyes dropped to her lips, and Lux felt a rush of heat through her body.

Kiss her, Lux.

It was as though everything around them faded, leaving just the two of them in that small room, the air thick with the unspoken. Zoey moved closer, and Lux felt her heart skip, her breath catching as their faces were now inches apart.

"Chief Valentine," Zoey whispered.

. . .

Lux's mind was a whirl, part of her screaming to stop, the other part wanting nothing more than to close the distance. She could feel Zoey's breath on her skin, warm and steady.

But she wanted more than just a kiss. Her thighs shuddered with a sudden burst of desire, wanting—no, needing—this stubborn lieutenant in front of her. She leaned in yet again, their lips almost touching, the anticipation coiling tight in her chest.

The blaring sound of the alarm shattered the moment.

Lux jerked back, her heart pounding, the spell broken. She glanced at the red alarm lights blinking in a corner then hurried toward the door.

"Shit, there's a fire."

Shit.

6

ZOEY

Zoey stepped out of the simulation room, the sound of the alarm still ringing in her ears. The fire station was a flurry of activity.

Everyone was in motion, grabbing their equipment and heading to the trucks. Zoey moved quickly, pulling on her gear with practiced ease. Her hands were steady and her mind sharp, but the memory of Lux's closeness lingered in the back of her mind.

"Gear up!" she called out through the chaos. "We need to move now."

The ride to the fire was tense, the sirens blaring as they sped through the streets. Zoey was in the passenger seat while Marshall drove, her eyes scanning the horizon as they approached the smoke rising in the distance. She could feel the heat even before they arrived, and the air was thick with the scent of burning wood.

As they pulled up to the scene, Zoey jumped out of the truck, her boots hitting the ground with a thud. The fire was worse than she had expected. The flames towered above the trees, and the heat was intense. Her team was right behind her, ready for action.

"Everyone, listen up!" Zoey said, her voice loud over the roar of the flames. "We need to establish a perimeter and start containment. Keep an eye out for any civilians. We don't know if anyone's still out there."

Her team nodded, spreading out as they moved toward the fire. Zoey grabbed her radio, checking in with the other units. "This is Lieutenant Zoey Knight. Phoenix Ridge 13 on site and beginning containment efforts."

The response came through quickly, and the other teams coordinated their efforts. Zoey moved with her team, directing them as they laid down firebreaks and set up hoses. The flames were relentless and the heat oppressive, but Zoey was in her element.

The fire was spreading fast, the wind pushing it through the forest at an alarming rate. Zoey could see the urgency in her team's eyes, but she kept them steady, guiding them through each step. They were making progress, but it was slow as the fire consumed everything in its path.

Zoey wiped the sweat from her brow, her eyes scanning the area for any signs of trouble. Her radio crackled to life, and Ramirez's voice came from the other end.

"We've got a spot fire near the northern perimeter. It's moving fast. Requesting backup."

Zoey turned to her team, assessing their progress. They were holding the line, but just barely. She had to make a call.

"Ramirez, take the trucks and head to the northern perimeter," Zoey said. "Contain that spot fire before it gets out of control."

Zoey stayed with her team, pushing them to keep the fire from spreading any farther. The smoke was thick, the heat almost unbearable, but Zoey didn't let up.

About half an hour later, they had managed to slow the spread, but the fire wasn't out yet. Zoey could feel exhaustion setting in, but she didn't stop.

The radio crackled again, and Zoey grabbed it. Ramirez's voice came over the line. "Lieutenant, we've got civilians trapped near the eastern edge. They're cut off by the fire."

Zoey's heart skipped and her mind raced as she considered the options. The fire was still spreading, and pulling resources away could mean losing containment.

"Where's the nearest unit?" Zoey asked. Containment be damned. She'd rather that than lose anyone else.

"The nearest unit is ten minutes out, but the fire's closing in fast. They won't make it in time."

"What about air support?"

"We should have them over the zone any time now. I only fear it'll be too late."

Zoey's heart raced. If the helicopters weren't up just yet, then there was no saving those civilians.

Not again.

"Hold the line here. Keep pushing containment," Zoey breathed into the receiver.

"Lieutenant?"

"I said hold the line," Zoey repeated. "I'm going in."

She grabbed her gear and headed toward the eastern edge, her team moving to cover her as she went. The smoke was thicker here, the flames closer, but Zoey didn't hesitate. She moved quickly, her eyes scanning the area for any signs of the trapped civilians. Leilani Silva joined in.

As they approached, she could see the group huddled together as the fire surrounded them. They were panic-stricken, their faces covered in soot, fear evident in their eyes. Zoey moved closer, momentarily stunned by a sudden wave of déjà vu.

"We're with the fire department! You're all going to be safe, okay?"

She could see the relief in their faces, but the fire was closing in fast. Zoey had to act quickly. She and Silva led them toward a break in the flames, the heat intense as they moved through the narrow path she had cleared.

The flames were close, too close, but Zoey kept them moving, urging them forward. Her heart pounded and adrenaline surged as they made their way out of the fire's grasp. When they finally broke free, the civilians stumbled into the open, gasping for air.

Zoey took a moment to catch her breath, her eyes scanning the area to make sure everyone was safe. The fire was still raging behind them, but they had made it out.

"Get them to the medics," Zoey ordered.

The medics moved in and took the civilians to safety. Zoey watched them go, her mind already shifting back to the fire and the work still to be done. She grabbed her radio to check in with her team.

"Containment is holding, but we're not out of the woods yet," Ramirez reported.

Zoey nodded, even though she couldn't see her. "Keep at it. We need to keep this fire from spreading any farther."

She turned back toward the flames and pushed everything else aside—the exhaustion, the fear of losing someone, and maybe, she hoped, the moment when she nearly kissed Lux Valentine.

It didn't work.

The fire still roared, but she couldn't let her team lose focus. She paused for a moment and looked around. There were still a few members of the squad staying back in areas where the fires were less likely to affect trapped campers and hikers.

Zoey frowned. No doubt, they subscribed to Lux's strategy.

"Haley, I need that hose over here now!"

Haley, a young firefighter with a strong build,

rushed over. Her face was streaked with soot and sweat dripped from her brow, but she moved with purpose, dragging the heavy hose behind her.

Zoey grabbed it from her and aimed the stream at a particularly stubborn section of the fire, steam rising as water hit the flames.

"Ramirez, how's it looking on your end?" Zoey asked over radio.

"We're losing control over here, Knight. We're keeping it from jumping the road, but it's pushing hard," Ramirez said.

Zoey could hear the strain in her voice. She knew Ramirez and her crew were exhausted, but they couldn't let up. "Keep at it. I'm sending Captain Hunter and her team to reinforce you. Hold the line."

"Copy that."

Zoey turned to Hallie Hunter, who had just arrived on scene with her team, and nodded.

"On it," Captain Hunter said. She motioned to her crew, and they headed off toward Ramirez's location.

Zoey watched them go, her mind racing as she considered their options. The fire was still spreading, and they were stretched thin. They needed more resources, but she knew the other teams were just as overwhelmed.

Her radio crackled again, and she heard Lux's voice come through. "Knight, it's Valentine. I'm coordinating air support. We are seeing the fire pushing uphill. It's going to be harder to contain if it gets over the ridge."

Zoey's heart skipped at the sound of Lux's voice, but she pushed the feeling aside. There was no time for that now. "I know. We're doing everything we can down here. What's the status of air support?"

"Still ten minutes out. I'm trying to get them to prioritize your location, but they've got other spots to cover too."

Zoey gritted her teeth, frustration bubbling inside her. Ten minutes could mean the difference between holding the line and losing control of the fire. But she couldn't afford to lose her cool. Not now. "Okay, we'll keep pushing. Just get them here as soon as you can."

"Will do."

Zoey lowered the radio, taking a moment to gather her thoughts. The fire was relentless, and they were running out of options. She looked around at her team, seeing the exhaustion on their faces and determination in their eyes. They were giving everything they had, but she knew they needed more.

Zoey's mind raced as she considered their next move. They needed to hold the fire back, but they also needed to prepare for the worst-case scenario. She spotted Lux's air team on the horizon, their helicopters slicing through the smoke as they approached.

"They're here," she said, more to herself than anyone else.

The helicopters swooped in low, dropping water on the flames, and the fire was momentarily subdued by the deluge. But Zoey knew it wouldn't last. The fire was too strong, too determined to be easily defeated.

She grabbed her radio again, calling out to her team. "Everyone, pull back to the perimeter! We need to regroup and prepare for another push."

Her team responded quickly, moving back to the established fire line. Zoey joined them, her mind still racing as she considered their options. The fire was still spreading, and they were running out of time.

Lux's voice crackled over the radio again.

"Zoey, I'm coming down to help coordinate. We need to get this under control."

Zoey's heart skipped again at the thought of Lux being here so close—both thrilling and terrifying. She wanted to see her, to feel the comfort of her presence, but she knew there was no time for that now. They had a job to do.

"How about I handle things from down here and you stay up there as my eyes?"

"Maybe you should take a look from up here. It's not looking good," Lux said. "Hold on, I think there might be some campers still trapped in the hot zone."

Zoey inhaled sharply and held her breath. "Where?"

"I said maybe. I'm not certain. I'll circle back as soon as I know."

"Copy that. We'll be ready."

"Hang tight, Lieutenant. I'm coming to get you."

Zoey recoiled. Despite the raging fire ahead, she felt chills run down her skin.

7

LUX

Lux thought the new lieutenant's voice sounded close to panicking over the radio.. For an experienced officer, that was a red flag. But right now, nothing mattered more than getting to her.

The helicopter rotors thundered above, drowning out the chaos below. Smoke and flames swallowed the forest, turning the sky into a murky blend of grays and oranges.

Lux's hands were steady on the controls, her vision razor-sharp. This wasn't just another fire; it was a beast raging with a ferocity that could devour everything in its path.

"Base, this is Valentine. We're approaching the

drop zone." There was no room for anything else when she was in the air.

"Copy that, Lux. The ground team is ready for aerial support," the response crackled back.

Lux could see them now, tiny figures moving against the backdrop of burning trees. And there, directing the chaos like an orchestral conductor, was Zoey. Even from up here, Lux could spot her. The way she moved, the way she commanded her team—it was like she was born for this.

"Stay steady," Lux told her co-pilot, Jay, as they prepared for the drop.

She nodded, her face set in concentration. "We've got a lot of wind shear. It's going to be a rough one."

Lux gritted her teeth. "We've handled worse. Let's give them a clean drop."

The fire was unpredictable, and flames licked at the edges of the trees, driven by the wind that was the pilots' worst enemy right now. They made the first pass. The water released hit the fire's edge with a satisfying hiss. But it wasn't enough. The fire was moving too fast, spreading up the hills and threatening to surround Zoey and her team.

Lux circled, keeping an eye on the ground. Zoey was a blur of motion, directing her team with sharp, precise gestures. She was in her element down there, and Lux couldn't help but feel a tightness in her chest as she watched her.

"Lux, we need to go up for another pass," Jay said.

"I see it. Hold on." She was already banking the helicopter for another approach.

"We're low on water," Jay reminded her.

Lux nodded, the tension in her shoulders growing. "We'll make it count."

They swung around again, the helicopter vibrating as they fought against the wind. Lux lined up the shot, and they dropped the last of their load right where it was needed. It bought Zoey's team some time, but it was clear that this fire wasn't going to be easily tamed.

"Valentine, this is Knight. Do you copy?" Zoey's voice sent a jolt through Lux, one that she wasn't sure she liked.

"Copy, Zoey. What's your status?" Lux replied.

"Same as the last time. We're holding, but barely. The fire is moving uphill faster than expected. We need you to survey from above and coordinate with the ground teams."

Lux glanced at Jay. "You take the controls. I'll guide you from the back."

She nodded, taking over as Lux unbuckled and moved to the back of the helicopter. She grabbed the binoculars, scanning the ground below as they approached the fire line.

"Zoey, I'm going to do a flyover and give you a better assessment," Lux said.

"Understood."

They passed over the fire, and Lux saw the full extent of the damage. It was worse than she thought. The flames were climbing the hillside, and there was a thick line of smoke making it hard to see the edges of the fire.

"Looks like the fire is spreading faster on the west side," Lux reported. "You need to shift your team to cover that area or it's going to cut off your exit."

"We're on it," Zoey said, and Lux could hear the determination in her voice.

Lux relayed the information to Jay, and they banked left to get a better view. The fire was relentless, but so was Zoey. Lux could see her moving, directing her team with precision. It was like she was part of the fire itself, bending it to her will.

Only, she couldn't turn it off.

"They're doing a swell job down there," Jay said.

"This looks like a swell job to you?" Lux asked, staring at the flames climbing uphill.

"If they weren't so damn good, we'd be choked for cover up here."

Lux knew she was right, but Jay hadn't grown up with a veteran firefighter for a father. It's everything or nothing. Until the last flame is put out, don't commend yourself.

As they swung around for another pass, Lux couldn't shake the feeling that they weren't doing enough. That *she* wasn't doing enough. She should be down there on the ground, not up here in the sky, detached from the heat of danger.

It was either that or she was completely losing her head over the new lieutenant.

"Zoey, I'm coming down," Lux said before she could second-guess herself.

The moment the rotors slowed down, she spotted Zoey standing a few feet away in full fire gear, her arms crossed over her chest, eyes narrowed at the approaching machine. Lux took a deep breath, steadying herself. The tension between them had only grown since the last time they'd spoken, and now she had to bring Zoey on board—literally and figuratively.

Jay stepped out and grabbed a hose. That left just enough space for Zoey.

Lux unbuckled her harness, pushed open the door, and hopped down onto the rough ground. Dust and ash swirled around her feet as she approached Zoey and gestured toward the helicopter. "Get in."

Zoey shook her head. "I'm better off staying with my team. We've got ground to cover."

Lux squared her shoulders. "You're wasting time. You need to see this from above to make a real plan. We'll be quicker, more efficient."

Zoey's jaw tightened. "My team is already stretched thin. If I leave now—"

"You won't be any good to them if you don't have the full picture," Lux interrupted, stepping closer. "You can direct them better from up there."

Zoey glanced at the helicopter then back at Lux. The hesitation was clear. "I'm not sure this is a good idea."

Lux softened her tone, trying to bridge the gap between them. "It's not about whether it's a good idea. It's about what's necessary. Get in. Let's do this."

For a moment, Zoey seemed ready to argue

again, but then she nodded, her face set in determination. "Fine. But this better be worth it."

Lux turned and climbed back into the cockpit, feeling Zoey's presence close behind her. As they strapped in, Lux handed Zoey a headset. "You'll need this."

Zoey took it without a word, adjusting it over her ears. Lux powered up the helicopter, the rotors spinning faster, kicking up more dust and debris. They lifted off the ground, the noise of the engine drowning out everything else for a moment.

Once they were airborne, Zoey leaned closer to the window, staring at the burning landscape below. The fire had spread farther than Zoey had anticipated, swallowing acres of forest and inching closer to the small town that lay beyond the hills.

"You see?" Lux said, her voice crackling through the headset. "We need to get ahead of this."

Zoey scanned the ground. "I see it, but we can't just focus on the fire. We have to look for anyone who might be trapped. There are isolated cabins out there."

Lux tightened her grip on the controls. "If we don't stop this thing from spreading, there won't *be* anything left to save. We need to focus on containment."

Zoey turned her head, her expression hard. "And what if people are out there waiting for help? We can't just leave them to burn."

"I'm not saying we ignore them," Lux said. "But we can't be reckless either. We need to fight this fire, and we need to do it smartly."

Zoey crossed her arms, her gaze locked on the flames below. "We can do both. We *need* to do both."

Lux's frustration flared. "You're not seeing the bigger picture, Zoey. The fire is unpredictable, and if we don't contain it, we could lose control of the entire situation."

"And if we focus only on the fire, we're risking lives," Zoey shot back. "There are families out there who might be trapped. We can't just prioritize one over the other."

Lux clenched her jaw, her eyes flicking between the horizon and Zoey. Both were beautiful, and neither was on her side. She frowned and stared at the controls instead.

"I didn't say we're prioritizing anything. I'm saying we need to act strategically."

Zoey's hand gripped the edge of her seat.

"Strategic doesn't mean ignoring the people who need us."

Lux inhaled sharply, the air in the cockpit thick with the heat of their argument and the intensity of the fire below. She felt the weight of Zoey's words, the concern and urgency they carried. But she also knew the reality of the situation they were in.

"Look," Lux said, we'll scan the area for survivors, but we can't lose sight of the bigger problem. The fire is moving fast. We have to be faster."

Zoey's eyes softened slightly, but her resolve remained. "I get that. But I need you to understand those people are counting on us. We can't fail them."

Lux exhaled, the tension between them crackling like the fire below. "I know that. But you need to trust me on this. I've done this before. We can do both, but we need to be smart about it."

Zoey's gaze met hers, and for a moment, the intensity of the fire below was matched by the heat in Zoey's eyes.

"Fine," Zoey said finally. "But if I see anyone down there, we're going in. No arguments."

Lux nodded, a part of her relieved that they

had reached some kind of agreement, even if it was a fragile one. "No arguments."

8

ZOEY

The constant thrum of the helicopter's blades was a dull ache in Zoey's ears as she leaned forward, eyes fixed on the expanding fire line below. The flames were relentless, tearing through dry brush and timber like a predator on the hunt.

The fire's orange glow was bright, even in the harsh light of midday, and casted long shadows across the rocky terrain they hovered over.

Zoey clenched her jaw, anxiety twisting her gut into knots. "It's moving too fast," she muttered, more to herself than to Lux, who sat beside her in the cockpit. "If the wind keeps up like this, we're going to lose the entire section."

Lux's gaze was locked on the same burning

horizon. "We can't let it get into that rocky terrain. If it does, we won't have a chance of containing it. The ground teams can't navigate those rocks."

Zoey knew she was right. The rocky terrain ahead was treacherous—steep and filled with boulders the size of cars. If the fire spread into that area, it would be nearly impossible to control, and they would have to wait for it to burn itself out. That could take days, and the damage would be catastrophic.

"We don't have enough air support," Zoey said. "If we get too close, we'll be putting everyone in danger. We can't afford to lose the helicopter."

Lux turned to look at her, and Zoey felt a strange jolt in her chest at the intensity of Lux's gaze. "We need to go in closer," Lux said. "We need to hit it hard before it spreads any farther."

Zoey shook her head. "That's reckless. We need to hold it back long enough for the ground teams to get the campers and hunters out. They're still evacuating."

"We've got to think bigger than that, Zoey. If we don't stop this fire now, it's going to keep spreading, and there won't be anything left to save. The ground teams can handle the evacuation. We need to focus on the fire."

Zoey bristled at the suggestion. It wasn't just about the fire; it was about the people on the ground. Their safety had to come first. "You're not listening," she said, her tone sharper than she intended. "If we go in too close and something goes wrong, we could crash. We can't help anyone if we're dead."

Lux didn't back down. "I know it's risky, but we have to try. If we don't stop it here, it's going to spread into the next valley. And then we're looking at a full-scale disaster."

Zoey exhaled, her mind racing as she weighed the options. She could feel the pressure mounting, the weight of responsibility crushing her. She glanced back at the fire. The flames licked higher into the sky, driven by the fierce wind that showed no sign of letting up.

She couldn't deny that Lux had a point. The fire was moving fast—faster than she'd ever seen—and if they didn't do something drastic, they would lose control of the situation completely.

But the idea of flying the helicopter closer to the fire made her stomach churn. It was a huge risk, and she wasn't sure she was ready to take it. "You're being reckless," she said, finally voicing the thought that had been circling in her mind since Lux had first suggested the plan.

Lux met her eyes, unflinching. "Maybe. But I'd rather be reckless and give us a fighting chance than sit back and watch the fire win."

There was a fire in Lux's eyes that matched the one below them—burning, intense, and impossible to ignore. Zoey felt her heart skip a beat and her breath catch in her throat. Despite everything, despite the dire circumstances, there was an undeniable pull between them, something electric that made her pulse race and skin tingle.

But she couldn't afford to let herself be distracted by those feelings now. She had to focus on the task at hand, on making the right decision for everyone involved.

She glanced back out the window, her eyes tracing the flames' path as they devoured everything. She could see the ground teams moving, tiny figures against the vast landscape, working tirelessly to create firebreaks and evacuate anyone still in the area.

It was chaos, pure and simple, and the wind wasn't helping. It was pushing the fire in unpredictable directions, making it even harder to contain. Every second that passed, the fire gained more ground, and the stakes climbed higher.

Zoey felt the weight of the decision pressing down on her. She knew what Lux was asking of her, knew the risk they would be taking if they followed her plan. But she also knew that sometimes in situations like this, you had to take risks. Calculated risks, sure, but risks nonetheless.

She turned back to Lux. "Fine," she said. "We'll do it your way. But you better hope this works or it's going to be hell."

Lux's eyes lit up, and Zoey could see gratitude there, too, mingling with her resolve. They were in this together now, and whatever happened next, they would face it side by side.

Zoey took a deep breath, steeling herself for what was to come. They were about to dive headfirst into the heart of the fire, into the unknown, with nothing but their skills and guts to guide them. She only hoped it would be enough, even though her gut screamed at her. Zoey's hands gripped the edge of her seat, her knuckles turning white.

The helicopter vibrated under them, a constant reminder of how close they were to the danger below. She could feel the heat from the fire even at this altitude, a suffocating presence that clawed at her nerves. The sky was a haze of smoke, thick and oppressive, making it hard to see anything.

Lux leaned over her, reaching for a switch just above Zoey's head. The scent of her, a mix of sweat and something distinctly Lux, filled Zoey's senses, overwhelming her.

The closeness was intoxicating, and for a moment, Zoey forgot about the fire, about the danger, about everything but Lux's presence. The proximity made her heart pound, and she was acutely aware of Lux's breath against her cheek.

They were close, too close. Zoey could feel Lux's warmth, the steady rise and fall of her chest as she reached for the switch. Her lips were just inches away, and for a heartbeat, Zoey wondered what it would be like to close that distance. To give in to the pull she felt every time Lux was near.

But then the helicopter jolted, a reminder of where they were and what they were doing. Zoey snapped back to reality, her face heating up as she realized how easily she'd been distracted. Lux's hand brushed against her arm as she adjusted the switch, sending a jolt of electricity through Zoey's body.

Lux didn't seem to notice the effect she had. She was focused, her eyes sharp and alert, taking in every detail of their surroundings. "We're losing altitude. We need to climb," Lux said.

But before she could make the adjustment, the helicopter shuddered violently. The engine sputtered, and Zoey's heart leaped into her throat.

"Something's wrong," Lux said.

Zoey's breath quickened as she fought to keep the panic at bay. She could feel the tension radiating off Lux and see the concentration etched into every line of her face.

For a moment, the world narrowed to just the two of them, the roar of the helicopter fading into the background. Zoey's pulse raced as her hands moved with practiced ease over the controls.

"Keep it steady," Lux instructed, leaving no room for argument.

Zoey gripped the controls, her palms slick with sweat as she tried to keep the helicopter level while Lux worked on something behind her. The helicopter jerked again, and Zoey's stomach lurched, fear clawing at her insides.

"I need you to hold it steady for just a few more seconds," Lux said.

Zoey could barely breathe, her attention split

between keeping the helicopter in the air and the unbearable closeness of Lux. Her heart pounded and her skin tingled with the awareness of Lux's presence. Every time Lux moved, every brush of her arm or leg against Zoey's, a shiver rippled through her.

Finally, after what felt like an eternity, Lux straightened, her eyes meeting Zoey's. "It should hold for now," she said. "But we need to get back to the main strategy."

Zoey's relief was short-lived as Lux's words registered. The argument they'd had earlier flared up in her mind again, and the tension between them thickened. "You're still pushing for that?"

"We have to," Lux said, her tone leaving no room for debate. "If we don't get ahead of this fire now, we won't have a chance later. We can't afford to wait."

Zoey shook her head, anger bubbling up inside her. "And what about the people on the ground? If we crash, they have to fight the fire without us while trying to save us and any civilians. Our priority should be landing as quickly as we can to help bring people to safety."

"They're handling the evacuations," Lux countered. "But if this fire spreads any farther, there won't be anything left for them to come back to. We need to think bigger, Zoey. This is about more than just the immediate danger. And I can fly this helicopter into anything. She'll hold, I know it."

Zoey's hands tightened on the controls, her jaw clenched as she struggled to keep her emotions in check. Lux's determination, her unwavering focus on the fire, was maddening. "You're not thinking about the risks," Zoey said. "If we push too hard too fast, we could lose everything."

"And if we don't, we'll lose even more," Lux shot back. "This isn't just about saving a few lives today. It's about preventing a disaster that could affect hundreds, maybe thousands, in the long run."

Zoey's frustration boiled over, her emotions a chaotic mess inside her. She understood where Lux was coming from; she really did. But the thought of making the wrong call and leaving anyone behind, of not doing everything they could to save as many people as possible, was unbearable. Again.

Lux's eyes softened, just a fraction, as she saw the conflict on Zoey's face. "I know you care about them, Zoey. I do too. But sometimes we have to make the hard calls. We have to look at the bigger picture."

Zoey looked away, her gaze fixed on the flames below. The fire was a living thing, hungry and relentless, and it was spreading faster than they could keep up with. She knew Lux was right and knew they needed to act fast if they were going to have any hope of stopping it.

But that didn't make the decision any easier.

Lux reached out, her hand brushing against Zoey's arm, sending a shiver through her. "Trust me on this," Lux said. "We can do this. Together."

Zoey turned to meet her gaze. The conviction in Lux's eyes made Zoey's heart ache. Despite everything, despite the fear and the tension, she wanted to trust Lux. Wanted to believe that they could pull this off.

"Fine," Zoey said. "But if this goes wrong..."

"It won't," Lux said.

9
LUX

Lux's fingers drummed against the console as the helicopter hovered over the blazing forest. The flames were fierce, their orange and red hues licking at the sky.

The heat was stifling, even inside the cockpit, and she felt sweat trickling down her back and adrenaline coursing through her veins.

Zoey sat beside her, her eyes fixed on the chaos below and her brow furrowed with concern. Lux couldn't help but glance at her, the tension between them palpable. Zoey's decision to prioritize the ground team's evacuation had been a point of contention.

Now, as she watched the flames grow stronger,

Lux couldn't shake the feeling that they were losing control.

"They're almost clear," Zoey said.

Lux nodded, but the tension in her chest didn't ease. She was too aware of how quickly the situation could turn. The fire was unpredictable, and every second they spent in the air felt like a gamble.

The radio crackled to life, and a voice filled the cockpit. "Ground team is clear. All personnel evacuated."

Zoey let out a breath she hadn't realized she had been holding, and Lux felt a small measure of relief. But it was short-lived. The flames were spreading faster now, fanned by the wind.

"We need to move in," Lux said. "We can't let this get any worse."

Zoey nodded, her eyes finally meeting Lux's. There was something in her gaze—concern, maybe, or regret. Lux couldn't tell. All she knew was that they needed to act fast.

"Let's do it," Zoey said.

Lux adjusted the controls, guiding the helicopter closer to the fire. The heat was like a physical force pressing down on them, making it hard to breathe. The flames roared, and sweat beaded on Lux's forehead.

Zoey was focused, her hands steady on the controls as they maneuvered the helicopter into position. Lux could feel the tension between them, the unspoken words that hung in the air. She knew Zoey was worried—about the fire, about the people, about the risks they were taking. But there was something else there too. Something Lux couldn't quite put her finger on.

The helicopter shuddered, and Lux glanced at the console, her stomach twisting as she saw the warning lights blinking. The heat was affecting the electrical systems, and they were losing control.

"Lux," Zoey said.

"I see it." Her hands moved quickly over the controls as she tried to steady the craft. But the helicopter was unresponsive and jerking violently as more systems failed.

"We're going down," Lux said.

Zoey's eyes widened, but she didn't panic. Instead, her mind worked to find a solution. Lux admired that about her, the way she could stay steady even in the worst situations. But it didn't change the fact that they were in serious trouble.

Lux pulled back on the controls, trying to guide the helicopter away from the worst of the flames. They were losing altitude fast, and the ground rushed up to meet them.

"Hold on," Lux said.

"We're losing control!"

Zoey's panic seemed to come all at once. One second, she was calm; the next, she was screaming at the top of her lungs. Lux struggled in vain to guide the helicopter back into the air.

The treetops loomed closer now, and Lux knew they didn't have much time. She steered the helicopter toward a dense canopy of trees, hoping the branches would help cushion their descent.

The helicopter slammed into the trees, and the sound of metal crunching and glass shattering filled the air. The impact had thrown Lux forward, her head cracking against the console. Pain exploded behind her eyes, and for a moment, everything went black.

When she came to, the world was a chaotic blur of smoke and flames. The helicopter was tilted at an awkward angle, the nose buried in the ground, the tail sticking up like a broken limb. Lux's head throbbed, and she could taste blood pooling in her mouth.

"Zoey," Lux croaked.

She turned her head, panic gripping her as she searched for Zoey. The cockpit was a mess, debris and broken equipment scattered everywhere.

She squinted through the haze, her heart pounding as she struggled to orient herself. The world around her was a mess of tangled wreckage and flames. The helicopter had gone down hard, and she knew the chances of survival were slim.

Her fingers, slick with sweat, unfastened the seat belt. The cockpit was barely recognizable, crushed and twisted like a discarded toy. Instruments dangled uselessly from broken panels, and the control stick was jammed against her seat. The windshield was shattered, and through the jagged hole, she could see the smoldering remains of the fuselage scattered across the forest floor. The engine, torn free from its mounts, lay a few yards away, still smoking.

Lux gasped shallowly. She could feel the heat of the fire creeping closer, the flames licking at the twisted metal. Her pulse quickened as she took stock of the situation. The wreckage was surrounded by trees, and the forest was dense and oppressive. The smell of burning fuel mixed with the earthy scents of pine and damp soil created a nauseating combination.

She tried to move, but her left leg was pinned under a piece of the dashboard. Pain shot through her as she tried to pull it free, and the metal cut into her skin. She bit back a scream, panic rising in her throat. The fire was spreading fast, and the heat intensified with each passing second. Her hands trembled as she reached for the radio, but it was dead. Smashed in the crash.

"Zoey," she whispered, her voice barely audible over the crackling of the flames. "Where are you, please...?"

Suddenly, she heard movement outside the cockpit and she turned her head, straining to see through the smoke. She blinked, trying to clear her vision. It was Zoey. Her breath caught in her throat as she watched Zoey clamber back into the cockpit, her face covered in soot.

"Lux! Hold on!" Zoey shouted.

Lux felt a surge of relief mixed with a jolt of fear. Zoey was coming for her. She wasn't alone. But the fire was growing, and she could feel the heat getting closer.

"I'm pinned," Lux said, her voice trembling. "I can't move my leg."

Zoey reached for the metal trapping Lux's leg. Her fingers were raw and bloody, but she didn't hesitate. She pulled with all her strength, grunting with the effort.

"I'm going to get you out of here," Zoey said.

Lux winced as the metal shifted, the pain in her leg sharp and unrelenting. She clutched the sides of the seat, and her knuckled turned white. The smell of burning fabric and oil filled her nostrils, making her cough.

"It hurts," Lux said, her voice cracking. "Zoey, it hurts so much."

"I know. Just hold on a little longer. I've almost got it."

The dashboard creaked as Zoey applied more pressure, her muscles straining. Lux felt the weight lift slightly, enough for her to pull her leg free. She gasped in pain as she moved, the cut on her leg bleeding heavily.

"Okay, you're free," Zoey said, helping her up. "Can you walk?"

Lux nodded, though she wasn't sure if she could. Her leg throbbed with each movement, but she forced herself to stand. Zoey wrapped an arm around her waist, supporting her as they made their way out of the wreckage.

The air was thick with smoke, and Lux's lungs burned as she inhaled. She stumbled over a piece of the landing gear when her foot caught on the jagged metal.

"Easy," Zoey said, steadying her. "We're almost clear."

They moved as quickly as Lux's injured leg would allow, the flames snapping at their heels. She could feel her hands shaking and her breath coming in short, sharp bursts.

"Zoey," she said. "What if... What if it explodes?"

Zoey glanced back at the wreckage, the fire now consuming the cockpit. She tightened her grip on Lux, her face set in determination.

"We'll be out of range," Zoey said. "Just focus on moving forward. We're going to make it."

Lux nodded, though her fear didn't subside. Every step felt like a battle, her injured leg protesting each movement. The forest seemed endless, and the trees closed in around them.

Finally, they broke through to a clearing far enough away from the burning wreck. Lux collapsed onto the ground, her body trembling from pain and exhaustion. Zoey knelt beside her.

"Are you okay?" Zoey asked, her hand resting on Lux's shoulder as she tried to catch her breath.

Lux nodded, though she wasn't sure if it was true. Her leg throbbed, and she could feel the blood soaking through her pants. But she was alive. They both were.

"I...I thought I was going to die," Lux said. "I thought that was it."

Zoey's hand tightened on her shoulder. "But you didn't. You're safe now."

Lux looked up at Zoey, her eyes stinging with tears. She could see the worry etched on Zoey's face, the lines of stress and fear that hadn't been there before. She reached out, her hand trembling, and gripped Zoey's arm.

"Thank you. Thank you for coming back for me."

Zoey shook her head. "I wasn't going to leave you."

A tear escaped, slid down her cheek, and mixed with the soot and sweat. She was shaking, her body still in shock from the crash. Zoey pulled her closer and wrapped her arms around her. Lux clung to her, burying her face in Zoey's shoulder.

"I'm so scared," Lux whispered.

"I know. But you're not alone. I'm here. We're going to be okay."

Lux closed her eyes, focusing on the warmth of Zoey's embrace. The fear was still there, gnawing at her, but it was tempered by Zoey's presence. For the first time since the crash, she allowed herself to believe that they might make it out of this.

10

ZOEY

Zoey kept her arm around Lux's waist as they moved through the clearing. Lux limped, dragging her injured leg with each step. Zoey could see the strain on her face, the way her lips pressed into a tight line, and the faint tremble in her movements. Lux's usual confidence was gone, replaced by a vulnerability that surprised Zoey.

"Let's take a break." Zoey gently guided Lux to a fallen tree. "You need to rest."

Lux shook her head. "We need to keep moving. What if the fire spreads?"

"The wind's blowing the other way." Zoey crouched in front of her til they were eye to eye. "We have some time."

Lux hesitated, her gaze shifting toward the distant plume of smoke from the crash site. Zoey could tell she was still fighting the urge to push on despite her obvious pain. But when Lux finally sat on the tree trunk, Zoey could see the relief in her eyes.

Zoey knelt and unlaced Lux's boot, her fingers moving with care. The leather was stained with dirt and soot, the laces frayed from wear. She eased the boot off slowly, mindful of Lux's sharp intake of breath. Underneath, Lux's sock was soaked with blood, the fabric sticking to her skin.

"You should have said something sooner." Zoey frowned as she inspected the injury. "This looks bad."

"It's just a scratch. I've had worse."

Zoey wasn't convinced. She peeled the sock back, revealing a deep gash running along the side of Lux's foot that continued up to her leg. The skin was raw and inflamed, the edges of the cut jagged where the metal had bitten into her flesh. Zoey felt a surge of anger at the sight, though she wasn't sure who it was directed at—herself for not noticing sooner or the universe for putting them in this situation.

"This isn't just a scratch," Zoey said, her tone firm. "We need to take care of this."

Lux leaned back and closed her eyes. "We don't have much in the way of medical supplies."

"I'll make do."

She tore a strip from the hem of her shirt, using it to bind the wound as best she could. The fabric was rough, but it was better than nothing. Lux winced as Zoey tied the makeshift bandage, but she didn't complain.

When Zoey finished, she sat next to Lux on the log. Zoey could see the exhaustion in her posture, the way her shoulders slumped and her breath came in shallow gasps.

"We can't go far like this," Zoey said. "You need to rest."

"We need to get to higher ground," Lux said, opening her eyes. "It's safer uphill."

Zoey glanced at the slope ahead of them. The ground was covered in a thick layer of underbrush. The trees were dense and their branches cast long shadows in the fading light. It was the logical choice—they'd have a better view of the area, and it would be harder for the fire to reach them. But Zoey could also see how difficult the climb would be, especially for Lux in her current state.

"You can't make it up there right now," Zoey said. "Not with that leg."

Lux's jaw tightened, and for a moment, Zoey thought she was going to argue, but Lux sighed..

"I hate this," Lux said. "I hate feeling so helpless."

"You're not helpless." Zoey reached out to squeeze her hand. "You're hurt, and we need to be smart about this."

Lux looked down at their joined hands, and she brushed her thumb over Zoey's knuckles. "I just...I don't want to be a burden."

"You're not. We're in this together. We'll figure it out. Let's just rest for a few minutes and think."

Lux nodded, though she still looked uncertain. Zoey could see the conflict in her eyes—the desire to push forward battling with the reality of her injuries. It was a struggle Zoey knew all too well, the instinct to keep moving even when every part of her body screamed to stop.

They fell into a comfortable silence with the only sounds rustling leaves and fire crackling. The stress of their situation weighed heavily on Zoey, but she pushed those thoughts aside.

"Lux," Zoey said after a while, "we need to talk about what we're going to do next."

Lux opened her eyes and met Zoey's gaze. "I know."

"I don't think you're in any shape to climb that hill. We're better off staying here and waiting for rescue."

"But what if no one comes?" Lux said, her voice tinged with fear. "What if we're stuck here?"

"We're not going to think like that," Zoey said. "We have to believe that help is on the way."

Lux looked away; her brow furrowed. "I don't want to stay here. It feels too exposed."

"I know," Zoey said. "But we need to be realistic. We're close to the crash site, which means any rescue team will start looking for us there. And we'll be easier to find if we stay put."

Lux was silent for a moment, her eyes distant as she considered Zoey's words. Zoey could see the fear and uncertainty in her expression, the way her fingers twisted in the hem of her shirt.

"What if the fire spreads?" Lux asked.

"Then we'll move. But right now, it's our best option."

Lux's shoulders slumped as she exhaled. "I just hate sitting here doing nothing."

Zoey reached out, placing a hand on her arm.

"You're not doing nothing. You're recovering your strength. And that's just as important."

Lux looked at her, her eyes searching Zoey's face. Zoey held her gaze, hoping to convey the strength and reassurance she didn't entirely feel.

"Okay," Lux agreed. "We'll stay here."

Zoey felt a small surge of relief, though she knew their situation was still precarious. The wreckage was a stark reminder of the danger they were in, the charred metal and twisted debris scattered across the ground like a graveyard of their hopes.

"Let's make a plan." Zoey stood and brushed off her hands. "We need to set up a safe area, away from the fire and make some sort of shelter."

Lux nodded, following Zoey's lead. Zoey could see the effort it took for her to move, the pain etched into her features with each step, but Lux never complained.

They found a small, sheltered area on the edge of the clearing, far enough from the fire to feel safe. The ground was soft and covered in pine needles, and the trees provided a natural barrier from the wind. Zoey cleared away some of the debris, making a space for them to sit.

"This will do." Zoey motioned for Lux to sit.

Lux lowered herself to the ground with a sigh and leaned against a tree trunk. "It's not exactly the Ritz."

Zoey managed a small smile. "It's not, but it's better than nothing."

They sat in silence for a moment, the weight of the situation settling over them like a heavy blanket. Zoey could feel the exhaustion tugging at her, the adrenaline that had kept her going now fading away. But she forced herself to stay alert because she knew they couldn't afford to let their guard down.

"We should gather some supplies." Zoey glanced back toward the crash site. "Anything we can use to make this more comfortable."

Lux nodded, though she didn't move. "I'll stay here."

"I'll be quick," Zoey said, getting to her feet. "Just sit tight."

Zoey made her way back to the wreckage, her eyes scanning the debris for anything useful. The sight of the destroyed chopper was a sobering reminder of how close they had come to death. The fuselage was crumpled, and the propellers had snapped like twigs. The engine, now a twisted heap of metal, lay smoking in the distance.

Zoey found a few items—a blanket, first-aid kit, satellite phone, bottle of water—scattered among the wreckage. She gathered them and moved quickly as the heat from the wreckage subsided.

Zoey watched Lux closely as they settled into their makeshift camp. Despite the pain and exhaustion, Lux maintained a calm demeanor.

Lux's composure under pressure was something Zoey admired. It was reassuring in the midst of all the chaos, and it made Zoey feel stronger, like she could handle whatever came next because Lux was there beside her.

She handed Lux the bottle of water she'd found, and Lux took it with a small nod of thanks. Zoey sat next to her, close enough that their shoulders brushed.

She could feel the warmth of Lux's skin even through their clothing, and it sent a subtle thrill through her. The chemistry between them, which had been there since they met, seemed to hum more intensely now.

"Phoenix Ridge," Lux said after taking a sip of water. "Do you think anyone saw the chopper go down? They'd send a team, right?"

Zoey nodded. "They should have. The fire

crews are always on alert for things like this. If they saw the smoke, they'd start moving."

Lux looked thoughtful. "Phoenix Ridge has the best fire department, they know the terrain and know how to get in and out of the forest safely."

"I've heard that," Zoey said.

"Phoenix Ridge is a tight-knit community," Lux said, a hint of a smile touching her lips. "They take care of their own. And anyone who's lost out here becomes one of theirs until they're found."

Zoey felt a warmth in her chest at the thought. "That's good to know."

Lux turned her gaze to Zoey, studying her face. "What about Forest Vale? What was that like?"

Zoey felt a tightness in her throat, an instinctual reaction to the question. She didn't want to talk about her previous station. The memories were too raw, too complicated. She looked away, pretending to focus on a nearby tree. "It's not important. What matters is that we're here now."

Lux's eyes lingered on her for a moment longer, sensing the unspoken tension. But she didn't press. "You're right. We're here, and we'll get through this."

Zoey was grateful for the change in topic. "We

will," she said and met Lux's eyes again. "We'll stay put, keep ourselves safe, and wait for rescue."

"And if the fire gets too close, we move."

Zoey felt her heart swell at Lux's words. "Exactly. We're in this together."

They fell into a comfortable silence, the connection between them growing stronger with each shared glance, each reassuring word.

Zoey could feel it in the way Lux looked at her, the way their hands occasionally brushed against each other as they shifted positions.

She had just one thought now. Stay alive. Every other one shouldn't matter—or so she hoped.

11

LUX

Lux looked up at the sky, noting how the orange hue of the setting sun mixed with the darkening clouds above. They had spent the entire afternoon waiting for a rescue team that never came. Her hopes had slowly faded with each passing hour, and now, it was almost evening. The cold started to creep in.

"I keep thinking about the station," Lux said after a while. "I wonder if they're worried about us."

"They probably are," Zoey said. "People don't just disappear without anyone noticing."

"I hope they're looking for us."

The night had settled in around them, and the

forest was alive with the sounds of crickets and distant rustling in the bushes.

Zoey shifted uncomfortably, her eyes flickering open in the dim light of the fire. Lux, who had been lying close to her, noticed the movement immediately.

"You okay?" Lux asked softly.

Zoey nodded, rubbing her arms as she tried to find a more comfortable position. "Just can't get warm. It's colder than I expected."

Lux reached over, her hand resting lightly on Zoey's arm. The contact sent a jolt through her, something warm and electric that she hadn't expected. "We should share the blanket," she suggested, her voice steady despite the flutter in her chest.

Zoey hesitated, glancing at the blanket, which was barely big enough for one person. "It's okay. You should use it. You need the warmth more."

Lux shook her head. "We both do. Come on, we'll be warmer together."

Zoey finally relented, shifting closer as Lux draped it over both of them, their bodies pressing together under the thin cover. Lux's heart quickened, the closeness making her hyper-aware of every detail—the warmth of Zoey's skin against hers, the steady rise and fall of her breathing, the smokey scent of her hair, and the way their legs brushed together.

"You're shivering," Zoey said after a while, her voice low.

Lux hadn't realized she was until Zoey pointed it out. "Yeah, I guess I am."

Zoey shifted, pulling the blanket tighter around them. "I'm sorry about earlier. I know I can be a bit...intense."

Lux shook her head, even though Zoey couldn't see it in the darkness. "Don't apologize. You're just trying to do what you think is best."

Zoey sighed. "It's just this whole situation is so messed up. I hate feeling powerless."

Lux could relate to that. She was used to being in control and knowing what to do in a crisis. But here, stranded in the middle of nowhere with nothing but each other and the remnants of the helicopter, she felt just as lost.

"My dad is a firefighter too. He's the strongest person I know, and he seems to always know what to do, no matter how bad things get" Lux said suddenly, the words spilling out before she could stop them.

Zoey was quiet for a moment before she reached out and brushed her fingers against Lux's cheek. The touch was gentle, almost hesitant. "You're strong too, Lux. You're still here, still fighting."

Lux's breath hitched at the contact, her heart skipping a beat. Zoey's words were warm and comforting, but it was the way she looked at her that made Lux's chest tighten with something more. There was an intensity in Zoey's brown eyes and a softness that Lux hadn't expected.

"Thanks," Lux said.

Zoey pulled back slightly, the moment between them lingering. She reached down to remove her jacket, the fabric rustling as she pulled it off and tossed it aside. The movement revealed a strip of bare skin at her waist, and Lux couldn't help but stare, her eyes tracing her curves.

The sight made Lux's mouth go dry and her pulse quicken. She felt a sudden, overwhelming urge to close the distance between them, to press her lips against Zoey's skin and taste the warmth there. But she held back, unsure if she should, unsure if Zoey would welcome it.

Instead, Lux shifted closer, their bodies now fully aligned under the blanket. Zoey didn't move away, and Lux took that as a good sign. The fire crackled softly beside them, the only sound in the otherwise silent night.

"Is this okay?" Lux asked.

Zoey nodded, her breath brushing against Lux's ear. "Yeah. It's okay."

The both settled in, the fire blanket doing little to keep out the cold, but the shared body heat made up for it. Lux couldn't stop her thoughts from wandering back to Zoey's body, her eyes drawn to the smooth lines of Zoey's exposed skin. The attraction she felt was undeniable, a pull she didn't want to resist.

But she did. She knew now wasn't the time. They needed to focus on staying safe and surviving. Still, the desire lingered, a quiet hum beneath the surface.

Zoey shifted again, and she wrapped around Lux's waist. The gesture was simple, almost casual, but it sent a thrill through Lux, a warmth that had nothing to do with the fire.

"Let's try to get some sleep," Zoey murmured, half asleep already.

Lux closed her eyes, even as she was acutely

aware of every point of contact between them. "Goodnight, Zoey."

"Goodnight, Lux."

They lay there in the darkness as the fire cast shadows around them. Lux's mind raced with thoughts of what could be and what she wanted.

But she kept those thoughts to herself, letting the comfort of Zoey's presence lull her into a restless, but contented, sleep.

12

ZOEY

Zoey's stomach growled.

She opened her eyes, the pain in her muscles from yesterday's crash still sharp. The smell of dirt and burnt wood filled her nostrils as she glanced over to Lux, who was still asleep. Her lips were slightly parted, and her skin, even with splotches of dirt on it, was beautiful.

Zoey considered waking her but decided against it. She would let her sleep a little longer. They both needed rest. She pushed herself up slowly, trying not to make a sound. Her body protested every movement. She needed food, something to keep up her strength.

She scanned the area, but didn't find anything in the clearing.

She stepped away, the forest silent except for the occasional rustle of leaves. Zoey took a deep breath and tried to steady herself.

Her stomach growled again. There had to be something to eat nearby, maybe some wild berries.

She didn't get far.

Lux stirred, a soft groan escaping her lips as she woke. Zoey turned back, watching her sit up slowly, wincing as she moved her injured leg.

"Where are you going?" Lux asked, her voice rough from sleep.

Zoey hesitated. "Just looking for food. We need to eat."

Lux rubbed her eyes. "Don't go alone. We shouldn't separate."

Zoey considered arguing but didn't. She couldn't leave Lux behind, not after everything that had happened. "Okay. Let's go together."

Lux smiled weakly and stood. Zoey waited and watched as Lux struggled to stand and stretch her legs before stabilizing.

They walked into the dense forest. The ground was uneven, and Zoey could feel her feet sinking into the soft earth with each step. The air was humid, making the walk even more exhausting.

As they walked, Zoey pulled out the phone

they'd found earlier, hoping for a signal. The screen remained blank, mocking her. She tried again, holding it up, but it was useless. The forest was too dense, and they didn't have a clear line of sight of the sky.

"Any signal?" Lux asked, though she probably already knew the answer.

"No," Zoey said. "I'll keep trying, though."

They continued walking, the forest growing thicker around them. Zoey's stomach growled again, louder this time. Lux glanced at her.

"Hungry?"

Zoey nodded. "Starving. We need to find something soon."

Lux looked around, scanning the trees. "There has to be something edible out here. We just have to look."

The forest seemed endless, and the trees towered above them, blocking most of the sunlight. Zoey's eyes darted from tree to tree, searching for any sign of fruit. She spotted something up ahead, a small patch of light breaking through the dense canopy.

"Over there." Zoey pointed.

They headed toward the light, pushing through the underbrush. The ground became softer, almost muddy, and Zoey realized they were nearing water. The light grew brighter, and soon they broke through the trees, emerging into a small clearing.

A stream flowed through the center of the clearing, and the water was clear and cool. Zoey's eyes widened as she spotted a small cluster of berry bushes near the edge of the stream.

"Finally," she said, heading toward the bushes.

Zoey picked the berries, filling her hands with as many as she could. Lux reached the bushes minutes after her, picking a few berries and eating them slowly. Zoey watched her, noticing how tired she looked. Her blue eyes were dull.

"Are you okay?" Zoey asked.

Lux looked up. "I'm fine. Just tired."

They ate in silence for a while, and the only sounds were the gentle trickle of the stream and distant bird calls. A couple handfuls of berries later, Lux glanced at the stream. "I'm going to wash up."

Zoey watched as Lux walked toward the stream. When Lux reached the water's edge, she started to undress, peeling off her dirty clothes and tossing them aside. Zoey's eyes followed the movements.

Zoey tore her eyes away, feeling a flush of heat rise in her cheeks. She shouldn't have been looking, shouldn't have been feeling this way. But it was hard to ignore the way her heart fluttered, the way her body reacted to the sight of Lux's bare skin.

She swallowed hard, trying to focus on anything else—the trees, the stream, the berries still clutched in her hand. But her gaze kept drifting back to Lux and to the way the water flowed over her body.

Lux had her back turned toward Zoey as she watched, feeling like she was intruding. Her heart pounded in her chest and her mind raced with thoughts she knew she shouldn't have. Lux turned slightly, and Zoey caught a glimpse of her face, her expression relaxed, almost peaceful.

Zoey's breath caught in her throat, and she quickly looked away, focusing on the berries in her hand. She forced herself to eat, trying to ignore her heart pounding and the heat spreading through her body.

But the sight of Lux's bare breasts glistening with water was burned into Zoey's mind. She tried to shake it off, but it was no use. The attraction was too overwhelming to ignore.

Zoey clenched her fists, trying to steady her

breathing. But even as she told herself this, Zoey knew it was a losing battle.

She risked a glance back at Lux, and her resolve crumbled. The sight of Lux's body sent a jolt of desire through Zoey's veins. She bit her lip, trying in vain to keep her breathing steady.

"Why don't you join me?" Lux said.

Zoey hesitated. "Are you sure?"

"Come on."

"We'd still need to set up a better place to sleep when we get back," Zoey said without thinking.

Lux rolled her eyes. Zoey heaved. There was no getting out of this now. She wasn't even sure she wanted to get out of it.

Zoey nodded and slowly stripped off her clothes, feeling Lux's gaze on her the entire time. The air was cool against her skin, but her body felt warm, heat radiating from deep within her.

Lux reached out to take Zoey's hand and lead her into the water. The stream was cold at first, the shock of it making Zoey shiver, but Lux's hand was warm and firm in hers, grounding her.

The chill of the water sent goosebumps over her skin, but it did nothing to quell the heat building inside her.

Lux moved closer, and their bodies almost

touched. Zoey could feel the warmth radiating off Lux and hear her soft breathing. Lux's hand slid up Zoey's arm, her touch gentle. Zoey's breath caught, and she looked up to meet Lux's gaze.

Without thinking, Zoey leaned in, her lips brushing against Lux's. The kiss was soft at first, tentative.

But then Lux's hand cupped Zoey's face, and the kiss deepened, becoming more urgent, more demanding. Zoey wrapped her arms around Lux's waist, pulling her closer, feeling the press of their bodies together.

Lux moaned softly against Zoey's lips, and the sound sent a shiver down Zoey's spine. She could feel Lux's hands moving, sliding down her back, over her hips, exploring her body with a hunger that matched Zoey's own.

Zoey's fingers trailed over Lux's wet skin, feeling the way her muscles moved under her touch.

They kissed deeply, their breaths mingling. Zoey's hands slid up Lux's back, pulling her even closer, wanting to feel every inch of her.

Lux's fingers found their way into Zoey's hair, tugging gently, tilting her head back to deepen the kiss. Zoey's knees went weak, and her heart pounded. They moved together, the water splashing around them, but neither of them noticed.

Lux's hands were everywhere—touching, caressing, exploring—and Zoey was lost in the sensation, in the feel of Lux's skin against hers. She couldn't think about anything except the way Lux's body fit against hers and the way their breaths came in short, ragged gasps.

Zoey's hand slid down Lux's back, feeling the curve of her spine and softness of her skin. Lux's breath hitched, her body arching into Zoey's touch, and Zoey felt a rush of satisfaction at the response she was drawing from her.

She kissed Lux again, harder this time, more demanding, and Lux responded with a fervor that took Zoey's breath away.

They broke apart for a moment, both gasping for air. Lux looked at Zoey, her eyes filled with desire, her lips swollen from their kisses.

"Zoey..." Lux whispered.

Zoey didn't answer with words. Instead, she closed the distance between their lips in another searing kiss. Lux's hands slid down her arms, pulling her closer. Their bodies pressed together, skin against skin, the water swirling around them.

The world around them faded away, leaving just the two of them wrapped up in each other. Zoey could feel Lux's heart pounding against her chest, matching the frantic beat of her own.

She moved her hands over Lux's body, exploring, feeling, and committing every curve and dip to memory.

Lux gasped as Zoey's hands slid lower, her body responding to Zoey's.

Zoey felt her own right hand instinctively seeking between Lux's legs and as she felt the wetness she had been seeking- that different kind of wetness- she smiled to herself and pushed her fingers inside. She enjoyed Lux's gasp as she entered her and she felt Lux's own right hand pushing between Zoey's legs. She parted her legs further, putting her foot up on a rock to allow Lux easier access. She wanted this so badly... no, she *needed* this so badly. This, Lux's fingers pushing inside of her.

She heard her own deep guttural groan.

"Fuck, Lux. Yes.. like that." She felt Lux's fingers moving inside of her, seeking her G spot and beginning to thrust in and out. Her own fingers were doing the exact same inside of Lux.

Lux's moans, soft and breathless, sent shivers

down Zoey's spine. Her blue eyes were glazed with lust.

Zoey could feel Lux's body responding to her touch, the way her muscles tensed and relaxed, the way her breath caught in her throat.

Zoey pressed her lips to Lux's neck, trailing kisses down her throat, tasting the salt and smoke of her skin, feeling the warmth of her body.

She felt the tension building between them until it felt like she might burst.

Lux's fingers moved in rhythm with her own.

"Oh god, oh yes.. fuck me…" Lux growled and Zoey obliged. She felt Lux's thumb tight against her clitoris.

And then, suddenly, everything turned beautifully white. Lux cried out, her body arching against Zoey's, and Zoey followed her, the world around them fading away as they were both consumed by the intensity of their release.

For a moment, everything was still. The only sounds were their ragged breathing, the water trickling around them, and the distant chirping of birds. Zoey felt the aftershocks of their pleasure still rippling through her and her body trembling from the intensity of it all.

She pulled back slightly, looking at Lux, who

was still catching her breath. Lux's eyes met Zoey's, and there was a soft smile on her lips, a look of satisfaction and contentment that made Zoey's heart swell.

"That was…" Lux began but let the words trail off.

Terrible? Wrong? Stupid?

"Amazing," Lux finished.

"That it was," Zoey said.

They stayed like that for a few moments, their bodies still entwined, the water gently lapping at their legs.

She loved every bit of the sex she just had with Lux, but the questions just wouldn't leave her mind. *What's wrong with you, Zoey?*

How could they be having sex while trapped here? How could she be getting this attracted to someone under these circumstances?

But then Zoey noticed something out of the corner of her eye—a movement on the bank. She looked around and saw nothing, then she heard the rattle. She pulled back, her body tensing as she spotted the source of the movement.

"Lux, don't move."

13

LUX

The rattlesnake was coiled and had its head raised, poised to attack.

Lux kept her eyes locked on the snake. Her body was tense, but her mind was clear. Panic would only make things worse.

"Stay still," Zoey whispered.

Lux kept her gaze on the snake. "It's a timber rattlesnake. The rattle is a warning."

Zoey swallowed hard, her eyes darting between Lux and the snake. "What do we do?"

"Just stay calm," Lux said. "It's probably just as scared as we are. We need to slowly back away."

Lux took a slow, deep breath as she steadied herself. She could feel the cold water lapping at her legs, the dampness of the air clinging to her skin. Every sense was heightened, every sound amplified in the stillness. The snake's tongue flicked out, tasting the air, but it didn't move.

Lux stepped back carefully, and Zoey followed her lead. Every muscle in Lux's body was tense, but she kept her movements smooth and controlled. The snake watched them, it's head swaying slightly, but it didn't strike.

Lux kept talking, her voice low and calm, hoping it would soothe both Zoey and the snake.

"They're most dangerous when they feel threatened," Lux said.

"Does it feel threatened?"

"How would I know?"

"Well, you're the snake expert."

"Shhh, don't upset it." Lux stopped backing away. "If we give it space, it should leave us alone."

"Should?"

"Back away slowly. I can't tell what it's thinking right now."

Zoey nodded. "I've never been this close to a snake before."

"Neither have I, not like this," Lux admitted.

The snake remained where it was, its gaze still fixed on them, but it made no move to follow. Lux kept her eyes on it, watching for any sign that it might strike, but it remained coiled, its body still.

Lux slowly straightened, still keeping her movements slow and deliberate. "Okay, we're almost out of its range," she said softly.

They took a few more steps back, and then the snake finally moved. It lowered its head, its body relaxing slightly as it slithered away.

Lux watched it go, her heart pounding in her chest. She didn't move until the snake was out of sight, disappearing into the underbrush. Only then did she let out the breath she'd been holding.

Zoey let out a shaky laugh, her hand coming up to cover her mouth. "I can't believe that just happened."

"Neither can I."

"How did you stay so calm?"

"That was calm?" Lux laughed. "I nearly peed my pants."

"You're not wearing any."

They both laughed, and Lux chuckled the loudest. She glanced at Zoey's face and smiled.

"Can't believe a snake saw me naked," Lux said.

"Who knows, maybe that's why it didn't attack."

"Don't even get started, you're"—she glanced at Zoey's body again—"damn."

Zoey backed away and cleared her throat. "We should get dressed."

Didn't she want this? Lux nodded and walked over to pick her clothes. Zoey did the same. Lux couldn't take her eyes off Zoey's beautiful round ass as she bent over. There was a memory that would stay with her forever.

"We should head back to camp," Lux said, as soon as they were done dressing. "We need to get dry and make sure we're ready for the next leg of the journey."

Zoey nodded, but she didn't move. Her eyes were still locked on Lux's, her expression softening. "Lux...?"

"Yes?"

Zoey hesitated, her hand still resting on Lux's arm. She could see the conflict in Zoey's lovely brown eyes.

"Nothing. Let's go."

Lux nodded, though she couldn't shake the feeling that there was something Zoey had wanted to say. But she didn't press, knowing that they had already been through enough for one day. They turned and began to make their way back to camp.

The tension from the rattlesnake encounter still buzzed in her veins, but she forced herself to try to relax. Zoey's hand brushed against Lux's, and her heart skipped a beat.

She reminded herself she wasn't supposed to feel this way. It was supposed to be just sex, nothing more. She didn't do *more*. She wasn't looking for anything deeper and didn't want to risk hurting Zoey when she inevitably got bored of her.

"Lux," Zoey started, "what do you think you'll do after all this is over?"

Lux's stomach tightened. She knew the question was coming, even if it wasn't the dreaded "what are we" talk. She needed to keep things light, keep the walls up.

"I don't know. Maybe take a long shower and eat something that isn't wild berries. You?"

Zoey laughed, but it was a little forced. "I guess I haven't really thought about it. It feels like we've been out here forever."

"Yeah," Lux agreed, keeping her tone casual, though her thoughts were anything but. She liked Zoey, more than she should. But she wasn't the type to settle down. It was easier to keep things physical to avoid the emotional entanglements that came with letting someone in.

Zoey hesitated, then reached out, her fingers

brushing Lux's arm. The touch was light, but it sent a jolt of electricity through Lux.

"You okay?" Zoey asked, her eyes searching Lux's face.

Lux nodded, forcing a smile. "Yeah, just tired."

Lux swallowed, her throat suddenly dry. She wanted to say something, but the words were stuck. Instead, she nodded again, her smile feeling tight.

Lux's heart twisted. She knew she was on the edge of something she couldn't control, something that terrified her more than the fire or the snake. But she couldn't bring herself to pull away.

Not yet.

She reached out, tucking a loose strand of dark hair behind Zoey's ear, her fingers lingering against Zoey's cheek.

The space between them seemed to shrink, the air around them thick with unspoken feelings. Lux wanted to close the gap, to give in to the pull she felt toward Zoey. But the fear of what might happen after held her back.

Instead, she stepped away, breaking the moment. "We should get some more rest," Lux said, even though her heart was racing.

Zoey nodded, the disappointment clear in her eyes, but she didn't press. "Yeah, you're right."

As they settled down, Lux couldn't help but wonder how much longer she could keep up this balancing act, caught between what she wanted and what she was afraid to have.

As much as she loved being with Zoey, she didn't want to think of anything after this episode. Commitment just wasn't her thing.

Zoey smiled, and it was that soft, genuine smile that Lux had come to love seeing. "Well, I'm glad you were here. I would've probably freaked out."

Lux chuckled softly. "You're tougher than you give yourself credit for."

Zoey shook her head, a playful glint in her eyes. "Not when it comes to snakes."

They both laughed, the sound carrying through the trees. It felt good to laugh, to share this light moment after the intensity of the situation. It had brought them closer in a way that Lux hadn't expected.

As they continued walking, the camp came into view, the faint glow of the fire a welcome sight in the dark forest. But neither of them seemed in a hurry to rejoin the others.

Zoey stopped walking, turning to face Lux

fully. The look in her eyes was intense, but not in the way it had been with the snake. This was different—more personal, more vulnerable.

Zoey took a small step closer, her eyes never leaving Lux's. "I don't know what I'd do without you."

Lux swallowed hard. She didn't know what to say or how to respond to her raw honesty. "Come on, Zoey. You'd be fine."

Zoey shook her head, her eyes shining with something Lux couldn't quite place. "Maybe. But I'd rather not find out."

The space between them felt like it was shrinking, drawing them together in a way that was both thrilling and terrifying. Lux could feel the heat radiating off Zoey's skin, could see the way her chest rose and fell with each breath.

"Zoey," Lux began, her voice trembling slightly. "I—"

But before she could finish, Zoey closed the gap between them, her lips pressing softly against Lux's. The kiss was gentle at first.

But then it deepened, the hesitation melting away as they lost themselves in each other.

Lux's hands found their way to Zoey's waist, pulling her closer as the kiss became more urgent.

She could feel Zoey's heart pounding against her chest and could taste the faint sweetness of her lips.

When they finally pulled apart, they rested their foreheads against each other's.

"Lux," Zoey whispered, her voice shaky. "Why do I want you this much?"

"Why do you ask so many questions?"

Zoey's hands cupped Lux's face, her thumbs brushing gently over her cheeks. "You're just something else, aren't you?"

Zoey's lips found Lux's again, more insistent this time. Lux responded eagerly, her hands roaming over Zoey's back, feeling the smooth skin beneath her fingertips.

They moved together, instinctively finding a rhythm that felt right and natural. Every touch, every kiss was filled with a longing that had been building for so long and finally found its release.

Lux guided Zoey to the ground, the cool earth beneath them a stark contrast to the heat between their bodies. They moved slowly, savoring each moment.

Surely one more time wouldn't hurt.

Zoey's hands were everywhere, exploring Lux's

body with a reverence that made her heart ache with affection.

Lux moved quickly pulling down Zoey's fire pants and underwear from her hips to her ankles and off in one smooth move.

She pushed Zoey's T shirt and bra upwards exposing her beautiful breasts.

She's so fucking beautiful.

Lux pinned Zoey's eager hands above her head as she took Zoey's nipple in her mouth, sucking, biting enjoying Zoey's gasps.

Zoey tried again to release her hands.

"Keep your hands there," Lux commanded. "I want to worship your body,"

Zoey shuddered as she nodded and her hands stayed above her head as Lux moved down her body with her mouth, kissing, licking, biting her belly and her hips getting closer and closer to where she really wanted to taste.

She was hungry with desire for Zoey.

She moved lower, parting Zoey's legs so she could kneel between them. She dipped her head and ran a long slow stroke of her tongue through Zoey's labia. She felt her own lust buzzing harder in her veins as she licked again and again. Long strokes with her tongue, pushing deep inside, tasting her.

Zoey's eyes were closed and she was moaning in appreciation, the sweetest sounds to Lux's ears.

She took Zoey's clitoris in her mouth and sucked feeling it swell in her mouth. Zoey whimpered and Lux felt throbbing between her own legs as though she might come herself just from licking Zoey.

Lux enjoyed the feel of Zoey's clit in her mouth so much that she kept it there alternating long slow sucks of it with massaging it with the flat of her tongue.

She moved her right hand to join in, her fingers delving Zoey's wetness before pushing deep inside. Zoey gasped and her legs began to shake. She whimpered again.

Oh fuck, she is so good to fuck.

Lux sucked gently yet persistently on Zoey's clitoris as her fingers began to fuck her.

She felt Zoey's pussy tightening around her fingers, she felt Zoey's whole body begin to tighten pre-orgasm. She felt a throbbing between her own thighs more insistent than anything she had ever felt before.

Lux slid her left hand inside her own pants and pressed against her own clitoris.

Zoey called out loudly and shuddered and gushed as her orgasm flooded through her.

Lux pressed tightly against her own clitoris and it was enough to tip her over the edge, her orgasm coming in a way it never had before. Her body convulsed as her climax rushed to every part of her lighting her up in all the best ways possible.

When she opened her eyes, she still had her fingers inside Zoey and a pool of Zoey's climax in the palm of her hand. Zoey's orgasm had passed and her body relaxed. Her beautiful brown eyes looked up through heavy lids to Lux. Lux felt her heart swell as her orgasm subsided.

Well, fuck...

14

ZOEY

Zoey lay next to Lux, her body still tingling from the aftershocks of their lovemaking.

The air around them felt warm and heavy with the lingering scent of sweat and earth. Zoey turned on her side, propping herself up on one elbow to look at Lux. She was still catching her breath, her chest rising and falling in a steady rhythm that was almost hypnotic.

"That was...amazing," Zoey said softly, her voice still a little breathless.

Lux smiled, her eyes half-closed in contentment. "Yeah, it was."

For a moment, they just looked at each other, the silence between them comfortable and easy.

Zoey reached out, her fingers brushing a strand of hair away from Lux's face. The touch was light, almost reverent.

"I'm glad you're here," Zoey said.

Lux opened her eyes fully, meeting Zoey's gaze. There was a softness in her expression, a vulnerability that Zoey hadn't seen before. "Glad you're stuck in the Phoenix Ridge forests with me?"

Zoey laughed. "I wouldn't wish to be trapped here with anyone else."

"I guess that's some comfort anyway," Lux said. "I bet if my dad were here, he'd tease me about having my partner's back."

"Sounds like a great guy."

"He is. He always says that being a firefighter is more than just a job; it was a calling. He believes in it so much, and I guess that belief just rubbed off on me."

"That's why you joined the fire department, isn't it? To follow in his footsteps?"

"Yeah," Lux said, a hint of pride returning to her voice. "I wanted to help people, like he did."

"You're amazing, you know that?"

Lux chuckled softly, shaking her head. "I'm just doing my job, Zoey."

Zoey shook her head, her expression earnest.

"No, it's more than that. You're brave, and strong, and you care so much about the people around you. That's not just doing your job; that's being an incredible person."

Lux looked at her, a warmth in her blue eyes that made Zoey's heart flutter. "Thank you."

"He's still in Phoenix Ridge?" Zoey asked. "Your father?"

"Yeah. Sometimes he shows up at the station just to give the Chief Thompson hell."

Zoey raised her brow. "Hell?"

"In a good way," Lux said, laughing. "Chief Thompson is...well, she's like a mother to me, really."

Zoey could hear the affection in Lux's voice, and it made her smile. "It sounds like you're really close."

"We are."

"And Jay?" Zoey asked, curious about the person Lux spent so much time with in the air.

"Jay." Lux said, a fond smile spreading across her face. "She's a good woman. A bit of a joker, but she's solid. We've been partners for a while now, and there's no one else I'd trust more up there with me. She's always got my back."

"That's nice."

They fell into a comfortable silence

Zoey let the quiet linger, savoring the warmth of Lux's hand in hers. She could feel the steady beat of her own heart, a comforting rhythm that seemed to sync with Lux's breathing. The world outside their little bubble had faded away, leaving only the two of them, connected in a way that felt both profound and intimate.

Lux's fingers tightened around hers, grounding her in the moment. Zoey's gaze drifted over Lux's face, taking in the way her lips curved into a gentle smile, the way her eyes held a softness that made Zoey's chest ache with something she couldn't quite name.

"Can I ask you something?" Zoey said, her voice breaking the silence.

"Of course," Lux replied, her thumb still tracing slow circles on Zoey's hand.

Zoey hesitated for a moment, gathering her thoughts. "Why did you become a firefighter? I mean, I know you said you wanted to follow in your dad's footsteps, but...why this? Why something so dangerous?"

Lux's smile faded a little. "It's a good question. I guess part of it is that I just loved the thrill. With my dad being my only parent, I grew up having a thing for danger."

Zoey nodded. "That makes sense."

"Dad didn't think it did at first."

"Really?"

"Yeah. So I first became a pilot."

"Smart."

"But it's more than that too. There's something about it...the adrenaline, the challenge. It's like every time I go out there, I'm reminded of what I'm capable of. It's hard to explain, but it's almost like...it gives me a purpose."

"You're really brave, you know that?" Zoey felt a surge of admiration for Lux, for the courage it took to face danger day in and day out.

Lux's lips quivered into a small smile. "I don't always feel brave. Sometimes I'm scared out of my mind. But I think that's part of it too."

"I think that makes you even braver. Doing what needs to be done, even when you feel scared."

Lux's smile widened, a warmth spreading through her eyes. "Thanks, Zoey."

Zoey returned the smile, her heart feeling light and full at the same time. She shifted closer, her body drawn to Lux's like a magnet. Their legs brushed together, and Zoey felt a spark of electricity pass between them, a reminder of the passion they had shared earlier.

She leaned in closer, her lips brushing against Lux's in a soft, tender kiss. Lux responded immediately, her hand sliding up to cup Zoey's cheek, holding her close as their lips moved together in a slow, deliberate dance.

The kiss deepened, and Zoey felt a rush of warmth spread through her body, a sensation that was both comforting and exhilarating. She could feel Lux's heartbeat against her chest and the way their bodies seemed to fit together perfectly.

When they finally pulled away, Zoey's breath was ragged, her lips tingling from the intensity of the kiss. Lux's eyes were full of longing, and Zoey felt a similar pull deep within her own chest.

"Zoey?" Lux murmured, her voice low and full of emotion.

"I'm right here."

Lux's lips curved into a soft smile, and she leaned in to kiss Zoey again, this time slower, savoring the moment. Zoey melted into the kiss, her hands sliding up to tangle in Lux's hair, holding her close as their lips moved together in a perfect rhythm.

When they finally broke apart, Zoey rested her forehead against Lux's, her breath coming in shallow gasps. Then she leaned in, pressing a soft kiss to Lux's lips, savoring the warmth and tenderness that passed between them.

Lux's hand moved to Zoey's hair, her fingers gently stroking through the strands. Zoey let out a soft sigh of contentment, feeling completely at peace in Lux's arms.

Zoey took a deep breath, gathering her thoughts. "I wasn't just transferred here," she began. "I requested a transfer."

Lux shifted slightly. "What were you running away from?"

Zoey's lips twitched into a small smile. "I was the leader of a team in the department. We were a tight-knit group, and we worked together for years. We went into disaster zones and pulled people out of collapsed buildings, that sort of thing."

Lux's eyes held a mixture of curiosity and understanding. "What happened?"

Zoey felt a lump form in her throat, and she had to take a moment to steady herself before continuing. "There was...an incident. We were responding to a call. A fire had broken out in this old building, and there were people trapped inside. We went in, did what we always did—worked together and got as many people out as we could."

Zoey paused, her breath hitching slightly as the memories came rushing back. She could see the flames and thick smoke; she felt the heat against her skin.

Lux's hand slipped into hers, squeezing gently. "You don't have to talk about it if it's too hard."

Zoey shook her head, swallowing against the tightness in her throat. "No, I need to. I've kept this inside for too long."

She took another deep breath, willing herself to keep going. "We were almost done, almost out. But then, we heard this sound. It was faint but unmistakable: a child crying. We couldn't just leave, you know? We had to go back."

Zoey closed her eyes, the memory playing out in her mind like a movie she couldn't turn off.

"We split up, covering more ground that way. But the fire was getting worse, spreading faster than we expected. The heat was intense, and the smoke was so thick it was hard to see, hard to breathe."

She felt the tears welling up in her eyes, and she blinked them back, determined to keep going.

"I found the child. She was so small and scared. I picked her up and tried to get her out as fast as I could, but the fire...it was everywhere. There was no clear path out."

Lux's other hand cupped Zoey's cheek, her thumb brushing away a tear that had slipped free.

"Zoey..."

Zoey's voice cracked, and she had to stop for a moment, the pain of the memory almost too much to bear.

"We were trapped. And then...the floor gave way. I don't remember much after that except the sound of everything collapsing around us. And the heat...the heat was unbearable."

Lux's arms wrapped around her, pulling her close. Zoey could feel the warmth of Lux's body against hers, could feel the steady rise and fall of Lux's chest as she breathed. It was comforting, grounding her in the present, even as the past threatened to pull her under.

"We lost her," Zoey whispered. "We lost the child. And I lost part of myself that day."

Lux's hold on her tightened, and Zoey could feel the tears streaming down her face now, hot and unchecked. She buried her face in Lux's shoulder, her body shaking with the force of her emotions.

"If only I'd been a little more careful," Zoey said. "If only I'd focused more on saving people than just fighting the fires, that kid would've lived."

Lux's grip felt tighter around Zoey's body. "That explains why you wanted a rescue-first operation."

Zoey nodded, saying nothing.

They stayed like that for a while longer, the silence between them filled with unspoken understanding. Zoey felt a sense of peace settle over her, a feeling of safety that she hadn't experienced in a long time.

"Thank you," Zoey said.

Lux smiled, her eyes soft and full of warmth. "You don't have to thank me. I'm just glad you felt like you could share that part of yourself with me."

When they pulled back, Zoey rested her forehead against Lux's, her breath mingling with Lux's in the small space between them.

"I don't know what comes next," Zoey said. "But I'd hoped that Phoenix Ridge would save me."

"It will, if you let it," Lux said and her dreamy blue eyes focussed on Zoey.

"Right now, we should focus on getting more food to eat. Those berries won't save us for long."

"I bet if we followed that little stream a little, we'd find some fish," Zoey said.

"You bet or you know?"

"Wild guess," Zoey said.

"Let's catch our breath before checking it out," Lux said. "Deal?"

Zoey laughed. "Deal."

15

LUX

Zoey was right after all. There was a space not so far off from the spot where they had their bath where they could catch fish.

They stood in the middle of the river, their hands submerged. Lux stood beside Zoey and demonstrated to her how to catch a fish by hand.

Zoey tried to emulate Lux, but she tipped over and fell in the water, and Lux watched with an amused smile.

The sun started to rise, casting long shadows over the water, making it feel surreal.

"Here, do it like this," Lux said, stepping closer to Zoey and holding her hands poised over the water. Her touch was gentle but firm, and Zoey's chest fluttered.

"Like this?" Zoey tilted her head back to look at Lux, who nodded.

"Yeah, just like that," Lux said. "Now, flick your wrist a little as you drop your arm in the water when you see a fish."

"I'm really not good at this," Zoey said, her cheeks growing warm.

"It takes practice," Lux said. "My dad taught me when I was little. He used to take my brother and me out every weekend, rain or shine. Fishing was his way of keeping us connected, I guess."

Zoey glanced at Lux, noticing the way her eyes softened as she spoke about her father. There was a warmth in her voice that made Zoey want to know more.

"You must be close to him," Zoey said.

Lux nodded, her gaze fixed on the water. "Yeah, I am. Especially after my mom passed. I was just a kid, and my brother wasn't much older. It was tough, but my dad did everything he could to make sure we didn't feel like we were missing out on anything."

"I'm sorry about your mom," Zoey said quietly, not sure what else to say.

Lux shrugged, but there was a tightness in her expression. "It was a long time ago, but it still hurts sometimes. I miss her, you know? But I had my dad and my brother. They made it easier."

Zoey could see the pain in Lux's eyes, the kind of pain that never really went away, no matter how much time passed.

"What was she like?" Zoey asked, hoping it wasn't too personal.

Lux smiled, a distant look in her eyes. "She was amazing. Strong, kind, funny. She had this way of making everyone around her feel special. At least that's what my dad told me."

"Wait, you didn't–"

"I didn't get to meet her. I mean, I did, but I don't have any memory of her. I was still so little when she died."

"I'm so sorry about that."

Lux crouched, eyeing the fish swimming by. The sun continued to rise, casting a soft, golden light across the water. She could hear the gentle lapping of the water against the shore, the distant chirping of birds.

Zoey stood beside her, watching closely. "So, you really know how to fish?"

Zoey mimicked Lux's position, and Lux chuckled.

"Relax your shoulders," Lux said. "You're too tense."

Zoey sighed and loosened her body. "I'm just worried I'll mess it up."

"You won't," Lux assured her. "Just follow my lead."

They both stood, staring at the water. When a particularly large fish swam close to them, Lux said, "Now!"

Zoey squeezed her eyes shut and thrust her arm in the water. She swiped like Lux had shown her, and she pulled out the wriggling, slimy fish.

"We did it!" Zoey said, her face lighting up with joy as she clutched the flailing fish.

Lux couldn't help but smile, the sight of Zoey's happiness warming something inside her. "You did it," she corrected, her voice filled with pride.

Zoey looked at the fish, then back at Lux, her expression one of disbelief. "I actually caught a fish."

"You did," Lux said, her smile widening. "Not bad for your first time."

Zoey laughed, the sound light and carefree. "I couldn't have done it without you."

Lux felt something shift inside her. Maybe, just maybe, she could let herself be open to this, to whatever it was that was growing between them.

Maybe she could let herself be vulnerable, just this once.

They walked back to shore, Zoey still clutching the fish that stopped moving.

Lux glanced at her, studying her face for a moment. "You don't have any siblings, do you?"

Zoey shook her head. "I've got two. My brother's in the military. My older sister works as a teacher."

"Middle child?" Lux raised a brow.

"Middle child," Zoey said.

They fell into a comfortable silence, the sound of the river filling the space between them. Zoey watched the soft ripples in the water as her thoughts drifted.

A faint crackling sound broke through the quiet. They both turned their heads toward the source, eyes widening as they realized what it was.

"The phone," Zoey said, scrambling to her feet.

They hurried over to where they had left it, beside a tree a few feet away from the riverbank. Zoey grabbed the phone, her hands shaking slightly as she stared at the screen and accepted the call.

"Hello? This is Zoey Knight. Can you hear me?"

There was a moment of static, and then a voice crackled through, faint but audible. "Lieutenant, it's Jay."

"Thank goodness, Jay. We've been trying to establish contact—"

"We?" Jay's voice crackled from the other end. "Is Lux with you?"

"Yes, I'm here," Lux said. "How soon can you get a chopper down to our location?"

"As soon as we're able to triangulate your coordinates."

"And how long would that take?"

"We've triangulated the site of the crash. Are you guys close to the wreckage?"

"Yes." Lux could feel her heart race.

"We're dealing with some serious fire activity here," Jay said, her voice tense. "But we've got teams out there. The priority is getting you both back safely. Can you make it back to the wreckage?"

Zoey glanced at Lux, who nodded. "We can

make it back," Zoey said into the phone. "We're heading there now."

"Good," Jay said. "Stay safe. We'll try to keep in touch."

She lowered the phone, turning to Lux. "We need to get back."

Lux nodded, already moving toward their gear. "Let's go."

They packed up quickly, the mood between them shifting to something more urgent. The sky was darkening and the shadows stretched longer as they made their way back through the trees.

As they walked, Zoey found herself glancing at Lux, her mind replaying the conversation they'd had by the river. There was a heaviness to Lux that Zoey hadn't seen before, a vulnerability that made Zoey want to reach out, to offer some kind of comfort.

When they reached the clearing, they dropped their gear by their salvaged supplies, both of them breathing a little harder from the quick pace they'd kept.

"We're safe," Lux said, more to herself than to Zoey. "We're finally going home."

Zoey nodded, her eyes meeting Lux's. "Yeah, we are."

There was a beat of silence as they just stood there looking at each other. Zoey felt something shift between them.

"What happens now, Lux?"

Without thinking, Zoey stepped closer, her heart pounding in her chest. Lux didn't move away or break eye contact. Zoey's breath hitched as she leaned in, her lips brushing against Lux's in a tentative kiss.

Lux responded immediately, her hand coming up to cup Zoey's cheek, pulling her closer. The kiss deepened, and for a moment, everything else fell away—the fires, the danger, the uncertainty. It was just them standing in the fading light, finding something real in the midst of all the chaos.

When they finally broke apart, both were breathing heavily, faces flushed. Lux opened her mouth to speak, but Zoey beat her to it.

"I can't believe we might actually get out of here," Zoey said, her voice shaky but with a small, teasing smile playing on her lips. "What's the first thing you want to do when we're back?"

Lux chuckled. "Honestly? I want a big, greasy burger. And maybe a hot shower. In that order."

Zoey laughed, the sound lifting some of the

weight off her chest. "Good call. I'll take a burger too. And then I want to sleep for a week. Maybe longer."

"I can see that." Lux smiled. "Though, you sleep too long, and you might miss out on some things. Like me beating everyone at the station at bowling."

"Bowling?" Zoey raised a brow.

"Bowling. Arm wrestling. You name it."

Zoey raised an eyebrow, feigning disbelief. "You think you can beat me? Dream on, Valentine."

Lux grinned. "Oh, I know I can. We'll make a day of it: burgers, arm wrestling, and then we'll hit the beach."

"You and the beach," Zoey teased. "Why am I not surprised?"

"Hey, I need my ocean fix," Lux said, her tone light. "You're just lucky you're cute enough to invite along."

Zoey rolled her eyes but couldn't stop the smile that tugged at her lips. "Fine, fine. But I get to pick the movie for when we crash on the couch after. And no complaints if it's a cheesy rom-com."

"Deal," Lux said, the word coming out softer

than she intended. She took a deep breath, the playfulness slipping away as she looked at Zoey. "I'm going to miss this, though. Us."

Zoey's smile faltered slightly. "Yeah, me too."

"Zoey, there's something I've been wanting to say." Lux's voice was quieter now, more serious. "I like you. A lot. But I've never been good at...this. Commitment. I just—"

"I understand," Zoey cut in. "And honestly? I don't want to commit either. Not right now, anyway."

Lux blinked, the surprise evident in her eyes. She didn't mean to lead Zoey on and then toss her to the side. She didn't mean to keep her around either.

Ugh.

She didn't mean anything. It was all just beautiful, and the thought of commitment still scared her so much. How could she want someone this much yet still not want them too?

"Really? I didn't mean..." The words wouldn't form. "You get it, don't you?"

Zoey nodded, her smile bittersweet. "I care about you, Lux. But I think we both have a lot of stuff to figure out first. Maybe when we're out of here and things aren't so intense, we can see where this goes. But for now, no pressure. Just...us."

Lux sighed. She'd glanced at the horizon while they were fishing earlier. The orange glow of the fires were closing in on them. She knew it was almost a farce.

There was always pressure.

16

ZOEY

They stared at the phone as it beeped.

Zoey wondered what was going through Lux's mind. Was she hoping the line would crackle and they'd be heading back to the station? Was she thinking about her? What did that mean for everything they had shared so far?

Lux didn't need to say anything; Zoey could feel the same need coursing through her, drawing her toward Lux.

Zoey reached out, her fingers trembling slightly as they brushed against Lux's arm. Lux's skin was warm under her touch, and the contact sent a jolt of electricity through Zoey. She wanted more—needed more.

"You think they're close?" Zoey asked.

"If I know Jay well enough, she'd be flying right here already."

Zoey's let out a deep breath. When she'd woken up this morning, she hadn't expected that this would be their last moments together.

This should be a happy moment, right?

She should be feeling excited that she'd finally go back home. Why, then, did it feel this heavy in her heart?

"Lux," Zoey said, her voice rough with desire, "I'll miss you."

Lux's response was immediate. She pulled Zoey close, their bodies pressing together, and Zoey could feel the heat radiating off her. Lux's lips found hers.

Her hands roamed over Lux's body, feeling the lean muscle under her clothes and the way her body responded to each touch. She tugged at Lux's belt and the fastening of her pants and pushed her back against a tree.

Zoey's mouth found Lux's neck, trailing kisses along her collarbone and down to her chest. Lux's hands tangled in Zoey's hair, tugging her closer, and Zoey responded, her tongue flicking out to taste the salt on Lux's skin.

"Zoey," Lux moaned, her voice filled with need, and it was all she needed to hear.

Zoey's hand pushed inside the waistband of Lux's Calvin Kleins. Her fingers went to work, sliding against her clitoris. Lux moaned and her hips bucked against Zoey's touch.

The sound of Lux's pleasure drove Zoey wild, and she pressed harder, her fingers working to push Lux closer and closer to climax. Lux's fingers gripped Zoey's back tightly, her breath coming in short, ragged gasps.

"Zoey, I'm—" Lux started, but the rest of her words were lost in a moan as her body tensed, her back arching off the tree as she came, her entire body trembling with the force of it.

Zoey didn't let up, drawing out Lux's pleasure until she finally collapsed back against the tree, her chest heaving as she tried to catch her breath.

Zoey smiled as she held Lux up, her own body thrumming with need, but she couldn't take her eyes off Lux. Her cheeks were flushed and her dark hair was a wild mess around her face and she looked more beautiful than Zoey had ever seen her.

Lux's lovely blue eyes fluttered open, and when

she looked at Zoey, there was a fire in her gaze that made Zoey's breath catch in her throat.

"Come here," Lux said, her voice still rough from her orgasm, and Zoey didn't hesitate.

She leaned in to Lux, but Lux wasn't having it. She rolled her over, pinning Zoey between her and the tree, and Zoey's breath hitched as Lux's body pressed into hers.

"You're incredible," Lux said, her voice low.

Zoey's hands slid up Lux's back, pulling her in for another kiss, and Lux responded eagerly, her body moving against Zoey's in a way that made her head spin.

Lux's hands were on Zoey's thighs, pushing them apart and then seeking down inside the waistband of her fire pants and her underwear, and Zoey's breath caught as Lux's fingers found her, teasing her, sliding through her wetness, making her squirm.

"Lux," Zoey moaned, her hands tightening on Lux's hips, urging her on.

Lux's mouth moved to Zoey's neck, kissing and nipping at her skin as her fingers slid inside, making Zoey cry out. She arched her back, pushing herself closer to Lux, needing more, and Lux obliged, her fingers moving in a steady rhythm that had Zoey panting, her body tense with pleasure.

"Don't stop," Zoey gasped, her nails digging into Lux's back as the waves of pleasure built inside her, making her feel like she was about to explode.

Lux's mouth moved lower, her teeth finding Zoey's nipple through her shirt, and the added sensation pushed Zoey over the edge. Her body tensed, her breath catching in her throat as the orgasm crashed over her and her entire body shook with the intensity of it.

Lux didn't stop or let up until Zoey was a trembling, breathless mess under her, her mind spinning from the sheer pleasure of it all.

When Lux finally pulled back, Zoey could barely move, her body still tingling from the aftershocks. She looked at Lux, who was watching her with a satisfied smile, and Zoey couldn't help but smile back.

"That was..." Zoey started, but she couldn't find the words to finish.

"Incredible," Lux finished for her.

Zoey nodded, still trying to catch her breath. "Yeah, it was."

Their bodies were still close, and their breathing was slowly returning to normal.

"You're amazing, you know that?" Zoey said.

Lux's smile softened, and she brushed a strand of hair from Zoey's face. "So are you. I've never felt anything like this before."

Zoey's heart skipped a beat at the admission, and she leaned in to gently kiss Lux's lips. It was different from the desperate kisses they'd shared earlier. This one was soft, tender, and full of unspoken feelings that neither of them was ready to put into words yet.

They stayed a while, just holding each other, the only sound was the soft rustling of the wind. Zoey felt a sense of peace that she hadn't felt in a long time, like everything in the world had finally fallen into place.

Eventually, Lux shifted, "What happens now?" she asked, her voice quiet, but there was a hint of uncertainty in her ocean blue eyes.

Zoey reached to trace her fingers along Lux's strong jaw, her touch light but reassuring. "We take it one step at a time. We figure it out together."

Lux nodded, her eyes searching Zoey's face for a moment before she leaned to kiss her again, slow and lingering like she was trying to memorize every detail.

Zoey melted into the kiss, her arms wrapping around Lux's shoulders, pulling her closer. When they finally broke apart, Zoey rested her forehead against Lux's, closing her eyes as she let herself enjoy the quiet moment.

They didn't need to say anything else. Everything they needed to say had already been said in the way they touched, kissed, and held each other like they never wanted to let go.

And for now, that was enough.

Zoey looked up at the trees as the reality of what just happened settled in.

The warmth of Lux's body pressed against her was comforting, but her mind raced. The sex had been incredible, even better than the first time, but now, in the quiet aftermath, doubts began to creep in.

Lux shifted beside her, her fingers lightly running over Zoey's skin under her shirt. The gentle touch sent a shiver through Zoey, but it also reminded her of all the relationships that hadn't worked out before.

She had been in this place before: the thrill of something new, the hope that maybe this time it would be different, only for it to fall apart. Zoey didn't want to go through that again.

"Penny for your thoughts?" Lux asked, but Zoey could hear the curiosity in it.

Zoey hesitated, not sure how much she wanted to share. "I was just thinking," she said, her voice trailing off as she tried to find the right words. "This...this is nice."

Lux looked at Zoey with a small smile. "Nice? That's all?"

Zoey laughed softly, shaking her head. "Okay, it's more than nice. It's amazing. But..." She hesitated again, not sure how to continue.

"But?" Lux pressed.

"Why do I have a feeling that you didn't quite understand what I meant the last time we spoke about this?"

"We didn't speak about this," Lux said. "I talked, and you just agreed. I...don't know how that made me feel, but it's fine."

"Don't do that."

"Do what?"

"Act like it's all fun and roses when you've got a lot to say." Zoey ran her hand over her face. Talking any longer might ruin things for the both of them, but she knew it was worth it.

Lux stayed quiet.

"I didn't want to feel rejected," Zoey said. "Not again."

"Rejected?" Lux replied, clearly baffled. "Why on earth would you feel that way? You're...you're you."

Zoey sighed, turning her head to look at Lux. "I've been in a few relationships before, and they never ended well. I guess I'm just trying to keep my expectations in check, you know?"

"Trust me, I know that feeling." Lux's expression softened. "I get it. It's hard not to get caught up in the moment, especially with everything that's going on."

Zoey nodded, grateful that Lux understood. "Yeah. I don't want to get hurt again."

Lux reached out, brushing a strand of dark hair from Zoey's face. Zoey smiled, but it didn't quite reach her eyes.

"Maybe it's better if we just...enjoy what we have right now without expecting anything more."

Lux didn't respond right away, her eyes searching Zoey's. "So, you're saying we should just focus on the sex and not worry about what happens next?"

Zoey nodded. "Yeah. I mean, the sex is great,

and we might die out here. Maybe it is better not to overthink it."

"Jay is on her way," Lux reminded her. "Let's not jinx it, okay?"

"I just don't want to complicate things. We're already dealing with enough out here."

Lux squeezed her hand back, her smile returning. "Okay. No drama. Just great sex."

Zoey laughed, easing slightly. "So, after all this goes away, after here?"

"Why don't we wait until after here to figure it out?" Lux said.

"Is it me or does it feel hotter here?" Lux asked.

Zoey squirmed. It did feel hotter than it was a few seconds ago. She looked around suddenly on alert. It was burning orange in the distance and heading uphill fast. Thick, brown smoke was already filling the sky.

"How did it get this far so fast?" Zoey asked, shocked.

"Trade winds, Zoey. Phoenix Ridge gets a lot of them blowing uphill."

"We have to move," Zoey said.

"We have to hope Jay and the team get here as soon as possible."

17

LUX

Lux heard the faint sound of a helicopter approaching. The noise grew louder, and she looked over at Zoey, who was already on her feet, staring up at the sky.

"It's getting closer," Lux said, her voice steady.

"We need to signal them," Zoey said. The helicopter was getting closer, the sound now a deep, pulsing thrum that seemed to echo off the trees around them. Zoey's heart pounded, her senses on high alert.

Zoey turned her head sharply, her eyes widening in horror as she saw the flames surging toward them faster than she had ever seen before. The fire had found a new fuel source, and it was barreling toward them with a force that made her stomach drop.

"Lux, we have to go," Zoey shouted, her voice carrying over the roaring flames.

Lux spun around. She came back toward Zoey, her eyes locked on the approaching danger.

Zoey moved frantically. They couldn't stay here any longer. The fire was too close and approaching too quickly. She glanced back toward the sky, but the flames and smoke made it impossible to see anything clearly.

"Run!" Zoey yelled.

"But, Jay," Lux said. "She's still up there."

"She clearly can't land. Hopefully, if we get to higher ground, she'll be able to rescue us."

"We should—"

A branch snapped and crashed to the ground. Lux moved just in time, pulling Zoey along with her. She looked up, trying to locate the chopper, but the smoke was too thick above them.

They took off, their feet pounding against the dry, cracked earth as they ran through the forest. Her eyes stung and her lungs burned, but she didn't slow down.

Zoey was just ahead, her movements quick and agile. Lux could see the strain on her face and the way her jaw was set with determination. They both knew their lives were at stake.

As they ran, Zoey's foot caught on something, and she stumbled, falling hard to the ground. Lux was there right away, pulling her back to her feet.

"Come on, Zoey."

The flames were closer now, licking at the trees around them, the heat so intense that it felt like it was burning her skin. She didn't dare look back, afraid of what she might see.

They reached a small clearing, and for a moment, Zoey thought they might have found a safe spot. But the fire was relentless, consuming everything in its path. She could hear the crackling of burning wood, the roaring of the flames, and above it all, the distant thrum of the helicopter still searching for them.

"We have to keep going," Lux said, her voice tight with fear. "We can't stop here."

Zoey nodded again, her throat too dry to speak. She followed Lux, her legs heavy with exhaustion. They had been running for what felt like forever, and she wasn't sure how much longer she could keep it up.

But they had no choice.

As they pushed through the underbrush, Lux

felt the rocks and roots threatening to trip her at every step. She stumbled, but Zoey was there, steadying her, keeping her moving.

Suddenly, the ground dropped away in front of them, revealing a slope that led down into a narrow ravine. Zoey skidded to a stop, her heart pounding in her ears.

"This way," Lux said, her voice strained as she pointed down the slope. "We can use the ravine to get away from the fire."

Zoey hesitated for a moment, the drop making her stomach churn. But the flames were too close. She could feel the heat at her back, the crackling of the fire growing louder by the second.

With a deep breath, she nodded and followed Lux down the slope, their feet slipping and sliding on the loose dirt and rocks. The descent was treacherous, and Zoey's hands scraped against the rough surface as she tried to keep her balance.

They reached the bottom, their breaths coming in ragged gasps. Zoey looked around, her eyes scanning the narrow ravine. The walls were high, offering some protection from the flames, but they couldn't stay here for long. Jay would have no hope of spotting them.

"We need to keep moving," Lux said as she started down the ravine.

Zoey followed, her legs trembling with exhaustion. The ravine was narrow and winding, the walls pressing in on either side of them. The air was cooler here, but the smell of smoke still hung heavy, a constant reminder of the fire that raged above.

As they rounded a bend, Zoey felt something catch her foot, and she stumbled again. She cried out as pain shot through her ankle, the sharp, sudden jolt bringing tears to her eyes.

Lux was at her side in an instant, her hands gripping Zoey's arms as she tried to help her up.

"I think I twisted it," Zoey said, her voice tight with pain.

Lux looked up at the ravine, her eyes filled with worry. "We can't stop here, Zoey. The fire—"

"I know," Zoey said, cutting her off. She gritted her teeth and forced herself to stand, leaning heavily on Lux for support. Every step sent a jolt of pain through her ankle, but she didn't let herself think about it.

They kept moving, the ravine winding its way through the forest. The smoke was thinner here, and Zoey could feel the temperature dropping as they put more distance between themselves and the fire.

But they weren't safe yet. The fire was still out there, still chasing them, and Zoey knew they couldn't let their guard down. They had to keep moving, keep pushing forward, no matter how exhausted they were.

As they reached the end of the ravine, Zoey could see the sky through the trees, dark clouds of smoke hanging heavy above them. The sound of the helicopter was gone, lost in the chaos of the fire.

"We need to find somewhere she can see us," Lux said as she scanned the area.

"Jay, she was here," Zoey said. "We missed her, Lux. We missed her."

"She'd still be around here somewhere," Lux said. "She has to be."

"And if she isn't?" Zoey asked. "What if she somehow had issues with the chopper and couldn't hang around any longer?"

"We just have to hope she didn't leave, Zoey. She can't leave."

"What if she did, Lux?" Zoey asked.

Lux stopped pacing and stared at Zoey. She raised a finger and pointed it up the mountain.

"Then we'd better get up that mountain or we're toast. Literally."

"Fine. Come on," Zoey said, moving ahead of Lux.

The trail was narrow, and the dense trees on either side offered some shade from the heat.

"We need to get as far away from here as possible," Zoey said, glancing over at Lux.

"Yeah," Lux said. She didn't add that the steepness was starting to wear on her.

The ground beneath them got rockier. Lux adjusted her footing, careful not to slip. Zoey was ahead, her gaze fixed on the trail.

"Watch your step," Zoey said.

Lux nodded, focusing on her footing. The rocks were loose, shifting slightly under her weight, but she managed to keep her balance. Zoey was just a few steps ahead, moving at a steady pace.

"Have you ever been stuck out here before?" Zoey asked.

"No," Lux replied. "I did get lost in a game reserve once, though."

"Are you serious?"

"True story. Luckily, my father found me in less than five minutes."

"That doesn't count as being lost, does it?" Zoey asked.

"When you're wondering which wild animal would find you first, time moves pretty slowly."

"I know that feeling."

Lux groaned as her ankle hit against a stem. She slowed down.

"You okay?" Zoey asked, slowing down, too.

"It's fine. I'm fine." Lux continued walking. "Walking has never been my strong suit."

"No arguments there," Zoey said. "Explains why you chose to fly a chopper instead."

Lux chuckled. "You could say that."

After what felt like hours of walking, they came across a small stream. The water trickled gently over smooth stones, the sound soothing against the backdrop of their heavy breathing.

"Let's take a quick break," Zoey said, dropping her pack on the ground. "We could use a bath."

Lux hesitated, looking up the mountain. She knew they needed to keep moving, but the thought of washing off the dirt and sweat was tempting.

"Just a few minutes," Zoey added, already pulling off her boots.

Lux finally nodded, setting her pack down. She knelt by the stream, dipping her fingers into the water. It was warmer than she expected, but felt good against her skin.

"Feels nice," Zoey said, wading into the shallow water.

Lux followed, the warm water lapping at her legs. The stream wasn't deep, just covering her ankles, but it was enough to wash away the grime that clung to her skin.

Zoey cupped her hands, splashing water over her arms and neck. Lux did the same, the warmth of the water soothing her aching muscles. They moved slowly, almost lazily, letting the water rinse away the dirt and sweat.

Lux glanced over at Zoey, noticing how the water clung to her skin and the way her wet hair stuck to her neck. Zoey looked up, meeting Lux's gaze. She flashed a small, almost shy smile.

"Better?" Zoey asked.

Lux nodded. "Yeah. Better."

They stayed in the water for a few more minutes, letting the warmth soak into their skin. Lux could feel the tension in her body easing, the steady thrum of anxiety quieting just a bit.

But they couldn't stay there forever.

Zoey was the first to move, stepping out of the stream and reaching for her boots and pack. Lux followed, reluctantly pulling herself out of the water and drying off as best as she could.

"We should keep going," Zoey said.

Lux nodded, slipping her boots back on. The moment of peace was over, but it had been enough to keep her going. She could still feel the warmth of the water on her skin as they started walking again.

They continued up the mountain. The ground was rougher, and the rocks were less stable. Lux's legs ached with every step, but she kept moving, determined not to slow down.

As they walked, Zoey spotted a cluster of bushes along the trail, their branches heavy with dark, ripe berries. She paused, reaching out to pluck a few.

"Berries," she said, holding one out to Lux.

Lux took it, the sweet taste bursting on her tongue as she bit into it. It was a small comfort, but it was something. They ate in silence; the only sounds were the crunch of leaves under their boots and the occasional rustle of the wind in the trees.

The trail was narrower here, the trees thinning out as they got higher. The air was cooler, a welcome change from the heat that had followed them for so long.

After what felt like an eternity, Lux spotted a break in the trees up ahead. The ground leveled out slightly as the dense forest gave way to a small clearing. The sky was visible through the branches, and the clouds hung low and heavy.

"I think we've found a clearing," Zoey said.

Lux stepped into the clearing, her eyes scanning the scene. The ground was covered in soft grass, and the air was filled with the scent of pine and earth. It was peaceful, almost serene, but Lux couldn't shake the worry gnawing at the back of her mind.

She looked over at Zoey, who was staring up at the sky. The concern was still there, lingering in her eyes despite the calm.

"We'll make it," Zoey said.

Lux nodded, forcing herself to believe it.

"We should rest here for a bit," she said, glancing around the clearing.

Zoey agreed, her body finally giving in to the exhaustion.

Lux sank onto the grass, letting the cool air wash over her. Zoey sat beside her, the two of them sharing a moment of quiet.

For now, it was enough.

18

ZOEY

"Do you think we're safe here?" Zoey asked. Her voice was rough from the smoke and lack of water.

Lux nodded slowly, looking around. "For now. But we can't stay too long."

Zoey sighed, leaning back against a tree. She closed her eyes for a second, trying to ignore the dryness in her throat. She wanted to ask more questions, but her mind was too clouded with exhaustion to think straight.

"I need to confess something. The phone's gone, I must have dropped it," Lux said.

Zoey sighed. "So, we're really on our own then." She felt a knot forming in her stomach as the realization that they were completely cut off from any help and any chance of getting out of this quickly settled in.

"They'll keep looking for us, right?" she asked, but she could hear the uncertainty in her voice.

"Maybe." Lux's voice was strained, her gaze fixed on the ground. "But with the fire spreading like this, it's possible they'll think we didn't make it."

"What do you mean?"

"Since some of our stuff got burnt, they might think we were caught in the fire."

"They wouldn't just give up on us," Zoey said, more to convince herself than anything.

Lux didn't respond immediately. Instead, she stared at the horizon, her jaw clenched. Zoey could see the tension in her shoulders, the way her hands had curled into fists at her sides.

"Lux?" Zoey said.

"They'd better not," Lux finally said. "Maybe we should assume that they already have, though."

Zoey's chest tightened. "We can't think like that. We'll get out of this."

Lux let out a bitter laugh, shaking her head. "I'm not trying to be negative, Zoey. I'm just being realistic. We're up against a fire that's only getting worse, and we have no way to communicate. The odds aren't exactly in our favor."

"So, what do we do now?" Zoey asked, hating how small her voice sounded.

Lux looked at her, her expression softening just a little. "We keep moving and try to stay ahead of the fire. And we pray that the fire burns itself out before we get to the summit."

Zoey nodded, feeling a little steadier. Lux stood up, brushing the dirt from her pants.

"We should get going," she said.

Zoey stood up, too, though her legs protested. "Yeah. Let's go."

They started walking again. Zoey kept close to Lux, her breath coming in short gasps as they climbed. Now and then, she glanced over at Lux, watching the way she moved with purpose, even though the strain was evident on her face.

"I'm sorry," Zoey blurted out, unable to keep the words from spilling out.

Lux glanced at her, confused. "For what?"

"For dragging you into this mess," Zoey said. "If I hadn't—"

"Stop," Lux cut in, her tone sharp. "This isn't your fault, Zoey."

Zoey nodded, but the guilt still gnawed at her.

She hadn't asked for this, but she couldn't shake the feeling that she was somehow to blame for their situation.

They walked in silence for a while, and the only sound was the crunch of their boots on the dry earth. The sky above them was a dull gray, the sun barely visible through the haze of smoke. The air was thick, making it hard to breathe, and Zoey felt the burn in her lungs with every step.

"Do you think we'll make it out of this?" Zoey asked.

"I don't know, Zoey. I don't."

The bluntness of her words hit Zoey hard, but she appreciated the honesty. It was better than false hope, at least.

Zoey stared at the ground as they walked, her mind swirling with thoughts. She was exhausted, both physically and mentally, and it was getting harder to keep up with Lux's pace. Her legs felt like lead, and her lungs burned with every breath.

"We need to rest," Zoey said, finally coming to a stop. She could feel her heart pounding in her chest and her vision blurring at the edges.

Lux stopped, too, turning to face her. She looked like she was about to argue, but then she saw the state Zoey was in and nodded. "Okay. Just for a few minutes."

Zoey sank to the ground. She closed her eyes, trying to steady her breathing. Her whole body was trembling, and she felt tears pricking at the corners of her eyes. She didn't want to break down now, not in front of Lux, but the stress and fear were becoming too much to hold back.

Lux knelt beside her, placing a hand on Zoey's back. "Hey, you're okay. Just breathe."

Zoey nodded, trying to do as Lux said. She focused on her breathing, taking slow, deep breaths. Lux's hand on her back was grounding, a reminder that she wasn't alone, even though everything else felt like it was falling apart.

"I'm sorry," Zoey whispered, wiping her eyes with the back of her hand.

"You don't have to apologize," Lux said. "We're both scared. It's okay to be scared."

Zoey nodded again, grateful for the reassurance. She took another deep breath, feeling the tightness in her chest start to ease.

"Thank you," she said.

Lux gave her a small smile. "We'll be okay, Zoey. We just have to keep going."

Zoey didn't know if she believed it, but she nodded anyway. She couldn't afford to break down now, not when they were still in danger. She had to keep going, no matter how much she wanted to curl up and give in to the exhaustion.

They rested for a few more minutes before Lux stood up, extending a hand to help Zoey to her feet. Zoey took it, pulling herself up with a grunt.

"Let's keep moving," Lux said.

Zoey nodded, following her as they started walking again. She kept her eyes on Lux's back, using her as a focal point to keep her mind from spiraling. They were in this together, and as long as they stayed together, they had a chance.

But as they walked, Zoey couldn't shake the feeling that they were being left behind, that their chances of survival were slipping away with every step. The thought made her chest tighten again, but she pushed it down, focusing on the ground beneath her feet and the woman walking in front of her.

They climbed for what felt like hours. Zoey's legs were screaming in protest, and her lungs burned with every breath. She could see the strain on Lux's face, too, the tightness in her jaw and the sweat dripping down her forehead.

"We need to stop," Zoey said.

Lux didn't argue this time. She nodded, sinking to the ground with a heavy sigh.

Zoey leaned against the rough bark of a tall pine tree, taking in the scenery around them. They were surrounded by dense forest, and the towering trees stood guard like silent sentinels.

Zoey noticed the sky was a dull gray, the sun barely visible behind the smoke. It was hard to believe that just a few days ago, everything had been normal.

She glanced at Lux, who sat a few feet away, her expression tense.

Zoey could see the strain on her face, the worry etched into her features. She felt a pang of guilt for dragging Lux into this situation, but she quickly pushed the thought aside.

There was no time for regrets.

Zoey's thoughts drifted to her parents. She wondered what they would think if they knew where she was right now. Her mom would probably be worried sick, imagining the worst.

Her dad, though, he would try to be practical, try to figure out a solution, but deep down, she knew he would be just as scared.

What if she never got to see them again?

The thought made her stomach clench. She remembered the day she came out to them, how nervous she had been. The memory brought a small sense of comfort, but it was fleeting.

Her eyes settled on Lux again. There was something about her that made Zoey feel...something. It was too early to say if Lux was the one, but she couldn't deny the pull she felt toward her.

She shrugged off the thought, not wanting to get lost in feelings she couldn't afford to dwell on right now. There were more pressing matters at hand, like figuring out how they were going to get out of this mess.

"Maybe we should head toward the fire," Zoey said, breaking the silence. "The firefighters could be fighting a path to us."

Lux looked at her, considering the suggestion. She shook her head. "They would be at the other end of the fires. Even if they could fight their way to us, the fires are moving rapidly uphill because of the direction of the wind. They won't expend all their resources to fight it to the last. They'd just contain it and make sure it doesn't spread."

Zoey nodded, realizing the logic in what Lux was saying. Everything felt so hopeless, but she wouldn't let herself spiral. They had to stay focused if they were going to survive.

"We're better off staying on the path we are on," Lux added, her tone softening. "Moving closer to the fire would just put us in more danger."

Zoey let out a sigh, her shoulders slumping. "You're right. I just...I don't know what else to do."

"We'll figure something out. We just need to stay calm."

Zoey appreciated Lux's attempt to reassure her, but she could see the worry in her eyes. It was the same worry gnawing at her own insides. Still, it was comforting to know she wasn't alone in this.

Zoey shifted her position and noticed Lux wince slightly. "Your leg," she said. "Let me take a look."

Lux hesitated but eventually extended her leg toward Zoey. Zoey gently pulled off her boot and sock and took Lux's leg in her hands, feeling the warmth of her skin. The area around the cut was swollen, and Zoey could see bruises started to form. At least the cut didn't look infected and was healing well.

She massaged the area, applying gentle pressure. Lux closed her eyes, leaning against the tree.

She didn't say anything, but Zoey could tell by the way she relaxed slightly that the massage helped.

Zoey focused on her task, trying to block out the thoughts racing through her mind. But it was impossible not to think about what might happen next.

Would they make it out of here alive? What if they didn't? The uncertainty was terrifying.

Her eyes drifted back to Lux, who still had her eyes closed. There was something about the way Lux held herself, the quiet strength she exuded, that made Zoey's heart ache. It was different from anything she had ever felt before.

Loving a woman like Lux felt...freeing. It was like looking into a mirror and seeing both the similarities and the differences. And it was those differences that made the connection so beautiful.

It was like finding someone who understood her in a way no one else could.

Zoey kept massaging Lux's ankle and leg, her mind swirling with thoughts and emotions. She didn't know what would happen next, but as she admired Lux's quiet strength, she couldn't help but feel a glimmer of hope. Maybe, just maybe, they would find a way out of this together.

As Lux's breathing evened out, Zoey found herself lost in the moment.

The fire was still out there and the danger was real, but for this moment, Zoey allowed herself to find peace in the presence of the woman beside her. She wasn't sure what the future held, but she knew that whatever happened, she wasn't alone.

19

LUX

Lux leaned back against the tree, her eyes closed as Zoey continued to gently caress her lower leg and foot. The pain was still there, a dull throb that pulsed with each beat of her heart, but Zoey's touch made it bearable.

She wasn't sure if it was the massage itself or just the fact that Zoey was the one doing it, but it didn't matter. What mattered was the warmth spreading from Zoey's hands into her skin, a warmth that seemed to reach straight to her chest.

She had been trying not to think too much about her feelings for Zoey, but it was impossible now. Every touch made it harder to deny what was happening.

She was falling in love.

The thought should have terrified her, and maybe it did a little, but not as much as she would have expected. There was no jolt of fear, no urge to pull away and protect herself. Instead, there was just a pull toward Zoey that she didn't want to resist.

She opened her eyes and looked at Zoey, who had her brow furrowed in concentration. Zoey had a way of looking at the world that fascinated Lux. There was a softness in her beautiful brown eyes, a kind of quiet determination that made Lux want to know everything about her.

But there was also a distance there, especially when Zoey talked about leaving people behind. Lux could see the pain it caused her, the way it made her withdraw into herself, and it made Lux wonder what it was like for Zoey to be with her, someone who was so scared of letting people in.

"What was it like for you growing up?" Lux asked. "Did you always know you were meant to love a woman?"

Zoey smiled.

"I think I always knew, but it took me a while to figure it out. I did have this crush on a girl in high school. She was a year older than me—really pretty and really smart and straight. I thought she was perfect. You can guess how the rest played out."

"What happened?" Lux asked, curious.

"I told her how I felt, and she didn't feel the same way," Zoey said, shrugging like it didn't matter, but Lux could see the hurt in her eyes. "It was tough, but it taught me a lot about myself. I realized that I'm the kind of person who goes all in, a thousand percent, even when I know it might not work out."

Lux felt a pang in her chest at Zoey's words. She wasn't sure if she was ready for someone like that, someone who would give everything and expect the same in return.

But at the same time, the thought didn't scare her the way it usually did. Instead, she found herself wanting to be the person Zoey could depend on, the one who wouldn't let her down.

She looked away, trying to hide the confusion written on her face. She wasn't sure what to do with these feelings or how to handle the fact that she was starting to fall for Zoey, but she didn't want to push her away either.

The last thing she wanted was to hurt Zoey, but she couldn't deny the pull she felt, the way she wanted to kiss Zoey every time they were close.

"What's on your mind?" Zoey asked.

Lux hesitated, not sure how to answer. She didn't want to admit what she was thinking, so she deflected with a joke.

"I'm just thinking about how nice it would be if we had some marshmallows right now. A campfire and some s'mores would make this whole situation a lot more bearable."

Zoey chuckled, a sound that made Lux's heart flutter. "You always know how to lighten the mood, don't you?"

"It's a gift," Lux said with a grin. "But seriously, I'm just trying to figure out when we're going to get out of here. I mean, I'm not exactly in a hurry to get back to reality, but it would be nice to know we're not going to be stuck out here forever."

Lux found herself relaxing, letting go of some of the tension she had been carrying. It felt good to just be with Zoey, to not have to pretend or put up walls. She hadn't felt this way in a long time, and it scared her, but it also felt right.

Zoey's hands moved up her leg, massaging her thigh through her pants, and Lux let out a sigh of relief. The pain was still there, but it was manageable, and Zoey's touch was soothing in a way Lux hadn't expected.

"What about you?" Zoey asked suddenly, breaking the silence. "Did you always know?"

Lux thought about the question for a moment before answering. "I think I always knew, too, but it took me a long time to accept it. I was scared of what it meant and how people would react. It wasn't until I met someone who made me realize it was okay to be myself that I accepted it."

Zoey looked at her, curiosity in her eyes. "What happened to her?"

Lux shrugged, trying to sound nonchalant. "It didn't work out. I guess I wasn't ready for it, for the whole relationship thing. I've always had a hard time letting people in and letting them get close. But I'm trying to be better about that. I think losing my mom so young, I have serious abandonment issues. Trust issues. You know, well all of it."

Zoey nodded, understanding. "It's not easy, but it would be worth it, I think." Her brown eyes were warm and welcoming.

Lux looked at Zoey, feeling a sudden urge to kiss her and close the distance between them, to just give in to what she was feeling. But she held back, warning herself not to get too close or let herself fall too hard, too fast. She didn't want to hurt Zoey or make promises she wasn't sure she could keep.

She closed her eyes, leaning back against the tree, and let herself relax. She wasn't sure what would happen next, but for now, she was content to just be here with Zoey.

Zoey's hands moved on her leg again, this time massaging the area around her knee, and Lux felt a shiver run through her. She opened her eyes and looked at Zoey.

There was something beautiful about loving a woman like Zoey. It wasn't just about the physical attraction, though that was certainly there. It was about the connection, the understanding, the way they could just be themselves with each other.

Lux let out a sigh, closing her eyes again as she let herself get lost in the moment. She watched as Zoey's fingers traced the outline of her ankle, her touch gentle. She could feel Zoey's warmth through her touch, and it sent a tingling sensation up her leg.

Lux shifted slightly, trying to ignore the way her heart sped up just being this close to Zoey. It was hard to believe how much her feelings for Zoey had changed in such a short time.

When they first met, Lux saw Zoey as just another person she had to work with, someone to keep at arm's length. But now, everything was different. She was falling in love, and that realization terrified her.

She found herself wanting to be around Zoey constantly. The thought of kissing Zoey always lingered in her mind, and the way Zoey's hand rested on her leg only made that desire stronger.

Lux noticed the way Zoey's eyes seemed distant whenever she talked about leaving anyone behind. Losing a kid in a fire would do that for you. For sure. Lux understood the need to keep her distance, but she wondered what it was like for Zoey to be with her.

Did Zoey feel the same pull? Did she want to kiss her as badly as Lux did?

"Are you okay?" Zoey asked, looking up from Lux's ankle with a concerned expression.

"Yeah, just thinking," Lux said, trying to sound casual.

"About?"

Lux forced a smile. "Just thinking about when we'll be rescued. Trying to stay optimistic, you know?"

Zoey nodded. "We'll make it out of here, Lux. I promise."

Lux's heart skipped a beat. She wanted to believe Zoey and trust that everything would be okay. But part of her was still scared.

Scared of getting too close, scared of what might happen if she did. To lighten the mood, Lux decided to crack a joke. "If we don't make it out, at least I can say I spent my last days with a real-life action hero."

Zoey laughed, and the sound made Lux's chest tighten in the best way. "If you're lucky, I'll even let you see some of my stunts."

Lux grinned, but her mind was still racing. She didn't want to hurt Zoey or get too close, only to pull away later. But the more she thought about it, the more she realized she didn't feel the usual fear. She wanted to get closer and kiss Zoey again.

Zoey's hand rested on Lux's ankle, her fingers tracing light patterns that made Lux's skin tingle. Lux felt a warmth spreading through her, her body reacting to Zoey's touch in ways she couldn't control. She shifted slightly, feeling a growing tension between them, one that was becoming harder to ignore.

Zoey's fingers moved higher up Lux's thigh,

and Lux's breath hitched. She could feel her pulse quicken and her body responding to Zoey in a way that was both thrilling and terrifying. Lux looked at Zoey, their eyes locking, and she could see the same desire reflected in her.

Without thinking, Lux leaned in, her lips brushing against Zoey's in a brief but electric kiss. It was enough to send a jolt of electricity through her, leaving her wanting more.

But before they could go any further, the sound of hooves running uphill distracted them.

Lux pulled back, and she looked around. Three deer raced past. Then another.

"What's going on?"

Zoey's eyes followed the animals, her brow furrowing. "The fire must be getting closer. They're trying to escape."

Lux nodded, trying to push down the disappointment she felt at being interrupted. "Should we follow them?"

Zoey considered it for a moment, then nodded. "Animals have an instinct for where it's safe. We should head in the same direction."

"I used to have a dog who was the opposite. He always got into trouble."

"Sounds like you were always part of the mischief," Zoey said.

Lux was about to suggest going straight uphill but changed her mind. Zoey's point made sense, and she didn't want to argue.

"Let's go, then."

They started moving in the same direction as the animals, the sounds of the fire growing louder behind them.

Lux tried to stay focused, but her mind kept drifting back to that kiss and the way Zoey's hand had felt on her thigh. She wanted to feel it again and lose herself in Zoey's touch.

Lux heard vibrations, a low rumble that seemed to come from deep within the earth tried to pinpoint where it was coming from.

"Did you hear that?"

Zoey paused, listening. "Hear what?"

"That rumbling," Lux said, feeling a knot of unease forming in her stomach. "Maybe it's nothing, but—"

Another loud rumble cut her off, this time unmistakable. It was louder, more intense, and it made the ground beneath them tremble. Lux froze, her eyes wide with fear as she looked at Zoey.

"What the hell was that?" Zoey asked.

Lux shook her head, her mind racing. "I don't know, but it doesn't sound good."

They stood there for a moment, both of them unsure of what to do. The rumbling grew louder and more persistent, and Lux could feel the vibrations in her bones. She swallowed hard, trying to keep her fear in check, but it was no use. This was bad, really bad.

"Maybe we should—" Zoey started to say, but another rumble cut her off, this one even louder than before.

Lux's heart pounded in her chest as she realized what was happening. "We need to move now!"

20

ZOEY

Zoey's heart pounded as the rumbling grew louder, the vibrations beneath her feet increasing with every passing second. She barely had time to process what was happening before she felt the ground shift beneath them.

"Lux, we need to move," Zoey said.

She grabbed Lux's hand, pulling her along as they scrambled to find stable footing. But the earth was treacherous, slipping away under their boots as the landslide began to take shape.

Lux nodded, but Zoey could see the pain etched on her face. Each step was a struggle, but there was no time to stop. They both knew that hesitating now could mean the end. The ground continued to tremble, small rocks tumbling down the hillside, followed by larger ones. The sound of the landslide was like a roar, growing louder and louder until it drowned out everything else.

"Stay close!" Zoey shouted.

She looked over at Lux, her heart tightening when she saw her wince with every step. But Lux kept moving, her jaw set in determination. Zoey focused on the path ahead, trying to find a route that would lead them away from the worst of it.

"We're almost there, just a little more!" Zoey said.

The air was thick with dust, making it hard to breathe. Zoey's lungs burned, but she didn't dare stop. Her eyes stung, and she blinked rapidly to clear them, but it was like trying to see through a cloud. Lux's grip on her hand was strong, and Zoey held on tight, determined not to let go.

The ground continued to shift beneath them, and the incline made it even harder to keep their footing. Zoey could hear the crack of trees snapping somewhere below them, the sound echoing through the chaos. She had to remind herself to breathe.

"Watch out!" Zoey yelled as a large rock tumbled down, barely missing them.

They dodged to the side, but the ground was giving way faster than they could move. Zoey's heart was in her throat as she pulled Lux to her feet again. The strain on Lux's face was impossible to ignore, and Zoey knew that she was pushing herself to the limit.

"Zoey, I—" Lux started.

"Don't. We're not stopping." Zoey's voice was fierce, leaving no room for argument.

They continued their desperate climb, the ground shifting underfoot, but Zoey's focus was entirely on getting them to safety. She barely noticed the scrapes on her hands and knees or the sting of dirt and rocks as they pelted her skin. All that mattered was moving forward.

The noise around them was deafening, the roar of the landslide filling her ears. Zoey felt the ground lurch again, and her heart skipped a beat as she saw a massive section of the hillside give way, sliding down with a terrifying speed.

"Move now!" Zoey said.

They surged forward, adrenaline coursing through Zoey's veins. She could hear Lux's labored breathing, but she didn't slow down. There was no time. The ground continued to crumble beneath them, but Zoey refused to let fear take over.

"We're going to make it," she said, more to herself than to Lux.

They kept moving, but Zoey could feel the strain in her muscles, the fatigue setting in. Her legs felt heavy, her breath coming in ragged gasps, but she pushed it all aside. There was no room for weakness here, not when their lives were on the line.

Suddenly, the ground beneath them gave a violent jolt, and Zoey felt herself lose her balance. She let out a gasp as she stumbled, pulling Lux down with her. They both hit the ground hard, but Zoey didn't waste a second. She was back on her feet in an instant, pulling Lux up beside her.

"Come on!" Zoey urged.

Lux winced as she tried to stand, her ankle buckling beneath her. Zoey's heart dropped at the sight, but there was no time to dwell on it. She wrapped an arm around Lux's waist, supporting her as they stumbled forward.

"We're almost there," Zoey said again, even though she wasn't sure where "there" was. All she knew was that they couldn't stay where they were.

The roar of the landslide was deafening now, the ground beneath them shaking with an intensity that made it hard to stay upright. Zoey could feel the fear clawing at her insides, but she shoved it down, focusing on Lux and the path ahead.

They moved as fast as they could, but the ground was slick with mud and debris, making every step a battle. Zoey's legs burned with the effort, but she didn't stop. She couldn't stop. Not when they were so close to getting out of this alive.

But then she heard it—a crack, louder than anything else around them. Zoey's eyes widened in horror as she looked up to see a massive boulder breaking free from the hillside above them.

"Run!" Zoey screamed, but there was nowhere to go.

The boulder crashed, and the ground trembled beneath the impact. Zoey's heart pounded as she tried to move, but the ground was shifting too fast and the mud pulled at her feet. She could feel the panic rising in her chest, but she forced herself to stay calm.

"Zoey!" Lux's voice was filled with fear, and Zoey turned just in time to see her stumble again, her ankle giving out beneath her.

"Lux!" Zoey's voice cracked as she reached out, grabbing Lux's hand just as she started to fall.

But the ground beneath them was giving way. Zoey could feel herself being pulled down, the weight of the mud dragging her down with it. She struggled to hold on, her grip on Lux's hand slipping as the ground shifted beneath them.

"No, no, no!" Zoey's voice was frantic as she tried to pull Lux back up, but it was no use.

Lux's foot was caught, and her ankle twisted painfully beneath the weight of the debris. Lux let out a cry of pain, her face contorting in agony as she tried to free herself. Zoey watched, helpless.

"Not again," Lux whispered.

Zoey's hands trembled as she tried to dig Lux's foot out, but the mud was too thick and the rocks too heavy. She could feel the panic rising in her chest, the fear threatening to overwhelm her. But she couldn't let that happen. She couldn't let Lux get hurt again.

"Hold on, Lux. I'm going to get you out of this," Zoey said.

But even as she said the words, Zoey could feel the ground shifting beneath them again, the landslide continuing its relentless descent. She heard the roar of the earth around them, the sound of trees snapping and rocks tumbling down the hillside. And in that moment, Zoey knew that they were running out of time.

She looked at Lux, her heart breaking at the sight of her in so much pain. But there was no time to hesitate, no time to think about what could happen next. Zoey had to act, and she had to act fast.

"Zoey, you have to go," Lux said.

"No. I'm not leaving you."

"Zoey, please," Lux said. "I can't do this again. I can't let you get hurt because of me."

Zoey shook her head, her jaw set in determination. "I'm not leaving you."

She could see the fear in Lux's eyes. But she also saw something else: trust. Lux trusted her, and Zoey wasn't about to let her down.

"I'm going to get you out of this," Zoey said. "I promise."

The ground had stopped rumbling, but the aftermath of the landslide had left chaos in its wake. Trees were uprooted, boulders scattered, and the path they'd been on was obliterated. Zoey's hands shook as she tried to clear the debris around Lux's leg, her breath coming in shallow gasps.

She glanced up at Lux, whose face was pale and streaked with dirt. "You have to hold on."

Lux nodded weakly, her lips pressed into a thin line. "I'm trying, Zoey."

Zoey saw the pain in her eyes. Lux's leg was pinned under a large branch, and every time Zoey tried to move it, Lux winced.

"I'm sorry. I'm so sorry," Zoey whispered as she continued to pull at the branch. Her arms ached, and her hands were raw, but she didn't stop. She couldn't stop. She could feel her panic rising, but she forced it down.

"It's not your fault," Lux said softly. "Just...get me out of here."

Zoey put all her strength into moving the branch. It took several tries, but finally, with a grunt, she managed to shift it enough for Lux to pull her leg free. Lux let out a cry of pain as she did, and Zoey immediately knelt beside her, helping her sit up.

"Are you okay? Can you move?" Zoey asked, her eyes wide with concern.

Lux shook her head, tears welling. "My ankle... it's worse." She tried to move her foot, but the pain was too much, and she quickly stopped.

Zoey felt a surge of helplessness wash over her. She didn't know what to do. They were alone, far from any help, and Lux was injured. She swallowed hard, trying to think. They had to keep moving. They couldn't stay here, not with the fire still so close.

"Lux, we have to go. I'll help you. Lean on me, okay?"

Lux hesitated, then nodded. "Okay." Zoey helped her to her feet, and Lux leaned heavily on her as they started to make their way uphill again. Every step was a struggle, and Zoey could feel Lux's weight dragging her down, but she didn't complain. She just kept going, putting one foot in front of the other.

The air was thick with smoke, and Zoey's lungs burned with every breath. She could hear the crackling of the fire behind them, but it wasn't as close as before.

That was something, at least.

But the climb was steep, and with Lux injured, it was slow going. Zoey's muscles screamed in protest, but she pushed through the pain, determined to get them to safety.

Lux was silent, her face pale and sweaty. Zoey knew she was in a lot of pain, but she didn't say anything. She just kept going, Lux's grip on her shoulder tightening with every step.

"Just a little farther," Zoey said.

Zoey was careful with every step, making sure she didn't slip and bring them both down.

"We should try to find a place to rest," Lux said after a moment, wincing as she shifted her weight. "Somewhere we can wait for help."

Zoey wiped her eyes, taking a deep breath. "Okay. But we need to take it slow. I don't want you hurting yourself even more."

"I'll be fine," she said. "I just need to catch my breath."

The terrain was rough, and Lux's ankle was giving her trouble, but she didn't complain. Zoey kept a close eye on her, ready to catch her if she stumbled.

They walked in silence for a while, both too exhausted to talk. The forest around them was eerily quiet, the only sound the distant crackling of the fire. Zoey's mind was racing, thinking about everything that had happened, everything that could still happen. But she tried to push those thoughts away, focusing on the present, on getting them to safety.

After a while, they found an area sheltered by

trees. It wasn't much, but it was better than nothing. Zoey helped Lux sit down, then collapsed beside her, her body aching all over.

"We'll rest here for now," Zoey said. "We'll figure out what to do next once we've had some sleep."

21

LUX

Lux shifted slightly, trying to sit up without putting too much pressure on her injured leg. The movement didn't go unnoticed. Zoey glanced over her shoulder, her eyes softening as she met Lux's gaze.

It had been an hour since the landslide incident, and her leg felt slightly better.

"How are you feeling?" Zoey asked, carrying a tenderness that Lux had grown to crave.

Lux managed to smile, though it was laced with discomfort.

"Better, I think. The leg still hurts, but it's not unbearable."

Zoey scooted over to meet Lux. "There should

be a river close by. We could find something to eat maybe?"

"More berries?"

"Yeah," Zoey responded.

Lux didn't care for fruit at the moment. She wanted to reach out, pull Zoey closer, and let her know how much she meant to her. But she held back, her mind wrestling with the tension between desire and caution.

But they were both exhausted, physically and emotionally. The last thing she wanted was to push too far, too fast.

Zoey shifted slightly, adjusting to look at Lux more directly. Her hand moved to Lux's cheek, and she leaned in, pressing her lips gently against hers. The kiss was soft and tentative, but it sent a rush of warmth through Lux's body, waking something deep inside her. At that moment, Zoey's touch was everything she needed—gentle reassurance filled with a quiet passion impossible to ignore.

But just as quickly as it started, the kiss ended. Zoey pulled back, her expression a mix of affection and concern.

"You should rest," she said softly. "I'll go get us some food, okay?"

Lux nodded, though she wasn't ready to let Zoey go. "Be careful."

Zoey smiled, that familiar warmth returning to her eyes. "I will. I'll be back soon."

Lux watched as Zoey walked away.

Once Zoey was gone, Lux lay back down, her thoughts spinning in a thousand different directions. The kiss lingered on her lips, and the memory of Zoey's touch sent sparks of desire through her.

Lux tried to push it aside, reminding herself they were still in a dangerous situation. But it was hard to ignore how her body responded to Zoey, how her heart seemed to beat a little faster whenever she was nearby.

She tried to focus on anything else—the sounds of the forest outside and the faint crackle of the fire—but it all circled back to Zoey. Lux closed her eyes, willing herself to calm down. No matter how strong they were, now wasn't the time to get lost in her feelings.

After what felt like an eternity, Zoey finally returned. Lux opened her eyes, sitting up as best she could. But when she saw what Zoey was carrying, her breath caught in her throat.

She held a dead rabbit by its hind legs. Lux

stared at it, shock rippling through her. "You...you hunted it?"

Zoey blinked, then let out a small laugh, though she seemed uncomfortable. "He was badly injured in the landslide, he was crying in pain. He wouldn't have survived. It was a kindness.. and, I didn't want him to go to waste." she explained, setting the rabbit down on a flat stone.

Zoey seemed to sense Lux's unease, and she quickly moved to change the subject. "I also found some fruit." She pulled a small bundle of berries from her pocket. "They should help keep us going."

Lux's tension eased a little at the sight of the berries. She was grateful for Zoey's thoughtfulness, even in such dire circumstances. "Thank you."

Zoey handed Lux a few berries and sat beside her, taking one of Lux's hands in hers. Lux looked down at their joined hands, her heart swelling with emotion. She could feel the warmth of Zoey's touch and the steadiness of her presence, which brought her a sense of comfort she hadn't felt in a long time.

After a while, Zoey shifted. "We should probably build a secure shelter," she said. "Something that will keep us safe through the night."

"We lost most of the stuff at the previous camp, Zoe," Lux said. "We don't have much here anymore."

"Luckily, I was more than just a girl scout."

"You were a scout?"

Zoey saluted. "I learned to set up camp with just wood."

"All right, lieutenant," Lux said. "And how much wood do we need?"

"Not much," Zoey said. "We only need something to keep above our heads while we sleep."

Lux nodded. "What do you need me to do?"

Zoey smiled, genuinely making Lux's heart skip a beat. "You can help me gather more sticks," Zoey said.

Lux glanced around, her eyes scanning the makeshift lean-to they had started to build. The ground was rough and covered with scattered leaves and twigs. She watched Zoey thatch the branches together to form a perfect fit, her movements swift and confident.

Lux felt a swell of admiration for Zoey's resourcefulness. They had gathered enough sticks to construct a simple shelter to give them a little protection.

"You've done this before, haven't you?" Lux asked, her tone light.

"Not exactly," Zoey said, concentrating on her task. "But I've seen it done enough times to have an idea. Plus, we don't have much choice, right?"

Lux nodded, feeling a little more secure with Zoey's presence. "It's impressive, though. You just... you seem to know what you're doing."

Zoey gave her a small smile. "Survival instinct, I guess. I just do what needs to be done."

As Zoey finished, Lux stepped back to examine their work. It wasn't perfect, but it was better than nothing. The makeshift shelter had a decent frame with good cover from the elements.

Zoey wiped her hands on her pants and looked over at Lux. "Let's get more sticks. The bigger ones will work better for the walls."

The two of them worked silently, gathering sticks and larger branches, creating a pile near their shelter.

Once they had enough, Zoey placed them along the sides of the frame, leaning them against the frame. Lux watched her, occasionally helping when Zoey asked but mostly observing how Zoey worked.

"What's next?" Lux asked.

"Now we gather leafy branches to make a mat for on top of the roof. It'll help keep the rain off."

"Lux chuckled. "Rain?"

"We can't leave it to chance, can we?"

"I guess not." Lux gathered leafy branches and started placing them on the frame. "Got it."

"Perfect," Zoey said, arranging the leaves to get the most coverage.

There was something captivating about how Zoey moved, her hands worked the materials, and her mind focused on the task. After a while, Zoey stepped back to assess their progress. "Not bad," she said, tilting her head slightly. "It'll do for now."

Lux smiled, a bit of pride swelling in her chest. "Yeah, it's not bad at all."

They both stepped inside the makeshift structure, crouching slightly to fit under the low ceiling. It was cramped, but it provided some protection from the elements. The ground inside was still hard, but they could make it more comfortable later.

"At least we're not completely exposed," Zoey said, settling down on the ground.

Lux sat down beside her, their shoulders brushing. The closeness sent a warmth through Lux that made her heart beat a little faster. She could feel the tension in the air, the kind that had nothing to do with fear or survival but with something much more intimate.

"So...you're okay with this?" Zoey asked.

Lux glanced at Zoey, noticing the way her eyes softened as she looked at her. "Yeah," she said quietly. "I'm okay with it. More than okay."

Zoey reached out and took Lux's hand, giving it a gentle squeeze. Lux's heart fluttered at the touch, her thoughts briefly straying to places she tried to avoid. She liked Zoey—more than liked her—but she wasn't sure what that meant for them, especially in their current situation.

Zoey let go of her hand and leaned back, closing her eyes. "We're going to be okay, you know," she said. "No matter what happens."

Lux nodded, her gaze fixed on Zoey's face. "Yeah," she echoed. "We'll be okay."

Lux wanted to reach out again, touch Zoey and feel her close, but she held back, not wanting to push too far. She had to remind herself to stay calm and not let her emotions get the better of her.

Zoey reached out and gently cupped Lux's cheek, her thumb brushing lightly against her skin. "I'm just glad I found you."

Lux's breath hitched at the touch, her heart

pounding. She leaned into Zoey's hand, closing her eyes as she savored the moment. Their connection felt undeniable.

Zoey leaned in closer, her breath warm against Lux's skin. "I'm here," she whispered. "I'm not going anywhere."

Lux opened her eyes, meeting Zoey's gaze. The intensity in Zoey's eyes sent a shiver down her spine, and she felt herself leaning in, closing the distance between them. Their lips met in a soft, tentative kiss, one that quickly deepened as they lost themselves in the moment.

Zoey's hand slid down to Lux's waist, pulling her closer as the kiss intensified. Lux's hands found their way to Zoey's shoulders, gripping them tightly as the heat between them grew. She could feel the tension melting away, replaced by something much more powerful.

When they finally pulled apart, they were both breathless, their hearts racing in sync. Lux rested her forehead against Zoey's. Her eyes closed as she tried to calm the whirlwind of emotions inside her.

Zoey's voice was soft when she spoke, her breath still heavy. "We should probably get some rest."

Lux nodded, though sleep was the last thing on her mind. "Yeah."

They shifted slightly, making themselves more comfortable on the hard ground. Zoey wrapped an arm around Lux, pulling her close, and Lux nestled into her embrace, feeling a sense of safety and warmth that she hadn't felt in a long time.

As they lay there, the makeshift tent providing a barrier against the outside world, Lux allowed herself to relax. She listened to the steady rhythm of Zoey's breathing, letting it soothe her as she drifted closer to sleep.

Zoey's voice broke the silence, a soft murmur that made Lux's heart flutter. "I'm glad you're here with me, Lux."

Lux smiled, her eyes still closed as she replied, "I'm glad you're here too."

22

ZOEY

Zoey kept her eyes closed, feeling Lux's chest's gentle rise and fall against her side. It felt nice, like everything was okay at that small moment. She could stay like this forever, just the two of them, hidden away from the world. Zoey let herself get lost in the rhythm of Lux's breathing, letting it calm her.

She was awake, but she didn't want to break the stillness.

Zoey could feel the soft brush of her hair against her cheek, the faint warmth of her breath on her neck. She reached out, her fingers barely grazing Lux's cheek. The touch was so light, so careful, like she was afraid to wake her.

Her heart squeezed in her chest as she took in

Lux's features. The curve of her lips, her eyelashes rested against her skin, the faint freckles across her nose—everything about Lux was beautiful to Zoey. She let her hand fall away, feeling a warmth in her chest that she hadn't felt in a long time.

She cared about Lux more than she had allowed herself to realize. It scared her how much she felt, how deeply she cared. It wasn't just the physical attraction.

It was more. She wanted this, wanted Lux.

Zoey thought about the last time they made love as she lay there, watching Lux sleep. Zoey felt a lump rise in her throat.

Zoey's mind wandered to how Lux had leaned into her, how their kiss had felt so right, so natural. It wasn't just about survival or the situation they were in. It was about their connection and the bond that had grown between them over the past few days. She didn't want to lose that. She couldn't lose that.

Lux's eyes fluttered open. "Morning," she said softly.

"Morning," Zoey said. She felt a nervousness in her stomach, but she pushed it down, trying to keep her expression calm.

Lux stretched, her hand brushing against

Zoey's arm again, and Zoey felt a shiver run down her spine. She wanted to say something, anything to break the silence that had settled between them, but her mind was blank. All she could think about was how close Lux was and how much she wanted to reach out and touch her again.

Lux shifted onto her side, facing Zoey. "You okay?"

Zoey nodded, swallowing hard. "Yeah."

"You sure?" Lux asked.

Zoey nodded.

Lux's hand moved to cover Zoey's, and she turned her head slightly, pressing a soft kiss to Zoey's palm. The gesture was so tender and so full of emotion that it took Zoey's breath away. She felt a tear slip down her cheek but didn't move to wipe it away. She just watched Lux, watched the way she looked at her with such care, such affection.

Zoey leaned in slowly, closing the distance between them until their lips met in a gentle kiss. It was soft, almost hesitant. But as the kiss deepened, Zoey felt a warmth spread through her chest, a warmth that chased away the fear and uncertainty.

Lux's hand slid down to Zoey's waist, pulling her closer, and Zoey responded by wrapping her arms around Lux, holding her tightly. The kiss became more urgent. Zoey felt her heart racing, her skin tingling with every touch, every brush of Lux's lips against hers.

Zoey leaned in again, pressing another kiss to Lux's lips, and she felt Lux smile against her mouth. The kiss was slow, unhurried. Zoey let herself get lost in the feeling, in the way Lux's lips moved against hers, in the way their bodies fit together so perfectly.

Lux's hand slid up Zoey's back, her fingers tracing soft patterns against her skin. Zoey shivered at the touch, her breath hitching in her throat. She could feel the tension building between them, the slow burn of desire simmering just beneath the surface.

Zoey pulled back slightly, her eyes searching Lux's face. "Are you okay?"

Lux nodded, her eyes shadowed with emotion. "I'm more than okay."

Zoey felt a surge at Lux's words, and she leaned in again, pressing a kiss to the corner of Lux's mouth. She let her lips linger there momentarily, feeling the warmth of Lux's skin against hers.

Lux's hand moved to Zoey's waist, pulling her closer, and Zoey felt a shiver run down her spine.

She sighed softly as Lux's lips brushed against her jaw, trailing soft kisses down her neck. Zoey tilted her head back slightly, giving Lux better access, and she felt a rush of heat spread through her body.

Lux's lips moved back to Zoey's mouth, capturing it in a slow, deliberate kiss. Zoey responded eagerly, her hands tangling in Lux's hair as she pulled her closer. The kiss deepened, their tongues meeting in a slow, sensual dance that left Zoey breathless.

Lux's gaze softened as she looked at Zoey. Zoey's breath quickened, her heart racing as Lux's fingers traced a path from her cheek to her collarbone. Her touch was gentle, but it sent a surge of warmth through Zoey that she couldn't ignore.

"Zoey," Lux whispered.

Zoey's eyes met Lux's, and she could see their intensity. Lux wasn't just looking at her; she was seeing her, every part of her, and it made Zoey feel exposed but in the best way possible. She swallowed, trying to calm the flutter in her chest.

Lux's hand moved lower, fingers grazing over the edge of Zoey's tank top. Zoey's skin tingled when Lux's fingers touched it. She couldn't stop the shiver that ran through her, nor did she want to. Lux glanced to where her hand rested and hesitated, looking back up at Zoey.

"Zoey," Lux said again. "I...I love you."

The words hung between them, and Zoey's breath caught. Her mind raced, a mix of shock, confusion, and something deeper—something that made her chest tighten with emotion. Lux loved her. Zoey had hoped for it, but hearing it out loud felt surreal. She didn't know how to respond, didn't know what to say.

Instead of words, Zoey's body reacted. She leaned in, closing the small distance between them, and kissed Lux with a softness that belied the storm of emotions inside her. Lux's lips were warm, and the kiss deepened naturally like it was the only thing they could do.

Lux responded with equal enthusiasm, her arms wrapping around Zoey's waist, pulling her closer. Zoey could feel Lux's heartbeat against her chest, fast and strong, mirroring her own. Lux's hands slid up Zoey's back, fingers pressing into her skin, trying to hold on to something real, something solid.

Zoey's mind was a blur, but one thing was clear: she needed Lux to feel her and be close to her in every way possible. She broke the kiss, only to catch her breath, and then their mouths found each other again, more urgent. Lux's hands moved to Zoey's waist, then lower, her touch igniting a fire that Zoey hadn't felt before, not like this.

Without thinking, Zoey's hands found the hem of Lux's shirt, pulling it up and over her head swiftly. Lux helped, raising her arms, and then it was gone, leaving Lux's skin bare to Zoey's touch. Zoey ran her hands over Lux's shoulders, down her arms, and back up again, marveling at the smoothness of her skin and the way it felt under her fingers.

Lux's breath hitched, and she let out a soft sigh, her head tilting back slightly as Zoey's lips trailed down her neck. Zoey's heart pounded, and she couldn't stop pressing closer, feeling the heat of Lux's body against hers. It was overwhelming in the best way, and Zoey wanted more.

Lux's hands were on Zoey's hips now, tugging at the waistband of her shorts, and Zoey didn't hesitate. She shifted, helping Lux pull them down, and then they were gone, discarded somewhere on the ground. Lux's hands roamed freely now, exploring every inch of Zoey's body with a tenderness that made Zoey's heart ache.

"Lux," Zoey finally managed to whisper, her

voice shaky. She didn't know what she wanted to say, didn't know how to express everything she was feeling. But she didn't need to, because Lux was right there with her, understanding without words.

"I've got you," Lux said, her voice low and comforting.

Zoey felt Lux's lips on her skin again, moving from her neck to her shoulder, then lower. Every kiss, every touch sent a shiver down Zoey's spine, making her breath hitch. She closed her eyes, letting herself get lost in the sensation, in the feeling of Lux's hands and mouth on her.

When Lux's hand slipped between her legs, Zoey gasped, her eyes flying open. Lux paused, her gaze searching Zoey's face. Zoey nodded. That was all Lux needed. She moved her hand slowly, deliberately, drawing a soft moan from Zoey's lips.

Zoey's mind went blank, her body arching into Lux's touch as the sensations overwhelmed her. Lux's touch was gentle, but there was a purpose behind it, a need that matched Zoey's own. Zoey couldn't stop the soft cries that escaped her lips, couldn't stop her hands from clutching at Lux, pulling her closer, needing her more than ever.

Lux's lips found Zoey's again, and this time, the kiss was rougher, more desperate. Zoey could taste the urgency on Lux's lips, could feel it in the way Lux's body pressed against hers, and it only fueled the fire burning inside her. She kissed Lux back with everything she had, letting her emotions take over.

They moved together, their bodies fitting perfectly, every touch, every kiss bringing them closer to the edge. Lux's hand moved with more purpose now, her fingers teasing and exploring in ways that made Zoey's head spin. Zoey's breath came in short, shallow gasps, her body trembling with anticipation.

Zoey's heart pounded in her chest, her body trembling with the intensity of it all. She could feel herself spiraling, losing control, but she didn't care. Lux was there, holding her, guiding her, making her feel things she'd never felt before.

It was too much, too intense, and Zoey's mind went blank as the sensations overwhelmed her. She cried out, her body arching into Lux's touch, her fingers digging into Lux's shoulders as she rode out the wave of pleasure that washed over her.

Lux held her through it all, her touch gentle and soothing, her lips pressing soft kisses to Zoey's skin. Zoey's body trembled, her breath coming in shallow gasps as she slowly came down from the high. Lux didn't let go, didn't pull away, and Zoey was grateful for that.

She wasn't ready to let go yet, wasn't ready for this moment to end. Lux seemed to understand, and she held Zoey close, her arms wrapped around her, their bodies still entwined.

They lay there together, their breathing slowly returning to normal. Zoey felt a warmth in her chest, a feeling she couldn't quite put into words. It wasn't just the afterglow of their lovemaking. It was something more, something deeper.

23

LUX

Lux lay on the rough ground, her body still brimming with warmth and the aftershocks of desire.

Zoey slept soundly beside her, resting on her body with a hand loosely cupping her breast. The cool air caressing her skin didn't sway her, not when it contrasted with the warmth on Zoey's body.

Lux couldn't sleep.

Her mind was too restless, too consumed with everything. She could still feel the weight of Zoey's hands on her, the softness of her lips, the way their bodies had moved together in perfect sync.

She turned her head slightly, looking at Zoey's face. It was hard to believe she had found something so raw and real under these circumstances, trapped in the forest with fire closing in on them.

Who'd have thought...?

It wasn't just the physical connection. It was more than that. It was how Zoey made her feel: safe, understood, cared for.

How did it come to this? How had she found love here, of all places? She had spent years avoiding anything that resembled a real relationship, keeping her heart locked away, safe from the possibility of getting hurt or hurting others.

But now, lying next to Zoey, she realized she had never really known what she was missing until now. The last time she was this drawn to someone, it didn't end well.

Lux let out a quiet sigh, scanning the darkened sky above through the tiny cracks in their makeshift roof. The stars were faint, barely visible through the haze of smoke still in the air.

It had been days, and the fire hadn't slowed down. It still crept up the mountain. The higher they went, the closer it seemed to get.

Even now, she knew that time was running out. As beautiful as what they shared here, they couldn't stay much longer. She didn't even know how much farther they could go. They had already climbed so far up, and she was drained.

Lux shifted slightly, trying to get comfortable, but the unease in her chest made it impossible. It grew stronger with each passing second.

She couldn't shake the feeling that no matter what they did, the fire would catch up to them eventually. She couldn't bear the thought of losing Zoey here.

Not after she'd finally found someone who—

Does she want you?

The thought hit Lux so forcefully that she winced.

She knew that Zoey was drawn to her. But what if it was just physical for her?

Would she still feel the way once they got off the mountain? Would they get even off this mountain?

And then what? What would they do when there was nowhere left to run?

She didn't have an answer, and that terrified her even more.

A rustle of leaves in the distance caught her attention, pulling her from her thoughts. The forest around them was alive with the chirping of insects, distant calls of nocturnal animals higher up the mountain, and the fire crackling in the distance.

It felt like a countdown.

How fast could they go? What happened if the fire caught up with them?

Zoey stirred beside her, letting out a soft sigh in her sleep. Lux's heart clenched, a mix of love and fear swirling in her chest. She didn't know how they were going to get out of this.

She had just found her, just discovered what it felt like to care for someone, and now she was faced with the possibility of losing it all.

The idea of a life outside this mountain felt distant, almost unreal. Would they even make it out? Would they have a chance to see what could come of this thing between them?

She didn't know.

She turned her head slightly, looking at Zoey again. How was it possible to care this much this quickly?

She had spent so long avoiding this, avoiding the risk of getting close to someone. And now, here she was, head over heels for a woman she had met under the worst possible circumstances.

And yet, it felt right. It felt like the most natural thing in the world.

But the fire was still coming, and that was a reality they couldn't ignore. Lux reached out, her hand brushing against Zoey's arm. The contact was enough to wake her, and Zoey's eyes fluttered open, her gaze meeting Lux's in the dim light.

"Lux?" Zoey's voice was soft, groggy from sleep.

Lux didn't respond immediately. She scanned the trees and saw the faint fire glowing in the distance.

"We need to keep moving," she finally said.

"Lux?"

"Sorry." She sighed. "I must've gotten carried away."

Zoey pecked her cheek and adjusted so Lux could lay on her back. They both remained there, breathing quietly.

"Want to see the beautiful sky?" Zoey asked, sitting up slowly. The makeshift shelter immediately felt cramped. There wasn't much space to begin with.

"Sure, why not."

They both made their way outside. They soon found a spot to lie down and stare at the sky. Zoey scooted closer to Lux, patting her sides until she found Lux's hands.

Lux sighed, hating how her heart raced for a millisecond, even though she loved the gesture.

The sky was endless and so very beautiful streaked with color.

"Tense?" Zoey asked.

Lux sighed. "It's a new day, and we're still here."

"That's what's bothering you again?" Zoey asked.

Lux shrugged. Zoey rolled over. She was facing down on Lux now, with half her weight on Lux's body. Their eyes met for the briefest of moments. Then her lips found Lux's.

She soon backed away but remained arched over Lux.

"What's bothering you? The fire?"

Lux shrugged. "It's still coming," she said. "We can't stay here forever."

Zoey nodded, rubbing the sleep from her eyes. "Where do we go then?"

"Up," Lux said. "We keep going up."

Zoey looked at her, and for a moment, Lux saw the same fear she was feeling reflected in Zoey's eyes. But then Zoey nodded.

"We'll go up," she said. "We'll get off this mountain. We'll be fine."

"You're sure of that?"

Zoey chuckled and pecked her lips. "No, but I'm done being moody about it."

This time, Lux leaned in first for the kiss. She rolled above Zoey, pinning her down playfully as she ravaged her lips with sensual kisses. Her hands held Zoey's cheek, and her fingers tousled in her hair.

When she backed away, Zoey was still smiling.

"Well, that's the best good morning kiss ever."

She stared into Zoey's eyes for a little longer, then sighed and said, "You're just so naughty."

"If by naughty you mean sweet, then I'm guilty as charged."

They both remained on the ground, holding each other close. It wasn't long before the sun crept up the sky, and Lux stirred.

"Zoey?" she called.

"I know," Zoey said. "We've gotta move."

They gathered their things quickly, leaving their structure behind, and were soon on their way again. Lux could feel the heat in the air, the fire inching its way closer to them. There wasn't much time.

The climb was challenging. Lux's legs ached, her breath coming in short, sharp bursts. Zoey was just ahead, her movements steady, but Lux could see the strain on her face, the way her shoulders hunched slightly with each step.

"You sure we shouldn't wait for a bit?" Lux said. "You haven't gotten your strength yet."

"Trust me, I can go on for hours," Zoey said breathlessly.

"Yeah, as long as we don't get turned into barbecue," Lux said with a laugh.

"No doubt about that."

They both laughed. After almost half the day, they reached a small plateau, a tree break that offered a brief reprieve from the climb. Lux sank to the ground, her legs trembling from the effort. Zoey sat beside her, her hand reaching out to rest on Lux's knee.

"Look who's tired now," Zoey said with a laugh.

Lux nodded. The fire was still distant, so they had some time, but not much. Lux looked at Zoey, her heart aching with the weight of everything she wanted to say.

As the fire crept closer, Lux held on to that hope, that small, fragile thing that kept her going, kept her fighting. They would make it out of this. They had to.

Lux sat on the cool ground, her back pressed against the rough bark of a tree, lost in her thoughts as dusk faded into night. The night air was thick with smoke, the distant glow of the fire casting an eerie light over the landscape. Zoey was resting a few feet away, her breathing steady and calm, a stark contrast to the turmoil inside Lux.

She had tried to sleep, but her mind wouldn't quiet. Whenever she closed her eyes, images of the fire, them running, and Zoey's face as they struggled to survive flashed behind her eyelids. The reality of their situation pressed down on her, a weight she didn't know how to lift. She couldn't stop thinking about how close they were to the edge, how easily the flames could consume them in its path.

Her thoughts drifted back to the night before, to the words she had spoken to Zoey in a moment of passion and fear. She had told Zoey she loved her, and while it had felt right, she was now left wondering what it meant. Could she love someone in a situation like this? Did it even matter?

Lux's eyes scanned the darkened landscape, the outline of trees barely visible against the smoky sky. The fire was still advancing, but it felt like they were in a strange bubble of calm. She wanted to hold on to that feeling but knew it couldn't last.

The sound of movement pulled her from her thoughts, and she turned her head to see Zoey sitting up, searching for Lux in the smoke. Zoey's gaze found hers, and for a moment, they just looked at each other, the silence between them heavy.

Zoey stood up and walked over to Lux, her steps careful on the uneven ground. She sat beside her, close enough that their shoulders brushed, and Lux felt a warmth spread through her despite the coolness of the night.

"Still worried about the station?" Zoey asked.

"Nah, not that." she shrugged. "Right now, I'm more worried about the rumbling in my stomach."

"Are you sure you're just hungry?" Zoey asked.

"Well, not entirely," Lux said.

Zoey's eyes asked the rest of the questions. Lux hesitated, her eyes fixed on the ground in front of her. She wasn't sure if she wanted to have this conversation.

"About last night," she said quietly.

Zoey didn't respond right away, and Lux could feel the tension in the air between them. "What about it?" Zoey finally asked.

Lux sighed, turning to look at Zoey. "I said

something last night, something I'm not sure I should have said."

Zoey's expression softened, and she reached out, placing a hand on Lux's arm. "You mean when you said you love me?"

Lux nodded, her heart pounding in her chest. "I didn't mean to make things complicated. I don't know what I was thinking."

Zoey looked at her for a long moment. "Do you regret it?"

Lux hesitated, then shook her head. "No, I don't. I just…I don't know what happens now. There's no way for us to be rescued anymore. The station probably thinks we've been lost to the fire by now."

Zoey's hand tightened on Lux's arm, a small gesture of comfort. "I've been thinking about that too," she said. "But we can't give up hope. We've made it this far."

Lux wanted to believe her and hold on to that hope, but it was slipping through her fingers like sand. "What if they've given up on us, Zoey? What if we're all alone out here?"

Zoey was silent momentarily, her gaze distant as she stared ahead. "Then we accept it," she said as she stood up. "Come on, we should keep going."

Lux stood up. "Okay."

24

ZOEY

Zoey trudged through the rocky terrain, her boots scuffing against the uneven ground. The trees thinned out as they climbed higher.

She glanced over at Lux, who was walking a few steps ahead. For most of the day, she'd seemed stuck in her thoughts. Even when she spoke up, something else was on her mind.

As much as she felt attracted to Lux, she didn't want to scare her off.

Attracted?

Zoey slowed down somewhat. This wasn't mere attraction. She was falling in love with Lux, as strange as it sounded to her own ears.

"Shit." She stumbled.

Lux turned. "You good back there?"

"Yeah, sure," she replied hurriedly. "Just tripped on some stones."

The ground was littered with shrubs, their tough roots gripping the rocky soil. This area differed from the dense forest they had left behind. It felt more open, more exposed.

"We should be easier to spot from the air now," Zoey said.

"That's if they're looking," Lux said.

"We'd better hope they are."

Lux nodded, still focused on the path ahead. "Yeah, and hopefully, the fire won't spread as quickly up here. There's less fuel for it."

Zoey's gaze drifted upward, taking in the vast, clear sky. The smoke from the fire was still visible in the distance, but it felt like they had finally put some distance between themselves and the danger.

"It's a relief to be out of those trees," she said. "I was starting to feel like we were trapped down there."

Lux glanced back at her, a small smile tugging at the corners of her lips. "I know what you mean. It's good to see clear sky again."

They continued walking, the rocky ground

crunching beneath their feet. The shrubs grew thicker as they moved farther up the terrain, and Zoey found herself brushing past the occasional prickly branch. It wasn't easy going, but it was better than the constant threat of falling branches or getting lost in the dense underbrush.

After a while, they reached a slight rise, and Zoey's breath caught in her throat as she saw something shimmering in the distance. "Is that...water?"

Lux followed her gaze. "Looks like it. Could be a lake or a pond."

"Think we can try to catch something to eat?" Zoey asked.

"Sure, I'm famished," Lux said.

They descended the slope, the terrain leveling as they approached the water. As they drew closer, Zoey could see it was indeed a lake, its surface calm as it reflected the pale blue sky. The air around it felt fresher, and Zoey breathed deeply, savoring the clean scent.

Lux crouched by the water's edge, her fingers trailing through the surface.

"It's clean," she said, relief evident.

Zoey knelt beside her, the cool water lapping at her fingertips. "This is a good spot," she said. "We should take a break here, maybe even camp for the night."

Lux nodded. "Agreed. And if we're lucky, we might be able to catch something." She looked around.

Lux chuckled softly. "I'm sure we can figure something out."

They spent the next few minutes gathering fishing supplies. They found long, sturdy branches that could serve as fishing rods and some discarded string and drinks cans another hiker must've left behind. It wasn't perfect, but it was better than nothing.

They used the metal from the drinks cans to fashion hooks and put some berries on the end as bait. Do fish like berries? Time would tell on that front! Once their makeshift fishing rods were ready, they settled by the lake's edge, casting their lines into the water. Zoey felt calmer as she watched the ripples spread across the surface, the quiet lapping of the water soothing her frayed nerves.

"This is nice," Zoey said. She watched her line bob gently in the water. "It almost makes me forget about everything else."

Lux glanced at her. "It's strange, isn't it? How

something as simple as fishing can make everything seem…normal."

Zoey nodded, her gaze still fixed on the water. "Yeah. I guess it's a reminder that life goes on, no matter what."

"Yeah. I can imagine the look on my dad's face when I tell him I survived so many days out here. There'd be so many stories to share."

"Yeah," Zoey said. "Stories. They'd be scared now, you know."

"Yeah, I know. But my dad won't give up on me just yet." Lux's hands dropped slightly. "I bet he'd give them hell at the station if anyone dared suggest giving up."

They laughed.

Zoey's mind drifted, her thoughts wandering to her family and the life she had left behind. She wondered if they were worried about her or still hoping she was alive.

Had Becky Thompson the Fire Chief reached out to her parents already? Were they preparing for life without her?

She shifted slightly.

"You miss them, don't you?"

Zoey nodded. "Yeah, I do. But I don't want to

think about that right now. I just want to focus on getting through this."

Lux reached out, placing a hand on Zoey's shoulder. "We'll get through it. We've made it this far, haven't we?"

Zoey smiled. "Yeah, we have."

They continued fishing in silence, the tension easing as they focused on the task. After a while, Zoey felt a tug on her line, and she quickly reeled it in, her heart skipping a beat as she saw a fish wriggling on the end.

"Got one!" she said.

Lux grinned. "Nice catch!"

Zoey carefully removed the fish, holding it up for Lux to see. "It's sizable."

Lux laughed. "Who says sizable? That's a big fish." Her smile widened. "Let's see if we can catch a few more."

They spent the next hour or so fishing, catching a few more small fish.

Lux was in a playful mood as they finally gathered their small haul of fish by the lakeside. She leaned over, inspecting their catch with exaggerated seriousness.

"Well, it looks like we won't starve after all," she

said, holding up a fish and examining it like it was the most precious thing she had ever seen. "We will knock up another camp fire to cook them on and then I'd say we're practically gourmet chefs now."

Zoey chuckled, laying out the fish beside the stones they had collected earlier.

"Gourmet chefs who can't even start a fire," she teased, her eyes twinkling.

"Hey now," Lux said, picking up two stones with determination. "I told you, I've seen this in movies. How hard can it be? Of course we can start a fire. We are experts in fire."

"Yeah, putting them out, not starting them!" Zoey laughed.

Lux struck the stones together aiming to create a spark for the kindling they had gathered. She scrunched her face in concentration, clearly hamming it up to get a rise from Zoey.

Zoey crossed her arms, watching with mock skepticism.

"Right, and in the movies, they usually succeed after two strikes. You're on, what, twenty now?"

"Patience, grasshopper," Lux said, grinning as she kept striking the stones together. "Mastering the art of fire making takes time…or at least a lot of trial and error."

Zoey rolled her eyes but couldn't suppress a smile. Despite the absurdity of their situation, Lux's humor was infectious. It was hard not to feel a little lighter around her.

After several failed attempts, Lux flopped beside the fish, sighing dramatically. "Okay, so maybe I'm not quite the fire master I thought I was."

Zoey nudged her with her shoulder. "We could try rubbing a stick into a hole in a piece of wood, old-school style."

"Why not?" Lux said with a shrug. "We're already living in survival mode."

They spent the next few minutes trying to source suitable candidates for the stick and the piece of wood. Once they were sorted, Lux retook the lead, attempting to start the fire by rubbing the stick between her hands and attempting to create enough friction with the piece of wood to ignite the dry leaves they were aiming to use.

"This would be much easier if we had matches," Zoey commented dryly.

Lux gave her a mock glare. "Where's the fun in that? Besides, I'm pretty sure our ancestors did this all the time. If they could do it, so can we. I won't be beaten."

After what felt like an eternity of effort, during which Zoey began to doubt their fire making abilities seriously, they finally saw the tiniest flicker of smoke. Lux's eyes widened, and she doubled her efforts.

"It's working," Lux said, her voice laced with surprise and triumph.

Zoey leaned closer, watching as the smoke thickened and a small flame began to take shape. They quickly added more dry leaves and small sticks, nurturing the fragile flame until it grew into a small but steady fire.

"We did it!" Zoey said, beaming as she looked at Lux.

Lux sat back, grinning like a kid discovering a hidden candy stash. "I told you we could do it. I was starting to worry we'd have to eat raw fish."

Zoey laughed, the sound mingling with the crackling of the fire. "Well, we can enjoy our gourmet meal now."

They carefully prepared the fish, skewering them on sticks and holding them over the fire. The midday sun was high, casting a warm glow over the rocky terrain. The atmosphere was surprisingly peaceful, the earlier tension from their journey dissipating as they relaxed.

Lux watched the fish roast, the skin turning a delicious golden brown. The scent of cooking fish filled the air, making her mouth water.

"I have to admit," Lux said, "this isn't exactly how I pictured my week going, but it's not so bad."

Zoey glanced over at her, a soft smile playing on her lips. "Yeah, who would've thought we'd end up here? But at least we're together."

They ate in comfortable silence, savoring the simple meal. The fish tasted better than Lux had expected, or maybe it was just the satisfaction of knowing they had managed to catch and cook it themselves.

As they finished their meal, the air around them began to shift.

"Do you hear that?" Lux asked, her voice low.

Zoey tilted her head, listening intently. The sound grew louder and more defined.

"Helicopters!" Zoey exclaimed.

They both scrambled to their feet, scanning the sky. The sound of the helicopters grew louder, the deep thrum of the blades unmistakable now.

"There!" Zoey pointed, and Lux followed her gaze, her heart pounding with hope and disbelief.

Three helicopters appeared in the distance, their shapes small but unmistakable against the clear sky. They flew in formation, heading straight toward the rocky terrain where Lux and Zoey stood.

"They found us," Lux said, her voice thick with emotion. "They found us!"

Zoey grabbed Lux's hand, squeezing it tightly as they watched the helicopters draw closer. The noise was deafening now, the wind from the blades kicking up dust and debris around them.

One of the helicopters hovered above them, slowly lowering itself until it was just a few feet off the ground. The side door slid open, and a figure leaned out, waving at them.

Lux's breath caught in her throat as she recognized the pilot's gaudy orange hair.

"It's Jay!" Lux shouted.

Zoey laughed, a sound of pure joy as she waved back at Jay. The helicopter touched down, and the wind from the rotors buffeted them, but they didn't care. They were finally going to be safe.

Jay jumped out of the helicopter, waving to them with a wide smile. "You two sure know how to survive against the odds," she said, her voice booming over the noise.

Lux threw her arms around her, hugging her tightly. "Took you long enough to find us!"

Jay chuckled, patting her back. "It takes more than a little fire to keep me away."

Jay pulled back, looking at both of them with pride and concern. "Let's get you out of here," she said, leading them back to the helicopter.

Lux took one last look at the rocky terrain that had been their refuge as they climbed in. The fire still raged in the distance, but they left it behind, heading toward safety.

As the helicopter lifted off, Zoey reached for Lux's hand again, holding it tightly as they soared into the sky. Lux glanced over at her, their eyes meeting in a shared moment of understanding.

They had made it. Together.

The landscape below them blurred as they flew farther away from the fire, and Lux allowed herself to relax finally.

They were going home.

25

LUX

Lux took a deep breath, trying to shake off the residual unease that had settled in her chest since they'd been rescued.

"Is it me or did you grow fatter out there?"

Lux turned to see Joe, her older brother, on a chair next to her hospital bed, and a smile crept up her lips. He'd left his business in Vegas to come all the way to Phoenix Ridge as soon as he heard she was stuck in the fire.

"You're still the blond in an XL shirt," Lux said.

Joe burst out laughing. "I knew it'd take more than a burning mountain to rid you of your scalding tongue."

"You bet." She looked around. "Where's Dad?"

"He finally agreed to have some sleep," Joey

said. "The old man barely had any while you were still out there."

"Old man?" Lux chuckled. "You should try calling him that to his face."

"No, thank you." Joe raised his hands and laughed. His silver cuffs caught the sun, reflecting in Lux's face.

It had only been a day since they were airlifted off the mountain, and while she was relieved to be safe, a strange emptiness gnawed at her. The adrenaline that had kept her going through the ordeal was gone, replaced by a dull muscle ache and a lingering sense of disorientation.

But it wasn't just the physical exhaustion that weighed on her.

Without thinking, Lux swung her legs over the side of the bed and stood up. Her body protested with a sharp twinge in her side, but she ignored it. She needed to see Zoey.

The hallway was quiet as Lux made her way to Zoey's room. The sterile antiseptic smell hung in the air, mingling with the distant hum of hospital machinery. When she reached Zoey's door, she paused, her hand hovering over the doorknob.

She could hear voices on the other side—familiar voices. She recognized Zoey's soft tone and the deeper, comforting sound of a man's voice, followed by the warm laughter of a woman.

Taking a deep breath, Lux knocked lightly on the door and pushed it open.

Zoey was sitting in bed, her face lighting up with a smile as soon as she saw Lux. Beside her, a woman turned to look at the door. It wasn't difficult to spot the resemblance. This woman had to be Zoey's Mom.

"You must be Lux," the woman said.

Lux nodded. "Yeah, that's me."

Before Lux could say anything else, the woman crossed the room and hugged her tightly. The embrace was solid and comforting, and for a moment, Lux was too stunned to react. It had been so long since anyone had hugged her with such genuine affection.

"Thank you," the woman said as she released Lux. "Thank you for keeping my daughter safe."

Lux felt a lump form in her throat as she looked at Zoey's mom. She wanted to say so much, but the words wouldn't come. She could only nod, her chest tight with gratitude and sadness. The warmth of the embrace lingered.

"Come in," Zoey's dad, said. "We were just talking about how glad we are to have her back."

Lux stepped into the room, feeling slightly out of place but welcomed. Zoey's dad had a kind face and warm eyes, the same as his daughter. He stood up and offered his hand, and Lux shook it, feeling a sense of relief wash over her.

"It's good to meet you finally," he said. "Zoey's told us so much about you."

Zoey blushed slightly, her eyes darting to Lux's before looking away. Lux felt her cheeks warm in response, but she managed a small smile.

"I'm glad to meet you too," Lux said, quiet but sincere. "I'm just glad we both made it out of there."

Zoey's mom gestured to the chair beside Zoey's bed. "Please, sit down. You must be exhausted."

Lux hesitated momentarily before sitting, the chair creaking softly under her weight.

Zoey's mom sat on the edge of the bed, her hand resting lightly on Zoey's. "It's a miracle you two are alive. We were so worried when we heard about the fire."

"It was rough," Lux said, her voice low. "But Zoey is a really strong woman."

Zoey glanced at Lux. "We kept each other going."

"Lux," Zoey's mom said, "how are you feeling? You went through just as much as Zoey did."

"I'm...I'm okay," she said slowly. "Just glad to be out of there, to be honest."

Zoey's mom nodded. "It will take some time to recover, both physically and mentally. But you're strong, Lux. I can see that."

Lux wasn't sure how to respond to that.

Zoey's dad cleared his throat, his expression serious. "We can't thank you enough, Lux. For everything you did for Zoey."

"I didn't do anything special. I just did my job," Lux said.

Zoey's mom reached over and squeezed her hand. "That's more than enough, Lux. More than enough."

Lux swallowed hard, her eyes stinging with unshed tears. She wasn't used to this—this feeling of having a mother. "Thank you," she managed.

Zoey's parents exchanged a look, and her dad spoke up. "We should let you both get some rest. It's been a long few days."

Zoey's mom stood up and leaned down to kiss Zoey on the forehead. "We'll be back later, sweetheart. Get some rest, okay?"

Zoey nodded, her eyes filled with warmth as

she watched her parents leave the room. Lux stood up as well, feeling a strange reluctance to leave.

"Thank you," she said.

Zoey's mom smiled and pulled Lux into another hug. "You're always welcome with us, Lux. Always."

When they finally pulled away, Lux watched Zoey's parents leave the room, the door closing softly behind them. She stood there for a moment, her heart full and heavy at the same time.

Zoey's voice broke through her thoughts. "You okay?"

Lux turned to look at Zoey, who watched her with those kind, understanding eyes. "Yeah," Lux said quietly. "I'm okay." Zoey patted the spot on the bed beside her. "Come here."

Zoey and Lux exchanged glances, but the door opened almost immediately.

It was the crew from the fire station.

"Hey, look who finally made it out of the wild," Jay said.

Zoey grinned, sitting up a little straighter. "You guys found us."

"We weren't going to stop until we did, Lieutenant," Ramirez said.

"I think we can drop the titles now, Ramirez," Zoey said. "It's Zoey."

"You had us all worried sick," Jay said.

Zoey smiled. "We were pretty worried ourselves."

Jay turned to Lux, her expression serious but kind. "You did well out there, Lux. You kept your cool and got Zoey through it. We're all proud of you."

Lux felt pride in her words, but she also felt overwhelmed by the attention. She wasn't used to being in the spotlight like this. "I just did what I had to."

"You did more than that," Jay said, her tone firm. "You kept her safe.."

Ramirez nodded in agreement, her eyes warm as she looked at Lux. "We're just glad you're both okay."

Lux shifted slightly. She was grateful for their support, but being the center of attention like this was uncomfortable.

Zoey's expression softened as she looked at Lux, then back at the crew. "I couldn't have made it without Lux. She was there every step of the way."

Jay nodded, her gaze steady. "You both made it. That's what matters."

The room fell into a comfortable silence as the crew settled in, filling the space with their familiar presence. Lux relaxed a little, the tension in her shoulders easing as she listened to the friendly banter between Zoey and her colleagues.

After a while, there was another knock at the door, and the legendary Fire Chief Becky Thompson stepped inside.

"Chief," Zoey said.

"Zoey, Lux, it's good to see you both safe."

"Thank you, Chief," Zoey said. "For a moment, I was afraid we'd be mistaken for dead."

Becky frowned and shook her head slowly. "Not around here, Lieutenant. We stick with our own. We never gave up on you- not for a second."

"Thanks, Chief."

Becky's gaze shifted to Lux, and for a moment, she thought she saw the faintest hint of a smile. "Besides, Lux's father and I go way back. He would have my neck if I didn't get his princess back in one piece."

Lux laughed. "I can imagine that."

Becky nodded. "I'm proud of both of you."

Zoey broke the silence. "Well, we're here now, right? That's what matters."

Ramirez grinned, the tension in the room easing. "Yeah. That and your new awards."

Everyone paused and exchanged glances. Ramirez's smile soon waned when she noticed that she was the only one still smiling.

"What's she talking about, Chief?" Lux asked.

Chief Thompson shook her head before clearing her throat. "Well, since that's already out there, the station has decided to award you two an award for your resilience and bravery."

"That doesn't come with an overdue leave, does it?" Zoey asked.

Chief Thompson laughed. "You can take as much rest as you want. The award ceremony will be in a week. You two should be discharged pretty soon and should be all good for the awards ceremony. Unless you run off up that mountain again."

The crew laughed. Lux found herself smiling too.

As the conversation flowed, Lux found herself listening more than speaking, content to soak in the presence of her colleagues. They were indeed family.

The chief stayed for a while, occasionally joining in the conversation but mostly observing. Lux noticed how her gaze would occasionally land on her. Just like her father, she was always looking out for her.

Eventually, the chief stood up, signaling it was time for her to leave. "I'll let you all get some rest."

The crew also stood, saying their goodbyes with promises to check in later.

As the last crew filed out of the room, Becky turned to Zoey and Lux one last time. "You both did well out there. Remember that."

Zoey nodded, her expression serious. "We will, Chief."

Becky gave them a final nod before stepping out of the room, the door closing softly behind her. The room fell silent once more, the weight of everything that had happened settling over them.

Zoey let out a long breath, her shoulders sagging with exhaustion. "That was…a lot."

"Yeah," Lux said. "So, how does it feel to be a hero?"

Zoey chuckled, shaking her head. "Right, because getting us through a wildfire is just a casual stroll for you." She rolled her eyes.

Lux smirked, leaning forward slightly. "Well, I did have some pretty great company. Couldn't have done it without you."

Zoey's cheeks flushed a light pink as she met Lux's gaze. "We make a good team."

"That we do," Lux agreed, her voice softening. She glanced around the room before returning her gaze to Zoey. "Think they'll ever let us live this down?"

Zoey laughed, her eyes sparkling. "Probably not. We're going to be legends at the station."

Lux grinned. "I always wanted to be remembered for something. Maybe not quite like this, though."

"Hey, fame is fame," Zoey teased. "I'm just glad we're both here to tell the tale."

Zoey's smile softened as she closed the distance between them, pressing a gentle kiss to Lux's lips. The moment was brief but filled with unspoken promises and relief.

As they pulled apart, Lux's eyes shone with happiness. "You sure we won't go on a vacation up that mountain sometime?"

Zoey chuckled, resting her forehead against Lux's. "You're impossible."

"And you love it," Lux replied, her voice barely above a whisper.

Zoey's smile widened. "Yeah, I really do."

Zoey squeezed her hand and gazed into her eyes. "I love you, too." Zoey smiled and Lux felt her insides flutter.

She loves me.

26

ZOEY

It'd been a week already. She spent most of the time with her parents and colleagues, who never stopped dropping by to see her. No matter how much she reminded them that she was better now, they still wouldn't stop with the gifts.

Zoey stood at the city hall's entrance, taking in the event's grandeur.

The room was filled with people dressed in their finest, the soft hum of conversations blending with the clinking of glasses and the occasional burst of laughter. The walls were draped in deep red and gold tapestries , giving the entire room a warm, almost festive feel.

The town organized the event to honor the

bravery and dedication of firefighters and emergency responders, and tonight, Zoey and Lux will be among those recognized. Zoey felt a mix of pride and nervousness bubbling up inside her as she glanced around the room, searching for a familiar face.

She spotted Lux standing a few feet away in full best uniform. She was so striking looking and conversing with a tall man who looked like her. There was no mistaking the resemblance—the same strong jawline and intense blue eyes. Zoey knew instantly that this had to be Lux's father.

Zoey observed their interaction, noting the ease with which they spoke and how Lux's eyes softened when she looked at him. It was clear that they shared a deep bond, one built on years of love and mutual respect. Zoey felt a pang of something she couldn't quite name—perhaps a mix of admiration and longing—watching them together.

As if sensing Zoey's gaze, Lux turned and caught her eye. A smile spread across Lux's face, and she waved Zoey over.

Zoey made her way through the crowd of people, her heart beating a little faster as she approached Lux and her father. When she reached them, Lux's father turned to face her, his expression warm and welcoming.

"Dad, this is Zoey," Lux said. "Zoey, this is my father, Robert Valentine."

Zoey extended her hand, her smile a little shy. "It's nice to meet you, Mr. Valentine."

Robert Valentine took her hand firmly, his smile reaching his eyes.

Lux's sharp blue gaze met Zoey's eyes and Zoey saw all the warmth of love in her eyes and she liked it.

Before she could find her voice to say anything else, the sound of a microphone being tapped filled the room, drawing everyone's attention to the stage at the front of the hall, the legendary Phoenix Ridge Fire Chief Becky Thompson stood there, her presence commanding and authoritative, yet there was a warmth in her eyes as she looked out over the crowd.

"Ladies and gentlemen," the chief began, her voice carrying easily across the room, "tonight, we are here to honor the bravery and dedication of those who have gone above and beyond the call of duty. We have faced many challenges this year, but our team has remained strong, committed, and unwavering in their resolve."

Zoey felt a surge of pride as she listened to the chief's words, knowing that she and Lux were part of that team. It was humbling to be recognized for something that had become integral to her identity.

The chief continued, her voice steady and filled with conviction. "Tonight, we want to pay special tribute to two of our own who showed extraordinary courage by putting their own lives at risk to save civilians and then determination to survive in the face of overwhelming odds when they were trapped by the forest fire. Lieutenant Zoey Knight and Chief Pilot Lux Valentine, please join me on stage."

Zoey's heart skipped a beat as she heard her name. She glanced at Lux, who gave her an encouraging nod. Together, they made their way through the crowd, the significance of the moment settling over them.

As they stepped onto the stage, the applause was deafening and echoed off the hall's walls. Zoey felt a rush of pride, gratitude, and a deep sense of accomplishment. But more than that, she felt an overwhelming sense of connection to Lux, who stood beside her, a steady presence amid the chaos.

Becky handed them each a small, metal plaque. "Zoey Knight and Lux Valentine, for your bravery, dedication, and unwavering commitment to saving lives, we honor you tonight. You are a testament to the strength and resilience of this team, and we are proud to have you with us."

Zoey felt a lump rise in her throat as she accepted the plaque. She glanced at Lux, who looked at her with a mixture of pride and something deeper, unspoken but understood.

They stepped off the stage, the applause still ringing in their ears, and Zoey found herself gravitating toward Lux. There was so much she wanted to say, so much she needed to express, but the words seemed to elude her.

Lux seemed to sense Zoey's thoughts, and she reached out, taking Zoey's hand in hers.

Zoey felt a deep sense of contentment as they walked through the crowd to return to their seats for the rest of the event. They had made it through the fire, fear, and uncertainty, and they came out stronger on the other side. And as long as she had Lux by her side, Zoey knew they could face whatever came next.

After the ceremony, everyone lingered to talk. Zoey glanced at Lux, standing a few feet away, conversing with some of their colleagues. The warmth of the event still lingered in the air, and the memory of receiving their awards felt surreal. But something else on Zoey's mind had been brewing since they had made it back from the mountain.

The moment felt right. She'd been holding back, unsure of how Lux might react, but Zoey knew she had to leap. She approached Lux, her heart beating a little faster with each step.

"Lux," Zoey said.

Lux turned. "Hey, what's up?"

Zoey hesitated for a second. "I was thinking... now that everything's calmed down a bit, maybe we could, you know, go out sometime? Like, on a proper date."

Lux's eyes widened slightly, a hint of surprise flickering across her face, but then she smiled. "I'd like that."

Zoey exhaled the breath she'd been holding. "Great. How about tonight?"

"Tonight sounds perfect."

Later that evening, Zoey stood outside a fancy

restaurant, butterflies fluttering in her stomach. She'd chosen the place carefully, wanting everything to be just right for their first official date. The soft glow of the lights from the restaurant's windows cast a warm hue over the entrance, and the quiet hum of conversation floated through the air.

Zoey adjusted the collar of her jacket, glancing down the street for any sign of Lux. She didn't have to wait long. Lux soon appeared, walking toward her with that same confident stride Zoey had come to admire. She looked stunning, her outfit simple yet elegant, and the sight of her made Zoey's breath catch in her throat.

"Hey," Zoey greeted.

"Hey yourself," Lux replied. "You look great."

"So do you," Zoey said, feeling a warmth spread through her chest. "Ready to head in?"

Lux nodded. The interior was cozy and intimate, with dim lighting and plush seating offering privacy. A waiter led them to a table near the back, away from the bustle of the main dining area.

As they sat down, Zoey glanced at Lux, taking in the way the candlelight danced across her features. Zoey couldn't take her eyes off Lux as they settled into their seats. The soft glow of the candlelight made Lux's features even more striking, and Zoey felt that familiar flutter in her chest.

"It's strange, isn't it?" Lux said, her voice low and intimate. "How much I missed you even though we were only apart for a few days."

Zoey smiled. "I know what you mean. I kept thinking about you the whole time. Even in the hospital, all I could think about was when I'd see you again."

Lux's gaze softened as she reached across the table, her fingers brushing lightly against Zoey's hand. "It's like we went through all that just to end up here, in this moment."

Zoey's breath hitched at the touch, and she turned her hand over, lacing her fingers with Lux's. The connection between them felt electric, charged with the tension of everything they'd been through and the feelings they were finally allowing themselves to explore.

"You have no idea how much I missed you," Zoey whispered.

Lux's thumb traced small circles on the back of Zoey's hand. "I think I have some idea," she said, her tone playful.

Zoey's pulse quickened as she leaned in closer, the space between them shrinking. The restaurant around them seemed to fade away, leaving the two in a bubble of shared emotion and anticipation.

"I couldn't stop thinking about you," Zoey admitted, her eyes locked on Lux's lips.

Lux's smile was slow and warm. "I couldn't stop thinking about you either," she said softly. "And now that we're here, I don't want to think about anything else."

Zoey's breath caught as Lux's hand tightened around hers, and for a moment, the world outside their little corner of the restaurant ceased to exist.

"That sounded so sweet," Lux said. "You're a keeper."

Zoey backed off somewhat. Lux squinted.

"I shouldn't have said that," Lux said. I—"

"It's not that," Zoey replied. "It's just the last person who said that to me was…well, my ex."

Lux's expression softened. "You don't have to if you're not ready."

"No, I want to," Zoey said. "We were together for a few years. It started great, but I got so consumed with firefighting. I thought I could balance it all, but I couldn't. And then after the accident—the one I told you about, with the child—I just…shut down."

Lux squeezed her hand gently. "That's a lot to carry."

Zoey nodded, feeling a lump form in her throat. "I tried to make it work, but I wasn't present anymore, not for her or anyone. The guilt, the grief—it was all too much. She deserved better than that, better than me."

Lux leaned in closer, her voice soft but firm. "You're not that person anymore, Zoey. What happened wasn't your fault, and you've done everything possible to move forward. You deserve happiness too."

As the evening wore on, the conversation grew quieter and more intimate.

"I guess we should probably focus on enjoying tonight, huh?" Zoey said.

Lux chuckled. "Yeah, I think we've earned a little fun."

Just then, the waiter approached with their meals, setting the plates down with a flourish. The delicious aroma filled the air, making Zoey's stomach growl in anticipation.

"Looks amazing," Zoey said, her eyes widening as she took in the beautifully plated dishes.

Lux grinned, picking up her fork. "I think it's time to dig in."

They both began to eat, the conversation shifting to lighter topics: favorite foods, funny stories from their childhoods, and plans for the future.

"My place?" Zoey suggested that the second they were done eating.

Lux's eyes met Zoey's, and for a moment, neither spoke. Then Lux nodded, a small smile playing on her lips. "I'd like that."

27

LUX

Lux sat on the edge of Zoey's couch, the soft fabric brushing against her fingers as she ran them along the seam. The room was dimly lit, with only the warm glow of a single lamp casting shadows that danced on the walls.

It was almost too quiet, and the silence seemed to amplify the thudding of Lux's heart in her chest.

Zoey was in the kitchen, her back turned to Lux as she poured two glasses of water. Lux watched her, taking in the way Zoey moved with a calm grace that she had come to admire. There was something comforting about being in Zoey's space surrounded by the little pieces of her life, yet

Lux couldn't shake the nervous energy coursing through her.

Tonight had been perfect. Dinner had been filled with easy conversation, laughter, and a connection that had grown stronger with each passing moment. And now, here they were, alone in Zoey's apartment, the air between them thick with unspoken emotions.

Zoey returned with the glasses, offering one to Lux as she sat beside her on the couch. Their knees brushed as Zoey settled in.

"Thank you," Lux said.

Zoey smiled, her eyes soft as she looked at Lux. "No problem."

"You have a beautiful place here," Lux said.

Zoey chuckled playfully. "Now you're just teasing. I barely got settled in before we got our compulsory forest trip."

Lux laughed. "No jokes, my house looks way worse."

"Not me," Zoey said. "Since my dad was in the military, everything had to be in order around the house. I bet he'd give me the side-eye if he saw my room looking this way."

"He seemed like a pretty chill guy to me."

"Oh, he is chill. Maybe even warmer now that he's grown older."

Lux loved the beauty in Zoey's eyes when she talked about her father.

"Mom likes you," Zoey said.

Lux's heart skipped a beat.

Zoey chuckled and continued. "She kept asking about you."

"And?"

"And I told her you're fine." Zoey pushed a stray bit of hair away from her eyes. "She seemed to have this idea that we were an item."

"Oh." Lux let out an uncomfortable chuckle. Zoey joined in, but it fizzled out as awkwardly as it began.

They sat there for a moment, the silence stretching out between them. Lux felt her emotions pressing down on her, urging her to speak and say the things she'd held back for so long. But the words were caught in her throat, tangled up with fear and uncertainty.

She glanced over at Zoey, taking in the way the light highlighted the curve of her jaw and the softness of her expression. Zoey's presence had become a balm for Lux's soul, soothing the raw edges of her heart in ways she hadn't expected. And yet the thought of opening up and exposing the vulnerability she'd kept hidden for so long was terrifying.

But Lux knew she had to do it. She couldn't keep running from her feelings, not when they had brought her to this moment, to this person.

"Zoey," Lux began.

Zoey turned to face her fully. "Yeah?"

Lux took a deep breath, trying to gather her thoughts. "I-I've been thinking a lot about us. About what we've been through and where we are now."

Zoey nodded, encouraging Lux to continue.

"I never expected any of this," Lux admitted. "I never expected to feel this way about someone, especially not in the middle of everything that's happened. But I do. I care about you, Zoey. A lot."

Zoey's eyes softened, a small smile tugging at the corners of her lips. "Lux…"

"I'm not good at this," Lux rushed on, her words coming faster now that she'd started. "I've never been good at letting people in, trusting them with my heart. But you? You make me want to try. You make me want to be better."

Zoey reached out, her hand gently covering Lux's where it rested on her knee. The touch was warm, grounding Lux in the moment and giving her the courage to keep going.

"I'm scared," Lux admitted, her voice barely above a whisper. "I'm scared of getting hurt, of messing this up. But more than that, I'm scared of not taking the chance. Of not seeing where this could go."

"Lux, you don't have to be scared. I'm here. I'm not going anywhere."

Lux felt a rush of emotion at Zoey's words, the sincerity in her voice wrapping around Lux's heart like a comforting embrace. She turned her hand over, intertwining her fingers with Zoey's, holding on tightly as if to anchor herself.

"I don't want to lose this," Lux said, trembling. "I don't want to lose you."

Zoey's thumb brushed over the back of Lux's hand. "You're not going to lose me, Lux. I promise."

For a moment, they just sat there, holding onto each other, letting the silence speak the words they didn't need to say. Lux could feel the steady beat of Zoey's heart through their joined hands, a rhythm that matched her own.

Lux hesitated for a second, then took a deep breath. "Zoey, would you be my girlfriend? Like, officially?"

Zoey's eyes sparkled with warmth, and she smiled.

"I know it sounds a bit rushed, but I'm certain I want no one else, Zoey. I want you."

"Yes," she said softly. "I'd love that."

Relief flooded through Lux, and she couldn't help but smile back, a genuine, unguarded smile. "Good," she said, her voice a little stronger now. "That's good."

Zoey leaned in for a kiss, her eyes never leaving Lux's.

Lux melted into the kiss, letting go of the fear that had held her back for so long. There was no room for doubt or anything except the overwhelming sense of rightness that filled her. She caressed Zoey's face with her fingers.

The kiss deepened, becoming more urgent. Zoey's hands slid around Lux's waist, pulling her closer, their bodies pressing together.

Lux's fingers tangled in Zoey's hair, and she could feel the heat of Zoey's body against her own. Her scent was intoxicating, a blend of something floral and earthy. Lux's heart raced as she became more aware of every sensation.

"I love you," Lux whispered against Zoey's lips, her voice trembling.

"I love you too," Zoey replied, her breath warm against Lux's skin. "So much."

Their lips met again, more forcefully this time, with a desperation that spoke of all their shared feelings.

Lux's hands roamed Zoey's back, feeling her muscles tense and relax beneath her fingertips. Zoey's hands moved in slow, deliberate circles on Lux's sides, tracing the curve of her body. Lux could feel the heat of Zoey's touch radiating through her clothes.

"I want you," Lux murmured between kisses. "Badly."

"Me too," Zoey said, her voice a low murmur. "I didn't know how much I needed you until you were here."

The kisses became more fervent, their lips moving together with an urgent and perfect rhythm. Zoey's hands slid under Lux's shirt, touching the bare skin of her back.

Lux shivered, her breathing becoming more erratic. She reached up, tugging Zoey's shirt over her head, tossing it aside.

Zoey also responded by pulling off Lux's shirt, and they continued to kiss, their bodies pressed together. The sensation of skin against skin was electrifying.

It was different this time. They were both clean, uninjured. Zoey's hair was silky and smelled like honey.

Lux's hands explored the curves of Zoey's body, each touch drawing a gasp or a moan from both of them. They broke the kiss only to gasp for air before resuming, their lips meeting with equal enthusiasm.

"Tell me you love me," Lux said, her voice filled with need.

Zoey chuckled, stilling somewhat and holding Lux closer. "I love you." Her hands trailed Lux's sides. "I love you so much."

"I love you too," Lux said, her voice choked with emotion. "More than I thought possible."

Zoey's kisses traveled from Lux's lips to her neck, leaving a trail of warmth that made Lux's entire body react.

Lux tilted her head back, giving Zoey better access. She could feel Zoey's lips brushing against her collarbone, each touch sending a shiver down her spine.

Zoey's hands moved to Lux's pants, deftly undoing the button and zipper. Lux's heart pounded as she felt Zoey's touch against her skin, and she shivered with anticipation.

She reached for Zoey's pants, her hands trembling slightly as she worked.

Once they were both undressed, they continued to explore each other's bodies, their hands and lips moving with a sense of urgency and longing.

Lux felt a profound connection with Zoey, their bodies moving in sync as they expressed their love through touch and kisses.

"I've never felt this close to anyone," Lux said.

"Neither have I. You mean everything to me."

Lux was on top and she pushed with her right hand between Zoey's legs.

"Open your legs," she urged and Zoey's thighs obediently parted for her hand.

At the same time she felt Zoey's hand seeking between her own legs and she opened to allow Zoey access.

They moved as though synchronised, sliding their fingers through each other's wetness and Lux felt herself groaning in anticipation. She felt more turned on the she ever had before.

Zoey's body was hot and writhing beneath her, her breasts pressing against Lux.

Her voice was breathy. "Please, Lux... Fuck me... I need to feel you inside me."

Lux didn't need asking twice. She pressed her fingers hard and deep inside Zoey enjoying Zoey's loud moan as she did so.

She instantly felt Zoey's fingers copying her actions and pressing hard and deep inside her own body.

"Oh, fuck, Zoey." Lux growled, "You feel so fucking good."

Lux had curved her fingers upwards to press against Zoey's G spot and was beginning to rock them in and out. Zoey was doing the same to her. They moved in tandem, completely together and Lux felt Zoey begin to tighten around her fingers are her breathing got more ragged. Lux felt her own orgasm building.

"Come with me," she growled as she pressed her thumb tight against Zoey's clitoris as she ground her own pelvis down seeking pressure on her own clit.

Delicious pleasure built deep within her.

"Always," Zoey whispered and captured her mouth in a deep sensual kiss, their tongues tangling with each other's.

Zoey exploded on her hand wet and hot and

Lux felt her own orgasm crash through her at the exact same time.

They kissed right through it, deep and long. Their fingers still buried deep as they rode out the waves of their climax. Lux had never known anything like the intensity of it.

When their fingers finally slid out of each other Lux sat up straddling Zoey's hips and brought her own fingers to her mouth tasting Zoey's pleasure from her fingers. She licked them and then sucked them deep into her mouth. She looked into Zoey's lovely brown eyes as she did.

Zoey didn't look away.

"Sorry, " Lux shrugged. "Couldn't quite help myself. You taste fucking exquisite." She smiled her most roguish smile at Zoey as she finished enjoying the taste of Zoey on her tongue and she watched as Zoey's own right hand moved to her own mouth as she lay reclined beneath Lux.

Lux could see the slick wetness of her own orgasm on Zoey's fingers. She watched in awe as Zoey began to sensually lick her fingers without breaking Lux's gaze once. Slowly pushing each one into and out of her mouth with a satisfying wet pop.

It was the sexiest thing Lux had ever seen.

Lux swallowed, lost for words for maybe the first time ever.

"There's something I'd really like," Zoey purred when she finally removed her fingers from her mouth.

"What's that?" Lux managed to find some words finally.

"I want to come in your mouth the exact same time you come in mine."

"Oh, really?" Lux raised her eyebrows as she felt herself suddenly very very turned on again. "69?" she asked.

Zoey nodded, her eyes full of seduction, "Lie back, I want to be on top."

Lux gulped again as Zoey sat up and pushed her backwards. Zoey was so incredibly sexy. Her dark silky hair was messy and her lips were so very sensual as she extracted herself and then spun herself around straddling a leg over Lux's face.

As Lux watched Zoey's beautiful wet pussy opening and lowering onto her face she thought she might combust there and then. But, she managed to hold off her own orgasm and set to tasting Zoey again and pleasing her with her tongue and mouth. Zoey's groans and moans as she began to grind down onto Lux's mouth made it very clear she was enjoying herself.

Lux pushed her tongue fully inside Zoey as far as she could and thought she might down in Zoey's resulting wetness. She felt Zoey grinding her hips down, taking her pleasure.

Oh, fuck, she is so sexy.

Lux slid her tongue out and moved back to alternating long strokes that teased Zoey's anus and reached all the way up to her clit with nibbling and sucking at whatever she could put her mouth on.

Zoey's breathing quickened, "Oh, Baby I'm so close," she purred and with that she dipped her head between Lux's legs and began to eat her out with no holding back.

Lux felt herself right up there on the edge of orgasm straight away as she ate Zoey out with equal hunger. They devoured each other as though they were the feast they had craved for so long.

When Lux felt Zoey begin to come and flood her mouth with joy, she released her own orgasm coming in hot wet pulses again and again. They kept their mouths on each other and they both kept coming in a way Lux had never really thought possible. It felt transcendent.

Lu thought she never ever wanted to stop licking Zoey but eventually they both did and Zoey rolled off her, turning around, they both lay in wetness as Zoey kissed her long and deep and mingling the tastes of both their sex. It felt like the most intimate moment in the world.

As their lovemaking peaked, Lux felt a wave of emotions flooding her. The connection she felt with Zoey was profound, and she knew that this moment was something they would both remember forever.

Something they'd both share forever.

They held each other close, their breathing gradually returning to normal as they lay in wetness and basked in the afterglow of their passion.

"I love you," Lux said again, her voice filled with awe and tenderness.

"I love you too," Zoey replied, her eyes filled with affection. "Always."

They remained in each other's arms, savoring the closeness and warmth of their shared experience. The silence that followed was filled with a deep sense of contentment and connection as they both realized they had found something special in each other.

EPILOGUE
ZOEY

Zoey stepped onto the porch of their cozy home, the late afternoon sun casting a warm glow over the landscape. The house sat near the edge of the forest, where they had both found peace after everything they'd been through. The air was filled with the soft rustling of leaves and the distant chirping of birds, a soundtrack to the life they had built together.

She looked out over the yard where their rescue dogs Bill and Ben, chased each other around, their tails wagging with pure joy. Nearby, their cat, Binx, a sleek black creature with striking green eyes, lounged on a sun-warmed rock, watching the dogs with amusement and disdain.

The house itself was modest but filled with

warmth. Zoey had fallen in love with it the moment she saw it. The wooden beams, the large windows that let in plenty of light, and the way it blended seamlessly with the surrounding nature were perfect. Inside, the walls were decorated with photos from their adventures, both before and after they had met, and mementos of the life they had started to build together.

Zoey glanced over her shoulder, smiling as she saw Lux moving around inside the house. She was preparing something in the kitchen, her movements sure and steady. It was a simple life, but it filled Zoey with a deep sense of contentment. This was what they had both wanted: a life together, surrounded by the things they loved.

Lux caught Zoey watching her and smiled back, her eyes sparkling with that familiar warmth. "What are you doing out there? Just staring into space?" Lux asked, her voice carrying through the open window.

"Just thinking," she said as she stepped back inside. She walked over to Lux, wrapping her arms around her from behind and resting her chin on her shoulder. "I still can't believe this is our life now."

Lux leaned back into her embrace, sighing contentedly. "It's pretty great, isn't it?"

Zoey nodded, pressing a kiss to Lux's cheek. "Better than I ever imagined."

Lux turned slightly to look at her, a playful smile tugging at her lips. "Even with the chaos of having three rescues?"

Zoey laughed, the sound light and carefree. "Especially with the chaos. I wouldn't have it any other way."

The two of them stayed like that momentarily, enjoying their lives closeness and quiet rhythm. The smell of something delicious wafted from the stove, filling the house with a comforting aroma.

"What are you making?" Zoey asked.

"Just some pasta." She glanced back at the stove. "Thought we could have something simple tonight."

Zoey's stomach growled in response, and she grinned. "Sounds perfect."

Curious about what was happening in the kitchen, Binx padded over and rubbed against Zoey's leg, purring loudly. Zoey reached to scratch behind its ears, earning a satisfied chirp.

"You spoil them, you know that?" Lux teased..

Zoey shrugged, unrepentant. "They deserve it."

Lux shook her head, but her expression had no honest admonishment. Instead, she turned off the stove and dished out the pasta. They worked together, setting the table in comfortable silence.

Once everything was ready, they sat down to eat, their conversation flowing easily as they talked about their day, their plans for the weekend, and the little things that made up their lives together. Zoey loved these moments. They were so simple and ordinary yet filled with so much love.

As they finished their meal, Zoey leaned back in her chair, looking out the window at the trees surrounding their home. The sky was beginning to darken, the first hints of twilight creeping in. It was a beautiful sight, one that never failed to calm her.

Lux followed her gaze, a soft smile on her lips. "It's so peaceful here."

Zoey nodded, reaching across the table to take Lux's hand. "I'm glad we found this place."

"Me too," Lux said, squeezing her hand gently. "It's home."

They sat like that for a while, their hands intertwined, the love they shared filling the space between them. Zoey felt a surge of gratitude for everything they had: each other, this home, the life they were building.

Lux suddenly stood up, a mischievous glint in her eye. "How about we dip in the lake before it gets too dark?"

Zoey raised an eyebrow, her curiosity piqued. "Now? You mean right now?"

Lux grinned, her enthusiasm infectious. "Why not? It's the perfect way to end the day."

Zoey couldn't help but laugh, shaking her head in disbelief. "You're impossible, you know that?"

"But you love me for it," Lux teased, already moving toward the door.

Zoey rolled her eyes playfully but couldn't stop the smile that spread across her face. "Yeah, I do."

She followed Lux outside, the cool evening air wrapping around them as they made their way down to the lake with Bill and Ben running enthusiastically ahead. The water was calm, reflecting the fading light of day. It was a place they often came to when they wanted to unwind, a private sanctuary just for the two of them.

Lux didn't waste any time, quickly shedding her clothes and wading naked into the water with a carefree laugh. Zoey watched her, her heart swelling with love for the woman who had become her everything. Lux's nude body was more beautiful than ever, all long lean muscles and beautiful firm breasts. Lux was so full of life, so fearless in her pursuit of happiness, and Zoey couldn't imagine her life without her.

"Well?" Lux called out, her voice echoing across the lake. "Are you coming in or what?"

Zoey chuckled, shaking her head in disbelief. "You're crazy."

"But you love me," Lux countered, her eyes shining with amusement.

Zoey smiled, warmth spreading through her as she began to undress. "Yeah, I do."

As she waded into the lake, the cool water enveloping her, Zoey felt a sense of peace settle over her. This was their life now, filled with love, laughter, and the quiet moments that made everything worthwhile.

And she wouldn't have it any other way.

FREE BOOK

I really hope you enjoyed this story. I loved writing it.

I'd love for you to get my FREE book- Her Boss- by joining my mailing list. On my mailing list you can be the first to find out about free or discounted books or new releases and get short sexy stories for free! Just click on the following link or type into your web browser: https://BookHip.com/MNVVPBP

Meg has had a huge crush on her hot older boss for some time now. Could it be possible that her crush is reciprocated? https://BookHip.com/MNVVPBP

ALSO BY EMILY HAYES

Check out the next in the Phoenix Ridge series:

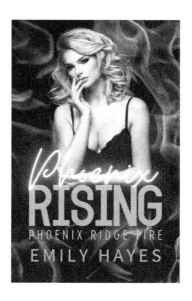

Two fierce women, one city in crisis—will the legendary Chief Becky Thompson's fiery clash with Dr. Lucinda Everett ignite passion? In this scorching enemies-to-lovers Sapphic romance, sparks fly between Phoenix Ridge's fire chief and a brilliant trauma surgeon.

mybook.to/PRF6

Have you read my Hearts Medical series yet?

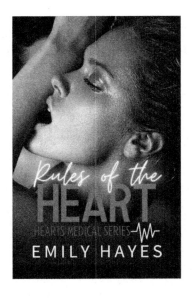

Can Dr. Valerie Bush break her own rules and take a chance on love? In this steamy age-gap, enemies-to-lovers Sapphic romance, the icy head of surgery clashes with passionate young Dr. Ella Ashton—sparking undeniable chemistry that could change everything.

mybook.to/Hearts1

Printed in Great Britain
by Amazon

David Thirlby

ISBN 0 85429 183 0

First published March 1977

© David Thirlby 1977

All rights reserved. No part of this book may be reproduced or transmitted in any form or by any means, electronic or mechanical, including photocopying, recording or by any information storage or retrieval system, without permission in writing from the copyright holder

The Haynes Publishing Group
Sparkford Yeovil Somerset BA22 7JJ England

a FOULIS Motoring book

Printed by J H Haynes and Company Limited Sparkford Yeovil Somerset BA22 7JJ
Bound by Cedric Chivers Limited Bath Avon
Editor Tim Parker
Jacket design Phill Jennings

Dedication

THE BOOK HAS been dedicated to the memory of Tom Rolt. Tom Rolt's career and writing added immeasurably to the standing of engineers past. His books were, in the main, about the people who made the wealth of this country by their own efforts

Archie Frazer-Nash

Contents

		page
Foreword		10
Preface		11
1	The GN up to the first world war	13
2	The post war GN	27
3	The racing GNs	43
4	The Plus-Power Frazer Nash of 1924–25	57
5	The Boulogne	71
6	Kingston to Isleworth and the TT Replica	97
7	The other chain drive cars	135
8	The Frazer Nash-BMW	153
9	The post war cars	171
Index		204

Foreword

THE CHAIN DRIVE FRAZER NASH published by Macdonalds in 1964 has been out of print for some years. That book described all the components that made up the whole; the companies and the people who made them work, the commercial histories, the technical considerations and complete appendices as to the history of the various cars. This book deals with the two prime elements - the cars and the people.

Ron Godfrey, who died on October 26 1968, was good enough to point out that the historical significance of the Grand Prix GN had not been brought out, consequently the first two chapters of this book have quite a different scenario. Much information in the chain drive chapters is common to both books, though in the passage of ten years there have been changes of emphasis. The passage of time has placed the Frazer Nash - BMW in a special niche, as the link between the pre-war and post-war Frazer Nash. It is salutary to remember that the last Frazer Nash was made almost twenty years ago.

Bill Aldington has kept many photographs over the years and over forty of the illustrations used in this book have come from his collection.

My thanks to IPC Transport Press for permission to quote from the *Light Car and Cyclecar,* and to the Editors of *Motor* and *Autocar;* especial thanks are rendered to those who had the wisdom to keep *Autocar's* photographic library, which is all important in the presentation of motoring history. Charles Thorn of Bristol, a professional photographer, has been photocopying and printing, photographs for me this last ten years, to my satisfaction. My thanks also go to the Proprietor and Editor of *Motor Sport* for permission to quote from that magazine and to Denis Jenkinson for his help and the use of his photographs. My thanks also go to *Autosport.*

Many people helped editorially with this book and I must give due thanks to the late Ron Godfrey, Cushy (L.A. Cushman), Bill Craddock, Aldy (H.J. Aldington), Bill Aldington, Michael Bowler, Lindeiner of the BMW Car Club, Tony Mitchell and last but not least Betty Haig.

The photographers, where known, are credited in the text.

David Thirlby
Hartford, Northwich
Cheshire

Preface

THE VARIOUS FIRMS which made the Frazer Nash motor car, were Frazer Nash Ltd: William G. Thomas and Frazer Nash Ltd: and AFN Ltd. The total production of cars was 460. Approximately 18 were 'early' Frazer Nash, being the prototypes - the Frazer Nash GN, the Deemster chassis Frazer Nash and the Ruby engined Frazer Nash GN. From 1924 to the end of 1928, when the firm was controlled by Archie Frazer-Nash, the production totalled 140, with the peak production year in 1925, producing 50 cars. H.J. Aldington, from 1929 to 1939, made 180 chain drive cars and his peak year was 1934 with 39 cars. The post-war Frazer Nash totalled 105* cars and of these years, the best was 1951.

There has never been greater interest in this marque than there is today, with more cars being used than ever before. The Frazer Nash Section of the Vintage Sports Car Club is, without doubt, the most active one-make competitive club in the World, regularly turning out over thirty cars for a race. There is nowadays a wish to give credit to the people who made this possible and it is my profound hope that this book will help serve the purpose. Principally to give credit to Archie Frazer-Nash for his brilliant intuitive engineering, Ron Godfrey for his engineering skills and to 'Aldy' Aldington for his business acumen that kept the firm strong. There were other people whose contributions were important in the life span of the firm and who should be acknowledged - Harold Scott, W.G. Thomas, Richard Plunket-Greene, Eric Burt, Bill Aldington and Fritz Fiedler, for without them the history would not have been the same.

The three men who were the Frazer Nash and GN companies have all died. Both Frazer-Nash and Godfrey died before the surge of modern day interest became apparent. 'Aldy' enjoyed talking about the chain-gang days in the last few years of his life and it was a pleasure to see him and his brother Bill at the annual dinner; it was clear that he enjoyed the recognition he received, as the man who had given pleasure to many people by producing the Frazer Nash car.

A.G. FRAZER-NASH	—	1889-1965
H.R. GODFREY	—	1887-1968
H.J. ALDINGTON	—	1901-1976

*Footnote - See page 199

FRAZER NASH

Ron Godfrey on the roof of the Etna Works at Hendon

The GN up to the first world war
Chapter 1

ARCHIE FRAZER-NASH and Ron Godfrey were together in the 'office' of the Elms Motor Works, discussing the recurring theme of each issue of the January 1913 *Cyclecar*. The theme was that it was certain that a Cyclecar Grand Prix would take place over the same course as the French Grand Prix, probably on Sunday 13 of July. Frazer-Nash was eulogising at length over the undoubted fun there would be in entering a continental motor race and, almost in parenthesis, that there would be positive advantages for the firm of a good performance by GNs in such a race. Ron Godfrey, in his quiet way, pointed out that "a good result was unlikely since it was difficult enough to go to London and back without having an involuntary stop". Hendon to London was one thing, but a Grand Prix, even for cyclecars, was 250 or more racing miles, and the inference of what Ron Godfrey had said was self evident. The 1912 GN was by no means everything that a car should be; oversimple, almost crude in parts, with a lower engineering content than either of the principal partners had intended when launching the car on the market in early 1911. Ron Godfrey, in later years, said that in January of 1913 they were introducing changes, but that month changed their whole lives. Almost without discussion they knew they would enter and the whole car had to be redesigned there and then, from stem to stern, reliability had to be built in "and some of the woodscrews replaced by nuts and bolts. If we had not decided to enter for the 1913 Amiens Cyclecar Grand Prix there would have been no post-war GN model ready for manufacture, no Frazer Nash and certainly no HRG".

FRAZER NASH

The first GN chassis with a JAP engine, the gear lever is a broom handle, nailed to the chassis as Ron Godfrey said "in the interests of verisimilitude"

Ron Godfrey and Archie Nash (as he was known prior to the Great War) had been friends since studying for their City and Guilds in Mechanical Engineering at Finsbury and, then subsequently, with their apprenticeship together at Willans and Robinson of Rugby (now GEC). They had collectively and separately played at motorcycles and cars and the prehistory form of cyclecar known as a 'creepabout', where an engine was placed in a buckboard, or the simplest form of chassis, with a drive to a rear wheel. A creepabout was usually innocent of such devices as bodywork or steering mechanisms, claiming to work on the Ackermann principle, and the brakes, if any were provided, would be the simplest form of transmission brake.

In August of 1910, *Nash had left Willans and was working for the Vilcar Company, and was concussed whilst operating a fly-press; during his convalescence he and his brother Malcolm Nash put together the first creepabout to operate in such a manner that it was actually possible to set out on a journey. The first journey to Scarborough took five days and parts of the nights as well; the car had to be pushed for the last few miles. Nevertheless the car had been made to run under its own power.

* Footnote — Archie Nash was employed as one of the first two driving instructors for the infant British School of Motoring on an Itala, Spyker or Henry Brazier in 1910. In the same building in Coventry Street occupied by the BSM was another 'motoring child', the Automobile Association

THE GN UP TO THE FIRST WORLD WAR

In September of 1910 redesign took place and Nash's erstwhile partner, J. Robertson Brown, had *Motor Cycle* write-up the car. Nash was 'hopping mad' since for one thing there was no mention of his half of the partnership and, to quote Nash, "or my mother for that matter, since she owned the Vee twin JAP - she acted as guarantor and had been forced by the HP company to take up the guarantee!" Ron Godfrey had also seen the article and called in to see Nash at Hendon, as he, too, had finished working for Willans. Immediately they got in touch with Boileau, the editor of *Motor Cycle,* who was distressed enough to agree to write another article to put the matter right. The article in *Motor Cycle* of December 29 1910 (page 16) and the catalogue that Raymond Morgan produced were sufficient to bring in about six orders over the following two months. Godfrey said in an article in *Light Car* of 1933 'The first order was completed after many months and numerous promises for delivery had been broken. It is a Saturday, and our customer, who so far we have only known by name, arrives, stating that he wishes to drive away at once as he has a 220 mile journey. Archie Nash greets him but, I, hovering for a furtive last minute adjustment, notice that he is not quite his serene self. Perhaps he is thinking our masterpiece does not look quite as sleek as the catalogue illustrations'. The first hero's name was George W. Walmsley of Cleaton Moor, Cumberland. He wrote a three page article in *Motor Cycling* in November 1911 which told of the journeys he had made and the difficulties he had had with belt drives, ignition and brakes, in the first 300 miles of ownership, but the whole article was warm with praise 'truly the GN is a magic carpet' - vindicated the possibilities of the duocar and he concluded. 'As to reliability, I do not see what there is to go wrong, beyond what can be easily adjusted on the road by the average motorcyclist. The engine is an 8hp JAP, and if one cannot keep that power plant in tune, the deficiency will be personal. The carburettor is the standard 1911 motorcycle B and B, and the ignition is by Bosch magneto, with coil and accumulator for starting the front cylinder. The gears are very simple, and of the sliding dog type. The large double disc clutch, operated by pedal, is simplicity itself. The GN has evidently passed through a long period of eliminations, and evolved into a production like the drawings of a master cartoonist, whose few lines seem so simple, yet mean so much, and bespeak the more prescience and study in the primary stages.

'I can make the usual disclaimer in a more original way, as my only personal acquaintance with Messrs Godfrey and Nash was when I went to Hendon after many postponements, hoping to drive the GN home to Cumberland, but I am afraid it was only hard words I used in my disappointment. I believe, since, that my wait was profitable. I am sure I have a far, far

DECEMBER 29th, 1910.

THE G.N. QUAD.

A LIGHT RUNABOUT ON SPORTING LINES.

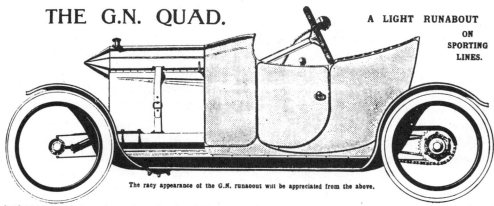

The racy appearance of the G.N. runabout will be appreciated from the above.

THERE have been a number of attempts in the past to produce a passenger vehicle which is little more expensive in initial cost and running than the popular motor bicycle. To attain these ends, lightness is a *sine quâ non*, but lightness and strength do not go hand in hand, and most of the early attempts to satisfy popular requirements lacked rigidity. On November 10th last we illustrated a new form of sociable quadcar on which we had been allowed a trial, and that machine has been spoken of very favourably. On this page we illustrate the latest form of G.N. runabout, of which the quadcar previously

The sporting type chassis with double V belt drive.

referred to was the forerunner. It must be admitted at once that the design is very striking, the bodywork being particularly neat. A point to recommend it is that it is no experiment or suggested design, but the outcome of two years' experience with this type of vehicle. It is made in three different models, the price varying according to equipment, but the same outline is common to all. Firstly, it is compact and as narrow as possible to reduce wind resistance. The 8 h.p. engine, which is of the V type twin-cylinder air-cooled variety, is situated in front, the cooling being assisted by means of a fan. A refinement worthy of mention is that the carburetter is fitted with a pilot jet for slow running. The petrol tank is torpedo-shaped, and placed above the engine. Its capacity is sufficient for 200 miles.

The frame is suspended on large tubular axles by cantilever plate springs duplicated in front. Steering is by twin wire rope, acting without jockeys or guides, and turning the wheels only as in standard car practice. The two-speed gear is placed amidships, the drive being communicated from the engine by means of a chain. The final drive may be by chain or V belt depending upon the model selected. The gear gives a direct drive on both speeds. Radius rods are used to control the movement of the rear axle. Push pedals operate clutch and brake, and an extra hand brake is also fitted. In the case of the *de luxe* model internal expanding brakes are used, but on the "sporting" models, belt rim brakes. The tyres are heavy voiturette 650 by 65 mm. section. The weights are given by the makers as follows: Sporting single-seater, 230 lbs.; 7ft. wheelbase. Sporting two-seater, 300 lbs.; 9ft. wheelbase. De luxe two-seater, 400 lbs.; 7ft. 9in. wheelbase. It should be observed that the two-seater runabouts have side by side seats, rendering conversation an easy matter.

The de luxe chassis which is chain driven.

All parts, excepting the engines (J.A.P. or Peugeot), magnetos (Bosch), and minor fittings, are made at the works of Godfrey and Nash, Elms Motor Works, Golder's Green Road, Hendon.

THE GN UP TO THE FIRST WORLD WAR

better article than if they had delivered to date, instead of to their satisfaction'.

During 1911 and 1912 the company fought for survival and many of the early cars were returned by indignant owners, who were not cast in the heroic mould of Mr Walmsley and had not served their apprenticeships on motorcycle combinations. A change of premises had to be made as Nash's mother, a doctor, complained that it was bad enough being a female doctor, striving to make a living in the man's world of 1911, without the additional noisy drawback of what her son and his friend were doing in the back garden.

Cecil Whitehead, who was the owner of a GN and liked it, offered to put a thousand pounds of capital to get them on a more business-like footing. Whitehead's money was put to good use, for they were now able to buy a milling machine and dog clutches could be made simply and correctly; as Godfrey said "making everything in the round was very trying". The company was registered as GN Limited and the company address was the Elms Works, The Burroughs, Hendon; though for sales purposes the Works were described as the Elms Motor Works. The main building had housed a chinese laundry and the bonus feature was the quantity of overhead lineshafting. To Nash and Godfrey this was in the nature of a godsend, since for any component they could make out of two or three inch round steel, there was an endless supply of raw material for the taking, in the air above their heads. It was Ron Godfrey who usually climbed up to get further stocks down, as he was the more agile. Nash said it was good training for an engineer to use what was to hand rather than what he would have preferred. It also led to a lifetime use of the expression "best laundry iron" which could be confusing to the hearer, eg Alastair Pugh asked Frazer-Nash what material was used for the axle clips on the front axle of a Frazer Nash - answer "best laundry iron".

Reinforced ash was used for the GN chassis until the end of 1916. The reinforcement by steel bushes, flitch plates and longerons eventually meant that, for the racing chassis such as *Kim I* and *Bluebottle,* the advantages of ash were overcome by the disadvantages and by 1919 the steel chassis was standard to all models.

The firm got a bit touchy if prospective purchasers suggested that maybe ash was not the ideal material for a chassis and Orrinsmith used to suggest that if a GN with an ash frame savaged a lamp post, then it would unwind itself; Godfrey used to cap this with an account of how a GN had had an argument with a bus and if you accepted Godfrey's story then there was no doubt that the GN came off best.

FRAZER NASH

Nash and Godfrey in the third or fourth GN

Osman Hill, the Secretary of the Cyclecar Club suggested that bonnet sides would improve the appearance. Nash is accompanied by his wife

THE GN UP TO THE FIRST WORLD WAR

The major difference between GN and other lesser manufacturers was that GN made their own engine. Godfrey originally designed the GN engine using a turn of the century design of motorcycle engine called the Clement. This engine had an overhung crank and was ideally suited to be made with lathes and the products of a foundry. Godfrey scaled up the single-cylinder Clement engine and made a 90 degree vee-twin with an outside flywheel.

Experiments had been carried out using a Peugeot 8hp vee-twin engine and the cylinder barrels, rods and pistons were borrowed for the new design.

By the end of 1912 the engine had been further developed to fit positively opening inlet valves, and the fitting of GN designed and manufactured components, rather than Peugeot. The engine was emerging from the prototype stage and increased in capacity by 110cc to 1086cc (84 x 98mm). The use of GN cylinder barrels and heads together with the valves, pistons, con-rods, etc. made the engine wholly GN. The cylinder head and barrel were held down by means of two studs per cylinder and a large bridge piece over the cylinder heads; the pressure was applied via a cup-piece in the bridge piece, through a large steel ball and cup on the cylinder head. The differential expansion of iron, steel and aluminium sometimes led to the cylinder heads cracking in service if the long studs were over tensioned. The heavy finning on the heads and barrels meant that fan cooling used on some of the earlier cars could be dispensed with, but there was some discussion as to whether to place the front cylinder horizontal or 5 degrees off the horizontal and the rear cylinder nearly vertical, since at that time there was no intention to place the engine other than in line with the chassis. The horizontal/vertical disposition eventually was adopted for the cheapest model made in 1915 as the Touring Model (also known in the Works as the Colonial Model) selling at a basic price of 88 guineas.

The redesign, following the decision to enter for the Cyclecar Grand Prix, was completed by April and incorporated into one chassis. This was the subject of a comprehensive article in *Cyclecar* of 9 April 1913, entitled 'The Grand Prix GN' and the article stated the car would be entered for the Grand Prix and 'After a lengthy test has now been adopted as the standard model'.

The differences between what went before and the new standard were so complete that they are best summarised as follows:

a) A new vee-twin engine mounted across the chassis. This was the engine that had been under development, but now it was to be positioned across the chassis with the cylinder heads protruding through the bonnet sides - engine cooling was never again a problem and in fact the GN found favour with

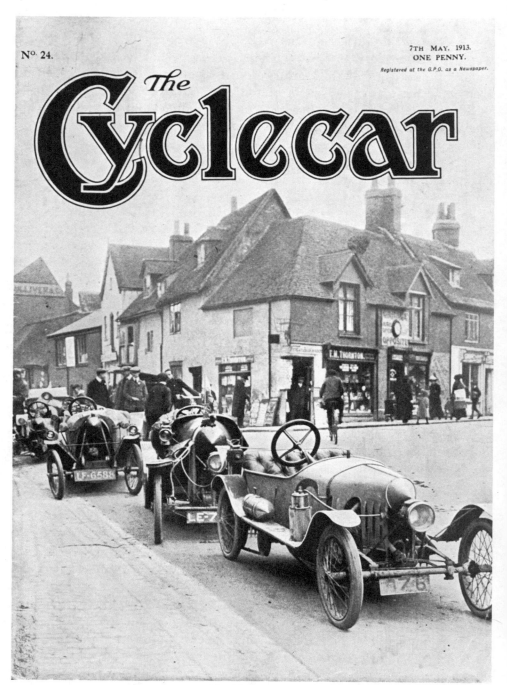

The cover of Issue 24 of the *Cyclecar* showing a Sabella cyclecar sandwiched between the 1912 GN and the 1913 Grand Prix GN *IPC Transport Press*

THE GN UP TO THE FIRST WORLD WAR

sales, if not all over the globe, at least in some surprisingly hot places due to active agents. The engine was three point mounted and a one piece aluminium casting incorporated the engine crankcase, the crankcase extension supported the overhung crankshaft at the rear and the bearers for side location in the chassis frame.

b) A new layout of flywheel, clutch, propshaft and bevel drive to the countershaft. The flywheel was of adequate size so that the engine did not die when one cylinder faltered and this marked out the GN from all its vee-twin competitors. The clutch and drive train of propshaft and bevel box were a significant step forward from the previous long chain that connected the engine to the countershaft; this chain had been bad engineering practise and was a frequent cause of breakdowns. The new layout was instantly recognisable since it was the basic design of the later chain drive Frazer Nash cars.

c) The revised layout of countershaft with 2 or 3 or 4 forward speeds or 3 speeds and reverse. Godfrey and Nash had examined the two speed transmission on the Land Speed Record Darracq as 'Bill' Guiness (Kenelm Lee Guiness) was a good friend. This mechanism used two crown wheels on the back axle and between them a sliding dog to which the pinions were attached; the space was remarkably tight between the crown wheels, and Godfrey said the idea of the compact double dog and sprockets for a car came after looking at the Darracq.

d) Large Vee belt pulleys on the countershaft. Before the First World War this statement would have been of significance to all motorists. GN had made the gear reductions with a combination of the bevel wheel reduction and the ratio between the sprockets. Hence there was no need to make any greater reduction with the Vee belt pulleys other than the ideal two to one ratio of a driving to driven pulley; the driving pulley being of a generous diameter, meant that in wet weather there was less tendency to slip, as might be encountered in lesser designs.

The announcement of the Grand Prix model and the way the GN had 'evidently passed through a long period of eliminations and evolved' was obvious to many people and the orders came in to such an extent that a further move of premises was necessary to cater for them. This move to Etna Works, the brand new premises in Hendon, specially built for the firm, at the end of 1913, allowed for up to a maximum of 70 chassis to be worked on at the same time, guaranteeing a steady production of maybe five cars a week. The coming of the war upset the strategy as Godfrey and Nash were beginning to grasp the essentials of forward ordering in bulk, so that the works would run smoothly without shortfalls in material, or in bought-out

FRAZER NASH

Nash in practise for the Amiens Cyclecar Grand Prix

Start line of the Cyclecar Grand Prix: Borbeau in the Bedelia (13), Whitehead in the GN (14), Nash in the GN (18)

THE GN UP TO THE FIRST WORLD WAR

items such as castings, lighting sets, etc.

The Grand Prix GN had been built for one purpose, and as the weeks rushed by both Nash and Godfrey were amazed at the interest being shown by everybody speculating whether the cars were ready and the preparations that were being made. It was decided that Nash and Whitehead would race and Godfrey would look after the pits and the general preparation. Nash won the first cyclecar race ever run at Brooklands but in a longer distance race of 65 miles the following week, the beaded edged tyres kept coming off Whitehead's car and Nash's car was beaten by the Singer.

The Cyclecar Grand Prix turned out to be a setback for GN as Whitehead's car only lasted a few hundred yards. Last minute panicking involved tightening of every bolt in sight, including the cylinder holding down bolts and one of the cylinder heads split right across soon after the

The Grand Prix Model of 1914

Chassis of the Grand Prix GN

FRAZER NASH

start. Nash's luck was no better, for the cause of his breakdown and eventual retirement was so unusual as to be unique. At the end of the first ten and a half miles lap, MacMinnies, driving the Grand Prix Morgan (as a three wheeler running in the sidecar motorcycle class and not eligible to win the Cyclecar race) was in first place with a lap of 13.53 minutes with Nash at 14.13 and Munday in another Morgan at 14.17. On lap 3 the *Cyclecar* report said: 'Mr

S efficient as it is simple, the G.N. cyclecar is backed up by the rare experience of the pioneer, its whole design is based on the practical knowledge of actual requirements. The vibrationless G.N. 90° twin engine, cooled perfectly by G.N. air cooling; the simple and accessible change speed gear by dog clutches; and the final belt drive—elastic and smooth running—over large fixed pulleys; all these things have been evolved in their present state of perfection after countless experiments and are based on actual road experience. The price of the G.N. is £107; accessories are extra. Trial runs can be arranged from the new works at Bell Lane, Hendon, N.W., or with Messrs. Lake's, at the West End Showrooms, 222, Shaftesbury Avenue, W.C. Two G.N.'s were entered for the London-Edinburgh-and-back trial—one by an amateur private owner—and ran second and fourth in a field of seventy for the Cup. Both were awarded double-journey **GOLD MEDALS**.

'Pioneers in Design' from the *Light Car and Cyclecar* of June 1914

THE GN UP TO THE FIRST WORLD WAR

Nash came in on his GN, took off his bonnet to make an adjustment and had hardly begun to move away when yells went up for him to come back, and it was hurriedly explained to him that he must carry his bonnet around with him if he did not wish to be disqualified. He put it on, but when he attempted to start up his motor he was again in difficulties, probably eight minutes being lost before he got away. Later it was discovered that there was no obligation to carry a bonnet throughout the race, nor even to start with one'.

Archie Nash said the roads were so bad, previously having had the Grand Prix and the solo motorcycle races run over them, that bits were falling off his car continuously, the dummy radiator moved and his mechanic had to carry the bonnet for the rest of the race. On the worst part of the circuit the engine went startlingly rough and Nash pulled into the side in Boves village to find the trouble. One of the advantages of Godfrey's design of engine was accessibility and by removing the timing chest complete it was perfectly practicable to inspect the crankpin and big ends and even work on them. Nash found that the crank pin had come loose, which was indeed unfortunate, because in the weeks before the event this crankpin had been specially built up for the race. Nash then set to and made some packing out of tin at the side of the road and eventually rejoined the race, but without any hope of achieving any success. MacMinnies was the first to finish but as far as the French were concerned he had only won the sidecar class, of which class he was the only finisher. Borbeau, designer manufacturer and number one works driver for Bedelia, won the Cyclecar Grand Prix. The British regarded it quite differently. A dinner was given in London to the victors of the Cyclecar Grand Prix who were honoured, there and in the Press, as MacMinnies and the Morgan.

Nash planned to return in 1914 for the next Cyclecar Grand Prix, which he assumed would be run on the same course and at the same time as the French Grand Prix. The car was to have softer springing, as reliability was far more important than cornering power, and a stone guard was to be placed across the front of the engine. A water colour painting was produced by an artist named Bower in 1914, presumably for publicity purposes, showing such a GN speeding down a tree-lined Route Nationale. However, no race of equal calibre to the 1913 Cyclecar Grand Prix was ever proposed again, and consequently the car in the painting was never built. The commercial, if not the racing, success of the Grand Prix GN was assured.

After the beginning of the Great War it was business as normal during the first half of 1915 with the Grand Prix GN as the standard model.

FRAZER NASH

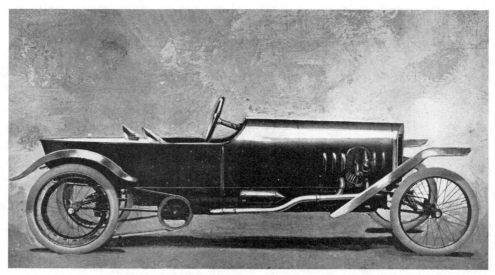

SPECIFICATION OF 1915 VITESSE MODEL G.N

Engine.—G.N 90° twin, 84 × 98mm., capacity 1086cc., accurately balanced. Cylinders of close-grained iron with detachable head with holding-down bolts. The cylinder is not subjected to tension stress. G.N air-cooling system, with very deep cooling-fins and special design of exhaust system. Special light pistons of steel, machined from solid bar, with two rings, hardened gudgeon pin with G.N safe fixing, special light connecting-rods of forged high-tensile steel, bushed with phosphor-bronze bearings of large area. Crank-shaft hardened and accurately balanced, running in two long bronze bearings lubricated by G.N direct system. Timing-wheels (two only), cams (two) and rockers are carefully hardened high tensile steel ; valves are of large diameter in special steel—design obviates use of valve-caps and attendant difficulty of removal. Engine mounted in frame by three-point suspension to permit liveliness of frame without stress.

Lubrication.—By G.N system of semi-automatic pump, delivering to a pocket in crank-case, which in turn feeds—through oilways in the bearings—to the crank-case.

Carburetter.—Brown & Barlow, with two-lever control and G.N pilot-jet for starting and slow running. (Solex, with one-lever control, to order). Gravity feed from petrol tank in scuttle.

Ignition.—By U.H. high tension magneto, specially built for 90° engines, driven from cam-shaft.

Clutch.—G.N three-plate clutch, faced with Ferodo, progressive and proof against unlimited slipping.

Transmission.—Bevel-driven countershaft with Renold roller chain drive to pulley-shaft. Three speeds and reverse (four speeds to order). Changes made by dog-clutches, final drive by G.N system of 1-inch belts over 8-inch pulleys. Chains are protected from dust and dirt, the centres are constant and the alignment is always perfect.

Wheelbase.—8′ 6″. Track 3′ 4″. Over-all length 10′ 8″. Width 4′ 2″. Height, 3′ 4″, with screen 4′ 1″. Ground Clearance 8½″.

Frame.—Of steel-armoured ash, cross-braced at corners.

Springs.—G.N cantilever, with radius-rods front and rear, maintaining perfect wheel alignment.

Wheels.—G.N detachable wire wheels with 650 × 65 Michelin tyres.

Steering.—By G.N duplicate cable system, designed to obviate the rigidity and consequent fatigue and breakage of other type.

Body.—Special light aluminium streamline body with staggered seats and ample leg-room. Tool-box at rear.

Equipment Extra.—Two acetylene lamps and generator, windscreen, horn, tools and pump are included in price.

Spare Wheel and Tyre, with bracket fitted if ordered with car, £3 18s. extra.

Polished Aluminium Body, £4 4s. extra.

Price £155.

Specification of the Vitesse Model taken from 1915 GN catalogue

---

*Footnote - Of interest at this point is the fact that Hans Renold Ltd and subsequently Renold Ltd have been the suppliers of chain exclusively, from the earliest days of the GN, through to the present time with the Frazer Nash Section of the VSCC's spares scheme. As Archie Frazer-Nash once said "Renold is the best chain and for the best chain drive car on the market we use the best chain"

The post war GN
Chapter 2

ARCHIE NASH was stung into writing a letter to the *Light Car and Cyclecar* in November of 1914, following criticism of transmissions that used bevel, chain and belt cumulatively. His letter said '... the fact that the gear reduction is made in one step necessitates either a weak bevel pinion - on account of its small size - or a large increase in weight, by the corresponding increase of the crown wheel and casing, which results from making the pinion of sufficient size ...'. This part of Frazer-Nash's reply, as will be appreciated, was not very strong; however, when comparing the GN with cars that had their gearboxes on the rear axle he was on much firmer ground '... All this means weight and unsprung weight at that ... its heavy unsprung weight, is notoriously inferior, in its steadiness and ability to hold the road, to the simple GN type of machine ...'. Presumably Sheret had not read his employers' letter when he chopped off the back axle of a Grand Prix GN and made the chain drive countershaft, in front of it, the rear axle. The chains had to be increased in size from ½in pitch to ¾in pitch, due to the fact that with this arrangement, the back axle was not always parallel in the horizontal plane to the bevel box countershaft. Not only did the modification work, but it worked very well indeed and GN could not help announcing their post war model in the middle of 1916.

The Etna Works in Hendon, by the middle of 1916, was heavily engaged in war contracts and Nash, now generally referred to as Frazer-Nash, had joined up and had been seconded to the War Office. He joined the Armament Section of the Technical Department and before the end of the

FRAZER NASH

'Bluebottle', Ron Godfrey's pre-war car, was in use by the firm until 1921 and raced by Godfrey. Seen here with L. A. Cushman

war was in charge of the Synchronous Gear Design Department, whose responsibilities were to continue to perfect the firing of machine guns through propellors on fighter aircraft; over a decade later this apprenticeship into the handling of Ministry contracts and the friends he made, were to stand him in good stead when he began to develop and manufacture the Nash and Thomson gun turret for aircraft. The most enjoyable part of Frazer-Nash's war time experiences was learning how to fly, and after the war he put in a successful bid for an Avro 504K.

A facet of the character in both Godfrey and Nash was that they both liked an 'in story' or an 'in joke'; if people asked the reason for some of their sayings then they would willingly explain, but they would never volunteer. An example is "best laundry iron" and another was the predilection for Irish registration numbers. In 1912 they saw a visiting southern Irish registered car touring in England and noted that the registration letters were black onto a white background. Two registration numbers were immediately obtained from Tyrone, HZ 6 and HZ 7 and these numbers could then be instantly applied to aluminium bodywork with black paint.

THE POST WAR GN

If the 'Irish' driver of an 'Irish' racing car such as *Kim*, temporarily visiting England, should be apprehended by the police on the road down to Brooklands from London - if an 'Irish' brogue could be summoned up by the driver to make the explanations and the policeman recognised the paperwork problems that would later ensue - then there was a very real chance that the policeman might make only a verbal caution. This 'insurance policy' was minor in relation to the facility that registration numbers would be capable of being applied to bodywork in seconds, and the private amusement it afforded them both to have a 'foreign' number. The Irish came into line with the British authorities after independence, on registration numbers but the GN Works cars in the early 1920s went on carrying Irish numbers from Leitrim of IT 341, 342, 327, 354; not from any reasons of ease of application, because that no longer applied, and certainly not for reasons of evading legal responsibilities, but purely for old times sake, and for the fact that it was the senior partners' own private joke.

The 1916 prototype, bearing the registration number HZ 6, only needed two pieces of modernisation in 1918 to be in effect the post war model:

a) The wire and bobbin steering which had proved to be extremely effective and positive had to be rejected in favour of a steering box, drop arm and drag link.

b) The ash chassis which had been a major success had to be rejected in favour of a rolled steel chassis.

Besides these two 'modern' improvements, the opportunity was taken to redesign the crankcase, firstly to reduce the echoing properties of the timing chest by reducing it in size and secondly to use fabricated engine bearers to the crankcase, as there had been too high a rejection rate of the complete pre-war casting. One year after the end of the war the order book for GNs was measured in the hundreds but the capacity of the Etna Works at Hendon was only two or three cars a week.

Just prior to the Olympia Show in late 1919, GN took a double page spread in the *Light Car and Cyclecar* and made the following announcement 'GN AFTER ELEVEN YEARS. The GN evolved over eleven years ago to meet the need of a simple and efficient two-seater, has, through strenuous application and in the light of practical experience, developed a high standard of performance, economy and comfort. A WELL EQUIPPED MODERN WORKS, capable of turning out 100 cars a day has now been acquired and the present output will be greatly increased in the next few months. IN FRANCE ALSO the GN is starting on quantity production and was a great attraction at the Paris Salon. THUS AFTER ELEVEN YEARS,

1920 Scottish Six Day Trial with Cushman driving

THE POST WAR GN

the GN perfected, offering the luxurious comfort of the touring car at the cost and economy of the motorcycle and sidecar, has not only proved itself in constant service and open competition, but is in mass production in two countries to meet its ever growing demand. GN Limited, East Hill, Wandsworth'. The copywriter's mistake in stating that the production rate was to be 100 per day earned GN a certain amount of notoriety and press coverage, since the copy should have said 100 cars a week. A hundred cars a week was real news and at Olympia GN proudly showed a polished GN chassis, strapped down to the floor so as to flatten the springs - without the weight of a body the chassis looked a bit arched - the wood screws soon gave way with a loud bang and much consternation. At the same show Rover were showing for the first time their Rover 8 with its air-cooled twin engine and perhaps the pundits of the day felt quite sure of themselves in saying 'air cooling' is the outstanding feature of the rejuvenation of the light car, and predicting a great future for the simple car rather than the scaled down large car.

An agreement was made between British Gregoire and GN, so that the substantial premises that Gregoire of France owned in East Hill, Wandsworth, used as the headquarters for their British sales and servicing, was now sold to GN. Marcel Lourde organised this sale and the investment by Gregoire into the new enlarged GN company. He further organised and put through the licensing agreement for Salmsons to produce the GN in France. Marcel Lourde's entrepreneurial advice and his knowledge of the world of finance, were a great advantage to GN and though he was rarely seen in England he was a firm friend of Frazer-Nash. The licensing agreement with Salmsons was carried through in weeks, but the purchase of the East Hill Works, was protracted and lasted for months. It was not until the end of 1919 that GNs were able to get possession of the premises and then there were further delays, due to the 50 times increase in capacity that was planned. In fact it was not until the end of 1920 that the cars really started to flow from the new factory and, just at this time, the post war boom was already beginning to falter and within a short time GN was to pay heavily for the two lost years of production.

Much to the surprise of both Godfrey and Frazer-Nash the physical limitations of space precluded any greater production rate than fifty cars a week; the peak production week of fifty-five achieved during the autumn of 1921, with the peak month of two hundred and twenty cars, used every inch of space. Godfrey busied himself with production, whilst Frazer-Nash handled the sales and the preparation of the racing cars.

Photographer Ron Godfrey, Vera Godfrey, Archie and Mamie Frazer-Nash during a stop on the London-Manchester Trial

GNs on pre-delivery test runs from the Works, Captain Easte poses on Wandsworth Common

THE POST WAR GN

Finch and Cushman await the start of a one day JCC Trial to Cheddar in a Legere model GN

GNs found themselves in 1920 emerging from the chaos of endeavouring to become a major motor car manufacturer and the aim was in satisfying the agents. The agents wanted cars to sell, they also wanted a first class back-up service of spare parts, manuals, advertising and promotional matter. H.R. Morgan was a tower of strength in making sure that the promotional material was available and he also recommended the absolute necessity of a decent spare parts manual. H.R. Morgan used professionally his Christian name of Raymond and 'Raymond Publicity' is to be seen on advertising material produced for GN. Several attempts were made to produce a parts list and in the end Godfrey accepted Morgan's suggestion that they should take a car off the production line, put it in a shed, take it apart, photograph the parts, and give each part a number. This was done and was a great success, as there could be no doubt that a manufacturer who produced such a manual was in the business to stay. Service engineers of the calibre of Captain Easte, who toured the country, materially increased the firm's standing. There were also produced official spare parts price lists and again it is possible in this to detect the hand of H.R. Morgan. Godfrey thought it rather steep, the percentage price uplift made to the standard

FRAZER NASH

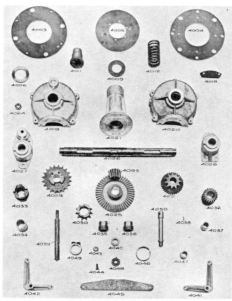

Spare parts list (part of the transmission section) item 4026, the countershaft, cost £1 10s 0d, items 4093 and 4025 the pinion and crown wheel cost £2 0s 0d and £3 15s 0d

GNs were sold all over the world. Active agents were to be found in Austria, Denmark, Holland and Australia

Salmson built chassis awaiting to be moved to the body shop

THE POST WAR GN

A Salmson advertisement demonstrating the absolute superiority of the GN Cyclecar

The GN advertisement in the Motor Show catalogue of 1921

The 1921 Motor Show. GNs with doors dominate the stand

FRAZER NASH

costings, but Frazer-Nash chuckled with glee at the sheer nerve of it, though by no means were the prices out of line with other manufacturers. The sequel to the story of the production of the spare parts manual was that in 1922 there was a form of stock taking and the car that had been taken apart had been painstakingly taken out of the works by an entrepreneurical workman, part by part, and presumably reassembled!

Frazer-Nash and Godfrey saw no reason why any changes at all should be made to such a fine car, but they were fully receptive to suggestions for mechanical improvement; for instance, that a device could be used on the hub-nuts to stop the nut unscrewing and which would prevent the wheels falling off. They were not at all receptive to the suggestions that the GN should be made more like a car than a cyclecar; this they felt was not merited, since there was supplied with each post-war car a well designed and manufactured hood and a spare wheel with its own mounting bracket. Frazer-Nash and Godfrey recognised that the requests from agents asking for improvements to be made, to uplift the GN specification to that of a light car, had the fatal drawback that the price was to remain at a cyclecar's price.

At the end of 1921 the ground swell of complaint from the agents had risen, due to the incipient signs of the depressing slump that was coming. The following items of complaint were raised: The engine to be more silent, the body to be more comfortable and a better technical specification.

Everybody agreed about the noisiness of the GN engine. The range of noises were legion, valve gear noise, piston slap, etc. There was no part of the engine that did not add its own contribution to the orchestration; to have fitted more efficient silencers would have made the 'chaplinks' and 'chaplunks' of the valve train even more noticeable.

The coachwork that was fitted to the 1914 GN had seemed at that time to be the last word, especially when fitted with a windscreen and hood - though by 1921 it was regarded as primitive. The absence of a door in the specification meant that the body frame could be light, simple and cheap to produce, hence Archie Frazer-Nash's explosion, in exasperation for the thousandth time, when the question had been asked by a customer for a door to be fitted. "Door, door, what do you want with a door?" This customer presumably never got beyond the prospective stage.

A better technical requirement covered many areas where the GN might be uplifted to a higher specification; examples of this were electric lighting to be more of a fitting than an extra, more instruments - "what do they want an oil gauge for when there is no pressure to be read", but the critical necessity was for front starting of the engine. The GN, from almost

THE POST WAR GN

Hugh and Eva Conway in a 1922 GN, with front starting during a trial in the thirties

the beginning in 1911, had had an extension to the counter shaft from the bevel box, with which a starting handle could engage; the car could be hand, or kick started. It was simple and straightforward, but by the early 1920s people did not expect to see a starting handle fed into the middle of a car, and many people, always ready to laugh at the bizarre, laughed at the GN side starting. Frazer-Nash said to Orrinsmith, who was the chief draughtsman, "When I come in tomorrow I want to see a design on my desk which means we can get away from the side starting handle". Orrinsmith's note on Frazer-Nash's desk the next morning stated simply 'Problem insoluble, cars will have to be sold, started'. The problem was eventually solved, but the result was more expensive to manufacture, involved poor engineering and was likely to cause trouble before the cars were very old - to Frazer-Nash and Godfrey the saga of the positioning of the starting handle was probably the last straw.

FRAZER NASH

The basic trouble at East Hill was that production had not really started until the end of 1920 and there had been too short a time to start paying back the capital investment. If East Hill had been in production a year earlier, then the two senior partners would have had their way when things started to go wrong. They wished at the end of 1921 to cut back production and move into the sports car market, where most of the disadvantages of the design could have been made into advantages, and where there could have been room for manoeuvre on pricing, when changes were required. The point of view which envisaged a reduction in output, was anathema to the Board of GN and it was agreed that all that was best in British light cars was to be seen in the Rover 8!. It was agreed that a Rover 8 would be examined throughout and all those features that could be incorporated, should be incorporated, in a completely new model. In the meantime some changes would be introduced into the 1922 range which would be a halfway stage. These would incorporate most of the suggestions that were being made by the agents.

Greater width bodies, with a door, were to be the standard and the 1922 catalogue in its preamble stated the following;
'COMFORT. Only when a car is well-proportioned, quiet and sweet running can comfort be attained. The 1922 GN is roomy, luxuriously comfortable, gives perfect protection in any weather; its chassis, too, is as excellent as its bodywork is beautiful'.

After this preamble the 1922 potential purchaser could not have been surprised by the first page of the text which stated that the 'All-Weather Model' was, by inference, a beautiful car. It was not until the last few pages of this catalogue were reached, that from two whole pages of small type, it could be seen that the GN was a very successful competition car indeed. A GN had won the Tourist Championship of France, as the catalogue said, 'the highest obtainable class award of the continent', and a whole page of racing successes, not only class awards but many Fastest Time of the Day awards, were listed. It also featured a remarkable 94 miles to the gallon recorded during the Midland Light Car Club's one day road trial that included the Old Wyche Cutting at Malvern with a gradient of reputedly 1 in 3.

One of the features of the 1922 range was that the engines had been modified to lower the noise level. The chief modification was to the design of the cams, which meant that in quietening the ramps, the power of the engine was seriously reduced. When this was compounded with the increased weight of the coachwork, the original performance which had been positively sporting by the standards of the time dropped to a more

THE POST WAR GN

THE LEGERE G.N.

WITH a special aluminium panelled body, and attractive appearance, the Légère G.N. is a slim, light two-seater with a specially tuned engine. The car is not a special speed model, but has been designed as a light (Légère) model for the motorist who appreciates a lively car and delights in wonderful acceleration.

Contrary to the prevailing idea, the aluminium body is easier to keep clean than the conventional paintwork. The wings are finished in G.N. blue. No dickey seat is fitted.

The general specification is the same as that of the Touring model; many improvements have been incorporated in the 1922 model.

EQUIPMENT, as in the case of Touring model, includes head, adjustable wind-screen, electric lighting installation with dynamo, batteries, switchboard and ammeter, *two head-lamps, mounted on the wings, with double filaments for bright and dim, and tail-lamp, speedo-meter, detachable wheels, spare wheel and tyre, pump, horn, jack, tools, etc.*

£240

THE ALL-WEATHER G.N.

HITHERTO, the small car has not been associated with any high degree of comfort or weather protection, and it has remained for the G.N. to provide a practical all-weather body, at a reasonable price, which will permit a quick change to be made from the open to the closed car.

This all-weather G.N. has a double folding screen, special black all-weather hood, with side window panels, the near-side panel opening with the door.

When not in use the hood folds neatly down in the same manner as the usual hood, and the side panels stow away underneath the seat. Both when open and closed, the car is elegant and attractive, is perfect for the professional man or for all-round use. Equipped as Touring model.

£250

The All Weather and Legere GNs from the 1922 catalogue

FRAZER NASH

Captain Easte road testing the Steiner

pedestrian level, and the fuel consumption was markedly worse. The Grand Prix GN of 1914 always gave 60mpg, the immediate post-war cars right up until 1922 gave at least 45, with an easy 55 obtainable on a long run, but the 1922 car was at its best a 40mpg car.

The strain of what was happening in the Works in 1922 was more than Frazer-Nash could stand, practically every change that had been made in the last quarter onwards from 1921 had been specifically against his advice. In most cases he had not only argued against the change but would have preferred a change, if it had to be made, to be in the diametrically opposite direction. In all cases Godfrey agreed with Frazer-Nash, but was not as vocal in his disagreement. The increased capital they had to take on in 1920 meant that the senior partners now held only a minority shareholding. The 1922 models, when designed, were against Frazer-Nash and Godfrey's judgement but they co-operated in the implementation of the Board's decision; they realised that they could be wrong, and that what the market was looking for were the 1922 Touring and All-Weather models. In fact they were not wrong and sales were poor even in relation to the end of 1921. The Board in 1922 decided to carry on with the development of the 1923 car, which in mid 1922 was running around in prototype form with the name of 'Steiner' on the radiator. Frazer-Nash argued that to carry on with this development was suicide but it was too late for the Board to turn round and

THE POST WAR GN

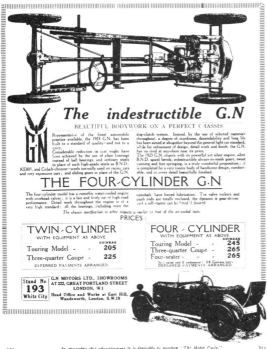

The shaft drive GN

G.N. 1925-28 Models—Cars of Amazing Performance.

The current models of the G.N. car are founded on the well-proven type of chassis incorporating the special G.N. transmission. There are, of course, many improvements in the chassis itself, some of which can, when desired, be embodied in earlier cars.

The new type G.N.s are a logical development from the early models. The latter were always known for their excellent performance, but this has been very greatly improved upon. The new cars, which are fitted with the British Anzani engine, are now fully equal, and usually superior, in speed, acceleration, and hill climbing, to any cars which are available at even two or three times their price.

Owners of early G.N.s who have derived general satisfaction from them can rely on obtaining the same good qualities from the new cars, with a very great improvement, not only in performance, but in detail, work, comfort, and silence.

Specialities.

A number of improvements are now available for owners of 1919-22 G.N. models. The plain bearing front hubs have been replaced on our later models by ball-bearing ones, and these have also been made available for earlier cars in the form of a conversion set. Again, the early type of G.N. hub cap was found sometimes to give trouble, partly by not being sufficiently secure, and partly by causing wear on the thread of the hub. The new type safety hub cap has a positive locking device, and the whole cap grips the thread tightly, and wear cannot arise.

On a few of the 1922 air-cooled cars, roller bearings were fitted to the big ends of the connecting rods with remarkably satisfactory results. They have been found to stand up to the most gruelling work in a way which no plain bearing could do. These are also available in the form of a conversion set.

The old type of chain tray which was attached to the back axle was not entirely effective, and often became a source of rattle. A new type is now available which offers far better protection, and which, being fastened to the body itself is adequately sprung and therefore free from rattle and noise.

The road springs which are now supplied are of far better quality than those which were procurable for standard equipment, as are the spring "U" bolts.

On many of the cars which have been on the road for a number of years, subject to hard usage, the selector rods and mechanism have become somewhat loose, and cases are not unknown where this has even caused the possibility of engagement of two gears at once. New type selector rods are available with yoke ends, instead of plain rods, and give satisfactory service for an indefinite period.

On some of the earlier cars a type of band brake was fitted. These can now be replaced with pairs of cast-iron brake shoes lined with Ferodo. Not only is the resulting braking force much more powerful, but it is smoother, more dependable, and far more permanent.

On some cars there has been trouble with the fracture of petrol pipes, and flexible petrol pipes of a special type are now available, the standard length is 15½in.; they can be supplied for either the Capac or Sthenos carburettor, but if required for any other special carburettor the thread of the union should be specified, and an additional charge of 1s. is made.

Many owners of early G.N.s find that the steering wheel is on the small side for comfort and easy handling. We have a stock of large steering wheels which we can offer at a special price, which are well under half their actual value. They are in new condition but have some slight imperfection which makes them unsuitable for putting on to our new cars.

The eyebolt bearings of many of the old cars became loose and gave a certain amount of trouble. The new type which is at present being used can be fitted to these old cars, and they consist of a new bearer which is pressed into the spring bracket, and a floating oilless bush, running on this bearer, on which the eyebolt presses. They have been found to give about five times the effective life of the present parts, and when wear develops, which should not be for many thousands of miles, they can be brought into new condition by fitting a new oilless bush, which is a very simple matter to replace.

Some people like to be able to release the compression to secure the easiest possible starting. A valve lifter set is available which we prefer to fit at the works (this can be done in 24 hours), but if the timing case of the engine is sent the set can be assembled locally.

	£	s.	d.
G.N. Safety Hub Caps ...	0	9	6 each.
G.N. Ball Bearing Front Wheel Assemblies, including new stub axles of special alloy steel, and fixed hubs, complete, ready to interchange with the existing hubs and stub axles ...	5	7	6 per set.
Roller Bearing Big End, consisting of crankpin and three roller races, together with two new special connecting rods ...	4	17	6 per set.
Grease Gun Set, complete with set of nipples and tin of grease. These greatly facilitate the lubrication of important points in the chassis ...	1	12	0 per set.
New Type Chain Tray ...	2	2	0 each.
Selector Rods (with yoke ends) ...	0	17	6 per pair.
Foot Brake Rod (with yoke ends) ...	0	8	9 each
Cast Iron Brake Shoes (complete with Ferodo lining)	2	2	0 per two pairs
Flexible Petrol Pipes ...	0	11	6 each.
18" Steering Wheels ...	0	17	6 each.
New Type Eyebolt Sets (with eyebolts complete) ...	1	2	6 per set.
M.P. Shock Absorbers (for front axle) ...	1	17	6 per pair.
Valve Lifter Sets ...	2	12	6 per set.

An active spares market was catered for by this part of the GN Instruction Book published in 1928 by GN Ltd. of 300 Balham High Road admit its mistakes and Frazer-Nash resigned and left the company. Ron Godfrey thought he could stick it out, but with his partner and friend gone he could only stand it for a month and by the autumn of 1922 he also resigned.

The 1923 GN was in essence a side valve Rover 8 with the cylinders at 90 degrees instead of the Rover's 180 degrees. The overhung crankshaft design had gone and the advertisement from the *Motor Cycle,* of October 1922, shows the changes which, as the *Light Car and Cyclecar* pointed out, were revolutionary; it would be in a similar vein if British Leyland were to announce the finish of the Mini - for GN to abandon chain drive was revolutionary. There was not a single component in the car that had not been changed, even parts such as the front axle and steering box had been unnecessarily modified, even if outwardly they looked the same. The four cylinder car was less than satisfactory and the minimum priced model at 205 guineas, reduced in December to the more plebeian £195, compared unfavourably with the Rover 8, selling at £180. The press said that 'the new vee-twin engine is particularly silent', but this did not compensate for only a trickle of orders. The guarantee claims, especially on the Chapuis Dornier four cylinder engined model, were very high. The directors substituted this engine rather than the DFP engine that Godfrey had approved and which had been tested in the Steiner.

GN Motors Ltd., being the successors of GN Ltd., were going through their death throes and the unkindest cut of all was that the *Light Car and Cyclecar,* both in the readers' letters and the editorial, seldom referred to the new GN models. The comments in the correspondence columns were warmly disposed to the older models, references were made to the economy and, as one correspondent wrote, 'as for the chain drive I can only wonder why the makers departed from it'. An article on the merits of four cylinder cars against twin cylinder cars compared the two new GN models in March of 1923, where the writer noted ironically and, as he said, with 'lingering regret', that 'no longer was there the typical bark for which the GN was famous'.

The racing GNs
Chapter 3

FRAZER-NASH AND GODFREY never had to rationalise their desires to go motor racing, there never was any question whether they would be improving the breed. It was absolutely clear that if you competed, the standards of manufacture improved, the cars got better and the public bought the cars. If none of this had been true they would have still gone motor racing, because it was fun, and business without fun was not what they wanted before the 1914-1918 war; after that war the situation was different, since they then employed over 500 people.

In the post-war period they had to go motor racing because there was no more effective way of demonstrating their wares and thereby selling them. Even as the troubles of the company became overwhelming the competition department at the East Hill Works were producing racing cars and many sports racing variations of the vee-twin engine.

The Streamer was the first racing car built by the firm, being a single seater version of the 1912 car. The Grand Prix GN, though neither a single seater nor a racing car entirely, was built for the 1913 Amiens Race and was the forebear of all later cars. *Kim* was designed for the Isle of Man International Cyclecar Race, to be known as the Dangerfield Trophy, after the Managing Director of Temple Press and the man who believed that the cyclecar would replace the motorcycle. This trophy was to be raced for over a ten lap course from St Johns to Kirkmichael, to Peel and returning to St Johns giving a lap of almost sixteen miles. The race was to take place on 24 September 1914, and by mid July the new GN, *Kim*, weighing only 3½

The 'Streamer' — the very first GN single-seater powered by the 90° GN engine in line with the chassis South Harting 1913. One of the first appearances of 'Kim'

THE RACING GNs

hundredweight, entered and ran in the South Harting Hill Climb, where it was beaten by Carden in a Carden. The engine of *Kim* used a more robust crankshaft and crankcase; it was the brass (not bronze) cylinder heads with the valve spring mounted above the rocker gear with incredibly long valve stems running in twin valve guides above and below the rocker, that was especially unique and was borrowed from the Austro Daimler design. Godfrey owned a 27/80 Prince Henry Austro Daimler and the valve gear of this machine appealed to him and Sheret. It was unfortunate that the war prevented the running of the Dangerfield Race and there was very little doubt that *Kim* was probably the fastest accelerating car in the World at that time, up to eighty miles per hour.

Kim emerged from the war as *Kim I,* for the intention was to bring it up to the post-war GN specification, as far as the chassis and running gear were concerned. Before this rebuild was carried out *Kim I* was involved in a high speed accident when the car went off Brooklands backwards. Archie Frazer-Nash was lucky only to sustain some facial bruising from the steering wheel and a broken collarbone. Page 47 shows the first outing of *Kim II*. *Kim* now weighed considerably more than its pre-war weight and was ready for racing again within a month of the accident. On a test lap of Brooklands *Kim II* was found to be considerably faster than *Kim I* had been. Sensation! The whole of the racing staff of GN were aware of this and much discussion took place regarding the reason; it was Godfrey who decided that the reason had to be that the rolling resistance was lower and it was Frazer-Nash who decided that racing cars go better after being crashed - all the stresses having been relieved! The outcome of the discussions was that a new test was instituted on a very slight downward slope near the GN shed at Brooklands. Racing cars, without a driver aboard, were released from a given mark and where they stopped, some ten yards further, was marked by a wooden peg in the grass at the side of the road; it will be appreciated that this led to a great deal of care being taken to reduce the rolling resistance of each car. The test was known as 'The Flying Millimetre', because, following chassis tuning, the cars all tended to finish within millimetres of one another.

Frazer-Nash decided after the accident with *Kim* that the Works had to build a special car for Brooklands. *Mowgli* had an extra long wheelbase which was achieved by making the normal rear axle into a second countershaft and fitting the rear axle behind this countershaft driven by a single set of sprockets and a chain. The engine was designed and built as a racing engine and no attempt was made to use standard parts as had been the case with *Kim*. The chain driven overhead camshaft earned the engine the nick-name of the 'chain-makers delight'! The crankcase, with its ribbed

August 2 1920. Archie Frazer-Nash crashes at Brooklands in 'Kim'. According to the *Daily Sketch* his first words were "Who won?"

Frazer-Nash supervises the rebuilding of 'Kim'

THE RACING GNs

'Kim II' makes its first public appearance with the post-war steel chassis and four speed chain final transmission. The pre-war bobbin and cable steering was retained for a month only

FRAZER NASH

'Kim II' in road going trim with the post-war steering. All set with hood, windscreen, lights and Frazer-Nash behind the wheel (note his hands on the steering wheel) ready to drive to Skegness

sump, was very much stiffer than any GN engine previously and with the use of ball and roller bearings throughout for the crankshaft and con-rods the Works had built their first out and out racing engine.

Mowgli's engine, which went on to power Basil Davenport's *Spider*, was highly successful in obtaining British National Records, but on long distance events the camshaft drive system, on several occasions, let the car down. Nevertheless the Works persisted in this drive that used a single six foot run of roller chain. The engine could be run in three guises, as the standard 84 x 98mm (1086cc) or 89 x 98mm (1219cc) or 89 x120mm (1493cc), in the last two of these categories it was used only for record breaking attempts. The difficulty with the chain drive was not that necessarily of the drive, but of the limited number of teeth that took the drive from the crankshaft and the limited number of teeth that were in mesh for the magneto drive. To prevent the chain jumping, it had to be tensioned to an absurdly high amount; quite why two such inventive engineers as Frazer-Nash and Godfrey persisted with this design, when with only the smallest modification they could have had two separate chains driving the

The Boulogne Grand Prix of 1921. Marcel Lourde talking to F. N. Pickett whilst Lombard organises the French GNs on the start line

Boulogne Speed Week of 1921. Godfrey in 'Bluebottle', Cushman in the 'Mowgli' powered car and Frazer-Nash in 'Kim II'

Archie Frazer-Nash finds that he is odds on favourite for the 1100cc class of the 1921 200 Mile Race

Frazer-Nash and Cushman after winning the 200 Mile Race

THE RACING GNs

Mamie Frazer-Nash, Archie's wife, races the 200 Mile Race car

camshafts, and a short, third chain driving the magneto, is difficult to understand.

The 1921 Boulogne meeting brought home to them the deficiency of the design. The sprint course and the Boulogne Grand Prix course involved the use of the road from Boulogne to Le Wast with its continuous downhill roller coasting gradient, where the revolutions the engine could reach in top gear were described as 'the like of which had never been seen before'! The camshaft drive chain gave continuous trouble and even tightening up to a board-like configuration gave no remedy, with the chain breaking due to over tension. Godfrey and Frazer-Nash, whilst they were at Boulogne, commenced the design of the 200 Mile Race engines with shaft drive overhead camshafts.

GNs never produced an engine with a single chain to each camshaft but they did produce a few sports racing engines using plate drives, that are now legends. This type of camshaft drive was known in the Works as the *Duke of Argyll drive*. The drive was taken up the line of the barrels and across the heads, making a triangulated series of off-centre plates with

FRAZER NASH

counter balancing bobweights. The reason it was known as the *Duke of Argyll drive* was that the Duke of that time had had installed in his fields rubbing posts for his cattle and as the cows dropped their shoulders to rub against the posts they produced a strange off centre motion at the top of their bodies with their feet still. To Frazer-Nash and Godfrey therefore, to call this type of drive by the descriptive title of the *Duke of Argyll drive* was self evident.

The original 200 Mile Race engine was built and tested within three months of the Boulogne fiasco. It was officially named the *Akela* engine after Kipling's lone wolf but was known in the Works as the *I Swear* engine. The vertical shaft-drive camshaft growing out of the engine and bisecting the angle between the cylinders had at its peak a bevel box resembling a clenched fist in the traditional manner which witnesses are supposed to adopt before saying "I Swear" in court. The complexity of drive and the sophistication of the whole engine design showed that though the firm was in business making cyclecars, they were not going to compromise on the design of the engine for the 200 Mile Race. This race from the time it was proposed, excited the imaginations of the light car manufacturers, in the same way as the 1913 Amiens Cyclecar Grand Prix had done in earlier years. The engine was in fact a development of *Mowgli* using the same crankcase-crankshaft arrangement, except that the timing chest was much modified to accept a better design of flycrank housing and the bevel drive to the vertical camshaft drive; all these drives used splines, so that the problems of expansion and contraction could be overcome. The cylinder heads were a highly advanced pent-roof design of bronze with four valves and two sparking plugs.

The success of Frazer-Nash in winning the 1100cc class of the 200 Mile Race was the apogee of the firm's existence. He won the 1100cc class, averaging 71.54mph; he put in a last lap of 77.45mph.

During the early months of 1922 reconsideration was given to the sports-racing and racing engines. The 1921 developments with the *I Swear* engine and the chain driven overhead camshaft Vitesse engine were the prototypes for the 1922 season. The *Akela* engine was redesigned to have a single shaft drive to the overhead camshafts, up the line of the barrels, similar to the classic layout of 'cammy' Velocettes and Manx Nortons, but in GN vernacular the new *Akela* engines were also known as the V drive engines. The *Swear* engine had introduced side by side connecting rods and it was therefore a surprise that the V engines reverted to the traditional forked and plain connecting rod arrangement. The works engines rarely exceeded 3500rpm and failures in rods, whilst the firm was active, were almost

Run up to the start of the 1922 200 Mile Race. Car no. 1 is Hawkins with a lightweight youth, car no. 2 is Godfrey and Finch and car no. 3 is Frazer-Nash with Cushman about to submerge

200 Mile Race — Frazer-Nash driving whilst Cushman lies prone beneath the toneau cover

FRAZER NASH

Hawkins in his 200 Mile GN and Frazer-Nash in the 9ft 9in wheelbase 'Mowgli' powered with an Akela engine *National Motor Museum*

unknown; Godfrey believed that with the overhung crankshaft design the forked arrangement was better engineering. One of the weaknesses of the GN and Frazer-Nash companies and of all drivers of GNs and subsequently chain drive Frazer-Nashes, was that when the car was running well there was always a terrible tendency to prove it over and over again. Inevitably by the time a race came around the car was worn out! A classic example of this was in the 1922 200 mile event, which was further compounded by Frazer-Nash deciding at the last minute to try out some experimental pistons. The race started splendidly with Frazer-Nash averaging 78.78mph for a standing start 50 mile record with Cushman lying prone beside him on a mattress - shortly after this a piston collapsed. Frazer-Nash with Cushman changed a piston in 42 minutes, which was excellent going and still finished the race, at an average speed of 62mph; however, the Salmson team were miles an hour faster than the GNs and Marcel Benoist had averaged 81.88mph to win; but Godfrey, Hawkins and Frazer-Nash finished third, fourth and fifth to the Salmsons, to win the Team Prize. It was Frazer-Nash's mechanic, Cushman, who should have been awarded a cup, for Frazer-Nash noticed in the regulations that they did not say

THE RACING GNs

The greatest GN Special exponent of them all (Frazer Nash on the bonnet), Basil Davenport wheels up 'Spider' for a record breaking run at Shelsley in the late 1920s

anything about the passenger having to sit upright by the driver. Frazer-Nash did not accept Cushman's reply "Neither does it say that the passenger has to be alive".

In 1921 the firm experimented with a half way design of engine, intended as a sports racer and was indicative of the direction that Godfrey and Frazer-Nash thought was the way for the firm to go. The simple Vitesse engine of 1919, with its push rod operated overhead valves, was to be supplanted with an engine that would be cheap to build but with chain driven overhead camshafts, as advanced a design as any engine on the market. The prototype running in 1921 had a bronze nearside and cast iron offside cylinder heads, but for 1922 they were both made in iron. A perfectly hemispherical cylinder head with twin valves coupled with a crankcase and crankshaft of *Akela* standard was of an advanced enough design to satisfy anybody and it was also remarkably cheap to build in quantity. The whole history of the GN company is plagued with 'might have beens', but if the company had produced sports racing GNs, powered with such an engine, then they could not have failed to have been a success.

FRAZER NASH

"Those extra horses."

IN some cars, the speed attainable in comfort & safety is limited by the suspension long before the engine is "all out," but in the case of the G.N., the cars hold the road so well that, fast as they are, many an owner would welcome still more power and speed.

So that the desired extra power may be conveniently imparted to these cars, a complete set of parts has been prepared which can be fitted easily by any Agent or, if preferred, at our Works.

The design of these cylinder heads, and valve gear, is based on the experience gained with several different forms of combustion chamber on the same engine.

In the conversion set, the valves are not inclined, but are set parallel, a design which simplifies the valve gear, and increases its life.

The combustion chambers are so shaped as to present a minimum wall area.

The valve guides are extended to receive the lower portion of the hardened valve collar, thus relieving the valve of the side thrust which is always present when rockers are used.

This prevents wear on valve stem and consequent air leakage.

In our experience valve breakage with overhead valves on G.N's. is very unusual, but when it has occurred it has almost invariably been at the collar, (or cotters where these were used).

Should breakage occur here, with the Frazer Nash system it is impossible for the valve to drop into the cylinder. Double valve springs are used, thus avoiding many troubles due to high speeds.

The rocker gear is an exceptionally sound job; the rockers themselves have very large bearings, properly lubricated, with a wick-feed carrying lubricant to the push rod ball end.

The push rods themselves are very light and rigid, being tubular, with spherical solid ends.

Owing largely to the care in design in these details, after conversion to the Frazer Nash system of overhead valves, the engine is generally quieter than before.

A list of the parts included in the Standard Set, price £25, is given on the next page. Also of the 1923 set, price £27.

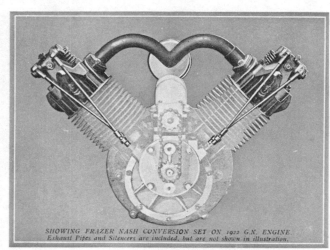

SHOWING FRAZER NASH CONVERSION SET ON 1922 G.N. ENGINE.
Exhaust Pipes and Silencers are included, but are not shown in illustration.

'Those Extra Horses' — The GN shares with the Mini the unique advantage that the engine output could be doubled, or even trebled and no chassis tuning was required to improve road holding

The Plus-Power 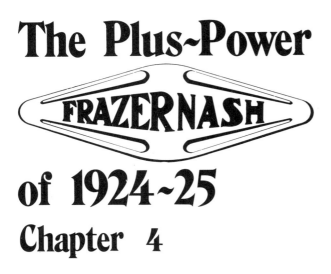 of 1924-25
Chapter 4

ARCHIE FRAZER-NASH opened up in business on his own at 102 London Road, Kingston-upon-Thames (the site in recent years has been redeveloped), and negotiated firstly with Black and later with Walter Laffan, a trading relationship between himself and GN in order to manufacture and sell the Frazer Nash-GN. GN had ceased selling the cahin drive GNs in late 1922, though there was a thriving spares business; hence there was no difficulty in coming to an agreement. Frazer-Nash knew, by Easter of 1923, that there was no possibility of selling Frazer Nash GNs, since a road test of this car had brought in very few enquiries. The reasoning that Frazer-Nash applied to this lack of response, was that it was because the car was still called a GN; which damned it in the eyes of large parts of the motor trade. The GN, the Morgan and the Trojan were all regarded as suspect, and sizeable parts of the motor trade would not have any of these three cars on their premises, preferring such cars as Calthorpe, Bayliss Thomas, Clyno, Rhode and others, that were no doubt worthy motor cars, but on no account could be labelled as important. Frazer-Nash tried again in 1923 with another touring model, which in this case used Deemster chassis which he had bodied by Loves of Kingston and fitted with a Frazer Nash radiator badge. Frazer-Nash thought that the sales could not have exceeded a dozen. Not exactly a success.

A further development that seemed logical at the end of 1922, was to market an overhead valve conversion kit for the thousands of GNs and Rover 8s, running on the roads at that time. A catalogue was published

FRAZER NASH

entitled 'Thoses Extra Horses', but this did not lead to any real sales of the kit, since the GN had gone from being a production car, through obsolescence to being obsolete in approximately eight months - by mid 1923 the GN was dead. Though people might buy parts to keep the car running, they certainly did not part with their money for upgrading purposes. Rover 8 owners were not noted for their competitiveness and consequently the conversion kit was promoted on the improvement to top gear performance and hill climbing at speed; the car ran out of road worthiness a long time before the maximum speed of the converted car could be established - so the *Light Car* implied without actually saying it in so many words. Frazer-Nash's 'entrepreneurism' was not rewarded and Europe's first 'bolt-on-goodie' manufacturer achieved the results of so many pioneers in being ahead of his time.

Frazer-Nash had set up his own firm with one intention and that was to make a high grade sports car, not only for the satisfaction of doing so, but also to do what he and Godfrey had said so many times that GN should have done. He wanted to see if all the ideas that had been discussed when they were together in the GN days, were commercially viable. Walter Laffan was approached in mid 1923 by Frazer-Nash, in a further attempt to produce a stop-gap car, to see if selected GN parts could be purchased at advantageous prices and this was soon negotiated. Frazer-Nash placed Ruby engines into GN chassis. The only fittings, which were not GN, were the Rudge Whitworth hubs and wheels and the Frazer Nash radiator badge; for 1924 these cars were fitted with a Frazer Nash radiator. This 1100cc car was a splendid small car, the engine was delightfully smooth and high revving. The word refined was linked with a GN chassis for the first time presumably refined in relationship to what had gone before! The drawback was the limited performance, since the engine in its standard tune gave less than 30 horse-power and to achieve the maximum rated horse-power of 39, involved a racing specification. Brian Lewis was an early purchaser, as also was J.A. Hall and both competed widely in their cars.

All through 1923, and the first half of 1924, Frazer-Nash was working towards the launching of the new car; practically every component was redesigned, since the idea was to leave the cyclecar image behind, but at the same time to offer exceptional value for the performance offered. All of these changes consumed a lot of time. The real question mark in the design of the car was the engine that was to be used. The Plus-Power engine became available at exactly the right moment and offered to Frazer-Nash the specification that he required of a 1500cc engine of sporting design. The brief life of the Plus-Power Engine Company was at variance with one of

THE PLUS-POWER FRAZER NASH OF 1924-25

Brian Lewis competing at Boulogne in 1925 with a Ruby engined Frazer Nash

Frazer-Nash's dictums - "Any fool can design an engine, but it takes a clever man to design a good chassis"; there were many difficulties in producing reliable engines from the very beginning of prototype manufacture. This was only to be expected, but Gustave Maclure had high standards and the possibility that things might go wrong was foreign to his soul. The development problems were never really ironed out, since the order book for the engines with only Frazer-Nash, Horstman and Hodgson as the only users, was so limited. There were never the funds for development.

The *Motor*, *Autocar* and *Light Car* and *Cycle-Car* featured the new model. The *Autocar* was typical of the motoring press in saying: 'From the extent of Mr Frazer-Nash's exploits in the racing field, it is natural that any car for which he is responsible would be one which gives a very high performance for its size and weight'.

The features of the new car were recorded by the motoring press:
(a) 'The clutch was modified for lighter pressure and also that there was no end thrust on the engine'.

This was the Frazer Nash clutch with which, with very few exceptions, all cars were fitted, and had as its main feature a laminated spring steel shock absorber. This allowed a certain amount of engine and prop-shaft movement relative to one another; consequently less spring tension was needed and much less finesse on operating the clutch, when getting away from rest. The GN clutch was a brutal in and out affair, when the coil spring was highly tensioned for racing starts. This GN clutch was resuscitated in later years by

FRAZER NASH

AFN for the Nurburg, the Single Seater and other out-and-out works competition cars. It was in those later days known as the 'racing' clutch.

(b) 'Universal joint between the propshaft and the bevel box'.
(c) 'Spiral bevel gears with ball-thrust bearings for the bevel box'.
(d) 'Torque reaction taken in a slightly different manner'.
(e) 'A very ingenious cam-plate mechanism has been evolved to make it impossible to mesh two gears at once'.

It is these four modifications, that collectively made one of the most important changes from the GN. The fitting of a fabric universal joint, in front of the bevel box, was a major advance in the quest for smoothness, but the cotton construction of the fabric-rubber universal made it necessary for the Works racers to be fitted with a special contrivance, a knacker-catcher, which was a split piece of wood, located around the prop-shaft with a clearance hole. The works racing GNs had been known to have the pole vaulting accident, if the clutch broke up then there was always the possibility that the front end of the prop-shaft would drop onto the ground. The superior design of the Frazer Nash clutch meant that there was no necessity to mount a strap across the chassis beneath the prop-shaft, as had been fitted to some racing GNs, but for the Frazer Nash cars it was not unknown to have the fabric coupling disintegrate and then for the prop-shaft to flail around, beneath the seats. Miss Gleed, later to be Mrs Tommy Wisdom, enquired of Tommy Randall, one of the Works fitters, "Why wasn't her car fitted with a knacker-catcher".

A 3.5 to 1 spiral bevel crown wheel and pinion was supplied by ENV Ltd of thirty-five teeth mating to ten teeth, and the bevel box casing was cut away at the top to mount the oil-filler plate and the pivot for the 'ingenious cam-plate'; this was also known as the inter-locking plate and in later years as the 'wriggly monkey'. The torque reaction of the GNs prop-shaft was taken by the bearings in the chassis, holding the bevel shaft in position, and the bevel box literally floated in the chassis; whereas Archie Frazer-Nash used the cross-member across the chassis at this point to secure the nose of the bevel box casing by means of a U-bolt. Consequently, self aligning bearings in the bevel shaft chassis-bearing housings could be used and the bearings lasted considerably longer.

(f) 'The conical bearings of the GN in the back axle replaced by substantial ball bearings'.
(g) 'Springs re-designed for front and rear axles'.
(h) 'Stronger front axle of new design'.

These three modifications were inter-related. Since the springs were

THE PLUS-POWER FRAZER NASH OF 1924-25

fifty per cent wider at 1¾in, there was more room to fit bigger bearings in the rear axle radius arm housings, and with the weight of the four-cylinder, water-cooled Plus-Power engine, stronger springs were needed to the front axle which necessitated in their turn a stronger front axle of 1¾in diameter. Since the springs were wider, so the top and bottom flanges of the chassis were widened to take them.

(i)   'Stub axles completely re-designed'.

The Rudge-Whitworth wheel and hub were much heavier than the GN design, but in every other respect, particularly with regard to safety, they were infinitely preferable. The front axle still looked like a GN axle, being perfectly straight with no front wheel brakes and with the 'U' ends (Elliott type). To quote, in this instance from *The Autocar,* on the stub axles '... with proper thrust washers, and the bearings have been increased in size and made more durable'. This statement could hardly have been more damning of the GN cyclecar design concept for keeping the wheels running true and on the axles.

(j)   'Hartford shock absorbers fitted to the front axle'.

Shock absorbers were fitted to the rear axle from September 1925 as an optional extra; not until 1927 were they a standard fitting.

The early Frazer Nashes had a three-speed transmission with reverse, mostly with the ratios 3.8, 5.4 and 10 to 1, with a reverse of 12 to 1, though second gear was often 7 to 1, and with this went a bottom gear of 12.5. These wider gear ratios were for those who were 'go anywhere' motorists, and not, by the firm's standards, too competitively minded. The first car had gear ratios of 3.5, 6.0 and 11.5 to 1.

The first catalogue published in late 1924 for the 1925 cars included the following under the heading of 'Change Speed': 'The change speed gear of the Frazer Nash is one of the outstanding features of the car, and although slightly more expensive than the conventional gearbox has such advantages that its extra cost is fully justified. The disadvantages of the sliding gearbox have come to be regarded, through general use, as necessary evils; amongst these are the difficulty of changing gear at high speed, with consequent liability of damage to the gear teeth (coupled with difficulty of replacement when a gear has been damaged), noise, and double loss of efficiency when not in top gear. Of these disadvantages, skilful mastery of the gear change reduces the risk of damage, but noise and double loss of efficiency when not in top gear remain. On this account many cars are geared on top below their most efficient ratio, to minimise the use of other gears; on the Frazer Nash, however, the gear can be changed with ease and certainty at any speed ...'.

FRAZER NASH

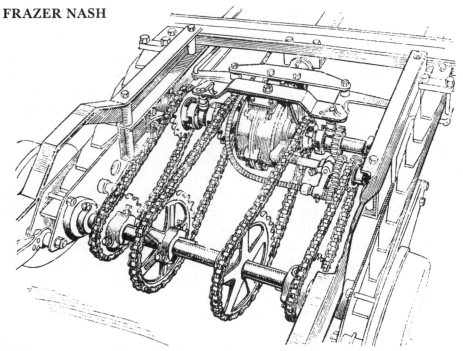

The three speed transmission with reverse. The admirals walk and speedometer drive can be seen
Autocar

The Plus-Power engine

THE PLUS-POWER FRAZER NASH OF 1924-25

The first Frazer Nash. Registration number PD 3103, chassis no. 1012 *Autocar*

Photograph is from the same article as the previous photograph. The radiator being in line with the front axle indicates that it is an earlier car *Autocar*

FRAZER NASH

The new Frazer Nash was available as the Fast Tourer and the Super Sports; these two names indicated the degree of engine chassis tune rather than the bodywork fitted, whereas the body shape depended on whether the car was ordered as a Two Seater or a Three/Four Seater. Frazer Nash model names were always confusing. From the beginning until the end of production of the chain drive cars in 1939, it was almost always the chassis specification that determined the model name as far as the works were concerned, but to the majority of owners it was the body specification that was important. Since, from 1926 onwards there was no attempt to use separate names for the two specifications there has been confusion ever since.

By 1925 there was a further variant available of the Three Seater, which meant that the bodywork at the rear was within the width of the rear mudguards and this diminution of width by some two inches reduced the seating from a Three/Four Seater to a Three Seater. The Two Seater was described: 'The body is of stream-line form, boat-shaped at the back. The panels are of polished aluminium mounted on rigid ash framework; the interior, as well as the seats, being upholstered in red. The seats are staggered slightly, and are remarkably comfortable. The locker at the rear will accommodate a suitcase in addition to the usual tool equipment. The wings are of beaten aluminium. The 'V' windscreen is metal-framed and rigidly mounted. The hood covered in black material, joins the screen with a simple clip attachment'.

A door on the passenger's side was a feature of the Three/Four Seater body which had a rounded tail and this feature was to become known as the 'Fallen Woman' or the 'African's Belly'.

A CAV starter motor and a large battery were included in the specification of the less expensive Fast Tourer model, though not in the Super Sports. Of the Super Sports it was noted: 'In order to reduce dead weight in this model the electric starting is omitted, thus saving not only the weight of the starter motor, and its details, but enabling also a small battery to be used. If required, a self-starter can be supplied as an extra'. This extra cost £15.

The catalogue under the heading of 'with standard equipment' listed the following:

Fast Tourer		Super Sports	
2 Seater	3/4 Seater	2 Seater	3/4 Seater
£285	£300	£330	£345

During 1924 and early 1925 the headlights were mounted separately from the wings. The bracing stays from the cast aluminium shell of the radiator to the aluminium wings were standard

The Vee tailed body was standard to all two seater bodies

The rounded tail or 'Africans belly' were standard to the 3 or 3/4 seater bodies. This yellow car with black wings was fitted with Whitehead front wheel brakes, to the special order of Brian Lewis

There was a further range of extras which included £12 for painting a car to the customer's colour requirements (the standard cars were in polished aluminium), and £20 for front wheel brakes.

The first announcement in the press of the model's prices was in October 1924; the Standard Two Seater and the Standard Three/Four Seater at £295 and the Super Sports Two Seater at £330. The Fast Tourer model was alternatively named the Standard. Frazer Nash Ltd started off in the way they were destined to carry on, with a plethora of model names. The cars delivered in November, December and January of 1924-1925 had the following model names: Standard Fast Tourer, 1925 Frazer Nash, 1925 Super Sports, Fast Tourer Three/Four Seater, Fast Tourer Three Seater, Super Sports Three Seater, Standard Three Seater.

The catalogue also said: 'Amongst those who appreciate the open road are many who ask that a car, in addition to being a useful and economical means of transport, shall be something more - something that will give the joys of real speed and power. Several well-known makers supply special models which satisfy this demand, but the cost, both initially and in running expenses, has been far beyond the reach of many ... The new model has been modified to give greater comfort, improved springing and silence without sacrificing the magnificent performance of which these cars are capable. From their continuous success in competition an impression may exist that the Frazer Nash car is intended mainly for the sporting enthusiast. It actually has this appeal, but the new model is equally intended for everyday use, and is particularly suitable for those who have to cover long distances quickly, with or without passengers ...'.

THE PLUS-POWER FRAZER NASH OF 1924-25

Frazer-Nash was always captioned as 'genial as ever'. He is sitting at the wheel of 'Rikki-Tikki', the Works racing car with the Plus-Power engine. The hand pump was to pressurise the fuel tank and was a standard fitting to all competitive Frazer Nashes

Archie Frazer-Nash said that he never sat down with a clean sheet of paper to design a motor car, since at all times there were the constraints of the materials and components that were available - which for obvious reasons had to be used. The motor car that he was designing was going to recognise its parentage; the components, that had proved to be satisfactory in the past, were to be used again. The main item of continuity was in the manner of the car's going, or as it is expressed nowadays - roadholding. The manner of its going was a summation of many items. The differential less rear axle was not detectable to the normal motorist; it was not until cornering speeds became high that the lack of a differential became noticeable. The modern limited slip differential is superior, but the widespread use of narrow tyre sections of the twenties, combined with a solid back axle, offered the best solution. The original beaded edge tyres were 700 x 80 (say 325 x 19 in modern terms), in the later twenties, the advent of the well-based wheel, the size had been changed to 27 x 4 (say 400 x 19) and in the thirties to 27 x 4.40 (say 450 x 19). The high geared steering that Frazer Nash designed to operate full lock to full lock, using only three quarters of a turn of the steering wheel was a fast ratio, so that any tendency for the rear tyres to break away at racing speeds could be easily caught; on more conventional cars with an adequate

FRAZER NASH

steering lock the ratio would have been a whole turn. The fast precise steering aligned with the certainty of knowledge of what the rear wheels were doing, aligned with very firm springing, was a direct continuation of GN practice. *The Autocar* road tested, in 1937, a short chassis Blackburne TT Replica and in that road test there was written the following which was entirely true for all Frazer Nash chain drive cars, and though this was written in 1937, it is as true now in the 1970s, as it was also true in the early 1920s.

The Frazer Nash itself, as entirely distinct from the BMW with which the name has more recently become connected, is in the fullest measure the diehard enthusiast's car. It can give the sheer joy of driving, performance and handling as it does, and becomes almost a living entity under the driver's exact control. He feels a rare mastery over the machine, and over the road itself.

In the course of the years the main design has not altered appreciably, and the car retains its chain drive from a countershaft, one stout chain for each ratio, whilst a variety of engines is available. The car tested had a twin overhead camshaft six-cylinder unit of 1½ litre capacity.

From the first moment of reacquaintance with the make after a long interval, its remarkable personality impresses itself upon one. It is so completely the true, 'no frills' sports machine, and is either liked better than any other for certain major qualities or rejected as 'impossible', according to the point of view.

One does not need to drive at anywhere near the maximum to obtain a striking average speed, for this car can maintain practically a set rate. That figure can be between 60 and 70mph on a main road, there being no need to slacken appreciably for bends, and the car holds speed just as the driver wishes up gradients. Third can always be used as an alternative to top, even for several miles on end, as over a winding or up-and-down section, or, again, for high-speed passing. Owing to the closeness of the ratios, and the revving powers of the engine, there is about the same maximum on third as on top gear.

An outstanding point is the steering, which is higher geared than on any other production car today, needing less than one turn (almost exactly 7/8) from lock to lock. It is phenomenally quick in response to the wheel, and also has strong caster return action. In ordinary driving the car is hardly steered at all in the literal sense; slight pressure one way or the other on the wheel takes it round curves, accurately to an inch or two and close in to the road edge. There is not the barest hint of heeling over or the springs giving, however fast a turn is entered, and it feels as if, short of striking something, the Frazer Nash could not be turned over.

The shock absorbers had not been tightened before this record breaking run at Brooklands Test Hill. Frazer-Nash narrowly avoided an accident on touch down

'Rikki-Tikki' brought out of retirement in June of 1928 to open Greenford Speedway Track. One of the very few photographs showing Aldington and Frazer-Nash together. Aldington was one of the earliest users of a crash helmet

FRAZER NASH

It goes almost without saying that the driving position is all it should be, the big spring-spoked wheel being in a position to give the driver full power, whilst he can see both wings and judge matters exactly.

A point that has much to do with the general characteristics is the high, close gear ratios, all direct drives, and all equally quiet. Gear changing, by engaging dogs, is about as rapid as it can be, too, up or down.

It is perfectly normal on this machine to change without using the clutch, though a technique of its own is needed to avoid snatch. Given that, the gears almost 'fall' in. The gear lever is not only a right-hand one, but is placed outside the body, as also is the hand brake, of fly-off type.

It cannot be denied that the steering is heavy for a full lock turn and in manoeuvring, but this fact, and a heavy clutch spring action, too, are taken as part and parcel of a machine which can scarcely be judged by ordinary standards.

The Autocar in September 1925 road tested a Standard Three Seater and the Road Test was captioned 'High Speed at Low Cost' and sub-titled 'The performance of a £1000 sports car for £315'. H.J. Aldington's theory was that there were only a limited number of people available who had the cash to buy sports cars and he, as the sales manager, said "this years customers may well be down the road next year buying the competitors cars". Archie Frazer-Nash, when asked in the late nineteen fifties if he believed that he might have sold Frazer Nashes too cheaply, said that he thought it was possible. By selling them at too low a price people might have thought that the cars were tarred with the cyclecar brush. The thought that he might have sold just as many cars, if the price had been twice as high, worried him a lot!

The Boulogne
Chapter 5

THE PLUS-POWER ENGINE Company went into liquidation and Frazer-Nash considered using the Alvis 12/50 engine. He was not serious, as he considered the engine to be grossly overweight and was not too concerned when Alvis said no. He was far more interested in the new Meadows 4ED engine and went to Fallings Park in Wolverhampton to discuss the design; he thought the crank was too massive and the engine overweight. Therefore there was only one engine he could use - the Anzani side valve four cylinder engine; this engine had been designed by Gustave Maclure, prior to his forming the Plus-Power Engine Company.

The fitting of a side valve engine to a sports car, seemed to be a retrograde step, but within a short time both Frazer-Nash and Aldington, the sales manager, not only accepted the engine but were both advocates for it. The Anzani was a brilliant light weight design, in which reliability was linked with whatever stage of tune was specified.

Thistlewayte approached Frazer-Nash in early 1925 and said that he wanted a special car to be built for the Boulogne Grand Prix and that Clive Gallop would be the driver. There were no restrictions on the cost, but it was particularly specified that four wheel brakes were to be fitted. The Boulogne circuit featured two hairpin corners, that were at the ends of long down hill straights. One of the first Plus-Power cars had been fitted with Whitehead front wheel brakes and Archie Frazer-Nash had found that they had not affected the road holding at all and therefore one of his questions, "What do you want four wheel brakes for?" - was no longer asked.

FRAZER NASH

Aldington wearing a hat views the start of body building, at Martin Walter's in Folkestone, of Clive Gallop's car for the Boulogne Grand Prix. Completely drilled chassis were very rare *Autocar*

The two cars to be built for the 1925 Boulogne Grand Prix were to the same standards. Lowered chassis with highly tuned Anzani's to run on pump fuel, slim bodies and full undertrays along the length of the car. Excessive lightening of body components was to be avoided, as the Boulogne circuit was notoriously bumpy.

The main differences in respect to the earlier cars were as follows:
(a) Ten inch diameter front wheel brakes of Rubery manufacture were fitted (Alford and Adler type) with their Perrot operating shafts.

These were a very efficient mechanically operated proprietary braking system, and were fitted to many cars of their time, eg the Morris Cowley. This system of FWB was to be fitted to all chain drive Frazer Nashes, with the exception of some cars in the later thirties, which were fitted with the Shelsley System.
(b) The new front axle with its downward curved centre section.

This axle was from this time onwards to become the traditional Nash axle, and its curved centre section allowed the starting handle clearance over the axle.
(c) Lowered chassis of 8ft wheelbase.

THE BOULOGNE

The chassis was lowered by the simple Frazer Nash expedient of placing tapered wedges between the springs and the chassis. This splendidly simple modification was to remain standard practice, up to the finish of production. The eight-foot wheelbase was not standard, as it was only used for very few of the early racers; the standard wheelbase being 8ft 9in, with a few cars at 8ft 6in and a very few at 8ft 3in. Each of the two specially built Boulogne cars had what was known as a 'liberally drilled' chassis frame.

(d)   Nickel-silver radiators.

Before this the radiators had as their outer shell a cast aluminium housing. This, when new, was a delight, but tended to pit and deteriorate rapidly in appearance. Nickel-silver skinned radiators were fitted, which were standard to many cars of the time.

(e)   No running boards.

It was not until 1928 when the new Super Sports were introduced that the running board cars became non-standard, and Boulogne specification cars sold in 1926 and 1927 were in many instances fitted with running boards.

Thistlethwayte had his local coachbuilding firm, Martin Walter of Folkestone, body his car - whilst the works car was entrusted to the normal coachbuilder, Loves of Kingston. The bodies of the two cars were both similar in appearance, though the Thistlethwayte car was slightly narrower across the seats.

Four Frazer Nashes were entered for the Boulogne Grand Prix of 1925. This race was for cars up to 1500cc capacity and had two classes, up to 650Kg and 500Kg. The organisers obviously thought that the heavier class, le Grand Prix des Voitures Legeres, would be the fastest and the 500Kg class, the Boulogne Grand Prix des Voiturettes, started behind the 650Kg class. The two Anzani cars of Gallop and Frazer-Nash were supplemented by Brian Lewis's Frazer Nash and Ringwood's Frazer Nash. Ringwood's car was a 200-mile 'GN'! Lewis's car was one of the 1923 Ruby engined cars of 1100cc capacity, which Lewis had been racing under the name of the 'Rodeo Special'. The previous night to the Grand Prix, Lewis and Brian Eyston completely stripped, rebuilt, repainted in green and renamed the car a Frazer Nash 'so as to fully uphold the honour of Britain' *(The Motor)*.

Gallop, on the opening lap of the triangular 37 kilometre course, broke all records for the circuit and got close to 100mph on the St Omer Road. He lost six-and-a-half minutes changing sparking plugs, and this enabled B.S. Marshall to go into the lead on his Brescia Bugatti. Frazer Nash disappeared on the third lap and came clattering up to the pits without a tyre on the offside front wheel. He had pulled two tyres off their rims whilst

Clive Gallop with Harold Scott surveying the field: Ringwood gets ready to start the 200 Mile GN for the 1925 Boulogne Grand Prix

Ringwood gets a good start with Gallop, Lewis and Frazer-Nash behind. On the far left at the back is Marshall's Brescia Bugatti

Archie Frazer-Nash loses two tyres off the rims in the race

Clive Gallop and Harold Scott savour the delights of victory

FRAZER NASH

Archie Frazer-Nash and Johnstone outside the Works in Kingston upon Thames, after their return from Boulogne

cornering too energetically and lost seventy-five minutes. He cheerfully remarked that he could do 75mph on the rims, as *The Motor* reported. From the fifth lap onwards it was a race between Marshall and Gallop who was to finish first on the road, irrespective of the fact that they were in two different races. Marshall was in the lead by 5 minutes 19 seconds and by the seventh lap the time had decreased to 2 minutes 26 seconds. Marshall refuelled on the sixth lap and Gallop on the eighth lap (taking 42 seconds) and when he restarted was 3 minutes 13 seconds behind Marshall. At the end of the ninth lap the gap had decreased to 2 minutes 22 seconds and at the tenth to 2 minutes 14 seconds. On the eleventh lap the lap record was again broken by Gallop with a speed of 109.57 kilometres per hour (67.72mph) and he was only 1 minute 53 seconds behind. From the pits he was properly

The catalogue illustrations of the Boulogne Vitesse

Per Nas, the winner of the 1928 award for the most successful racing car in Sweden. He won most of the races on the frozen lakes with his supercharged Anzani Boulogne Vitesse

R. L. Bellamy in an Inter Varsity trial in the thirties, where a supercharged car would tend to be at a disadvantage *W. J. Brunell, National Motor Museum*

Aldington demonstrates the performance of a £1000 car for £315

Mamie Frazer-Nash and Kit Burt in a Concours d'Elegance during the Boulogne Speed Week of 1926

FRAZER NASH

The four seater Touring specification, note the depth of the coachwork and the size of the door

advised that it was hopeless and he finally finished the race 1 minute and 53 seconds behind Marshall. They finished at respectively 103.5 and 102.5 kilometres per hour average speeds, which speeds were approximately 20 kilometres faster than the previous year's race. There was every reason for the British in the tribunes to give two rousing sets of three cheers for the two drivers, as reported by *L'Auto*. Gallop won 500 Francs and his mechanic, whose name was reported as Iscottis, but in reality H.R. Scott, won 250 Francs. This was a splendid performance by the Frazer Nashes and H.R. Scott's finest hour, for he was Frazer-Nash's right hand man as well as being the chief draughtsman for the firm and he had personally organised the entry for the race and the preparation of the two new cars.

Charles Faroux wrote in the 30 August of 1925 issue of *L'Auto*, the *Sporting Life* of France, that Gallop's record breaking lap was 'Absoluement stupefiant' for such a size of car. The race averages for the two races and

THE BOULOGNE

A 1925 installation of an Anzani with the petrol tank in the scuttle, note that the filler is immediately above the exhaust manifold

Gallop's record were so much in advance of any race that had gone before, as to make a new dimension. They also surpassed the speeds of the prestigious Coupe Georges Boillot, which was up to that time the fastest and most important race of the Boulogne Speed Week.

The team prize was donated by Francis Pickett, a director of Frazer Nash Limited and the uncrowned King of Boulogne, as he had held the rights to the demolition of the Calais-Marck war time ammunition dumps. The Pickett Cup which had been won in previous years by both GN and Frazer Nash teams was once again obtained as Ringwood and Frazer Nash finished third and fifth in the 650Kg class.

The Boulogne chassis was listed by the Works prior to the 1925 race, but it was not until the end of 1926, that the Boulogne Vitesse model was available; this model, alternatively known as the Boulogne Special, could be bought in supercharged form with a Number 8 Cozette. The firm never sold a Boulogne Special and consequently the specification is a trifle vague. It is clear that any chassis fitted with the H.E. (high efficiency) Anzani engine (the highest power rated unsupercharged Anzani) was always known as a Boulogne, irrespective of whether it had a two, three or three/four seater body. If this seems too confusing then it should be said that trying to apply

Ivy Cummings in a JCC High Speed Reliability Trial at Brooklands

Peter Gibson replaces a broken rear axle on the Brenner Pass *D. S. Jenkinson*

'Mowgli' wearing its Boulogne Speed Week racing number, whilst competing at Shelsley Walsh a fortnight later in 1926, with Frazer-Nash driving

'The Terror' immediately after purchase by Dick Nash

FRAZER NASH

Many running board cars were modernised in the late twenties and thirties. John Bolster had this 1927 car rebodied after a crash. The aluminium wings and running boards were replaced with more modern style steel wings

logic to the classification of Frazer Nash chassis names, let alone the body styles, is difficult.

1925 was an important year in other respects. Archie Frazer-Nash had to look for larger premises and in crossing London Road in Kingston-upon-Thames he amalgamated with William G. Thomas to form W.G. Thomas and Frazer Nash Limited, increasing the floor space available for production ten fold. This change, combined with the tooling and pattern changes in converting to using the Anzani, used up his remaining capital. By the end of 1925 it was clear that the Frazer Nash car was not going to sell at the rate of hundreds annually and consequently there was no need for a nationwide list of agents. Thence forward there was a marked reluctance to offer agency terms to the motor trade.

1925 and 1926 were the peak production years of the Frazer Nash, a steady order book and a production of a car per week was seemingly

THE BOULOGNE

The Works at Kingston in 1928

satisfactory. In fact there was not sufficient cash flow and though the firm seemingly prospered for two years there was little ready cash. When Thomas left and wanted money out of the firm, he then placed Frazer-Nash in an invidious position.

The most popular Frazer Nash was the Three to Four Seater body design, which was fitted to all standards of chassis. The running boards were especially useful, not only for picnics but as work benches. On the driver's side of the car there tended to be placed the battery box and sometimes a tool box; the passengers' side of the car normally carried the spare wheel, in a well, on the running board. The Anzani engined Kingston design, with the rounded African Belly, reached its peak of refinement in 1927 with the fitting of the four speed and reverse transmission. It was not until 1928, that the Works had sufficient faith in this reverse mechanism to recommend its fitting to all customer cars; a brisk business then developed of converting

THE SUPER SPORTS.

3 SEATER MODEL.

ENGINE.—Four cylinder monobloc. 69 mm. bore by 100 mm. stroke. Capacity 1496 c.c. R.A.C. rating 11.9 h.p. Tax £12. Detachable cylinder head. Compression ratio 5.4 to 1. Side by side valves in special cobalt steel. 65 lb. valve springs in aero quality steel. Valve ports cleaned out. Three bearing crankshaft. Forced feed lubrication throughout. Thermo-syphon cooling. 35 m.m. Solex carburettor. Ignition by B.T.H. magneto. Revolution indicator drive arranged positively from engine. Dynamo skew driven from engine. Electric starter flange mounted. Engine develops 47 b.h.p. at 4,000 r.p.m.

TRANSMISSION.—Dry three plate clutch. Tubular clutch shaft with ball centred Hardy joint. Spiral bevels. Final drive by chains with dog clutch engagement. All gears direct. Right-hand control.

SPRINGS.—Quarter Elliptic front and rear. All braking and cornering torque taken by radius rods on both axles. Hartford shock absorbers to both axles.

BRAKES.—Internal expanding on all four wheels. Foot control to front and rear. Hand control to rear.

WHEELS.—Rudge Whitworth triple spoked, detachable, with 27" × 4" Well Base Dunlop tyres.

DIMENSIONS.—Wheelbase 8' 9". Track 3' 7". Ground clearance 7½".

BODY.—Polished aluminium. Front seats adjustable. Back seat for two children or one adult. Interior and seats upholstered in best quality real leather. Pneumatic cushions. Two panel flat windscreen, or V-screen optional if specially required. Hood covers all three seats. Black hood cover. Wings of beaten aluminium.

EQUIPMENT includes—Speedometer, revolution indicator, C.A.V. five lamp lighting set and starter, complete tool kit, spare wheel and tyre, etc.

SPEED.—80 m.p.h.   PETROL CONSUMPTION.—35-40 m.p.g.

PRICE.—With three speeds and reverse, £390 ; with four speeds and reverse, £410.

---

4 SEATER MODEL.

ENGINE AND CHASSIS.—Specification similar to Super Sports three seater (above).

BODY.—Polished aluminium. Sliding front seats. Wide door on near side. Body wider than three seater, with higher sides, scuttle and radiator. Interior and seats upholstered in best quality real leather. Pneumatic cushions. Hand brake and gear lever inside body. Two-panel flat windscreen. Hood covers all four seats. Black hood envelope. Side curtains. Wings of beaten aluminium.

EQUIPMENT includes—Speedometer, revolution indicator, C.A.V. five lamp lighting set and starter, complete tool kit, spare wheel and tyre, etc.

SPEED.—75 m.p.h.   PETROL CONSUMPTION.—35 m.p.g.

PRICE.—With three speeds and reverse, £435 ; with four speeds and reverse, £455.

From the 1926 and 1927 catalogue. The three seater style and the four seater models can be seen in the Brenner Pass photograph on page 82, and on page 80

The four speed transmission showing the double dog selected in a mesh for first gear *J. Hebbard*

THE BOULOGNE

earlier models to the four forward speeds and reverse specification. The standard ratios, if such a word can be applied, of the four forward speeds were soon established. The 10 to 1 bottom gear used a 14 tooth sprocket driving a 40 tooth sprocket, which when combined with the gearing of the 3.5 to 1 crown wheel and pinion, gave the ratio. This high bottom gear was the recommendation from the Works, but a lot of motorists found this difficult to accept, since the more conventional cars of the time tended to have a 16 to 1 bottom gear and ratios of up to 20 to 1 were not uncommon. Archie Frazer-Nash and Aldington could and did explain that the conversion of power by chain drive was highly efficient and that conventional car gearboxes, especially in the low ratios, were extremely inefficient, with only a fraction of the power getting to the back axle; for those that could not be converted, and for the trials drivers, there was the 'ultra low' bottom gear of 11.75 (14 teeth to 47 teeth). The second gear of 7 to 1 (17 teeth to 34 teeth) was also used for reverse; when selecting reverse a further cumulative reduction was made by the meshing of the straight cut teeth. The third gear of 4.75 (22 teeth to 30 teeth) was with second gear almost a standard fitting. Top gear for the Anzani engined car was invariably 3.8 to 1, the only exceptions being the supercharged Boulogne Vitesses, with a ratio of 3.5 to 1 (24 teeth driving 24 teeth).

Archie Frazer-Nash had abandoned *Rikki-Tikki* as the Works racing car at the time of the change from the Plus-Power to the Anzani. He experimented with a super-charged Anzani engine; he was not over sanguine that the power and reliability would be as evident as Gustave Maclure, now back again with Anzanis, and H.R. Scott said it would. *Mowgli's* engine had been sold to Basil Davenport for use in the *Spider,* so the chassis of *Mowgli* was shortened and fitted with Rudge Whitworth wheels, and fitted with chain driven Cozette supercharged Anzani. The car proved to be extremely fast and such a success that *Terror* was built. The *Terror* used a variety of different stages of tune of supercharged Anzani engines and various sizes of Cozettes, the chassis was kept as light as possible, but it was fitted with front wheel brakes. Archie Frazer-Nash never got the car finely tuned and it was in the early thirties that Dick Nash, (no relation whatsoever to Frazer-Nash), both in 1931 and in 1932, achieved Fastest Time of the Day at Shelsley Walsh with the *Terror*.

AFN Limited was formed in March of 1927 as the successor to William G. Thomas and Frazer Nash Limited; Richard Plunket-Greene, a schoolmaster from Aston Clinton, officially entitled the Sales Director, was the largest shareholder in the new company, Archie Frazer-Nash and Dorothy Burt were the two other directors. Dorothy Burt's influence was

FRAZER NASH

Archie Frazer-Nash at the wheel of Alastair Pugh's 1928 Super Sports on the occasion of the 21st birthday party of the Vintage Sports Car Club

almost negligible in the running of the company, other than being the purchaser of the 1928 TT Saloon. The reason for her directorship was that she was the nominee of her husband who, as a director of Mowlems the civil engineering contractors, was not allowed to have outside business interests.

H.J. Aldington left the firm and founded Aldington Motors; his intention was to obtain orders for new Frazer Nashes which he could use as stated: 'May we send you particulars of our specialised components for the car including lower chassis, special bodies, engine conversions and tuning, twelve volt lighting and starting, four speed gears and Marles steering, etc., Aldington Motors, Station Avenue, Kew'. Aldington's unannounced intention was to obtain orders for new Frazer Nashed which he could use as a lever against the Works and Plunket-Greene in particular. He had not envisaged in 1927 the possibility of obtaining control of the firm.

Eric Burt had to mount a further rescue operation in 1927 to prevent the Anzani company from going out of business and he put his wife into the new Anzani company as a nominee director. The physical movement of the

THE BOULOGNE

Bobby Bowes Frazer Nash seen at Brooklands *A. S. Heal*

Anzani machinery from Willesden to Kingston-upon-Thames was expensive, but Burt seemed to have limitless funds, according to Frazer-Nash. The Works at 145 London Road, Kingston had the Frazer Nash workshops to the right of the entry courtyard and to the left, in the three storey block, were the Anzani workshops; the front portion of the single storey structure to the right housed William G. Thomas, whose many activities included lorry restoration and civil engineering. At the first floor level at the rear of the courtyard there was an external walkway linking the two blocks. From this walkway Archie Frazer-Nash was known to survey the activity beneath whilst promenading along the 'Admirals Walk'. H.R. Scott who had left Frazer Nash Limited to join Anzani's was taken over by the new company, British Anzani Engineering Co Ltd, and as he said many years later, "I was obviously intended by the good Lord to work for Frazer-Nash and there was no point in trying to fight fate". Scott accepted fate and designed the 1928 range, and some of the improvements he incorporated involved merely catching up with Aldington.

FRAZER NASH

THE SUPERCHARGED MODEL.

SPECIFICATION.

ENGINE.—Four cylinder monobloc. 69mm. bore by 100 mm. stroke. Capacity 1496 c.c. R.A.C. rating 11.9 h.p. Tax £12. Detachable cylinder head, specially lapped to block, dispensing with gasket. Side by side valves in special cobalt steel. 80 lb. valve springs in aero quality steel. Valve ports hand polished. High tensile steel crankshaft with roller bearing big ends and exceptionally large diameter main journals. Connecting rods machined from solid in special 100-ton heat treated nickel chrome steel. Exceptionally large gudgeon pins. Force-feed lubrication throughout, dry sump optional. Ignition by B.T.H. magneto. Revolution indicator drive arranged positively from engine. Electric starter flange mounted.

Cozette supercharger mounted vertically at front of engine and skew driven from crankshaft through shock absorbing coupling. Cozette or Solex carburettor, mounted directly on supercharger and readily accessible. Large diameter short induction pipe, fitted with safety valve. Induction pipe pressure gauge on instrument board. Oil supply to supercharger by separate pump mounted on supercharger, delivering through hollow rotor spindle. Oil control automatic from foot throttle.

Engine develops over 85 b.p.h.

(NOTE.—On the Supercharged model the dynamo is mounted on the chassis and driven from the propellor shaft.)

TRANSMISSION.—Dry three plate clutch. Tubular clutch shaft with ball centred Hardy joint. Spiral bevels. Final drive by chains with dog clutch engagement. Four forward speeds, all direct. Right hand control.

SPRINGS.—Stiff, flat Quarter Elliptic front and rear. All braking and cornering torque taken by radius rods on both axles. Duplex Hartford shock absorbers to both axles.

BRAKES.—Internal expanding on all four wheels. Foot control to front and rear. Hand control to rear.

WHEELS.—Rudge-Whitworth, detachable, with Well Base tyres.

DIMENSIONS.—SHORT CHASSIS—Wheelbase 8' 3". Track 3' 10".

LONG CHASSIS.—Wheelbase 8' 9". Track 3' 10".

BODY. SHORT CHASSIS.—Two Seater. Interior and seats upholstered in best quality real leather. Pneumatic cushions. Low flat windscreen, in unsplinterable glass. Hood with black cover.

LONG CHASSIS.—Three seater. Front seats adjustable. Interior and seats upholstered in best quality real leather. Pneumatic cushions. Low flat windscreen in unsplinterable glass. Hood covers all three seats. Black hood cover.

EQUIPMENT includes—Speedometer, revolution indicator, C.A.V. five-lamp lighting set and starter, complete tool kit, spare wheel and tyre, etc.

SPEED.—Two Seater (Short Chassis) Model, over 100 m.p.h.
Three Seater (Long Chassis) Model, over 95 m.p.h.

From the 1928 catalogue: An example of the long chassis 3 seater is shown on page 89

THE BOULOGNE

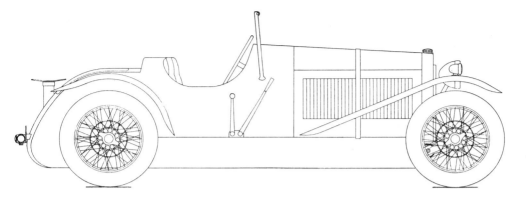

THE SUPERCHARGED TWO SEATER (Short Chassis)

Standard Finish Dark Green, Black Chassis.

Price £620

The 'New Type' Super Sports models introduced in 1928 had a lower chassis, a new style body in which running boards were abandoned, (being thoroughly out of date for sports cars), a wider track front axle was fitted giving the cars a pronounced crab track and a rear mounted petrol tank. This last change was important since the risk of fire was significantly less than with the scuttle tanked cars, whose petrol fillers were neatly located immediately above the exhaust system. The gallonage, increased to seven plus from a bare five, was in 1929 increased to nine. The increased weight to be accommodated at the farthest end of the car, involved stiffening up the welded angle iron cranked chassis extension which held the tank, the spare wheel mounting and the top mounting for the rear shock absorbers; this piece of ironwork, due to its vague similarity to the walkway, was known as the 'Admiral's Walk'.

There was a marked difference between the old and new type Frazer Nashes since the earlier cars were mainly polished aluminium bodied running board cars. Owners of the older cars had been convinced by Aldington that what they really needed to do was to spend some money on having their cars updated. The new front axle was marketed under the heading of stability

FRAZER NASH

The method of determining the quantity of fuel in the tank is usually determined with a graduated dip stick. The car is a 1928 Super Sports *D. S. Jenkinson*

THE BOULOGNE

A 1929 Super Sports, short chassis, model

and improved road holding. It was patently clear that it was fitted to improve the extremely poor steering lock of the earlier cars. The four speed transmission was, however, a major step forward. The fitting of the petrol tank at the rear and the steady increase in size up to the thirteen to fourteen gallons of the TT Replicas reduced the height of the African Belly; by 1932 the African Belly of the TT Replica was reduced to a mere swollen chin. The belly was at its aesthetic best in 1928 to 1930, when however, it was often not seen as it was demurely veiled by the positioning of the spare wheel.

The side valve four cylinder Anzani engine reached standards of perfection in quality control that were literally unrivalled. Though this may have been expected during the heady years at the beginning of the nineteen twenties when up to a dozen reputable car manufacturers were buying the engine, the standards were still maintained, when in the late twenties the users had declined to Frazer Nash and Lea Francis, and finally to just Frazer Nash. The engine was available in several standards of tune and Frazer Nashes used three unblown engines; the Sports or SA model giving 38 horse-power, the Super Sports or SS model which gave 47 horse-power - both at 4000rpm and the H.E. (standing for high efficiency) which gave 52 horse-power at 4500rpm.

The start of the 1928 Tourist Trophy. The advantage that was to be gained, by not having to erect a hood at the start and the later taking down of same, was nullified by the five minuted it took to start the supercharged Anzani engine *Autocar*

The supercharged Anzani, as sold to a private individual, was fitted with a number 8 Cozette and it was Eric Burt who arranged that the sales and maintenance of these French built superchargers were handled by British Anzanis from the end of 1927. The sports-racing HE specification of Anzani when fitted with a number 8 Cozette was sold with a guaranteed 80 horsepower, at approximately 4500rpm and a boost pressure between 9 and 11 pounds per square inch. The Works were only too happy to demonstrate this power on the test bed and if the owner was willing to learn, then Scott would explain the disadvantages of supercharging, since the advantages were too well known to be catechised. The Works engine always ran on fuel blends and, whenever possible, on methanol based fuels such as alcosene or P.M.S.2; the Works engines were more reliable since the drivers recognised

THE BOULOGNE

'The Slug'; so called due to its low build, had a special fabricated front axle and a supercharged four cylinder overhead camshaft Anzani engine developing 110bhp. The Conan-Doyle brothers competing in a Cambridge University Speed Trial of the early thirties

the frailty of some components and drove accordingly. A good proportion of the private owners unleashed full power whenever possible and the engine had a short and merry life.

Frazer-Nash and Scott devoted most of their time to the building of competition engines and competition cars, almost exclusively within the confines of the British Anzani side of the premises. The competition car of 1928 was the *Slug*, which was probably too ambitious a car considering the declining nature of the business and the shortage of capital. Plunket-Greene was effectively in charge of the Frazer-Nash side of the business and there was a continuous shortage of bought out components in the stores, so that for the fitters to have to make cylinder head gaskets from a sheet of copper was not at all unremarkable.

FRAZER NASH

In late 1928 Archie Frazer-Nash became seriously ill with nephritis and was in hospital for several months. His illness coincided with a marked reduction of the order intake and Plunket-Greene became desperate since many purchasers, such as Per Nas from Sweden, liked to discuss their requirements personally with Frazer-Nash before placing an order. Plunket-Greene went to see Frazer-Nash in hospital, but was so shocked by Frazer-Nash's appearance that he could not bring himself to discuss the poor state of the business. H.J. Aldington made a bid for the business and Eric Burt said that he would not put any obstacles in the way of Aldington making a take over bid. The bid was in fact effectively for only the goodwill of the Frazer Nash business, since all the major pieces of equipment were the property of British Anzani. Aldington, en route to one of the preliminary meetings at Kingston, ran out of petrol in Richmond Park, and seeing two working men having a sandwich lunch at the side of the road beside a motorcycle combination, asked them if they had a can and some petrol; Tommy Randall and a fitter from British Anzanis were on their way back to the Works having taken a war time radial Anzani engine crankcase to Barimars for a weld repair. Tommy Randall asked the tall dark stranger to give him a leg up into the willow tree, under which they had been sitting, and from the bole of the tree rescued the remains of an oil can; he then ran a pint or so of petrol from the motorcycle and the tall dark stranger was soon on his way to his important appointment at Kingston. The transfer of ownership of the Frazer Nash Company went through smoothly; almost immediately Frazer-Nash started to get better and was soon discharged from hospital. It was agreed that Aldington would manufacture elsewhere than in Kingston. Aldington, walking through the Works at Kingston for the first time in well over a year, saw and recognised Tommy Randall; Tommy Randall was told that there would be a job for him at the new Works. Aldington well appreciated the skills of a man who could literally pluck out of thin air a required object at zero cost.

Kingston to Isleworth and the TT Replica
Chapter 6

THE TRANSFER OF ownership of AFN Limited took place in the beginning of 1929 but it was not until March of 1930 that the new premises were ready at London Road, Isleworth in Middlesex. Nelson Ledger with Tommy Randall were the only employees of the old company that moved to Isleworth.

Archie Frazer-Nash's main weakness was that he was not commercially orientated, he understood that attention to detail, forward ordering, supervision of staff, were essentials in the running of a business, but these functions were not his metier. Aldington was the complete businessman and he began to run the business of making and selling Frazer Nash cars on the basis that it was a business. His brother Donald had joined him at Kew and became Aldington's right hand man; even more important for the future of the company was that his other brother, Bill, joined him and took over the advertising, brochures, letters to the editor and all the matters usually known in industry as 'publicity'. For the first time in the history of the Frazer Nash concern a concerted effort was made to sell the cars.

Bill Aldington's advertising copy bears examination as a first class example of what publicity material should be - pithy, punchy and informative. His weakness was to tell too much of a story, but there were many exceptions and the advertisement showing the TT Replica and the BMW together is a good example; however, many of his advertisements were so congested that he had to use 5 point to get the words all in. It was said at the time 'that only the young men can read his advertisements, without

FRAZER NASH

The shape of the external exhaust system, unique to the supercharged Anzani cars of 1929 and 1930, is shown on Mrs Wisdom's 1929 car

using spectacles' - but since he was trying to sell Frazer Nashes to young men then it was thought that he was probably right. He produced a single fold brochure on the NEW Frazer Nash early in 1930 and this was followed at the end of the year with the catalogue of the 1931 range.

The one thing that Bill Aldington was never able to sort out was the question of whether or not there was a hyphen between Frazer and Nash, and there is always the element of excitement in reading his print whether he would put in the hyphen or leave it out. Archie Frazer-Nash was clear that his name was hyphenated and that the car was unhyphenated when H.J. Aldington took over control of the firm. Since it was a trade-name, the subsequent use or non-use of the hyphen was Bill Aldington's affair. The other feature of his copy was, if possible, never to refer to his brother by name, he always tended to handle the matter as if the cars were driven by nobody, a good example is to be found in the 1931 catalogue 'While space does not permit us to cite every individual award, the outstanding success of

KINGSTON TO ISLEWORTH AND THE TT REPLICA

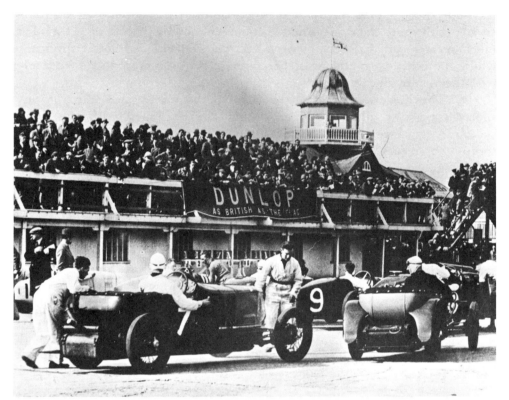

The all steel panelled and fabric bodied cars are seen together with respectively H. J. Aldington and Tommy Wisdom. Lining up for the start of the opening Brooklands meeting of 1930

the Frazer-Nash in the M.C.C. One Day Sporting Trial 1930, is worthy of attention. Out of 72 entries the Frazer-Nash was the only car to climb successfully all the hills non-stop, and the only car to win a Premier Award. Again in the London Exeter, 1930, a Frazer-Nash gained the Special Prize for the Acceleration Test on Black Hill against 183 cars'.

This same catalogue included the following paragraphs and these sentiments he tended to repeat, just changing the odd word, right through to 1957. 'It is gratifying that most of our successes have been gained by amateurs (driving privately owned cars) together with the fact that our successes, and those of our owners, have always been won on perfectly standard cars with normal gear ratios, etc.

'Such conspicuous success in open competition may cause some people to imagine that the Frazer-Nash is only intended for the sporting enthusiast. It is, rather, a general-purpose car for the man wishing to use his car privately for business and really fast averages over long distances, and at

FRAZER NASH

the same time capable of competing in reliability trials, speed events and hill climbs with more than a reasonable chance of success. In the latest models much greater care has been given to increase comfort and better springing, whilst the coachwork and general equipment compare more than favourably with the best modern standards.

'The Frazer-Nash has an all-round performance unequalled by any sports car - the docility of a touring car combined with the fierce acceleration, capacity for speed and that "glued-to-the-road" feeling of the thoroughbred racer. Ease of handling, positive safety at high speeds, efficient brakes and the car's low centre of gravity inspire complete confidence on the part of the driver.

'The Frazer-Nash is not produced on mass production lines, and, therefore, makes a particular appeal to enthusiastic owner-drivers who want a car that is definitely "out-of-the-ordinary". Personal attention to owner's wishes is a feature of our organisation and an important point is the readiness of the manufacturers to carry out any deviation from standard in body-work, equipment, etc. to fall in with customers' individual requirements'.

The Works never produced a printed official spare parts list for distribution to the customers or an instruction book. The problems of producing an instruction manual where every car was different from the one before were self evident and it was Archie Frazer-Nash who had said in exasperation to a customer, "If you need an instruction book you don't deserve to own one of my cars".

Aldington wished to upgrade the cars and to change the image. In some cases these were contradictory requirements and in the first heady excitement of ownership some of the decisions he took proved to be wrong. The main change that he was anxious to introduce was the fitting of the Meadows 4ED engine, an o.h.v. engine of imposing appearance which entirely fitted Aldington's requirements for the new Frazer Nash. The supercharged Anzani was retained for the Works cars.

Aldington was not going to produce polished aluminium bodied cars for the reason that they were too expensive to produce, repairs were very difficult to carry out and the cars became very second-hand looking quickly. Steel bodies would be durable and easy to repair, whilst fabric bodies, Sportop bodies, would be cheap to produce. Aldington's chief requirement was to lose the cyclecar image once and for all and to achieve this, simply, was relatively easy, as the sine qua non of cyclecars were the almost complete lack of instrumentation. The Boulogne models had been adequately instrumented but his intention was, that from then onwards, this

The Ulster, a short lived design. The road holding suffered from the fact that chassis was down-swept from behind the rear engine bearers

FRAZER NASH

was to be a minimum standard. If the size of the instruments was increased then it almost served the same purpose as extra instruments and was a grading up process at a minimum cost.

The 1930 cars listed in the press were as follows:

Three/Four-Seater Interceptor with sv engine	£325
Three/Four-Seater Interceptor with ohv engine	£350
Two-Seater Falcon with sv engine	£350
Two-Seater Falcon with ohv engine	£375
Two-Seater Boulogne with ohv engine	£395
Two-Seater Boulogne with ohv engine	£425
Two-Seater Boulogne with sv engine (supercharged)	£450
Two-Seater Boulogne with ohv engine (supercharged)	£475

All Two-Seater models could have the longer wheelbase (9ft instead of 8ft 6in) and a Three/Four-Seater body for £25 extra, and four forward speeds for £20 extra.

In addition to these models there were the Ulsters with lower chassis, roller bearing engines and four speeds.

Ulster I sv engine	£495
Ulster II ohv engine	£495
Ulster III sv engine (supercharged)	£575
Ulster IV ohv engine (supercharged)	£575

From the basic twelve models, with a large variety of coach-work only thirteen cars were delivered in 1930. Presumably it was hoped to be able to build at least one of each. The supercharged ohv Meadows engine was wishful thinking as it was not until 1932 that this line of development was gone into.

The 1931 catalogue showed changes:
Interceptor I at £325 and the II at £350
Falcon I at £350 and the II at £375
Boulogne I at £395 and the II at £425
Ulster I and II, both at £495

The only difference between the specifications of I and II were the side valve Anzani for the I and the overhead valve Meadows for the II. The Interceptor, Falcon and Boulogne models were equipped as standard with the cheapest body and the only interpretation of the price differences is that of engine specification from the SA (Sports A Anzani) to the SS (Super Sports) to the H.E. (High Efficiency) and for the Ulster the H.E. again. The Meadows engine standards would be logically the standard Meadows, the Brooklands Meadows with one carburettor and with two carburettors.

The narrowness of the Frazer Nash body, meant that the passenger, Bill Aldington in this case, had to put his arm behind the driver so as to provide space for arm movements for the driver, his brother H. J. MY 3940 was the Works' racer with a supercharged Anzani engine for mountain events at Brooklands and with a touring engine for trials

The Sportop bodies are not mentioned by name in the catalogue produced at the end of 1930

Coachwork and Equipment

PRICES given throughout this catalogue are for short chassis models (wheelbase 8ft. 3in., track 3ft. 11in.), with two-seater sports body as illustrated on page four. The bodywork is very pleasing in design and sporting in appearance, whilst comfort and durability have not been sacrificed. English ash frames and the finest materials are used throughout the construction of the body. The door on the nearside allows of easy access to the seats, which are upholstered in leather, with pneumatic cushions. Spare wheel and tyre are mounted at the side, and there is ample room for luggage, tools, etc. in the domed back. The body is cut away on driver's side to allow of easy gear changing and use of brake lever—these levers are fitted outside the body, but inside levers can be had if desired. The general appearance of the car is greatly enhanced by the deep sided body, well-domed and valanced cycle-type wings, while no running boards are fitted. The windscreen is of the single panel folding type, and a well fitting detachable sports hood of black twill is supplied. The equipment includes Lucas 12 volt electrical lighting and starting (with dip and switch), 100 m.p.h. speedometer, clock, oil gauge, complete tool kit, spare wheel and tyre, etc.

THE three-four seater body (as illustrated on page nine) on long chassis (wheelbase 8ft. 9in., track 11in.) costs £35 over and above the catalogue price of any model. The specification includes rear 8 gallon petrol tank (with electric or hand pressure pump system) and spare wheel and tyre mounted on substantial bracket at rear. General details as regards materials used, etc., are identical with the two-seater, but in addition a wide "cut-through" door is fitted, and the separate bucket seats for the driver and passenger are adjustable—these are upholstered in leather with pneumatic cushions, as is the rear seat which provides accommodation for a third passenger, children, or, alternatively, can be utilised for luggage. The hood covers all seats and is easily erected. The instrument board is of walnut, with cubby hole in front of passenger, while the instruments are neatly panelled. General equipment is as specified above for the two-seater type of body. The long bonnet and the well-proportioned domed wings add to the attractive appearance of the car, while the body is cut away on the driver's side. The tool compartment is in an ideal position—under the bonnet in the forefront of the scuttle. Hood cover and mats are included. The undershield completely encloses the whole of the chassis.

A FULL four-seater body on the long chassis can also be supplied, and as will be seen by the illustration on page six, has very attractive lines. This type of coachwork has proved very popular, and costs £60 over and above the catalogue price of any model. Full details as to measurements, equipment, etc., will be sent on request.

ON page eleven, the "Ulster" model illustrated shows the special sports body, including many extras in its equipment. The "beetle back" section of the body is hinged, giving access to the spare wheel and tyre. Many interesting points are incorporated in this model, and, unfortunately, the illustration does not do full justice to this very handsome Frazer-Nash—its exceptionally low build and sporting lines undoubtedly make it one of the most outstanding sports cars on the road. The bodywork, etc., conforms with International measurements and regulations—an added advantage for anyone considering active participation in racing or competition work. This model costs £575 (unsupercharged) and £655 (supercharged) with this special body and complete equipment. Full details, photographs, etc., will be sent on request.

A MODIFIED three-four seater body, with rear petrol tank, mounting of spare wheel at rear, etc., can also be supplied for the short chassis model, and we are, of course, always prepared to build bodies of any type to customer's own orders and special requirements.

COACHWORK is fabric covered, or panelled—colour to customer's choice. Wings and bonnet cellulosed any colour. Standard finish of chassis and wheels black.

THE "Intercepter," "Falcon" and "Boulogne" models are equipped with three speeds and reverse—standard ratios being 1st 10.1, 2nd 5.4, and 3rd 3.5. The "Ulster" model has four speeds as standard, the gear ratios being 1st 11.6, 2nd 7, 3rd 4.8, and 4th 3.8. The former models can, however, be fitted with 4 speeds and reverse at an extra cost of £20. One of the big advantages of the Frazer-Nash is the way in which any of the gear ratios can be independently altered to suit any special conditions. Such alterations are easily and inexpensively carried out at any time.

Mr Marriott of Putney Hill in his three/four seater Sportop bodied supercharged Anzani car. Marriott once beat Aldington off the same mark in a mountain race in this car. The 'cut-through' door was typical of the more touring bodies of 1930 to 1931 *W.J.Brunell, National Motor Museum*

The newly finished Falcon Works at Isleworth in 1930

The two seater fabric sports body was the cheapest body style offered by the Works. The registration plate is off a much earlier car

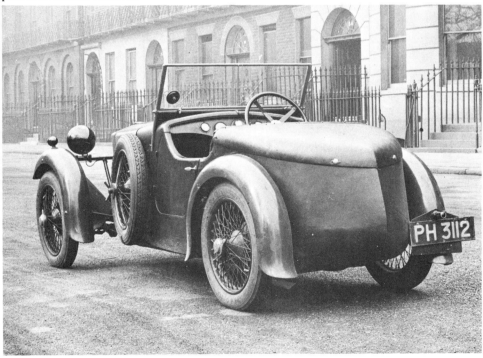

FRAZER NASH

Neil Berry's Sportop bodied car. The raised upswept scuttle was fitted to only a few highly competitive cars — normally Works cars

Aldington's efforts to up grade the cars were not entirely sufficient in July of 1930 to satisfy the road tester of *The Autocar* who said '... another minor point noted on earlier models which apparently has not yet been put right, at all events not on the machine tested, was the heat communicated to the drivers and front passengers feet. Although the engine showed no sign of running hot it attained a sufficient temperature to make the driving department a trifle uncomfortable on a hot day. A ventilator would be a welcome addition. In addition there were one or two features which seemed more in keeping with cyclecar practise than modern design. The brake ratchet was one of these, being formed of a simple serrated edge into which the lever was held by a coil spring, although quite efficient the arrangement suggested possibilities of future wear. The strangler, again, was operated by a simple length of wire attached beneath the dash and quite innocent of any more elaborate form of control'. *The Autocar* confused

KINGSTON TO ISLEWORTH AND THE TT REPLICA

Vaughan Skirrow in his steel bodied Interceptor of 1930, at a Vintage Sports Car Club meeting in 1955 at Prescott

elaboration with quality and performance, but in this they were only reflecting the mores of the time. The Aldingtons took notice of this road test but the various fittings, which were to change the image, took time to procure and fit. The policy of continuously uplifting the specification meant that if the client wanted to pay more money, then there were more expensive models that could be bought and high cost extras, that could be fitted.

The 1930 and 1931 cars seem in retrospect to be as if Aldington was looking for the way to go and the Ulster I together with the Sportop, Falcon and Interceptor are nowadays exceedingly rare models. The steel panelled cars were too heavy, the fabric panelling was too liable to damage and the decision to drop these two styles was influenced by the success of the aluminium panelled Sportop. An amalgam of this body style and the Boulogne II body style eventually became the TT Replica.

The 1928 entry of a Saloon Nash in the Tourist Trophy had ended in fiasco; the quick start, that was supposed to take place, having no hood to erect, was wrecked by the fact that the car took five minutes to start. The 1929 race from the Frazer Nash point of view was only notable for the fact

FRAZER NASH

that Archie Frazer-Nash was in the Works Austin 7 team and finished third overall; the two Nash entries were supercharged Anzani cars and both retired in the third hour.

There was not a TT entry in 1930 by the Works but in 1931 Aldington entered three cars, two of them privately owned. John Teague attributes in his *Profile* on the TT Replica, that the car road tested by the *Motor* in June of 1931 was the direct prototype of the TT Replica. T.G. Moore wrote in the *Chain Gang Gazette**, of the not very successful 1931 TT, when all three cars retired and said, specifically of the road test car '... The test was of Aldington's car with a Meadows engine ... but it carried the number plate from my car, HX 3863. This came about because W.H. Aldington, then sales and publicity manager, thought the car would photograph better with a front number plate on it and so borrowed mine ...'. Aldington's car used for the road test was registered as MV 158 and recorded for the road test 81.8mph in top gear at Brooklands; on the road it achieved 82.5mph in third under unfavourable conditions and the merits were clear of the high Frazer Nash top gear as an overdrive gear. The Works cars, and cars sold as competition cars, seemed always to carry a 4.1 top gear, whilst the less competitively minded had the 3.8 ratio. By 1934 the Works offered the fitting of alternative sprockets fitted permanently to the rear axle; the ratios could be changed in a matter of minutes by sliding a sprocket sideways and altering the chain length.

The purchasing of the Aston-Martin company by H.J. Aldington from Bertelli in February of 1931 was bizarre. The story given to the press was 'H.J. Aldington has the exclusive handling of Aston-Martin car sales. The development will bring into association two widely different types of sports cars, each with an enthusiastic following'. Aldington did not want it to be known at all that he owned both companies, and other than for a small handful of people the secret was kept until the post-war years. The commercial sphere of sales, advertising and competition would be handled jointly without any detriment to the sales of either Frazer Nashes or Aston-Martins. Aldington kept the manufacturing elements quite separate and it has been a matter of conjecture ever since why he never fitted an International engine into a Frazer Nash chassis; he has since said that the cost of this engine was considerably higher than the 4ED Meadows but since the Aston-Martin car was sold at twice the price of a Frazer Nash then the engine was suitable for an Aston-Martin but not a Frazer Nash!

*Footnote - *The Chain Gang Gazette* is the club magazine of the Frazer Nash Section of the VSCC. This Section is the successor to the pre-war Frazer Nash Car Club

A Boulogne II Special being restored. This wider body with two doors can be seen to have a similar style to the TT Replica

A two seater Exeter model, being a car intended for the long distance M.C.C. rallies of the thirties, was normally only lightly tuned. Seen here in Bolzano prior to the Corsa Della Mendola hill climb of 1969 *D. S. Jenkinson*

FRAZER NASH

A long chassis Interceptor with a fabric body, coachwork by Wylder. The grouping of the instruments in the centre of the instrument panel was typical of the time and all touring Frazer Nashes of 1931 to 1932 were fitted with this style of front wings

The sales of Frazer Nashes by 1930 were exclusively from the factory and there was no question of paying agency and dealer discounts. Aston-Martins were sold through the trade and the commissions were normal. The Aldingtons increased the commissions so that the sales would hopefully approach one hundred cars a year, at which figure it was thought the Aston-Martin Company would become profitable.

Aston-Martin built two distinct types of cars; the Works cars, which were built regardless of cost to make them as fast and competitive as possible, and the production cars, which though externally similar were not in fact the same. The people who bought Aston-Martins bought on the score of reliability and long service; this was where Aston-Martin competition policy was sound, for they only entered long distance races. The type of owner who was tempted to buy a sports car because of reliability tended not to be too competitive in his outlook. Aldington said: "The Aston was advertised as the 'Aristocrat of Light Cars', and it probably was, but it certainly was the heaviest and most expensive. If you came up behind an Aston-Martin owner he always waved you on".

The Double 12 cars of 1930 and 1931 were very similar, T. G. Moore's car for the 1931 Race was fitted with a supercharged Anzani, note the lightweight body with no doors *T. G. Moore*

Abandonment of fabric for aluminium panelling, coincided with the building of the extension to the Falcon Works and the delivery of this early Colmore to Douglas Hopkins in early 1932

FRAZER NASH

R. L. Appleton trials his light blue TT Replica

KINGSTON TO ISLEWORTH AND THE TT REPLICA

AFN had the responsibility not only of entering Aston-Martins for competition but also in directing race tactics; the choice, beloved of novelists, as to deciding who was to win never came into Aldington's calculations. The Double 12 Race of 1931 had three Aston-Martin entries made by Aldington for Bertelli/Bezzant, Leon Cushman*/Malcolm Campbell, and H.W. Cook/J.D. Benjafield. The Frazer Nash entries were W.F. Braidwood/T.G. Moore, C.M. Harvey/H.J. Aldington, and Mrs T. Wisdom/D.A. Aldington. The array of B.R.D.C. blue blooded talent in the Aston-Martin team was matched by the return to racing of Major Harvey in the Frazer Nash team. The performance by the Frazer Nashes was not good with only Aldington's car finishing. The first five places were taken by MG Midgets. The Astons finished first and second in the 1500cc class and were the only finishers in that class. Aldington won a large silver cup as the entrant. This cup stands as the only award or momento, belonging to the family, for owning the Aston-Martin concern.

Aldington was usually very thorough in matters of management and the one item he did not control was the building by Aston-Martins of their racing cars and in fact it was Aldington's money that built LM5, 6 and 7, which were to be the Aston-Martin team cars through 1932 and 1933.

Unfortunately the motor trade did not sell sufficient Aston-Martins and by the end of 1931 it was a case of either letting Aston-Martins be liquidated or finding someone to buy Aldington out. Prideaux-Brune came to Aston-Martin's rescue and the seven months of AFN ownership was finished.

The first car to be designated by the Works as a TT Replica was MV 2013 raced and owned by Roy Eccles, later Barry Goodwin, and since the war by Reggie Wright. The fitting of radiator stoneguards had been entirely restricted to the Works racing cars, in particular to the Double 12 cars, so as to provide protection against Brookland's flying lumps of concrete. The TT Replica was fitted with radiator stoneguards and other distinguishing features were the louvring of the bonnet, not only on the flanks but on the top panels; the increased capacity of the fuel tank; better instrumentation; quick release filter caps and the new two seater body. This body had been developed from the Double 12 cars, through the Boulogne II, into the neat slim body that was only 33 inches across the body, at the seat squabs.

The TT Replica was available as a listed model from 1932 until the finish of production of the chain drive cars, at the beginning of the war. It was in later years known as the Byfleet II and at the very end in 1938-1939

*Footnote - Leon Cushman shared the same initials as the Cushman of GN and Frazer Nash but was no relation

Ivo Peters took this photograph of his own car MV 3357 a classic TT Replica with Bosch headlights and sidelights and the flared front wings, so typical of the 1932 to 1933 period *I. O. F. Peters*

The front axle could be polished, painted or in rare cases satin or bright chromed

KINGSTON TO ISLEWORTH AND THE TT REPLICA

reverted to its earlier name of Boulogne II. Initially it was fitted with the Meadows engine, always referred to as the four cylinder ohv Frazer Nash engine by Bill Aldington, in print. In 1933 the Blackburne engine was offered as an alternative engine for the Frazer Nash carriage trade when the chassis was increased to a nine foot wheelbase, instead of the standard eight foot six inches, and this engine was referred to as the six cylinder engine but later as the six cylinder twin overhead camshaft engine (this was to make the distinction between it and the BMW type 55 engine). The only other engine offered was the four cylinder single ohc engine which was wholly a Frazer Nash design, but the owners of that time and since, have found this too much of a mouthful, it has been generally known as the 'Gough' after the name of its designer Albert Gough. The supercharged versions of the Meadows and the 'Gough' were never known as TT Replicas even though one of them - Fane's car (CMH 500) - looked like a TT Replica.

The Aldingtons many times endeavoured to introduce a low priced Frazer Nash. Models such as the Exeter and the later Falcon, were specifically aimed at this market; the remarkable feature of some of the cars sold was that in many instances the owner returned after several months to have all the performance options fitted, these cost him considerably more than if he had had them in the beginning. The best example of up-grading was A.G. Gripper who bought a Colmore and later returned to have the car rebodied with a TT Replica body and to have the engine fitted with the deflector head. In mid 1933 the firm introduced the Popular model, which was intended to be a low cost TT Replica model at £445 (the lowest price model available at that time was priced at £375); the Popular model was also popular in the Works since it used a variety of parts which had last been used in the twenties, the 1½in back axle instead of the 1 5/8in, the 10in brake drums instead of the 12in, and Lucas electrics rather than Bosch. Practically all the items that were fitted to the Popular model for cheapness were also lighter in weight and it can be safely assumed that the lightweight racer that the Works built for Aldington to race at Donington in Club events, which was known as the *Light Blue Racer,* was at one and the same time the Popular.

The TT Replica fitted with the twin carburetted Meadows engine and the four speed and reverse transmission varied in price over the years of manufacture up to £600. The Aldingtons were not averse to the possibility of an owner providing an older car and having the Works up-rate the specification and rebody and re-register the car, as a new car - several TT Replicas were produced in this manner.

In 1933 the price was £475. The TT Replica, with the Meadows engine, gave a performance that was obviously dependent upon the state of engine tune specified by the buyer.

The normal standard of tune meant that the car was good for an 85mph maximum speed, with a standing start half-mile in thirty-two seconds, and 0 to 60mph in eighteen seconds. The cars weighed between 15½ and 16½ hundredweight. The TT Replica finally got away from the legacies of the cyclecar, a fly-off handbrake instead of the 'primitive' spring-and-ratchet system, and dual windscreen wipers. The TT Replica was available with or without a water-pump and fan, and after the 1933 Alpine these fittings were no longer listed; the header tank to the radiator was increased in size to make the capacity four-and-a-half gallons against the standard four gallons (generally known as the Alpine header tank). Bosch electrics were also available, and most cars built from mid-1932 had these German electrics fitted, as being generally superior to the cheaper British Lucas system. A divided tank was also available, under the scuttle, to give a reserve oil and fuel tank of two gallons each, as well as the twelve-gallon fuel tank (giving a total range of approximately 400 miles without filling up).

The TT Replica advertising literature had this to say on gear ratios. 'Four forward speeds and reverse, with all ratios to customer's requirements. Cruising ratios are 3.8, 4.8, 7 to 1 and 10 to 1. It is perhaps worth mentioning here that the Frazer Nash is intentionally high geared. The performance (in spite of this fact) is outstanding, and provides at the same time a guarantee that the car will stand up successfully to years of hard work, even under the most strenuous conditions. A cruising speed of 60mph at only half-engine revs is a very pleasing point for a prospective owner's consideration. This policy is in marked contrast to the average absurdly low-geared sports car, where the performance (inferior at that) is obtained only at the expense of abnormal engine revs and resultant rapid wear'.

The divided tank under the scuttle used the oil tank for the chain lubrication system. This system fed oil, by small bore copper pipes, to the ends of the countershaft, and centrifugal force wormed the oil through the countershaft bushes, the sprockets and on to the chains. The owner of a GN or early Frazer Nash could not help being impressed by these later cars, and if other features failed to register then the instrumentation could hardly fail to impress. From right to left across the panel: ammeter, oil pressure, water temperature, rev counter (large), central Bosch lighting-switch block, speedometer (large), fuel tank pressure. This was a minimum, and quite often the temperature gauge had two needles and two dials so that the oil temperature could be observed as well. If a supercharger was fitted then there was also a boost gauge. The cars in the twenties had adequate

KINGSTON TO ISLEWORTH AND THE TT REPLICA

The firm were always interested in the cheap model. Here is the Popular. This same car was the 'Light Blue Racer' *Autocar*

instrumentation, but one feature which never failed to impress, or depress, the Constabulary was the charming habit of placing the speedometer on the far left-hand side of the dash, whilst directly in front of the driver's eye was the rev counter. Archie Frazer-Nash said, "First things first and do not let yourself be distracted by inessentials".

The Blackburne-engined Frazer Nash was announced in May of 1933 and marked a radical change in the Works approach. The Blackburne introduced sophistication into the engine compartment, and though these cars were heavier and slightly slower, they appealed to that class of owner who only competed occasionally. The Blackburne cars were, as H.J. Aldington said, "Designed for a different market. The sort of owners we had in mind were people like Mrs Vary Bolster".

Various detail changes were made to the chassis in 1933 and 1934. The Admiral's Walk was the standard fitting in all the cars in the twenties, and in the thirties for the Colmore and other touring models. The Boulogne II had straight members bolted to the underside of the chassis, which

T. D. Ross and Aldington during the 1932 Alpine Trial; Ross was the designer of the RI Anzani engine used in later years in the Squire and available as an option for the Ulster 100

The Team entry for the 1933 Alpine of Adrian Thorpe, Lionel Butler-Henderson and Aldington

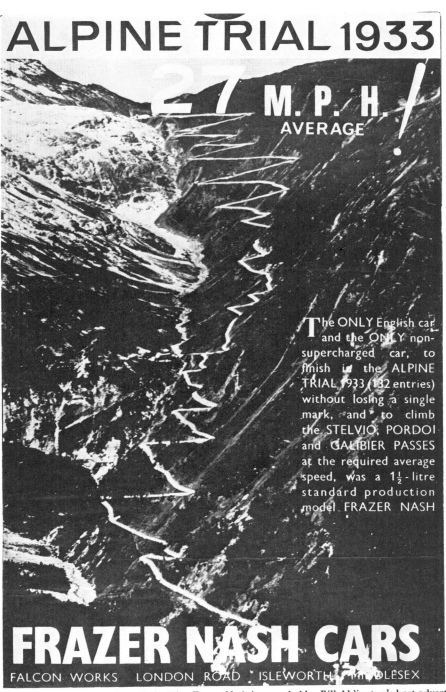

The finest performance by a chain drive Frazer Nash is recorded by Bill Aldington's best advertisement

The Hon. William Feilding, later the Earl of Denbigh, demonstrates during the 1934 Alpine, the limited amount of space available for luggage in a TT Replica

The 'Sporting Dukes', the Hon. Philip Mitchell-Thomson and Lord Waleran overtake the Cadbury-Heal Aston Martin after secretly topping up with water *A. S. Heal*

KINGSTON TO ISLEWORTH AND THE TT REPLICA

supported the petrol tank from below. In 1934 a one-piece chassis section was produced which swept down behind the bevel box and carried on to support the petrol tank. The Works fitted a 'new and improved' sprocket layout, but this was an esoteric point, and nobody could prove that it was an improvement, as the only improvement was that it seemed to be cheaper to manufacture! Generally the sprockets were laid out across the car; second, first, third and fourth. The 'new and improved' layout was first, second, third and fourth. A radiator was fitted in mid-1935 that had a slight slope back; this was styling, without necessarily being an improvement.

The Light Car reported in October 1932: 'One of the finest of all British sports cars is as usual not on show (the Motor Show) - The Frazer Nash. The absence may occasion surprise, but the reason is that the manufacturers are not members of the SMMT, because their policy is to preserve a free hand with regard to competition'. In 1933 AFN Limited joined the SMMT, and from then onwards had a stand at the Motor Show. In 1933 they exhibited four cars at the show, a TT Replica at £475, a TT Replica with a deflector head for £525, a Colmore with a Blackburne for £595 and a six-cylinder TT Replica at £550. This stand was very popular with friends of the firm - for all owners were friends. No matter what trouble arose with their cars, their loyalty, though it might become strained, to AFN Limited and H.J. Aldington in particular, was tremendous.

Albert Gough was employed as an engine improver, but in three years his status improved to the situation where he was recognised as an important member of the team. His first job was to improve the Meadows engine by raising the power output. The onset of detonation was the major problem for engine designs using the petrol of the thirties, with their very low flame speeds. His solution to this was to introduce a completely new design of cylinder head, which used squish lobes in the combustion chamber allowing increased compression ratios to be used. Gough also introduced the charge through four separate inlet ports, rather than the siamesed passages of the standard Brooklands Meadows cylinder head, and lightened the components in the valve train. The engine power with only a moderate increase in compression was raised by ten horse-power. Gough likened the deflector head to putting new wine in old skins since he raised the power but at the expense of bottom end reliability. Aldington said "It was the best advertisement for Gough, but the worst for Frazer Nashes he could have thought of". Aldington's heartfelt words were wrung out of him following the fitting of the first batch of the new cylinder heads to four cars at a Brooklands meeting and all four cars either broke con rods, or their crankshaft. The redesign of the bottom end of the engine, which should have

FRAZER NASH

Aldington and Neil Berry

taken place to stiffen up the crankcase, was not attempted, but Laystall crankshaft, and in some cases, special con rods, were fitted

    Albert Gough prevailed upon Aldington and he agreed that the first truly Frazer Nash engine should be designed. The design was to be suitable for supercharging and was to be built to diesel-like proportions. The engine suffered from the same drawbacks as the earlier Plus-Power in that there were never enough engines made to overcome the development snags in a prototype design. There were multiple teething problems involving the water cooled main bearings, connecting rods, the nitride hardening of the crankshaft and it was not until very recent years that it was found that the design of the valve springs actually tended to promote surge and valve bounce. There was no development budget and the first example made was installed in a customers car; in hindsight it is not difficult to believe that P.F. Jucker had endless trouble!

Facts!

"The Autocar" has now published its analysis of 1933 road tests of eighty English, Continental and American cars, and once again the Frazer Nash has conspicuously the best all-round performance.

The 1½-litre four and six-cylinder Frazer Nashes tested have easily the best acceleration figures from 10 to 30 m.p.h. and from 0 to 50 m.p.h. of ALL English and Continental cars, irrespective of engine capacity or price, and the highest maximum speed of ALL cars tested, with the exception of the 40-50 h.p. Continental "Phantom II" Rolls Royce (7,668 c.c.) costing £2,425, and the Talbot "105" Speed model (2,969 c.c.) costing £795 which has a maximum speed of 88.23 m.p.h. as against 87.38 m.p.h. for the Frazer Nash with its high top gear ratio of 3.8 to 1.

30 feet from 30 m.p.h. is generally recognised as 100% braking efficiency, and the figures obtained by "The Autocar" of 27 feet from 30 m.p.h. for both the 4 and 6-cylinder Frazer Nashes are, therefore, extremely satisfactory.

Road-holding is something which cannot be shown in figures, and anyway as far as the Frazer Nash is concerned it would be unnecessary. It is as safe on a wet and greasy road as on a dry surface—experts are unanimously and convincingly enthusiastic as to the road-holding qualities of the Frazer Nash.

Frazer Nashes have acquired an enviable reputation for their brilliant performance in trials, and successes this year have consolidated their pre-eminent position in this sphere of motoring sport, exemplified by the outstanding achievement by a Frazer Nash in putting up the finest performance of any English car in the 1933 Alpine Trial. "Motor Sport" said "*the Frazer Nash team put up by far and away the most amazing performance of the whole Trial.*"

At the track Frazer Nashes have been consistently successful this year both in "Mountain" and outer circuit races. Ever since "Mountain" events were introduced Frazer Nashes have proved their suitability for this difficult course, demanding as it does from successful cars the necessity for road-holding, cornering and braking powers, maximum speed and acceleration out of the ordinary. Handicaps have become increasingly severe for Frazer Nash competitors, and it is nothing uncommon to find a non-supercharged Frazer Nash giving an appreciable start to cars of much greater engine capacity, and, frequently, supercharged.

We have been successful in developing our o.h.v. engine considerably—a claim proven by the steady increase in average speeds in races won by Frazer Nash cars up to the last meeting, when a non-supercharged Frazer Nash won a Long Handicap at an average speed of 96.47 m.p.h. with a flying lap of 102.27 m.p.h.—with a standard two-seater body and no attempt at streamlining.

In the 500-Mile Race the Hon. Peter Mitchell-Thomson's privately owned non-supercharged Frazer Nash averaged 88.88 m.p.h. and was one of only seven cars to finish, having an absolutely trouble-free run.

Frazer Nashes were conspicuously successful at Shelsley Walsh hill climb in both May and September, and while space does not permit mention of other major successes, we might recall the noteworthy achievements by various private owners competing in events in which we are not allowed to compete officially as manufacturers.

It is most important to remember that the Frazer Nash is *not* a racing car, but is built as a general-purpose car, to meet the requirements of owners who want a car capable of high average speeds over long distances and equally capable of putting up an excellent performance in any event—speed trial, hill-climb, reliability trial or racing. It is in fact the finest all-round sports car in production and the *SAFEST.*

"Individuality" is essentially the keynote of its construction—it is a hand-built job, and the specification can therefore be adapted to an owner's personal requirements, while it is built to stand up to years of really hard driving. The depreciation of a new model is negligible, while the secondhand value is probably higher than for any other sports car—points well worth the serious consideration of a prospective purchaser. Thoroughly workmanlike in appearance—everything on the car is there for a purpose and not for superficial appeal, while it is in all probability the finest equipped sports car on the market.

We shall be only too glad to have the opportunity to prove our performance claims to you—choose a wet day if you want to be convinced of its safety!

Please write, telephone, or, preferably, call and see us if you would like further details.

Frazer Nash Cars   Falcon Works   London Road
Isleworth Middlesex   Hounslow 0011 and 0012

Please mention MOTOR SPORT when corresponding with advertisers.

Bill Aldington's 'Fact' advertisements were usually far more crammed with print, than this one of 1933

The Blackburne twin overhead camshaft six cylinder engine in the 1933 road test car

The instrumentation of a Blackburne engined TT Replica. *Left to right:* clock, the hand pressure pump and the petrol tank air pressure gauge, ammeter, speedometer in mph. Bosch switch unit, revolution counter, water temperature, oil temperature, oil pressure gauge, dash board light illuminating the oil pressure gauge, and the horn button *G. M. Schieffelin*

KINGSTON TO ISLEWORTH AND THE TT REPLICA

Aldington drives his son's Blackburne engined TT Replica at the 21st birthday party of the VSCC

Due to the greater weight of the Gough, and the mass of the internal parts, the engine had to be in a higher state of tune to give the same output. To get any real significant gain in power the engines had to be supercharged, and supercharged engines in the thirties were essentially a Works job, which rather militated against the private owner who had been the backbone of racing.

There were many individual examples of TT Replicas doing very well in competition. A detached observer noting the large number of Frazer Nashes competing in 1933 would probably have judged that the Works were turning out cars at the rate of hundreds annually instead of the actual 32 in 1932, 36 in 1933 and 39 in 1934. The Lands End Trial of 1932 had a total entry of 242, with Frazer Nashes being the second highest one make entry after MG with 23 cars.* Consistent entrants in all forms of competition drove their Frazer Nashes in the 1933 Lands End Trial; L. Butler-Henderson, P. Lees, K.M. Roberts, H.W. Inderwick, H.H. Porter-Hargreaves, A.G. Gripper, D.G. Hopkins, A.L. Marshall, C.M. Needham, H.J. Aldington, the

---

*Footnote - The entry of Frazer Nashes in recent years in events run by the Vintage Sports Car Club have often exceeded thirty in number; the 1969 Frazer Nash Raid to the Alps at one time had an entry of 42 Frazer Nashes and a final list of 34 cars that made the round 2500 mile trip

FRAZER NASH

The 'four cylinder single overhead camshaft Frazer Nash engine', being the official description of the 'Gough' engine

Hon. P. Mitchell-Thomson, N.A. Watkins, N.A. Berry, F.B. Robinson, J.D. Windle, E.R.M. Walker, F.T. Rainey, D. West, W.A. Pointing, S.H.H. Cundey. The Works used to send a small memento to private owners, if they got a gold medal, which was often an embossed Ronson cigarette lighter. This was the limit of the Works support; no private owners ever got less from a firm than did the owners of Frazer Nash cars, though they got a lot of friendship. The professional and semi-professional drivers, who were often to be seen driving various makes of cars, were never seen under the heading of Frazer Nash. Club race meetings were a rare event pre-war, in comparison to the post Second World War scene, but at a mid thirties JCC club meeting, up to ten Frazer Nashes were entered, all driving modern models, except for Bellamy who was driving his 1926 supercharged Boulogne Vitesse. These private owners were a tremendous advertisement for the firm. Ivo Peters in his Meadows and later Gough-engined TT Replica was a keen competitor. His performance in practice for the 1936 Limerick Grand Prix was a tour de force, since he broke the lap record for the previous year's race set up by

KINGSTON TO ISLEWORTH AND THE TT REPLICA

Michael Collier's 'Gough' engined car at the 1935 Le Mans, where it retired during the night with a broken engine, due to stretched bearing studs

Austin Dobson in a 2.3 supercharged Alfa-Romeo. The private owners who raced extensively are almost too numerous to mention, but Butler-Henderson, Porter-Hargreaves, Thorpe, Mitchell-Thomson, Jucker, Berry, 'Tim Davies' (Dudley Folland), Law and Griffiths-Hughes must be noted. Some owners had been racing for years - Roy Eccles, Alan Marshall and Commander Grogan.

The Frazer Nash also attracted women drivers, and the Shelsley Walsh Ladies' Record was held continuously, from the time the award was started in 1930 till 1933, by Mrs Elsie Wisdom and Miss Cynthia Sedgwick. Mrs Gripper, Mrs Arline Needham, Miss Midge Wilby and Miss McOstrich were all women drivers who owned their own Nashes and drove them well in all forms of competition.

It was in the Alpine Rallies of 1932, 1933 and 1934 that the TT Replica achieved their highest and best performances. A.G. Gripper had competed in the 1931 event in a Riley and passed on the message that the Alpine was made for Frazer Nashes and for the 1932 event both Gripper and

FRAZER NASH

Twenty five years later Bill May in the Collier car views with equanimity, the nine and a half mile Italian Hill Climb known as the Corsa della Mendola. Denis Jenkinson is quietly confident.

Aldington entered and each secured what the British called 'golds' and the Austrians 'Coupe des Glaciers'. They had troublefree runs, and the whole event could have been designed for Frazer Nashes being partly MCC trials, partly road-racing and partly speed hill climbs, at all of which the Frazer Nash was pre-eminent.

W.F. Bradley wrote in *The Autocar* of the 1932 Alpine: 'Aldington and Gripper brought their Frazer Nashes up the gradients in real 'Land's End' style; in fact, this is certainly the best performance Frazer Nashes have ever accomplished'.

The entry for the 1933 Alpine showed that Aldington had not been slow at passing on the good word, for a team was raised and several private entries as well. W.H. Aldington prepared a leaflet after the 1933 Trial called 'Alpine Trial Facts' which is worth quoting from:

'When it is remembered that teams were entered by the manufacturers of the finest cars in production in Europe - German, Austrian and French firms, with an unrivalled knowledge of Alpine conditions - it is

KINGSTON TO ISLEWORTH AND THE TT REPLICA

Griffiths-Hughes in the 1935 J.C.C. Rally, which used part of the Brookland's Test Hill

worthy of note that the performance of the Frazer Nash team had been described as 'by far and away the most amazing of the whole Trial' (*Motor Sport*, September), an opinion which has received general endorsement in the daily and technical motoring press.

'Originally all the Frazer Nashes in the Alpine Trial were entered as 'individuals', and it was a last-minute decision to enter a team made up of Mr H.J. Aldington and two of these bona-fide private owners, Mr T.A.W. Thorpe and Mr L. Butler-Henderson.

'*Motor Sport* said: 'By an unfortunate series of events the wonderful performance of the Frazer Nash team in the Alpine Trial was not revealed in the bald list of results. Thorpe's unlucky crash on the Stelvio lost the team ninety-two marks out of their total loss of ninety-nine. Of course, there should be no 'ifs' in motor sport, or any other sport, but the team will have everyone's sympathy, for without this accident the team prize would have been comfortably theirs.

'There has been a tremendous amount of misleading advertising

FRAZER NASH

The Shelsley front axle was an optional extra for all models. The 1935 catalogue described it as follows — 'a straight tubular front axle with inverted semi elliptic springs (acting as cantilevers), with rigid radius rods below the axle; duplex Hartford shock absorbers mounted above the springs, axle clips integral with the axle (with full provision for caster adjustment on the radius rods) and 14 inch diameter finned brakes'

subsequent to the Trial results being published, and certain makes of cars have claimed successes where they have, in fact, been far from successful!

'An analysis of the performances of all the cars in the 1500cc class shows that Frazer Nash cars would have been placed as follows:

H.J. Aldington	No marks lost	First
A.L. Marshall	4 marks lost	Third
L. Butler-Henderson	4 marks lost	Third
A.G. Gripper	7 marks lost	Fourth

'All the Frazer Nash cars which competed were privately owned and entered, and with one exception (Mr A.G. Gripper, who competed in the 1932 Coupe des Alpes, winning a Coupe des Glaciers, bought a new model this year), had all been driven in M.C.C. and other Trials and Brooklands events (two of the cars were in the Relay Race only a few days previously), in addition to the heavy mileage put up on all Nashes in the course of everyday motoring. A Frazer Nash is built for hard driving, and they invariably get their share!

'Even more noteworthy than the success of the team was the fact

KINGSTON TO ISLEWORTH AND THE TT REPLICA

that the non-supercharged 11.9hp Frazer Nash driven by Mr H.J. Aldington and his spare driver, Mr N.A. Berry (incidentally a private owner of a Frazer Nash), put up what was unquestionably the finest performance of any car in the Trial, irrespective of size. This Frazer Nash was the only English car (fifty entries) and the only non-supercharged car of the complete English and foreign entry (132 entries) to finish the Alpine Trial without losing a single mark, necessitating not only the ability to maintain the imposed average speeds on the road section, but also the ability to climb the three timed passes - the Pordoi, Stelvio and the Grand Galibier - at the very high average speed required by the regulations, and also to pass successfully the final examination as regards brakes, lighting and starting equipment, et cetera'.

There were two other Frazer Nash entries: F.W. Oxley left the road in the early stages and was dragged back on to the road by oxen. He then took a second dive off the road and retired; Mrs Gripper and Mrs Needham in Mrs Gripper's car retired on the Stelvio with fuel-feed trouble and withdrew from the Trial. Besides Aldington's penalty-free run there were only two others: Ing. Walter Delmar, in a 2.3 supercharged Bugatti, and Rene Carriere, in a 1750cc supercharged Alfa-Romeo.

A further three car team was raised for 1934, and there were also three private entries plus Aldington. The whole Trial was fraught with suspense from start to finish. The Honourable Peter Mitchell-Thomson and co-driver Lord Waleran were driving one of the team entries and they went off in their car a week earlier so as to have a holiday in the South of France. Mitchell-Thomson's Meadows TT Replica was fitted with a water pump, much against Aldington's better judgement. When the rest of the team met up with them just before the start, Aldington found to his horror that the gland in the pump had, in the previous week, started to leak. Instead of just tightening it up they had allowed themselves to be convinced by an old French fisherman of the efficiency of some gland material that they used on the boats, and there they were on the start line with the pump leaking and the radiator sealed by the organiser. This meant that the coveted Gold Plaque Alpine Cup for a deficit-free team entry was lost even before the start. Douglas Hopkins, who was Alan Marshall's co-driver, came to the rescue by driving out the pin at the rear of the filler cap on which the filler cap normally hinged. The cap now hinged on the 'plombeurs' seal, and the way was open to top up when required. They were instructed that whenever they needed water, they must drive miles away from the course and top up, only when they were sure they were not overlooked.

Through the several days of the Trial 'well wishers' brought

The 1935 Catalogue had to have a supplement to describe the Meadows and RI Anzani, since only the Blackburne and 'Gough' engines were described. The lengths that Bill Aldington went to, not to mention the names of the engine manufacturers, meant he referred to these optional engines as the four cylinder twin overhead camshaft and the four cylinder overhead valve Frazer Nash engines

Aldington news that car No. 105 had been seen driving off on the wrong road. On the last night of the Trial they all got decidedly merry, and it was suggested that the Germans knew about the tricks the 'Sporting Dukes' were up to. Whether they knew or not, car No. 105 had a broken water seal on its radiator the next day - broken by the 'Sporting Dukes' (penalty ten marks). This so demoralised them, that they were also four minutes late at the last control and the Frazer Nash team lost fourteen marks. Alan Marshall and Lionel Butler-Henderson, the other two team members, lost no marks. The BMW team lost no marks at all and won the 1500cc team award, a Coupe des Alpes, with the Frazer Nash team second, winning a silver gilt plaque.

Alan Marshall had his share of troubles, and did well to finish unpenalised as he had holed his sump and did a very quick temporary repair. Tweedale, driving Gripper's 1932 Alpine car, also won a Glacier Cup. Mrs Arline Needham drove through the whole trial, being partnered by an English mechanic, who could not drive. The road conditions in Yugoslavia were very bad with literally inches of dust, and a lot of the passes were reminiscent of M.C.C. trial sections except that they went on for miles.

The 1934 Trial was notably for the massive works support given to every entrant of any importance. Aldington was not in the position, with such a small works, to offer such backing, and Mrs Needham said: "The most honest people who ever went through an Alpine were the Frazer Nash team as they had no works support whatsoever".

After the 1934 Alpine AFN Limited, in their advertisement in *The Autocar*, included the following: 'Faced with the annual outburst of 'Alpinvertising' - a word we have coined to describe the misleading advertisements which appear after the Alpine Trial, frequently revolving round mediocre results so that they read as outstanding successes - we propose limiting ourselves to a plain statement of the facts.

'The facts that the average speed was reduced, together with the non-inclusion of the timed climb of the Pordoi Pass, made it a foregone conclusion the results this year would show a higher proportion of awards among makes of cars which failed last year, but what we regret most of all was the last-minute modifications of the route involving the elimination of the timed climb of the notorious Galibier Pass, which robbed the trial of its greatest difficulty'.

The Frazer Nash performance in the Alpine Trials of 1932, 1933 and 1934 was of a very high calibre indeed. The 1935 Alpine was cancelled at the last minute due to the German entries not being able to send money to the French organisers. AFN Limited offered to finance the entire German entry, but the Automobile Club de France had by then abandoned the Trial.

FRAZER NASH

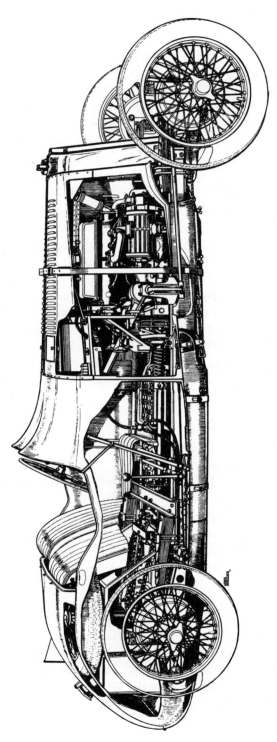

Max Millar's drawing from *The Autocar* of the Nurburg. £650 bought no luggage accommodation at all

The other chain drive cars
Chapter 7

ALDINGTON DID NOT really mind what sort of cars he made, as long as there was a demand. He would produce what the customer required. The depression which had commenced in the mid twenties did not begin to fade away until the mid thirties. Consequently the firm would build any model, fit any fitment, do up second hand cars and sell them as new, and when Mr Baines wanted a saloon, then a saloon was built. The only 'policy' was for the Works to race cars that were the same as the customers' cars - 'the same as you can buy' policy.

A.F. Agabeg entered a Salmson in the March Mountain Speed Handicap of 1931, and after the race sought out H.J. Aldington in order to obtain some training in the correct line. Aldington was much impressed and showed Agabeg how you could put a wheel over the edge of the banking quite safely. In the next meeting Agabeg so improved that he was able to beat Brian Lewis's single-seater Talbot with his supercharged Salmson. Some time in early 1932 Agabeg changed his name by deed poll to A.F.P. Fane. Since the Christian name he used was Fane, nobody could be sure as to the degree of friendship people shared with him, when they called him Fane.

In later 1931 A.F.P. Fane ordered an Ulster II which was to be bodied with a Corsica built 'shell' of his own design. The car was designed to be fitted with a supercharged Anzani, but the decision was taken to make it a blown Meadows car.

The Power-Plus supercharger was chain driven, incorporating a motorcycle cush type drive, from the Meadows engine. This supercharger

FRAZER NASH

The 1931 Saloon built for Mr Baines *Autocar*

was a British version of the Cozette, unfortunately improvements that were made to the design by Captain Eyston developed their own failings. It was Aldington's view that the Power-Plus was less efficient, and less reliable, than the Cozette. A hundred plus horse-power was raised from the blown Meadows, but this exposed the fragile nature of the bottom half of the engine. This car and Eric Siday's blown Anzani Ulster I were entered for the 1932 German Grand Prix.

    Aldington and Fane, on their way to Nurburgring, unfortunately had their car rammed up the back in the streets of Brussels, by a tram. In the race they had to retire with transmission trouble, as the chassis was twisted, which upset the bevel box. Siday's car, which had the same tail treatment as Fane's, used the tail to seal the pressurised fuel tank. When the body started to rattle to pieces, then the pressure went, and Siday had to retire also. *The Light Car and Cycle-Car* reported: 'Nothing like them had been seen in Germany before'. Though this race had not proved to be a success for the firm, the name of Ulster II was dropped and superseded by the model name of Nurburg.

    In September of 1933, the Works Nurburg was entered in the British Racing Drivers' Club 500-mile race at Brooklands on the outer circuit, to run with an unblown Meadows but fitted with Gough's new deflector head. The car ran like a clock through the whole 500, driven by D.A. Aldington and the Hon. P. Mitchell-Thomson, and notwithstanding fuel and tyre stops it

THE OTHER CHAIN DRIVE CARS

A Special two-seater built for Lord Cholmondeley in late 1931, he never took delivery and the first owner was Cowcill. This was the last Frazer Nash to be built with running boards

averaged 88.88mph to finish seventh, with a best lap recorded of 99.88mph. This was a splendid result. The works only sold two more Nurburgs, though the supercharged Meadows-engined cars were referred to by the works as having a Nurburg chassis.

Aldington's secondary aim to making and selling sports cars was to obtain a share of the high speed touring market; for this purpose the Blackburne twin overhead camshaft six cylinder engine was deemed to be perfect. The one major disadvantage was the gear wheel noise of the camshaft drives. When Peter Aitken ordered a wireless to be installed in his Blackburne engined TT Replica, the cup of joy overflowed for the Aldingtons - surely this meant that the Frazer Nash had moved all the way from the cyclecar image to becoming acceptable for the carriage trade. Unfortunately the high frequency noise that the Blackburne developed meant that the driver could only just hear the wireless, but, about three blocks away people turned around expecting to see a band! The Colmore and the later Byfleet I, another model name for the Colmore, were ideally suited, with the three/ four seater bodywork and adequate hood and sidescreens, to the smoothess and to all that was understood by six cylinder appeal. The six cylinder engine was, to most of the motor car manufacturers of the twenties and thirties, their philosopher's stone.

R. G. J. Nash in a Concours d'Elegance with his 1931 Falcon

An Exeter being driven by the Northern Secretary of the pre-war Frazer Nash Car Club, Porky Lees
National Motor Museum

THE OTHER CHAIN DRIVE CARS

The Aston Martin influence of 1931 is reflected in this early 1932 Exeter, where the front wings were mounted off the rear of the brake back plates

The surprise of the 1934 Motor Show was the supercharged, Shelsley model, which was an entirely different style of car. The supercharged 'Gough' used twin Centric superchargers in parallel, so that though the car had two superchargers, it was only single stage supercharged. An aerodynamically styled body, wider radiator, flowing wings together with a new front axle using cantilevered semi-elliptic springs, were the major innovations. Up to 90mph the normal front axle suspended on ¼ elliptic spring was more than adequate, but over this speed axle tramp became common. Gough told the story of how he and Fane went out together at Brooklands with himself driving and Fane wielding a camera, to photograph the axle tramp. The tramp was of such proportions that Fane would have needed a panoramic camera to encapsulate it. The Shelsley axle, with softer springs and much better shock absorbers, enabled the later single seaters to reach 120 and 130mph with no axle tramp.

Gough was on the stand at the 1934 Motor Show, and the twin-Centric supercharged Shelsley at £850 was a good crowd drawer. The TT Replica was now £650, with the 'Gough' engine, whilst the Meadows-engined variant had been renamed the Boulogne II at £475 (the successor to the Popular).

FRAZER NASH

A 1932 Cambridge blue coloured Colmore with the spare wheel mounted at the rear. On the Colmore model it depended on the chassis design whether the spare wheel was on the side or at the rear. After 1934 the Colmore used the deep TT Replica chassis and the spare wheel was mounted as per the TT Replica

The Shelsley Nash was also available with a Marles steering-box; why this conventional steering-box was offered is incomprehensible, as it had nothing approaching the lack of freedom from play and sensitivity of the circular rack and pinion standard fitting.

H.J. Aldington's policy had been to build and race sports cars, 'the same as you can buy' - but when Mitchell-Thomson ordered a Single Seater in early 1934, powered by an unsupercharged Gough, it was then obvious that 'same as you can buy' also included Single Seater racing cars. The Single Seater blown 1500cc ERA in 1934 had led to a revival of interest in this 'voiturette' class. AFN Limited had the chassis and the twin-supercharged Gough, and in 1935 Adrian Thorpe bought a Single Seater from the works. Following the 1935 Le Mans, Robin Jackson took Tim Davies's Shelsley to his establishment at Weybridge and converted the car to a Single Seater based on Adrian Thorpe's Single Seater. Thorpe's first event with his car was

Brian Swann demonstrates that chain adjustment is a messy business with a four seater Colmore of 1934, and a rear mounted spare wheel

The 1935 Catalogue illustration of a Colmore

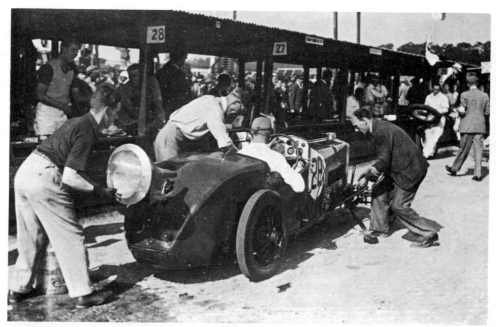

The Nurburg visiting the pits during the 1933 400 Mile Race. Albert Gough springs to the bonnet, Tommy Doman starts refuelling, whilst H. J. leans over brother Donald Aldington

Gough is checking the tappet clearances, the rocker box cover is lying on the bonnet, whilst Phillip Mitchell-Thomson prepares to drive off

THE OTHER CHAIN DRIVE CARS

The Nurburg cockpit. The windscreen is fitted with wire mesh in place of glass. The item on the far left is the newly introduced chain oiling system pump, which on later models was mounted on the floor

a five-lap race at Brooklands in which the engine threw a rod. The second time out was the British Empire Trophy of July 1935, and Tim Davies had also entered his Single Seater. Davies had a certain amount of trouble, including breaking a chain, but Thorpe was lying third in this handicap event, and in the words of *The Autocar* 'going magnificently and thoroughly deserved its place'. A piston then seized. This was unfortunate, as a success in the early stages of the Single Seater's life might have made a lot of difference.

The 1935 '500' had three Single Seaters entered - Thorpe and Fane, Tim Davies and A.H.L. Eccles, Mitchell-Thompson and Griffiths-Hughes. This last-named car had very few races since it was first built in 1934 and was running unsupercharged. The race was a debacle, as only six cars finished out of forty-one entrants, though Mitchell-Thompson was still running at the end he did not qualify as a finisher. Cobb won magnificently, averaging

FRAZER NASH

Charles Needham commissioned Knibbs and Parkyn of Manchester to build this body on a Blackburne TT Replica chassis. Needham eventually sold the car in part exchange for a Frazer Nash-BMW to Aldington. Aldington promptly broke the car up

121.28mph for the 500 miles in the Napier-Railton.

Jucker had converted his TT Replica to a Single Seater for the 1936 season, and supercharged the Gough engine with a belt-driven Marshall. Jucker, pronounced Yooka, was a splendidly wild driver, and at a Donington meeting in 1935 was flagged off for continuous cornering on the grass. There is a story that after a race he questioned whether he might have damaged his rev counter by bringing the needle against the stop; when asked on another occasion at what revs he ran his engine he said "at the made in England bit".

Adrian Thorpe had sold his Single Seater back to the works, and from the end of the 1935 season it became the works car with Fane as the driver. During the 1935 season the Single Seater became a catalogue model, first at £1,200 then later at a thousand guineas.

At the end of 1935 Fane secured the Mountain Class F Record at Brooklands at a speed of 78.30mph. Fane's attempt took several laps, and

The Hon. Peter Aitken's twin supercharged Shelsley, which at 19½ hundredweight was the heaviest model produced by the firm. It was also the most expensive at £850

The twin Centric Superchargers were mounted side by side at the front of the engine, drawing from a single carburettor for the Shelsley sports car. The lower geared Marles steering box was a major design aberration, when compared with the standard Frazer Nash steering box

The Shelsley front axle, with the cantilevered semi-elliptic springs and the 14in diameter Shelsley brakes. The slightly greater width of the Shelsley radiator can be seen *Autocar*

"Yes, Sir, you want a Shelsley model with our unblown twin overhead camshaft six cylinder engine". The Works would build any model using any combination of components. A Blackburne Shelsley seen at Prescott just after the war

Adrian Thorpe's Single-Seater outside the Works at Isleworth

FRAZER NASH

The start of the 1935 500 Mile Race. Fane is in 16, Tim Davies (Dudley Folland) in 17. Removing the brakes off the front axle and reducing the unsprung weight added to comfort, since brakes were not needed on Brooklands outer circuit

when he came in to check up, Aldington said: "Go to 5500rpm", whereupon Fane was supposed to have replied: "I have already been to 6000". Fane held the record for a year. The highest lap speed attained by Fane on the outer-circuit was 121.77mph in August 1936. Margaret Jennings (nee Allan), wrote in the B.R.D.C. Jubilee Book, referring to the end of the 1935 season: 'The opportunity of driving the Folland twin-blower Frazer Nash, quite the pleasantest outer-circuit car I ever handled, brought me nearer to having a little record to call my own than anything else. Unofficially timed in practice to lap at more than the 127mph necessary, it was decided to attempt the outer-circuit record, and many long days were spent in turning bays with that end in view. Sad to say, however, whenever a timekeeper was sent for, the car developed a temperament, on one occasion shedding top-gear chain on the track, and finally cracking its head just before Brooklands closed for the winter. I suppose everyone has a motoring 'might have been' and that

Fane in the single seater having spun off at Pardon Hairpin, Prescott in 1939. The Works had moved the seating position to improve the weight distribution for hill climbs and sprints *The Motor*

Fane leaves the start at Wetherby in 1939 to set a record time. The course was not used again after the war *R. Steavenson*

FRAZER NASH

was certainly mine'. Folland did not race in his own name, but used the name of Tim D. Davies as his nomme de G.P.

In the first Shelsley meeting of 1936, in July, Fane got equal second fastest time of the day. The second meeting of that year suffered from bad weather and the Single Seater was not in very good tune. However, AFN Limited were pleased, for Fane, in a 328 BMW, won the M.A.C. Sports Challenge Trophy. The June meeting of 1937 was run under good weather conditions, and Mays, in getting ftd at 39.09, broke his own record of 39.60 seconds. Fane got third fastest time with 40.89 seconds.

Goodwin bought the ex-Tim Davies Single Seater from Sammy Newsome, who had driven it once at Shelsley. Newsome's growing interest in Jaguars, and especially racing a very special SS 100, caused him to sell the car.

September 11, 1937, was a fine day and Mays was away racing at Phoenix Park, Dublin. Barry Goodwin opened the 1500cc racing class with a run of 42.6 seconds, then it was Fane's turn, and *Motor Sport* reported: 'Fane's first run was inadvertently untimed and his next run took the record. Fane drove every inch of the 1,000 yards ascent, taking the S-bend beautifully in a car that was at the very limit of control'. 38.77 seconds and a new record.

Fane's record was to last until a year later when Mays won it back with a time of 38.76; exactly one-hundredth of a second faster!

The works made one last attempt to build a low price Frazer Nash in October 1935 with the new Falcon. This used the BMW type 55 engine, and was listed at various prices from £400 to £450, but only one example was made.

The relationship between Aldington and BMW would not have precluded the fitting of a 328 engine to a Frazer Nash and both Fane and Aldington were keen on this, but by the time that 328 engines were freely available it was late 1937 and by that time the impetus for the chain drive cars had slipped away. The Reply, as the BMW engined Falcon was known by the employees in the works, slightly helped to redress the balance between the numbers of Frazer Nash BMWs that were being sold and the paucity of chain drive cars. In December 1935 the Frazer Nash-BMW Car Club amalgamated with the Frazer Nash Car Club; this seemed to be sensible at the time, but it proved to be disadvantageous to those members owning the older historic cars, for they had little in common with the owner who had bought a brand new car of quite a different design.

The Ulster 100 was announced in June of 1936. The sole example made was first shown fitted with the Anzani RI twin overhead camshaft

THE OTHER CHAIN DRIVE CARS

The Falcon model

engine; Aldington had taken over British Anzani as a company to theoretically manufacture the 'Gough' engine and had inherited numbers of this engine used for the Squire. The records indicated that two Ulster 100s were made, but the evidence points to there only being one car, but bearing two different registration numbers! At this late stage in the life of the chain drive cars a major change was introduced in that the springs were mounted beneath the rear axle and rear tubular radius arms were also used.

The Ulster 100 was the last throw of the dice, since the firm had ceased promoting the chain drive cars actively after the Motor Show of 1935. The Falcon and the Shelsley were shown together with three Frazer Nash BMWs for the 1936 Motor Show and in that year the firm made eleven chain drive cars, in 1937 two cars, in 1938 one car, and in 1939 Derek Senior bought the last chain drive car to be made by the firm - a Colmore.

FRAZER NASH

An advertisement for the non motoring press eg. *Aeroplane* and *Country Life;* BMW aero engines, BMW at the Nurburgring and a Doctor's Coupe, Type 45, with British bodywork in the motif

The  Chapter 8

THE 1934 ALPINE TRIAL was a torment to Aldington for many reasons. It was immediately obvious that the sections had been eased considerably since 1933, and this meant that the professional teams with works drivers were going to do better than his happy band of private owners, who were to say the least, difficult to regiment and more keen on the idea of having fun, than driving to team orders. The second reason was that, quite early on in the Trial, Aldington detected the sheer merit of the BMWs, not their performance, as measured in miles an hour, but the excellence of their road holding. When the roads were rough, as they were in Serbia, then the BMWs just romped away. Several times during the course of the Rally, Aldington had to lecture his Frazer Nash private owners, to stop them being so eulogistic about the road holding of the BMWs and not to comment on the galling fact that the Nashes had to power slide every hairpin; the Frazer Nash steering lock, or lack of it, would permit no other way, whilst the BMWs with a 30 feet turning circle were picking their path around the hairpins. Aldington decided that he wanted to go to Munich straight away after the Rally and he was worried that either Triumph or Roesch's representatives might take too healthy an interest in the BMWs. In hindsight he realised that his fears were ridiculous, but it was so obvious to him that the World was looking at the future in chassis design.

In the 1933 Alpine Rally only three cars had got through clean, but in 1934 at the San Remo prize-giving, over sixty cars were penalty free. The BMWs had won the 1500 team prize with the Frazer Nashes second. Neil

FRAZER NASH

Berry, who was an owner and a great friend of Aldington, as well as being his co-driver, suggested that they might go for a swim after the prize giving to which Aldington replied, "certainly not, we are on our way to Munich". There was a certain amount of trouble at Munich with the factory police and commissionaires, who found it difficult to grasp the fact that Aldington had travelled so far, with no fixed appointment, to see the Herr General Direktor Popp.

Aldington, at this meeting and subsequent meetings, impressed Popp with his enthusiasm. Aldington discovered that Herbert Austin's representative was at the factory discussing the possibility of taking a license for manufacturing the BMW. Aldington said he thanked Popp for the courtesy he had shown but there was no way that he could outbid Austin. However, Popp indicated that he could outbid on enthusiasm and the ability to get things done. Popp went on to propose that Aldington should take two cars back to England, to try them out and show them to people and then, if Aldington still liked them, he was to return and discuss a license; but the license was his, if he wanted it. Aldington, with Fane, drove back to England in a Model 315, open Two Seater sports, and a closed cabriolet. Fane confirmed Aldington's view before they got anywhere near the Channel ports, but Aldington took a fortnight before writing to Popp.

The license gave him the sales rights and the right to manufacture; this right was important since Aldington, with this, could carry out negotiations in Britain. He owned the British BMW rights and discussions did take place with Alvis and Riley at different times. In December of 1934 Aldington announced that he would be selling the Frazer Nash-BMW car and stated that in the not too distant future he would be manufacturing. Some cars were delivered in a completely knocked down state and Aldington fitted some components of British manufacture, but in the main, most cars came by rail and sea to Shoreham; from there they were driven to Isleworth.

It was Bill Aldington's idea to give the cars type numbers according to their BMW horse-power ratings and not to use the BMW numbering system, which would then differentiate the British Frazer Nash-BMWs from the German cars. The BMW system was based originally on engines so that the 1500cc engine and the cars that it was fitted to were type 315, the same engine when increased to 1911cc was the 319. The exceptions to this rule were the sports car engines, which, when fitted with three carburettors and a higher compression ratio, were the 315/1 and the 319/1 respectively. The

Footnote - The British type numbers were in sympathy with the BMW horse-power figures until 1936. The Type 40 could be in AFN's eyes a 2 carburettor 319 or a 3 carburettor 315/1; there were other anomalies also in 1934 and 1935.

H. J. Aldington driving one of the 315/1 1934 BMWs, similar to the 1934 Alpine Trial entry, at a German Hill Climb in late 1934

The 315/1 engine or 'Sportmotor', as described by BMW. The 319/1 was almost identical externally

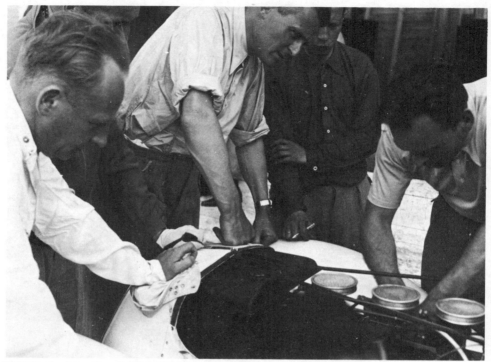

BMW Works driver Dreyfus, Schleicher in shirt sleeves, and a mechanic working on one of the cars entered for the 1936 French Grand Prix

engine, when completely redesigned and increased to 1971cc, then became the 326 (after the war this same engine was still fitted to BMWs as an alterantive engine in the 501). In 1936 BMW changed their own system to a chassis system.

Aldington's statement said that the two door saloon would be £350 and the Two Seater sports car £450, which were comparable prices to the chain driven cars of the time. The £100 Ford Popular Saloon available at that time indicated that BMWs would be for 'a select and discriminating market' to quote from a W.H. Aldington advertisement. Within a few days of the first heady announcement of the availability of the Frazer Nash-BMW, the prices were announced as £298 for the Type 34 1½ litre saloon, £325 for the Cabriolet, and a drophead Four Seater for £395; the 2 litre Type 40 (see footnote) with a single carburettor and Sports Two Seater body at £398.

The introduction of the 2 litre engines into the BMW range had coincided with the introduction of the Frazer Nash-BMW. The cars were an immediate success and this was shown by the motoring correspondents of the national newspapers, who literally queued up for the road test cars. The

H. J. Aldington in sober mood, probably about 1935

FRAZER NASH

Osterley House grounds are the background for this catalogue illustration for the Type 40 at £398, when fitted with the 315/1 engine. The same body was fitted to the Type 55, with knock-off hub nuts and the four pin securing wheel system, together with a 319/1 engine, at £475

Aldingtons found, much to their surprise, that there was a greater demand for Cabriolets and Saloons, than for the Sports cars.

Popp and Aldington were very similar in their outlook and one of Aldington's trading maxims was shared by Popp; if the client wanted something special and could afford to pay for it, then he should have it. Simple requirements such as special paints and upholstery were easy to arrange and within the wide variety of body styles available, a one-off car was not at all impracticable. The proliferation of model names for each type, made the model naming of the chain drive cars seem positively staid. The Type 40 was a popular model from the works and there were approximately fifty cars sold as Tourers, Saloons, Limousines, Pillarless Saloons, Cabriolet Saloons, Cabriolets, Two Seater and Four Seater Sports, together with a special German body built by Drauz and British bodied Coupes by Abbott.

The appeal of the BMW models to the British press was that with the

THE FRAZER NASH-BMW

Frazer Nash name they possessed a panache of sports racing; BMC in using the name Cooper proved the same point many years later. The standard one and a half litre Type 34 was as slow as many cars on the British roads, of that time, but it did have excellent road holding allied to reasonable acceleration due to its light weight. *Motor Sport* said in November 1935 '... the Two Seater car only weighs fifteen hundredweight. A comfortable Four Seater saloon only weighs seventeen and a half hundredweight, which should be an object lesson to those of our manufacturers who burden a 1100cc engine with a ton weight of chassis and coach work'.

AFN Limited set out to sell sports cars with perhaps a sale of the occasional tourer and the rare saloon; in their selling they often sold to their very sporting clients some very sedate tourers and saloons. The sales demonstration techniques for Frazer Nash and Frazer Nash-BMW cars were entirely different; the potential buyer of a chain drive car was treated with far more deference, than the erstwhile BMW purchaser. Fane would normally demonstrate the Frazer Nash at the highest possible speed on the best surfaced winding roads available. If such a road was not available, then a full 360 degree circumnavigation of a roundabout, with various amounts of opposite lock, had to suffice. The BMW tended to be demonstrated by D.A. Aldington, though both the other brothers were not above making demonstration runs over the roughest, most pot holed road available, Osterley Park near the Works was the favourite; if such a road was not available then driving the left hand front wheel up and over the kerbstone and down again into the gutter, adequately demonstrated the advantages of a rigid chassis and independent front suspension.

Aldington's relationship with Popp and the Works was of great importance to BMW on two counts; firstly Britain was, at that time, a hard currency area and it was very difficult for Germans to take cash out of Germany, and secondly the BMW people much admired Aldington for his knowledge and driving skill; Aldington was accepted as part of the BMW design team. The explosion of BMW designs and production, that took place between 1933 and 1936 is almost impossible to comprehend, especially as the BMW Works were maximising these designs into production cars in large numbers, at a rate of approximately 7,000 cars a year. The two chief engineers whose responsibility this was, were Doctor Fritz Fiedler and Rudolf Schleicher.

In the higher echelons of the BMW management there was a certain amount of fluidity, regarding responsibility. Fiedler's specific responsibility was to the cars and especially to chassis design but Schleicher, though primarily interested in motorcycles and the racing motorcycles for BMW,

Line up for the start of the 1936 TT with Bira, Fane and Aldington in the right hand drive 328, all specially painted British Racing Green for the occasion. The R.A.C. thought that the 328s were seriously underweight when compared with British 2 litre cars, presumably they had the 2 litre Aston Martin in mind as here, and the 328s had to carry one hundredweight of lead each

H. J. Aldington's 328 for the TT. The FRS is an aide memoire for faster, refuel, slower pit signals

THE FRAZER NASH-BMW

was responsible for the 326 engine and for the design of the 328 cylinder head.

The fabricated 'A' shape, with two bars across the tubular chassis of the open cars used various gauges of steel according to the beam and torsional strengths required and was a logical development of Bugatti's thinking. The saloon BMWs were developed from 1935 along more conventional lines using a strong box section frame and a large pressing at the front of the chassis. This chassis was used for the 320, 326, 327 and 335, but the sports and touring cars such as the early Type 34s and the 40s and 55s together with the 328 and 329 used the large diameter tubular chassis.

The original 1248cc engine and gearbox was probably bought direct from Opel and was enlarged by Opel to the one and a half litre class, with six cylinders of 58 x 94mm. The hypothesis is that it was an Opel development to increase the same engine to 65 x 96mm which gave a capacity of 1911cc (the 319 engine). At the beginning of 1936 a new engine was developed by BMW that was externally almost identical but had the dimensions of 66 x 96mm to give the capacity of 1971cc; this engine was described by BMW as new and more or less unburstable and was fitted to the 326 model, when it was introduced. The differences between the 319 and the 326 were a better crankshaft, better connecting rods and larger width of bearing area on the crankshaft and other differences that made for greater reliability and the potential for engine development.

The Frazer Nash-BMW type system of identification began to go even more awry with the advent of the 320 Saloon cars and the 326 Five Seater Saloon cars with their fixed bodywork. The 326 Five Seater Saloon car needed the horse-power, and was fitted as standard with the 50 horse-power or 1971cc engine - in 1938 and 1939 this model alternatively could be fitted with the 328 engine, when it could truthfully have been called the first 'BMW business man's express'. The 329 was available as a Saloon car Cabriolet and was not so over-bodied as the 326; this was available with either the 45 or 50 horse-power engines and the only reason there can be for this needless duplication is that the 45 or 1911cc engine was ex-Opel and cheaper. The Type 55 Sports car was available only with the 1911cc engine.

---

*Footnote - It was John Teague who discovered the remarkable similarity between the Vauxhall 12 of the mid-thirties and the 1911cc engine from a Type 55 BMW. The one and a half litre engines of Opel and Vauxhall of the mid-thirties were a General Motors design. This could make it clear how in the period of two years from 1932 to 1934, BMW could have passed from being a minor to a major manufacturer. If the BMW engines could have been bought from Opel, then there is no reason why the gearboxes, prop-shafts and back axles should not have come from the same source

FRAZER NASH

The new 1971cc engine had a conventional cylinder head with push rod operated valves in line, the 328 engine used the bottom half of this engine.

The 328 car and engine were as major a development, as anything ever seen in motoring. The new cylinder heads picked up with the push rod block and had overhead valves set at 90°, which were operated by push rods, but used additional short push rods across the head, picking up with the normal push rods in the block; hence it was possible to have a hemispherical cylinder head engine which gave a genuine 80 horse-power. The all-enveloping Two Seater comprehensively equipped bodywork was lightweight and aerodynamic. This new car made an impact in Germany, but it was not until the French Grand Prix of 1936 that the outside world saw these new cars in a sports car race. One of the three entered was listed as a Frazer Nash-BMW to be driven by Aldington and Fane, whilst the two others were listed as BMWs (must have been a trifle confusing for the French). All three cars retired before half distance, Henne's car lost its oil pressure and the other two retired due to the collapse of the rubber engine mounting pads in the hot weather, over the long distance. Aldington subsequently won the Munich Grand Prix but this was not a premier event.

Three 328s, specially sprayed British Racing Green, were entered for the 1936 Tourist Trophy at Dundrod and the result was that Fane finished third to Freddie Dixon (Riley) and Eddie Hall (Bentley) and Fane's best lap at 80.61mph was enough to make everyone realise that the 328 was a very fast car indeed. Bira and Aldington finished respectively 7th and 9th. Prince Chula tried to get a retainer from Aldington before Bira would drive but he was told that AFN did not pay such items! The Team Prize was won by the Frazer Nash-BMW team. *Motor Sport's* Continental Correspondent, Robert Fellowes, had earlier commented on Aldington winning the Munich Grand Prix in a 328 'the new BMWs are believed to be capable of 115mph and assisted by superlative road holding and steering are unbeatable in their class'. In commenting on the TT, *Motor Sport* said 'the changed appearance of these cars led to suggestions that they were not very standard ... These BMWs were not special editions of the Type 55, but new cars which may be regarded as no more removed from standard, than any other cars in the race'.

Fane's achievements on the continent in 328s were sufficiently important for there to be a general belief that before very long he would be offered a drive in the Mercedes team. He won the 2 litre class of the 1938 Mille Miglia and the class of the Eiffelrennen in 1937. In the Grossglockner Hill Climb of 1938 he made the sports car ftd.

In the spring of 1937 Popp assured Aldington that the production series 328 would shortly be available, so Aldington obtained from the Works

The advertisement used in *Motor Sport* of April 1937

Sammy Davis of *The Autocar* after putting 102 miles into the hour chats to a benign H. J. Aldington as Leon Cushman looks on (not the Cushman of GN and Frazer Nash)

Bill Aldington's comment "not so proud of the car, look at the rear wing line, proud of the owner". Lionel Martin stands beside a Bertelli bodied Type 45

THE FRAZER NASH-BMW

Dick Seaman leaving the S bend at Donington in the 1938 TT *J. Steavenson*

one of the team cars, chassis and engine no. 85003, whose spare wheel was concealed inside the tail rather than recessed into it. With this car, which came to be known as 'Aldington's white BMW', he organised an RAC observed demonstration that to the cognoscenti of the time was literally shattering and with the usual Aldington aplomb, it was also a very cheaply run affair. Sammy Davis of *The Autocar* was invited to take the wheel of the 328 and told to run for an hour at just over the 100mph mark. On April 15 1937, the car ran at revs between 4600 and 4900rpm with a 3.9 top gear and pump Discol fuel, and achieved 102.226 miles in the hour. This achievement which was made at Brooklands was all the more meritorious since in the following year several cars attempted to emulate the 328. Alan Hess, in the TT 4½ litre Lagonda achieved 104.4 in the hour, again on pump fuel, and with a passenger, which was one up on Aldington. Two further Lagonda attempts were made in 1938 with standard cars, these were not so satisfactory with mileages of 98.43 and 101.5. In 1939 Jill Thomas took her own 328 and achieved 101.22 miles which was impressive, as it was a completely standard car. By 1939 Aldington or Fane in one of the Works 328s could have probably achieved 110 miles in the hour, as by this time there were a considerable number of options regarding competition equipment and notably a whole range of crown wheels and pinions; Aldington was racing to sell standard cars and he let the 1937 performance stand on its own. A much modified Bentley Continental in road going form, just before the war, put 114.64 miles into the hour and this was the highest mileage recorded by a car in road going trim at Brooklands in the hour.

The TT in 1937 was run for the first time at Donington. The circuit had been increased in size for the forthcoming Donington Grand Prix and it was the increased lap distance of over 3 miles, which made the circuit

The front cover of the 1938 Catalogue with the 327 Fixed Head Coupe

Part of the back cover of the 1938 Catalogue with the standard 326 Saloon

The 1938 Motor Show. The only 335 imported, together with a 327 and a 328

suitable for International events. Four Frazer Nash-BMWs were entered, being driven by H.G. Dobbs, an earlier works Riley driver, Bira, who took over Henne's entry only the day before the race, Fane, whose instructions were to set out and bust the opposition and Aldington, to make up the four. Dobb's car broke on the line and the German mechanics under Bertelli's control took two and a quarter hours to strip and rebuild the broken differential, since Dobbs was nominated as one of the team entry. No sooner had Dobbs disappeared then Fane came into the pits for refuelling when lying second in the race. He had been responsible for causing the retirement of one Darracq, but when he restarted his back axle failed. Bill Aldington stated later it was due to the failure of an experimental ball race, (not a standard one, you note)*, and the mechanics wheeled the car away. Dobbs car developed gearbox trouble and he retired. The Darracqs finished a brilliant first and second whilst Bira finished third and Aldington finished eighth. The team prize was not awarded.

The production model 328s were available in Britain by June of 1937 and from then till the war the Works sold a minimum of 30 and possibly a few more. The standard price was £695. Certainly the most expensive 328 sold by the Works was chassis no. 85097 to the Maharajah Bahadur of Jammu and Kashmir, which involved so many extras that they were invoiced separately, as were the spare parts that were sent out to India, using the services of the Minister-in-waiting Major General Jund.

The 327 model was aimed at a market that wanted a touring version of the 328; all out performance was not necessarily the criteria and the standard 1971cc engine was fitted, with the alternative option of the 328 engine. In Britain these two cars were known as the 327/50 and the 327/80 whilst in Munich and Eisenach they were listed as the 327 and 327/28.

* Footnote — Bill Aldington used the word standard to describe all the cars, so to the components; some were more standard than others!

FRAZER NASH

Bill Aldington used Lionel Martin's comments in one advertisement he placed in the *J.C.C. Gazette,* without actually mentioning the name of Aston-Martin, which must have reduced its impact value.

'I have been a user of light cars since 1913, but I have never found any which approached in excellence my two Frazer Nash-BMWs.

'Each seems to be as nearly as possible perfect in its own class - the '45' dead silent, extremely flexible, an easy gear change and very lively; the '55' possessing the pleasant 'burble' of a sports car, a gearbox dead silent on all gears - with a perfect change, the delightful 'long stride' of the high axle ratio and phenomenal acceleration and, of course, each model has the familiar Frazer Nash-BMW characteristics of extreme lightness of 'feel' and delightfully accurate steering, with wonderful road-holding and cornering, SPRINGING NEVER IN MY EXPERIENCE EQUALLED, and all these qualities combined with that indefinable feeling of good breeding which gives unfailing promise of long and pleasant service.

'May I also express my sincere appreciation of your firm's most pleasant attention to 'service' - such as is only given by real enthusiasts'.

The normal body style of the 327 was with a Cabriolet body or a drop-head bodied coupe. Aldington sold very few 327s, certainly less than ten which was surprising. A.C. Bertelli, once of Aston-Martins, was interested in building bodies to the 327 but the only commission he received was to build a drop-head body to a 328 chassis for Lionel Martin, also ex Aston-Martin, who lived on Kingston Hill near to Archie Frazer-Nash.

In 1939 the BMW Works produced a new model, the 335, entirely to Aldington's requirements for a restyled Five Seater 320, with a three and a half litre engine (six cylinders 82 x 110mm). This was to be the real business man's express with a top gear of 2.9 to 1, but the coming of the war inhibited the development and only a few cars were made of which one came to England. The total number of BMWs sold as Frazer Nash-BMWs totalled approximately 340-360 of which a large proportion were Cabriolets and Saloons. In May of 1939 Aldington was entered by the BMW Works for the Hamburg Grand Prix which was a two litre sports car race. On one corner Aldington got too close to the trees and as he said, "the first tree removed the hub nut, the next one the wheel, the next one the brake drum and by the time the accident finished the car had turned over and it was a very thorough accident. I was just badly bruised. It was my first and only motor racing accident. I did not want the car to go to Munich to be repaired; the head mechanic said that I was to have no fear, that even if there was trouble coming, then they would keep my car till it was all over and I could then come and collect it".

Bill Aldington metamorphosed the 319/1 BMW, with left-hand drive, into a right-hand drive Frazer Nash-BMW type 55 by the simple expedient of instructing the printer "Change number plate to reversed white letters on black, AFN 37, and ALL TO BE REVERSED"

A British bodied drophead foursome Coupe on a type 55 chassis

Leslie Johnson's 328 which being a standard car featured the exposed spare wheel and the divided hinged windscreen. The works racing cars had a simple low cut windscreen and the spare wheel was always located inside the body

H. J. Aldington after winning the Munich Grand Prix of August 1936

The post war cars
Chapter 9

ISOLATED BURSTS OF small arms firing could be heard around Munich in July of 1945, as disaffected groups roamed the ungoverned countryside, endeavouring to live. The war had only been over for a month in Europe and General Patton, commanding the American Zone in the South of Germany, was opposed to signing a property release note, for a certain Lieutenant Colonel Aldington, R.E.M.E., of the British Army. Aldington and his brother Bill, also a half colonel, were miles away from where they should have been officially and were claiming that a certain car was their own. They had arrived officially, with the correct papers, but had managed to avoid being in an official party and were well received by all their friends at BMW. Eventually the weight of evidence convinced Patton that a 328 BMW had been sent back to the factory, by the owner, to be rebuilt following a crash, and that the Works had kept the car hidden away in a cellar all through the war. General Patton agreed that the car could be taken out of the U.S. Zone and raised the necessary paperwork.

The car that the Aldington's had 'found' was not the 328 which had been crashed in the 1939 Hamburg Grand Prix, as that had been broken up as soon as the war started, but the BMW that had finished third in the 1940 Mille Miglia. This nine lap race was over the triangular circuit Brescia-Cremona-Mantova and won by a coupe BMW. This coupe BMW, with a five speed gearbox, had previously competed in the 1939 Le Mans race and won the 1940 Coppa Brescia or Mille Miglia convincingly, driven by Huschke von Hanstein and Baumer. In third place, after an Alfa-Romeo, was one of the

FRAZER NASH

new open Works racers that were to be the prototype 328 replacement, and another of these open, highly aerodynamic, sports cars was in fifth place. Aldington had known that there was to be a replacement 328 and had seen sketches of the car in 1939 but was unaware that any cars had been built or that they had competed in a 1940 Mille Miglia. The BMW people in Munich showed Aldington this car, which had been driven in the race by Brudes and Roese, and were able to demonstrate that it ran and almost immediately this became transmogrified into the white 328 that the BMW people had been keeping for Aldington all through the war.

Bill Aldington drove the BMW back across Germany, but in driving through a bomb crater in Cologne, he knocked off the sump and the car had then to be towed to Ostend and taken over to England in a tank landing craft.

It was at Eisenach that the production of BMW motor cars had been centred and it is said that the post-war division of Europe was held up for twenty four hours at the Potsdam conference whilst Stalin insisted that the town of Eisenach and its surrounding countryside had to be inside the Russian Zone. The racing preparation and some of the experimental work had been carried out in Munich. The Works in Munich had been heavily bombed but many departments were in underground premises and in reasonable shape. The various members of the staff that Aldington managed to find, to see if they would like to come to England to make the post-war Frazer-Nash-BMW, all gave an emphatic "yes".

Aldington, on his return to England, opened up negotiations on several fronts, to get his demobilisation through as quickly as possible, to

---

Footnote - At the end of 1938 AFN Limited took over the agency for the Messerschmitt Taifun, a high performance touring aeroplane, also very similar in appearance to the ME 109. Aldington and Fane both obtained their single engined private flying licences before the start of the war. At the beginning of the war H.J. Aldington joined the Royal Army Ordnance Corps and transferred, as did many other volunteers from the Motor Industry, to the new Royal Electrical and Mechanical Engineers (R.E.M.E.) and rose to become a Lieutenant Colonel. D.A. Aldington also joined the R.A.O.C., but was transferred to the Ministry of Supply and it was through this organisation he became connected with the directors of the Bristol Aeroplane Company; he introduced his brother, who discussed post-war possibilities. H.J. Aldington subsequently became a director of Bristols. W.H. Aldington initially organised at Isleworth the trining of L.A.Ds (Light Aid Detachments) for the Army and for the greater part of the war, the training of Motor Mechanics or Engine Room Artificers (E.R.As) for the Navy.

Many pre-war owners were to die in the war. The greatest losses, to those who knew all the people connected with the firm, were caused by the deaths of Fane, Berry and Grogan; Fane was killed when his Photographic Reconnaisance Spitfire crashed on returning from France, Berry was lost flying the Atlantic and Grogan went down with the Hood

The Grand Prix model Frazer-Nash shown to the press in November of 1947, priced at £3500, inclusive of purchase tax

The Superleggera bodied Frazer-Nash Fast Tourer, exhibited at the Geneva Motor Show of 1948 prior to being shipped to the Shah of Persia

FRAZER NASH

The 'High Speed' model—a 120 b.h.p. 2-litre car eligible for Formula B Racing, and the 'Fast Tourer' model, possessing a performance of the first order . . . .

The "Motor" (February 4, 1948) says:

THE new " High Speed " model Frazer-Nash 2-litre is a direct descendant of the competition model sold by the company before the war. Although similar in general design it is, however, much developed, engine output having been raised by more than one-third and the all-up weight reduced. This, together with changes in body form which have sensibly reduced drag, has resulted in a car of altogether outstanding performance which should well hold its own in international events, as well as providing the enthusiastic owner with a first-class high-speed touring car.

Taking first the engine; this is unchanged dimensionally, but the power output of the Frazer-Nash of 120 b.h.p., obtained at 5,500 r.p.m., gives the quite remarkable figure of 3.82 b.h.p. of piston area. Another outstanding figure on this engine is 150 b.m.e.p. at 3,000 r.p.m., at which speed the engine develops nearly 70 b.h.p.

The general characteristics of the design are by now well known, a particularly ingenious feature being the means whereby a single camshaft disposed in the crankcase is made to serve inclined overhead valves by means of cross-pushrods and bell cranks. The valves rest on inserted seats in the light-alloy head, which is exceptionally deep so as to avoid distortion and includes short and direct passages placed almost vertically between the valve head and three down-draught Solex carburetters. This feature of the engine offers fundamentally good breathing quality, of which the designer has taken full advantage in securing the output figures aforementioned. The water flow is biased to the exhaust side of the head with a view to providing fully adequate cooling, and the crankshaft being 2 ins. in diameter is an exceptionally robust design. It is fully counter-weighted and damped against torsional vibration by rubber-bonding a disc and the fan pulley on to the front end of the shaft. This design is one of the few to employ hardened surfaces, which run in Vandervell copper-lead thin-wall bearings. Fully forced lubrication is, of course, provided, with the additional refinement of drilled connecting rods, so as to provide a pressure supply to the gudgeon-pin bearings, which are mounted about half-way down the long, light-alloy pressing used by Specialloid for the piston. This method of manufacture combines excellent quality of material with sustained strength at high temperatures.

The lubrication system also embodies an interesting heat exchanger, which runs the full length of the exhaust side of the casing and takes the form of a fin tube immersed in the cooling water so that when starting from cold the water warms the oil, whereas under high speed conditions excessive oil temperature is avoided by means of heat lost to the water. (" High Speed " model—oil in circulation passes through external oil radiator.) It is worth noting that the temperature of the cooling fluid is directly under the control of the driver, who is given hand operation of the radiator shutters.

The gearbox has carefully chosen ratios which provide maxima of 118 m.p.h. on top, 91 m.p.h. on third, 54 m.p.h. on second and 27 m.p.h. on bottom gear at the peak of the h.p. curve. These exceptionally high figures are, of course, in accordance with Frazer-Nash tradition for high gearing, and it will be noted that the potential maximum on *third* gear has been exceeded by only three post-war road-test cars using *top* gear.

A feature of the gearbox which is worthy of mention is the use of a free wheel on first gear only, so that this emergency ratio can always be obtained instantly without possibility of error. The three upper ratios are synchronized. Another point of interest is that the shaft running in the rear extension to the box is internally splined and embraces a sliding shaft, to which the front universal joint is attached. Motion caused by the rise and fall of the rear axle is, therefore, taken care of by fully enclosed and lubricated splines.

The rear axle itself is of orthodox design, but is located on the frame by means of a triangulated torque member, which also locates it sideways. This component is necessary because the rear suspension is by torsion bars, which lie on the longitudinal axis of the car and are connected to the rear axle by swinging arms, which are also joined to the piston-type shock absorbers. Similar dampers are used at the front end of the car, where the suspension is by a transverse-leaf spring mounted above two long wishbones. The effect of this arrangement is to provide almost parallel motion for the front wheels, the system being virtually equivalent to links of equal length.

The steering gear is a rack and pinion placed behind the wheel centres and having two short, swinging track rods, so that there is practically no geometric interference as the wheels rise and fall. The steering wheel is attached to the pinion by means of an open shaft and a disc-type universal joint, so that minor misalignment between body and chassis has no ill-effect upon the steering mechanism.

The frame of the Frazer-Nash is entirely special. The side members consist of two 5½ ins. diameter tubes of 12 gauge silicon manganese steel which are cranked downwards from the front of the car to the centre section and taper inwards in plan over the same distance. At the centre they are braced by a cross tube of similar construction and dimensions, a further cross member tying together the parallel section and the main frame which ends just ahead of the rear axle. An extension piece of smaller diameter tubes is cantilevered over the back of the car to form a support for the body and large fuel tank. The overall result is a very sturdy assembly with inherently low weight.

Abstracted from the post war catalogue published in the spring of 1948. On the cover was a side view photograph of the Grand Prix Model but no reference was made to this model in the text

Reduction in unsprung weight has been studied with particular care. Light alloy brake drums with inserted liners are used, the back plates having ample provision for ventilation so as to avoid brake fade when the car is doing competition work.

The brakes themselves are of the Lockheed two-leading-shoe type, the master cylinder being carefully shrouded from heat dissipated by the exhaust system. A centrally mounted pull-up handbrake works the rear shoes through a short direct mechanical system.

The wheels are notable in being of the knock-off type. They are not, as usual with this form of construction, wire wheels with splined hubs, but of the pierced disc type which are pulled up on to pins which transmit braking and driving torque.

The low weight of the chassis (10½ cwt.) is remarkable. Although this is a production type car the frame weight (140 lb.) is only 40 lb. greater than the best figures achieved in racing car practice where cost and easy production design have not to be considered, and the engine weighs less than 3 lb. per h.p.

It is obvious from the figures quoted that the new Frazer-Nash " High Speed " model will take its place amongst the leading fast cars of the world.

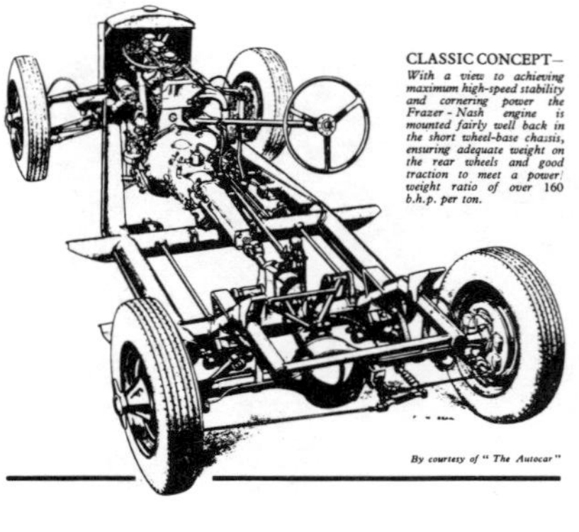

CLASSIC CONCEPT—
With a view to achieving maximum high-speed stability and cornering power the Frazer-Nash engine is mounted fairly well back in the short wheel-base chassis, ensuring adequate weight on the rear wheels and good traction to meet a power/weight ratio of over 160 b.h.p. per ton.

By courtesy of " The Autocar "

TECHNICAL SPECIFICATION

" HIGH SPEED " Model—120 b.h.p. at 5,500 r.p.m.

" FAST TOURER " Model—100 b.h.p. at 5,000 r.p.m.
(Compression ratio, 8·5 : 1)

Engine: 6 cylinders. Bore, 66 mm.; stroke, 96 mm. Capacity, 1,971 c.c. Rating 16.2 h.p. Detachable aluminium alloy cylinder head—hardened bronze seats for the valves, and special inserts for the 10 mm. plugs; the latter positioned vertically in centre of the head. Cylinders of special grey cast-iron in unit construction with upper half of crankcase. Inclined overhead valves operated by push-rods from a single camshaft—driven by duplex chain with automatic tensioner. Pistons—light alloy forgings. Sturdy forged steel connecting rods of special section with integral oil feed duct to gudgeon pin. Fully balanced crankshaft with torsional vibration damper—four main bearings. Copper-lead (steel backed) strip type bearings to all crankshaft journals. Water cooling (capacity 2 gallons) with pump circulation with pressure delivery to cylinder head—temperature regulation by hand-operated radiator shutters. Forced lubrication to all engine bearings with full-flow cleaner and suitable reduction in the pressure for the valve gear—oil in circulation passes through external oil radiator. (" Fast Tourer " model—oil heat exchanger in circuit.) Magnesium sump (oil capacity, 10 pints). Three Solex down-draught carburetters, each fitted with easy-starting device and individual air cleaners. Fuel supply by mechanical pump driven from camshaft (fuel capacity, 16 gallons).

Transmission: Single dry-plate clutch—in housing bolted to gearbox, itself integral with engine—complete power unit flexibly mounted. Four speeds—free-wheel operative on first gear, with synchromesh on second, third and top. Open two-jointed propeller shaft, dynamically balanced. Spiral bevel final drive.

Chassis: Frame and cross-members of special light steel tubes of unusually great diameter, welded to form a remarkably stiff, short girder—absolutely rigid.

Suspension: Front—independent, employing a top transverse half-elliptic leaf spring, wish-bones and hydraulic shock absorbers of special design. At the rear, suspension is by torsion bars, with hydraulic dampers.

Steering: Rack and pinion. Positive, yet finger-light, in action. Adjustable for rake and height.

Brakes: Hydraulic—foot-brake—on all four wheels—two-leading-shoe type. Light alloy drums with liners, and air scoops for cooling. Mechanical—hand-brake—by rods to rear wheels.

Equipment, etc.: Specially-designed 12-volt (72 a.h.) electrical equipment. 5.25 in. × 16 in. tyres on pierced disc wheels. " One-shot " chassis lubrication by foot-operated pump. Instruments: 5-in. diameter 120 m.p.h. speedometer, 5-in. diameter revolution counter, oil and water thermometer gauges, oil pressure gauge, ammeter, petrol gauge, clock, etc. Flexibly-spoked steering wheel.

Coachwork: Fully streamlined, yet essentially practical, two-seater body of light alloy on tubular framework. Finest materials only employed throughout in construction and finish. Fully concealed hood and all-weather equipment.

General Data: Wheelbase, 8 feet. Track (front and rear) 4 feet. Turning circle, 30 feet. Chassis weight, 10½ cwt. Complete car, 14½ cwt. (approx). Gear ratios: Top 3.55, third, 4.61, second, 7.72, first, 15.26, reverse, 12.22. Petrol consumption 25 m.p.g. at 70 m.p.h.

Note: Specification subject to alteration, and illustrations not necessarily binding as to detail.

Engine and Performance Data (" High Speed " Model)

Compression ratio, 9·5 : 1.	Piston area, sq. in. per ton, 43·3
120 b.h.p. at 5,500 r.p.m.	Brake lining area, sq. in. per ton, 198.
Max. b.m.e.p. 150 at 3,000 r.p.m.	Top gear m.p.h. per 1,000 r.p.m. 21·4.
B.H.P. per sq. in. piston area, 3·9.	Top gear m.p.h. at 2,500 ft./min. piston speed, 85.
Peak piston speed ft. per min. 3,260.	Litres per ton-mile, dry, 3,800.

Printed in England by Fosh & Cross Ltd., London

THE POST WAR CARS

finalise negotiations with the Bristol Aeroplane Company and to talk with the war reparations committee as to the methods of bringing over BMW drawings, and components. In particular he wanted people; Fiedler and Schleicher for the design side: Ernest Loof, the 'Freddie Dixon' of BMW: von Rucker and Alex von Falkenhausen. Falkenhausen, as well as being a superb driver, was a born organiser and the 'Neubauer' of BMW.

Bristols accepted Aldington's propositions and they were anxious to use their engineering capacity as soon as possible. Within weeks, it was agreed that Aldington should sell out to Bristols. Bristols were to produce a car, which was to be known as the Frazer Nash-Bristol. Bristols would transfer parts for Isleworth to produce sports cars for Bristols, which would then be sold as Frazer Nashes. Aldington, and his brother Donald, arranged for Bristols to apply pressure on the American Zone for the expedition of Aldington's requirements and their influence speeded up the process. A deed of agreement was drawn up and Aldington and the board of Bristols signed, whereby Aldington sold out completely his rights in both Frazer Nash and Frazer Nash-BMW.

Aldington's requests for people and material from Munich was contested by the Americans but, far more seriously, was contested by the British automotive industry. At the same time as one part of the British Motor Industry was stating they were not interested in the VW, then another part from Birmingham was against the importation of these German brains; in the end Aldington had to settle for Dr Fiedler only, who like Dr Porsche was reckoned to be a war criminal, though never tried as such, and was in jail. Eventually his release was obtained in 1946, and he went straight to Bristols to improve the engine.

Aldington managed to get from BMW all the drawings for the 326 and 328 including engine drawings and the drawings for the sports car replacement of the 328. He also managed to get back to England, by a feat of organisation which involved several government departments and the Army together, some engines and parts of a 328.

The intention in mid 1946 was for Bristols to produce a Saloon, which would update the 326 and the 329, together with a Cabriolet and a Sports car. Aldington insisted that the coachwork, for this new car, had to be perfect and it was agreed that two experimental bodies should be built by Farina and Superleggera. Bristols agreed to this and Count Lurani made the

Footnote - There was another 328 successor model made about the same time, which featured a slab sided body style, not dissimilar to the post-war C-type Jaguar Works cars. BMWs in the post-war period called this a Mille Miglia but now in 1976 since they have the Brudes car back in Munich, they have presumably renamed this car

The High Speed model on the Frazer-Nash stand at the first Motor Show, post war *The Autocar*

The Fast Tourer model was superseded by the 1949 Fast Roadster model, featuring a bonnet closing centrally east-west, it opened with the front half hinged over the radiator and the rear over the bulkhead

THE POST WAR CARS

The High Speed model was raced in its original form by Tony Crook, here seen at Silverstone in 1950
T. C. March

arrangements. By the end of 1946 the prototypes had been built and the road testing had been carried out. The drawing office at Bristols were detailing the items as if they were aircraft components, rather than pieces of motor cars. To examine the rear window and the sun blinds of the Bristol 400, indicates the aircraft industry background rather than automobile.

Aldington at this time had not decided the form the sports car was to take; it was clear that the Frazer Nash-Bristol saloon car was to be of an advanced post-war design and it was thought that the sports car should be complementary. The design could be either a 328 style, 1940 328 style or a torpedo style sports car.

In the middle of 1947 Bristols stated that they did not want to proceed with the agreement, since they did not wish to use the Frazer Nash name. Further that the activities that they were going to carry out should be done in their name and by themselves only. The decision to unscramble the

Aldington pulls away from the pits during the 1949 Le Mans 24 Hour Race, notice the use of a rear tonneau cover in the early cars

Aldington in Culpan's car at Le Mans

The Mille Miglia being aerodynamically tested by Bristols at Filton. The aim was to get a comparison against the Arnolt-Bristol with Bertone bodies. The Mille Miglia was significantly better streamlined

The first Mille Miglia outside the Works. The spare wheel compartment in the wing was neater than the Fast Tourer, which had a hump on the wing

FRAZER NASH

new company was not contested by Aldington; he said "they had not taken the decision lightly and if they did not want the Frazer Nash name then there was no point in fighting them to make them use it". The unscrambling was therefore carried out with Aldington's co-operation, so that the Isleworth factory and the use of the Frazer Nash name reverted to Aldington. The remaining parts of the agreement with Bristol, most of which had been implemented on supply of BMW components and drawings, were retained. To provide future know-how and co-operation and for AFN Limited to be able to buy Bristol engines and gearboxes on favourable terms, were in this new agreement.

If an aeroplane company could produce aerodynamic designs, then AFN Limited could do the same. The Grand Prix Frazer Nash model shown to the press in November of 1947 bore a startling resemblance to the 1940 BMW, but there were no journalists present who had been at the Coppa Brescia, or even knew at that time that BMWs had produced special cars for that event. This was to remind the press that though the thunder about new cars was seemingly coming from Bristols, there was still in Isleworth a centre where great sports car designs were produced. The Grand Prix model was the 1940 Mille Miglia BMW with a respray, a Frazer Nash badge or two and a new radiator grille. The announcement of this model gave the breathing space that was necessary for the Works to adjust to the idea that they would be building complete cars, rather than acting as an assembly plant. Bristols grudgingly let Fiedler go to Isleworth at the end of 1947 as he had uprated the Bristol engine, from the pure pre-war design of the 400, to a modern post-war specification and had materially raised the horse-power.

Fiedler, in a month, designed and produced most of the major drawings for the post-war Frazer-Nash. When the prototype was built it was found that everything fitted correctly and no rethinking was necessary at all. It was clear that the High Speed (later to be also called the Competition) and Fast Tourer Models were to repeat the pre-war story, for the first post-war catalogue's introduction ended, 'While these new cars will fully justify the description of production models in the true sense of the word, they will be built in limited numbers only and so maintain the Frazer-Nash tradition of personal contact between owner and manufacturer'. From this time forward the Works, or Bill Aldington in particular, had decided that there was a hyphen between Frazer and Nash and so this Book adopts the hyphen for the post-war story.

Bill Aldington's panache at showing off the wares was shown by the Salter spring balance on the Frazer-Nash stand, at the 1948 Motor Show, which indicated that the chassis, or more accurately the complete car less the

Jack Newton of Newton Oils was a constant competitor in his early car *T. C. Marsh*

The start of the British Empire Trophy Race of 1951; David Clarke 18, Stirling Moss 22 and Bob Gerard 21, were the front row of the grid. Second row; Sydney Allard in an Allard and Donald Pitt. The next row included W. H. Murray and Normal Culpan. Moss won the race with Gerard in second place

FRAZER NASH

Franco Cortese at the start of the 1951 Circuit of Sicily. A one lap motor race of 670 miles. Cortese competed against twelve Ferraris and four Maseratis, set up a 2 litre class record, won the cup awarded for the first foreign car in the race and finished fourth overall

bodywork, weighed only 10½ hundredweight. Other than parts which were fitted to the bodywork, such as the accelerator pedal and linkage, the whole chassis was complete. The price, with the punitive double purchase tax, at that time in operation, was a stunning £3,073 14s 5d. One of the earliest cars had been shipped, prior to the show, to the Shah of Iran.

The High Speed model was easily identified by the low slung headlights at the foot of the radiator. In 1949, at the same time as the introduction of tubular shock absorbers, the headlights were mounted high in a traditional manner and in a legal manner; the original mounting was low and created severe dazzle problems with night time running. Norman Culpan visited the Earls Court Show Stand and liking the look of the Frazer-Nash, placed his order by phone the next day. Later on he told Aldington, when he was having the car serviced, that he was entering for the first post-war Le Mans 24 hour race. Aldington asked Culpan if he could be the co-driver and this was agreed. The single Frazer-Nash entry finished third in the race, to Lord Selsdon's Ferrari driven jointly by Works driver Chinetti and Lord

THE POST WAR CARS

A Mille Miglia outside the Works, the resemblance of line to the later MG MGA is noticeable *The Motor*

Selsdon and in second place a three litre Delage. Culpan's red painted 'Competition' car was restricted to 5000rpm which gave it an easy cruising speed of 100mph and over the 24 hours it averaged 78.53mph. Culpan's car had been fitted with a 3.75 back axle ratio, at his request, rather than the standard 3.55. Supplementary fuel tanks were fitted as Culpan had established, through racing around the perimeter of a deserted airfield, that the fuel consumption at a 75mph average, with racing type acceleration and deceleration, was only 13mpg. If he had not had the supplementary tanks fitted then he would have had to retire, due to coming in to refuel before the regulations permitted - not many years later a Frazer-Nash had to retire for that same reason.

The renaming of the High Speed/Competition car, by the Aldingtons, as the Le Mans Replica was made for the 1949 Motor Show, as was the introduction of the Mille Miglia and the quickly forgotten Cabriolet. The Mille Miglia showed a significant change in the Works thinking; there were a number of features which indicated that the comfort and wellbeing of the

Practically any motoring magazine of the early fifties could have carried such a photograph of Salvadori and Crook

Bill Aldington's post war advertisements had considerable bite to them and the advertisement in *Autosport* of January 1952 was typical

In 1952 Bill Aldington ran this nostalgic advertisement. He was never above quoting from earlier victories and in 1948 referred at some length to Gallop's performance in 1925

driver and his passenger had been borne in mind in the design. Hitherto the design premises had been based on the hair shirt principle - functional, straightforward, hard wearing and designed for a job. The job of work being an all purpose competition car. The driver of a TT Replica, or an earlier Boulogne, or a Le Mans Replica was accustomed to the idea that he was in charge of a purposeful device, in the same way as a jockey of a three year old classic hopeful; his satisfaction was to come from the chance of achieving success and not from the niceties of comfort and wellbeing. The fitting of a windscreen, that could be raked, so as to achieve an optimum angle for racing purposes, but also providing comfort was a revelation; as were the features on the Fiedler designed Cabriolet of the same time, which shared with the Mille Miglia the spare wheel mounting inside the right hand front wing, so as 'to leave the rear space free for luggage accommodation'. The Foursome Cabriolet was soon to be forgotten, but it was one of the rare Frazer-Nash post-war attempts to produce a Four Seater car.

FRAZER NASH

The first Targa Florio model, for many years owned by Hugh Cundey, whose connections with the firm went back to the early thirties; firstly as an owner and in the immediate post war period as the Secretary

The private owners began to notch up a continuing series of victories; to the outside world it must have been clear that the production rate from Isleworth was similar to Aston-Martins or perhaps higher ... Prior to Le Mans there had been indications of the successes which were to follow, with Serafini's wild drive in the Tour of Sicily. Serafini, a pre-war Gilera rider, had had the Frazer-Nash leading the field prior to his crash.

Gillie Tyrer bought from AFN the Mille Miglia 1940 car. The Frazer-Nash badge was removed from the Frazer-Nash radiator shell and a BMW badge substituted. He proceeded to race it intensively and made record attempts to which the most notable was the standing kilo, recording 78.159mph at Jabbeke in Belgium; during one warm up for the flying kilo he passed through at 130mph plus, but was unable to complete this attempt due to engine trouble.

1950 was a year such as the marque Frazer-Nash had never known, and even the chain gang owners were not above taking an active interest in the successes. The interest had to be a little remote, as a good multi-owner

THE POST WAR CARS

The Frazer-Nash 'proposal' for Leonard Lord, fitted with the Austin engine, wheels and back axle. This car was later re-engined and became Kitty Morris' Drophead Coupe *The Autocar*

TT Replica was buyable at that time for £300 and the price of a new Le Mans Replica was £2700. Nevertheless the cat could look at the queen and purr a little. The only British sports cars that could beat the Le Mans Replicas were the Works, or near Works, Jaguars; on a good day, on a winding circuit, the Jaguars could be and were beaten. Johnny Lurani bought, for the Scuderia Ambrosiana, a Le Mans Replica and in the Tour of Sicily Cortese was lying second, until he retired with a split fuel tank. In the Mille Miglia Cortese finished sixth overall and second in the two litre class, to hordes of Ferraris and Maseratis of Works support type.

Motor racing reached a social pinnacle at the Silverstone meeting when the King and Queen, together with Princess Margaret, came to the Grand Prix meeting and the first glimmerings of the doubts about the BRM were clearly to be seen. The B.R.D.C. meeting in the autumn had two production car races of one hour for up to two litres and over two litres; the winners in the first of these races were Alberto Ascari and Serafini in Works Ferraris and they were followed by Jack Newton driving one of the earliest High Speed

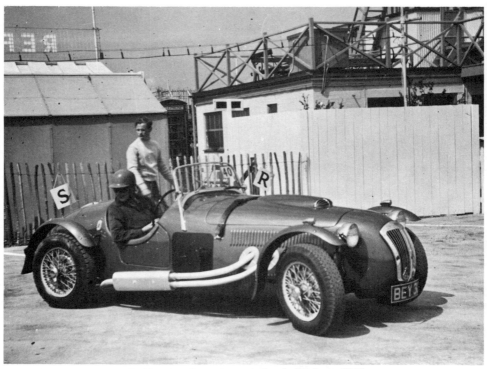

Betty Haig driving the last Le Mans Replica to be made by the Works in 1954

The lightweight and streamlined Mark II Le Mans Replica driven by Tony Crook at the 1952 International Trophy Meeting at Silverstone *T. C. March*

Mark I Le Mans Replica with Rudge-Whitworth wheels, which were a rare fitting

The Le Mans Coupe on its first appearance at Le Mans in the scrutineering bay. The Rudge-Whitworth Biennale Cup roundel motif, indicated that the same entrant had a car running in two successive years. There was always a certain amount of well bred cheating involved in the declaration of the owner's name

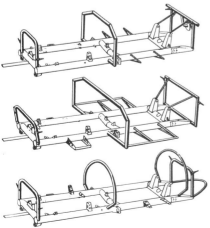

The Autocar in August of 1952 illustrated the simplification the Works had achieved. The later cars used basically only one chassis frame — top the Mark II Le Mans, centre the Mille Miglia and bottom the Single Seater

The Single Seater chassis, weighing only ninety pounds, with the BS 4 Bristol engine. The clutch pedal to the left of the gearbox casing definitely identifies the car as a Single Seater as it was not unknown for sports car chassis appendages to be welded on at a late stage

The Mk II Le Mans Replica of Tony Cook lined-up on the grid for the start of the 1952 British Grand Prix at Silverstone *Autocar*

THE POST WAR CARS

models and Frazer-Nashes also in fourth and fifth places. The TT a few weeks later had a two litre class entirely composed of Frazer-Nashes of which Bob Gerard's car was to finish third in the race, behind the irrepressible Stirling Moss and Whitehead in Jaguars.

In 1950 the design of the radiator grille of the Mille Miglia reverted to a more traditional shape, similar to a scaled down Le Mans Replica rather than the squared-off design which had been used. *The Autocar* stated that this shape of grille was to be standardised for all models 'to recall the famous chain drive Frazer Nashes of pre-war days'. The fuel tank was now in the front wing of the Convertible and the spare wheel in the tail.

Bristol Engine Performance Data

Engine Type	bhp	rpm	Compression Ratio	Valve Timing - Degrees			
				io	ic	eo	ec
85	70	4200	7.5	10	50	50	10
85A	80	4200	7.5	10	50	50	10
85C	85	4500	7.5	10	50	50	10
100A	100	5000	7.5	15	65	65	15
100B	105	5000	8.5	15	65	65	15
BS1 Mk II	130	5500	9.0	40	80	80	40
BS1 Mk III	142	5750	9.0	40	80	80	40
BS1a Mk III	148	5750	10.0	40	80	80	40
BS4 Mks I & II	142	5750	9.0	40	80	80	40
BS4a Mks I & II	155	6000	11.0	40	80	80	40

Notes: The 85 and 100 series engines were fitted to Bristol cars. The FNS engine fitted to early post-war Frazer-Nashes was current with the 85A and 85C engine, but gave 126bhp at 5000. After the conclusion of Frazer-Nash production, the 100D engine was developed that shared with the Mk II BS4 and 4a the Holset vibrator damper, which was a major improvement. The unsiamesed inlet six port racing head, used in the Bristol 450s and the Works racing Mk II Frazer-Nashes, raised 160bhp.

1950 had been good but the results in 1951 were spectacular:

Silverstone Production Car (Division 1)	1st, 2nd and 3rd
British Empire Trophy	1st and 2nd, S. Moss, F.R. Gerard
Enna Grand Prix	1st, F. Cortese
Targa Florio	1st, F. Cortese
Circuit of Sicily	1st in 2 litre class, F. Cortese
Mille Miglia	8th, F. Cortese
Rallye du Soleil	1st, O'Hara Moore
Sports Car Champion of Italy	F. Cortese

In 1953 the Works built the first single seater, since the chain drive days, for Ken Wharton as the Works driver

At the Swiss Grand Prix of 1953 the single seater had grown a massive air intake and was known, to the other members of the Formula 2 circus, as 'Wharton's Whale' *D. S. Jenkinson*

THE POST WAR CARS

The firm's promotional photograph for the single seater. Three were sold at £2000 each. At 10½ cwt dry weight, they used the same chassis as the Mark II Le Mans, but shorn of sports car appendages

There were other excellent performances, notably Eric Winterbottom's in the Alpine. He won one of the ten Alpine Cups awarded only three weeks after finishing second in the 2 litre class at Le Mans. The man of the year was Franco Cortese who competed through the season in the Scuderia Ambrosiana's Le Mans Replica, and won the Targa Florio, which no English car prior to this, or since, had ever won. He achieved the best individual performance ever recorded by a Frazer-Nash, completing the eight laps of the forty seven miles circuit in 7 hours 31 minutes 7.8 seconds with the fastest lap of 55 minutes 8.6 seconds on his last lap. Bracco was second in a 2.6 Ferrari and Bernabei third in a 2 litre Maserati.

The co-operation between Bristols and Frazer-Nash in 1952 was at a peak, the engine was steadily being uprated and the cars were continuously going faster. Lieutenant Colonel O'Hara Moore's car was timed over the flying kilometre during the Rallye du Soleil at 120.83mph; in the Targa Florio Cortese was timed on one of the straights at 121.62mph. Tony Crook went to Monthlery twice, the first time with Jim Manfield's Mille Migiia he achieved over 120mph in a ten kilometre run with a flying start and with the Le Mans Replica set out to cover 200 miles, but had to stop for two gallons of fuel and then ran out of petrol on the last lap to record 118.8mph. Within a month he was back again and this time properly organised, he averaged

FRAZER NASH

Aldington tells the Duke of Edinburgh what a splendid car the Le Mans Coupe is. The owner Edwin Redwood is half hidden behind this historic car, which competed at Le Mans twice and in 1953 won the two litre class and set a new class record

120.13mph to narrowly beat the records achieved in the Sunbeams during the vintage days, which were at best only British records set up by Jack Dunfee and Kaye Don.

1952 was a good year for the firm, but in racing the competition was growing daily more clamorous and the Works to keep ahead of this competition built the lighter and slightly more streamlined Le Mans Replica Mark II and employed Ken Wharton to drive. It was Wharton's suggestion, since the Le Mans Replica was a one and a half seater with lights, that it would be an advantage to eliminate the half seat, the lights, starter and all extraneous electrical equipment. The Single Seaters, of which there were three, supplementing the first which was a modified Le Mans Replica, never compared with the Cooper Bristols as they were overweight and consequently laboured under that disadvantage. Best performances were achieved in the Formula 2 Swiss Grand Prix of 1952 and third at the Nurburgring. The 1952 100 Mile Race for sports cars on the Boreham circuit, near Chelmsford, showed that the competition could still be held at

Len Potter's Mille Miglia, often raced by Mike Hawthorn, descends the dreaded Gavia Pass in an Alpine Rally *The Motor*

FRAZER NASH

bay with Wharton first, Mike Hawthorn second in Potter's Mille Miglia, to make it a 1, 2, 3, 4, and 5 for Frazer-Nash.

1952 emphasised the point that the Le Mans Replica was not only a very satisfactory and fast road car, but still also a race winner. Stuart Donaldson's car arrived late in New York and was driven to Florida at running in speed, where it was to be driven by Kulok and Grey in the new Sebring 12 hour race. The first race was robbed of its major excitement by the withdrawals of the Cunninghams but the Frazer-Nash beat several Jaguars to win.

The magazine *Autosport* said under the heading of 'Competition Proven' - 'Frazer-Nash, the country's most outstanding two litre sports car, winner of the British Empire Trophy in the Isle of Man, the two litre class of the Dundrod TT and Division One of the Daily Express One Hour Production Car Race at Silverstone'. In the same issue the AFN advertisement over the heading of 'Frazer-Nash Cars' stated 'The Frazer-Nash entry has invariably finished 100%, with privately owned and driven cars, competing against Works entered teams of other makes and greater engine capacity and Frazer-Nash owners have achieved numerous successes in Club meetings'. The standing of the Frazer-Nash was well exemplified by the start line of the two litre sports car race at Monte Carlo in June of 1952, where on the front row were Moss and David Clarke, with the leading Osca sandwiched between them, and behind were such heros as Valenzano in a Lancia and Castellotti and Biondetti in Ferraris; unfortunately Moss retired and Manzon in the Gordini won, Tony Crook came up from the third row to take third place and Clarke fifth at the finish.

Leonard Lord had told Aldington some months before the Motor Show that the Nuffield organisation were wishing to build a sports car. They would like the prototype to use Austin components from the Austin A135 and whatever Aldington required would be made available at cost price (the Austin A135 engine was a big four of 87 x 111mm, giving 2660cc). The Works built a car, the Roadster, similar to the Targa Florio in body shape and into this was placed the Austin engine and gearbox together with the column mounted gear change; it was felt by many that the Works had not put their full enthusiasm into the project. On the Healey Motor Show stand was to be seen Donald Healey's answer to the same problem - a really splendid car that was the prototype of the Healey 100 with practically the whole car, except the chassis, constructed of normal Austin components. During the Show, with Lord Nuffield and Leonard Lord present, it was announced that Austins were to manufacture the Healey. Aldington said that Leonard Lord was apologetic that the Frazer-Nash had not been selected,

THE POST WAR CARS

The Tew/Kelly Le Mans Replica at Leathemstown Bridge in the 1955 Tourist Trophy. HBC 1 was a car owned and raced by Bob Gerard for many years; for the 1953 Le Mans Race Gerard had the Works fit the wing valances to make it abide by F.I.A. requirements *The Motor*

but he agreed to take back the Austin components and refund Aldington's investment in the six or so engines he had bought. The Roadster was to have supplemented the Le Mans Replica Mark II, the newly introduced Targa Florio in its two forms of Turismo and Grand Sport, and the Mille Miglia.

1953 had the signs written large, for all to read, that the age of specialist motor car was coming. The sports car for racing was rapidly becoming a lightweight device, so that no one even attempted to drive them on the road. The market for the sports car that could be used for shopping, to go touring especially on long straight continental roads, to enter competitively in all sports car races and just as important, to race competitively over long distances such as in the Alpine Rally or Le Mans, with comfort, could no longer be met with one car.

The Federation Internationale Automobile in a pronouncement, at the beginning of 1953, outlawed sports cars competing in international events with, what the British called, cycle wings. The intention was probably

FRAZER NASH

Marcel Becquart behind the wheel of the Sebring he shared with Dickie Stoop to finish 10th overall in the 1955, disaster year, at Le Mans. This same car also ran in 1956 and 1957 at Le Mans *The Motor*

sound in preventing Grand Prix cars competing in road events, but the real sufferers were cars like the Healey Silverstone and the Le Mans Replica Frazer-Nashes. Le Mans Replicas had to have valances fitted to bridge from the mudguards to the bodywork. The Bob Gerard/Clarke entry for Le Mans in 1953 had very pretty valances flared in under the existing cycle wings but this modification robbed the car of significant performance. John Gott told Betty Haig "the 'wind brakes' that we had to have fitted for the Alpine detracted from the maximum speed of the car by a measurable amount". The Le Mans Replica that had started its competition career in 1948 was by 1953 illegal to race internationally. Several cars had to be rebodied. Peacock had his Le Mans Replica rebodied to a Targa Florio specification.

In 1953 Bristols began to compete and make record attempts in the Bristol 450. This car bore no resemblance whatsoever to their standard production car and consequently it was Aldington's fear that from that time

THE POST WAR CARS

Bill Aldington at the wheel of the 1953 Sebring (with which Stoop won the 1959 *Autosport* Championship), it is correctly fitted with the radiator trim. When fitted with a 140bhp Bristol engine this car was capable of a maximum speed of 135mph

forward the best engines would tend to go to Bristols Competiton Department. The Works responded well to this stimulus and further refined and lightened the Mark II Le Mans Replica and fitted a De Dion axle. This was really too late to be effective, as by 1954 the grids of all sports car races were fitted with lightweight Coopers, Lister-Bristols, Lotus 8s against which the whole concept of sports racing cars for gentlemen owners was a non-starter. The only form of competitive motor sport, at which the Frazer-Nash was ideally suited, were the great European Rallies of that time. O'Hara Moore's Le Mans Replica competed in at least three Alpine Rallies, three Rallye du Soleils, three Tulips, two Liege-Rome-Lieges and others besides, where the necessity to drive very fast up and down mountain passes was absolutely necessary.

In early January of 1954 there was an announcement made which was reported by the press, but generally not commented on, that AFN

FRAZER NASH

The 1954 Motor Show. This Sebring ran at Le Mans in 1955 driven by Odlum and Vard *The Motor*

Limited had been appointed concessionaires for Porsche. The BMW agency which had lain quiet for years was also reactivated in the middle fifties and the firm were also responsible for the range of BMW motorcycles and Steib sidecars. Add to this the UK concession for the DKW and it was no wonder that the Frazer-Nash activity began to wither. The last Frazer-Nash Le Mans Replica was made and delivered to Betty Haig, who was, in less than ten years to start to gather together the facts of the post-war history.

At Earls Court in 1954 the Sebring model was shown for the first time. It was introduced as a high speed car suitable for long distance racing or for Alpine Rallies, buitt to do it in the modern manner with a high degree of engine tune, de Dion axle, enclosed bodywork and in comfort. In commemorating the victory two years earlier at Sebring there was no doubt that the Aldingtons anticipated some orders from the United States for the new model. The Society of Motor Manufacturers and Traders has a system

THE POST WAR CARS

The Continental, with Porsche roof and doors, at the 1957 Motor Show *The Autocar*

whereby it is possible for a manufacturer to reserve model names, and even type numbers for future use, since the lead time on production, printing and publicity makes this essential; there is a story that one of the big five of that time had registered the name of Sebring and was more than a trifle put out, that this name had been 'stolen' - the fact that a Frazer-Nash had won Sebring had to be counter-balanced by the fact that only three Sebring Frazer-Nashes were ever made.

The wish to have a fast tourer, that would cover long distances effortlessly, was always at the back of Aldington's mind and a sine qua non of such a design requires an engine of adequate size that can pull overdrive gear ratios. The Austin engined car had awakened the wish and the Armstrong Siddeley Sapphire engine, which in twin carburetted form, accelerated the Sapphire car from nought to seventy in less than 18 seconds

FRAZER NASH

was impressive; the square 90 x 90mm six cylinders of 3½ litres giving up to 150 horse-power, without needing any serious development, made the engine ideal for fitting. The intention to enter such an engined car for Le Mans was told to the press, but the project was abandoned due to the weight of the engine. The entry for the 1954 race had a Le Mans Replica, the Sebring, and Gatsonides and Becquart in the Coupe. The Le Mans disaster in 1955 when over 80 people died changed the shape of motor racing. The TT in that year at Dundrod was also fated and Ken Wharton crashed the Mark II Works car, fortunately without seriously injuring himself. These two events cumulatively marked the end of the Works active participation in motor racing.

The firm finally found their large engine with the BMW 3.2 litre V8 which was shown in chassis form at the 1956 Motor Show and clothed afterwards with what the firm called a Gran Turismo Fixed Head Coupe. A year later this Coupe was sprayed silver and, slightly modified, became known as the Continental. The bodywork on this car bore a startling resemblance in the doors and roof line to the Porsche and was beautifully good looking. The 140bhp engine gave the effortless power required but it was too late.

In 1957 Peter Kirwan-Taylor joined the firm from Lotus and the intention was to build a special bodied Continental for Le Mans that year; the car's entry was at first refused by the organisers due to the insufficient driving ability of the drivers for the prototype class; eventually clearance was obtained by Earl Howe but it was too late to finish off the car even though it had been bodied by Peels of Kingston in six weeks. The car used a V8 BMW specially prepared in Germany where the capacity had been brought down to 2480cc. Kirwan-Taylor designed a new chassis for subsequent models but no cars were made. This new design incorporated a large number of Lotus features.

In 1958 the original Continental was at the Motor Show together with a Sebring and that was effectively the end of the Frazer-Nash story; though for the next few years it was possible to read in *The Autocar* and *Motor* the standard listed pirces for Frazer-Nashes. It was all rather pointless since the firm had made their last car in 1957, with the abortive Le Mans Saloon, and were moving towards the position they hold today of being the United Kingdom component of Porsche.

Footnote - Aldington looked back in the early nineteen sixties over the body designs he had been responsible for, picked as his favourites a special bodied saloon he had made in 1928, the Mille Miglia (whose body shape was repeated in the MGA) and the Le Mans Saloon known as the Le Mans Coupe. The surprise is that the TT Replica and Le Mans Replica were not included in such a list

*Footnote - Again of interest at this point, the 105 post-1945 production figure is an 'official' figure. A recent analysis carried out by Gerald Bingham and Bill Aldington, whose invaluable help at all stages has made this possible, by cross reference, they arrived at the figure 85/87. With those cars whose chassis have had two lives, it is feasible that a revised maximum figure could be 95

Index

A. G. Frazer-Nash, H. J. Aldington and W. H. Aldington with H. R. Godfrey occur frequently in the text and are not listed in this index

A
Aeroplane 152
Agabeg (see A.F.P. Fane)
Aitken, Hon. O. 110, 137, 145
Aldington, D.A. 97, 113, 136, 142, 172
Aldington, J.T. 125
Allard, S. 181
Appleton, R.L. 112
Argyll, Duke of 51, 52
Ascari, A. 187
L'Auto 182
Austin, H. 154
Autocar 59, 61, 68, 70, 106, 128, 133, 134, 165, 189, 190, 191, 202
Autosport 195
Automobile Association 14

B
Bahadue of Jammu and Kashmir, Maharajah 167
Baines 136
Baumer 171
Becquart, M. 198, 202
Bellamy, R.L. 78, 126
Benjafield, Dr. J.D. 113
Benoist, M. 54
Berry, N.A. 106, 122, 126, 127, 131
Bertelli, A.C. 108, 113, 164, 167, 168
Bernabei 193
Bezzant, J. 113
Biondetti, C. 192
'Bira' (Prince H.H. Birabongse) 160, 162, 167
Boileau, E.M.P. 15
Bolster, J.V. 84
Bolster, Mrs. V.C. 117
Borbeau 22
Bowes, R.L. 89
Bracco 193
Bradley, W.F. 128
Braidwood, W.F. 113

Brown, J.R. 15
Brudes 172
Burt, E. 88, 89, 94, 96
Burt, Mrs. D. (Kit) 79, 87
Butler-Henderson, L. 118, 125, 127, 129, 130, 133

C
Campbell, M. 113
Carriere, R. 131
Castellotti, E. 196
Chain Gang Gazette 108
Cholmondeley, Lord 137
Chinetti, L. 182
Chula, Prince 162
Clarke, D. 179, 196, 198
Cobb, J. 143
Collier, M.T.U. 127, 128
Cook, H.W. 113
Cortese, F. 182, 187, 191, 195
Conan-Doyle, (the brothers) 95
Conway, H.G. 37
Country Life 152
Cowcill, L.A. 137
Crook, T.A.D. 177, 184, 188, 193, 196
Cushman, Leon 113, 164
Cushman, L.A. 28, 30, 33, 49, 50, 53, 54, 113
Culpan, N. 178, 181, 182, 183
Cummings, I. Miss 82
Cundey, S.H.H. 126, 184
Cyclecar, see *Light Car and Cyclecar*

D
Dangerfield, E. 43
'Davies, T.' (D.C. Folland) 127, 140, 143, 148, 150
Davis, S.C.H. 164, 165
Davenport, B. 48, 55, 87
Delmar, W. 131
Dixon, F.W. 162, 175
Dobbs, H.G. 167
Dobson, A. 127
Doman, T. 142
Don, K. 194
Donaldson, S. 196

INDEX

Dreyfus 156
Dunfee, J. 194

E
Eccles, A.H.L. 143
Eccles, R. 113, 127
Edinburgh, Duke of 194
Elizabeth, Queen 187

F
Falkenhausen, A. von 175
Fane, A.F.P. 115, 135, 136, 139, 143, 144, 148, 149, 150, 154, 160, 162, 165, 167
Faroux, C. 80
Fellowes, R. 162
Feilding, Hon. W. (Earl of Denbigh) 120
Fiedler, F. 159, 175, 180, 185
Finch 33, 53
Frazer-Nash, Mrs. M. 32, 51, 79
Frazer Nash-BMW Car Club 150
Frazer Nash Car Club 108, 150
Frazer Nash Section of the VSCC 108

G
Gallop, C. Lt. Col. 71 to 81, 183
Gatsonides, M. 202
George VI, King 187
Gerard, F.R. 181, 191, 197, 198
Gibson, P.H. 82
Gleed, Miss (see Mrs. T. Wisdom)
Godfrey, Mrs. V. 32
Gott, J. 198
Grey, L. 196
Griffiths-Hughes 127, 129, 143
Gripper, A.G. 115, 125, 127, 128, 130, 133
Gripper, Mrs. A.G. 127, 131
Grogan, Lt. Cmdr. R.T. 127
Goodwin, B. 113, 150
Gough, A. 115, 121, 139, 142

H
Haig, Miss Betty 198, 200
Hall, E. 162
Hall, J.A. 58
Hanstein, H. von 164
Harvey, C.M. 113
Hawkins 53, 54
Hawthorn, M. 195, 196
Healey, D. 196
Henne, E. 162, 167

Hess, A. 165
Hill, O. 18
Hopkins, D.G. 111, 125, 131

I
Inderwick, H.W. 125

J
Jackson, R.R. 140
Jenkinson, D.S. 128
Jennings, Mrs. M. 148
J.C.C. Gazette 168
Johnson, L. 169
Johnstone, C.W. 76
Jucker, P.F. 122, 127, 144
Jund, Major General 167

K
Kelly, J. 197
Kirwan-Taylor, P. 202
Kulok, L. 196

L
Laffan, W. 58
Law, T.W. 127
Ledger, N. 97
Lees, P. 125, 138
Lewis, B.E. (Lord Essondon) 58, 59, 66, 73
Light Car and Cyclecar 13, 15, 19, 20, 25, 26, 27, 29, 42, 59, 136
Lombard, A. 49
Loof, E. 175
Lourde, M. 31, 49
Lord, L. 192
Lurani, Count J. 175, 187

M
Maclure, G.M. 59, 71, 87
MacMinnies 25
McOstrich, Miss 127
Manfield, J. 193
Manzon 196
Margaret, Princess 187
Marriott 104
Marshall, A.L. 125, 127, 130, 131, 133
Marshall, B.S. 73, 76, 80
Martin, L. 164, 168
May, W.S. 128
Mays, R. 150
Mitchell-Thomson, Hon. P. (Lord Selsdon) 120, 126, 131, 136, 140, 142, 143, 182, 183

FRAZER NASH

Millar, M. 134
Moore, T.G. 108, 113
Morgan, H.R. 33
Moss, S. 181, 191, 196
Motor 59, 73, 202
Motor Cycle 15, 42
Motor Cycling 15
Motor Sport 129, 150, 159, 162, 163
Munday, R.C. 25
Murray, W.H. 179

N
Nash, M. 14
Nash, R.G.J. 83, 87, 138
Needham, C.M. 125, 144
Needham, Mrs. A. 127, 131, 133
Newsome, S.H. 150
Newton, J. 181, 187
Nuffield, Lord 196

O
O'Hara Moore, Lt. Col. H.P. 191, 193, 199
Orrinsmith, E.H. 17
Oxley, F.W. 131

P
Patton, General 171
Peacock, R.F. 198
Per Nas 78
Persia, Shah of 173, 182
Peters, I.O.F. 114, 126
Pickett, F.N. 49, 81
Pitt, D. 179
Plunket-Greene, R.G.H. 87
Ponting, W.A. 126
Potter, L. 195
Popp, 154, 158, 159, 162
Prideaux-Brune, L. 113
Pugh, A.T. 17, 88

R
Rainey, F.T. 126
Randall, T. 60, 97
Redwood, E. 194
Ringwood 73, 74
Roberts, K.M. 125
Robinson, F.B. 126
Roese 172
Ross, T.D. 118
Rucker, von 175

S
Salvadori, R. 184
Seaman, R. 165
Sedgwick, Miss C. 127
Senior, D. 151
Serafini, 186, 187
Scott, H.R. 74, 75, 80, 87, 89, 94, 95
Schleicher, R. 156, 159, 175
Siday, E. 136
Selsdon (Lord) see Mitchell-Thomson
Sheret 27
Skirrow, J.V. 107
Stalin 17
Stoop, R. 198, 199
Swann, B. 141

T
Teague, J. 108, 161
Tew 197
Thistlethwayte 71
Thomas, Mrs. J. 165
Thomas, W.G. 84, 89
Thorpe, T.A.W. 118, 127, 129, 140, 143, 144, 147
Tweedale, J. 133
Tyrer, G. 186

V
Valenzano, G. 196

W
Waleran, Lord, 120, 131
Walker, E.R.M. 126
Watkins, N.A. 126
Walmsley, G.W. 15, 17
West, D. 126
Wharton, K. 192, 194, 196, 202
Whitehead, C. 17
Whitehead, P.N. 191
Wilby, Miss D. 127
Windle, J.P. 126
Winterbottom, E. 193
Wisdom, T. 99
Wisdom, Mrs. T. 60, 98, 113, 127
Wright, R.E. 113